**Two glitzy, glamorous tales
from Jane Porter and Caitlin Crews!**

INFAMOUS

Hand in Hand Collection

MICHELLE REID and ABBY GREEN

POWER

May 2012

JANE PORTER and CAITLIN CREWS

INFAMOUS

June 2012

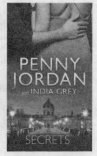

PENNY JORDAN and INDIA GREY

SECRETS

July 2012

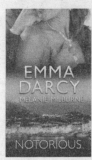

EMMA DARCY and MELANIE MILBURNE

NOTORIOUS

August 2012

LYNNE GRAHAM and MAISEY YATES

POSSESSION

September 2012

SHARON KENDRICK and JENNIE LUCAS

PRICELESS

October 2012

JANE
PORTER
and CAITLIN CREWS

INFAMOUS

Mills & Boon, an imprint of Harlequin (UK) Limited,
Eton House, 18-24 Paradise Road, Richmond, Surrey TW9 1SR

INFAMOUS © Harlequin Enterprises II B.V./S.à.r.l. 2012

Hollywood Husband, Contract Wife © Jane Porter 2006
Pure Princess, Bartered Bride © Caitlin Crews 2009

ISBN: 978 0 263 90171 9

009-0612

Harlequin (UK) policy is to use papers that are natural, renewable and recyclable products and made from wood grown in sustainable forests. The logging and manufacturing processes conform to the legal environmental regulations of the country of origin.

Printed and bound in Spain
by Blackprint CPI, Barcelona

HOLLYWOOD HUSBAND, CONTRACT WIFE

JANE PORTER

Jane Porter grew up on a diet of Mills & Boon®
romances, reading late at night under the covers
so her mother wouldn't see! She wrote her first
book at age eight and spent many of her school and
college years living abroad, immersing herself in
other cultures and continuing to read voraciously.
Now Jane has settled down in rugged Seattle,
Washington, with her gorgeous husband and two
sons. Jane loves to hear from her readers. You can
write to her at PO Box 524, Bellevue, WA 98009,
USA. Or visit her website at www.janeporter.com.

Dear Reader,

I met Caitlin Crews in 2005 at a publishers' splashy launch party in New York City. Caitlin and I shared the same editor and my editor had sent me Caitlin's first novel, thinking I would enjoy it. I had. But I was secretly rather envious of Caitlin's smart voice and distinctive style and meeting her in person only made me more insecure. Caitlin is blonde, beautiful, brainy, and so very funny. There was no way I could compete. Over the next few years Caitlin and I were thrown together time and again. But I still wasn't quite sure what to do with her.

Then came one holiday when we were both in Hawaii with our respective spouses. We met up for dinner in Waikiki and Caitlin told me she'd started reading my Mills & Boon novels and loved them. She said she was a fan. I said she was ridiculous. She made me feel clever and I loved how funny and smart and interesting she was. During the next year I began to turn to Caitlin for writing advice and input on my women's fiction manuscripts. We shared our favourite books with each other. We talked about life. And men. And love.

Over the years I learned to trust and treasure Caitlin for her honesty and strength and insight. I loved her warmth and loyalty to her friends. I loved having her in my life. And then one day she casually mentioned that she'd been working on a manuscript for Mills & Boon® Modern™ and would I be willing to look at the first couple of chapters? I told her to send them ASAP and I read them in one sitting. I was blown away. I loved Caitlin's voice and style and insisted she finish the story. She did.

The rest is history. That first book sold and Caitlin has since written ten amazing stories for Mills & Boon Modern. Caitlin is a true star. But even more importantly, she's one of my dearest friends. I adore her and am so happy and proud to be in this book with her. Welcome Caitlin to the Modern family!

Yours,

Jane

With love for my sister, Kathy Porter.

PROLOGUE

THE WEDDING WAS NOT supposed to happen.

This was a charade, a job she'd been hired to do. But the charade was supposed to have ended long before they ever went to the altar.

Long, Alexandra Shanahan silently repeated, clenching her bouquet of lilies, blue hydrangeas, white orchids and violet freesias tighter between stiff clammy hands.

This was all such a horrible mistake she couldn't even concentrate on the minister's words.

My God, she didn't even *like* Wolf Kerrick. Even four weeks of being squired around Hollywood as his newest love interest hadn't endeared the man to her.

In fact, four weeks of playing his girlfriend had only made her dislike him more. He was horrible in every sense of the word.

He was too rich, too successful, too powerful. He was too much of everything, and that alone made her uncomfortable, but the fact that he didn't respect women infuriated her. He treated women like playthings, taking what he wanted, when he wanted, and discarding without remorse when inexplicably bored.

And now she was his wife.

Alexandra swallowed, stunned, silenced, undone.

She, who could handle anything, she who never wavered in the face of danger, she who took risks and loved challenge, welcoming adversity with open arms, was now married to the world's most famous film star.

Spots danced before Alexandra's eyes and she gulped in air, trying to clear the fog from her head. If she didn't know herself better, she'd think she was going to faint.

She couldn't faint.

It was too much of a photo opportunity.

She must have inhaled too sharply, because suddenly Wolf's hand was at her elbow.

"You better not faint," he growled in his rough accented English, a sexy combination of Irish and Spanish vowels that left women weak at the knees. But that was Wolf's magic.

He was the quintessential bad boy, times a thousand, and everybody's celluloid dream.

Six feet three and impossibly broad through the shoulder while lean in the hip. He looked as good naked in love scenes as he did in a tuxedo shooting the latest James Bond thriller.

Alex's jaw jutted and she tugged her arm from Wolf's touch. "I won't," she whispered defiantly, even though she wasn't sure she wouldn't faint. Truth be known, she was scared, scared in a way she hadn't been since first moving to Los Angeles four years ago.

It'd been a long four years, too.

Four years of struggle, attempting to crawl up the ladder of Hollywood fame. And now she was here. Sort of.

Wolf's grip on her arm tightened. "Then smile. You look as though you're dying."

"If only I were so lucky." Then she forced another tight smile just in case any of the guests could see her face. This was her wedding, after all.

"I'm your dream man. Remember?"

Those had been her words, too, her exact words, but they'd been uttered in a moment of panic, at the height of a crisis. She would have never claimed him otherwise.

Alex's stomach rose, threatening to embarrass her right then and there. Oh, God. What had she done?

Biting her lower lip, Alexandra battled the second wave of nausea even as the Santa Barbara breeze lifted her veil, sending the lace and her long, artfully styled curls blowing around her face. Married to Wolf Kerrick. Mrs. Wolf Kerrick.

Alexandra Kerrick.

Her eyes squeezed closed, her hand shook where it rested on Wolf's arm.

Why had she thought she could play his girlfriend?

How could she have ever thought she'd be able to manage him?

And why had she come to Hollywood in the first place?

CHAPTER ONE

Beverly Hills, California
Five weeks earlier...

ALEXANDRA SHANAHAN had thought being invited to lunch with Hollywood's most powerful actor was too good to be true.

She was right.

"You want me to *what?*" Alexandra Shanahan asked incredulously, staring at Wolf Kerrick as though he'd lost his mind.

"Play my new love interest," he repeated, his deep voice nearly flat.

Wolf Kerrick's love interest. How ludicrous. Beyond ludicrous.

Wolf Kerrick...and her? Alexandra would have laughed if her stomach wasn't doing wild cartwheels.

Everything, she thought woozily, about the lunch was wrong. The impossible-to-secure reservations at the famous Beverly Hills Hotel's terrace restaurant. The bright blue sky overhead. The dizzying fragrance of the terrace garden's roses and gardenias.

When she'd first sat down at the table, she'd introduced herself—silly, but since they'd never officially met, it'd seemed like the right thing to do.

Wolf had repeated her name thoughtfully. "Shanahan. Sounds familiar."

"There's a famous football coach by the same name," she'd answered nervously, trying to ignore the excited whispers of the other restaurant patrons. Everyone had been watching them. Or at least watching Wolf. But then, he was a megastar and sinfully good-looking, so she couldn't really blame them.

"Maybe that's it," he'd answered, leaning back in his chair. "Or maybe it's familiar because it's Irish."

She'd managed a tight smile before dropping her gaze, already overwhelmed by his formidable size and presence.

Wolf Kerrick was bigger, broader, stronger, more male than nearly any other actor in the business. There was no mistaking him for any other actor, either, not with his Spanish-Irish black hair, dark eyes and sinful, sensual mouth.

"Daniel said you had a job offer for me," she'd said nervously, jumping straight to the point. There was no reason to stall. She'd never be able to eat in his company, so ordering lunch was out of the question. Best just get the whole interview over and done with.

"I do."

She'd nodded to fill the silence. She'd hoped he'd maybe elaborate, but he hadn't. Her cheeks had scalded. Her face had felt so hot even her ears had burned. "Daniel said he thought I'd be perfect for the job."

Wolf's dark head had tipped, his black lashes dropping as he'd considered her. After an endless silence he'd nodded once. "You are."

She wasn't sure if she should be flattered or terrified. He seemed so much friendlier on the big screen, more approachable in film than he was here in flesh. Right now he was anything but mortal, human. Instead he was like a dark warrior, an avenger with a secret—and dangerous—agenda.

"I'm looking to fill a position," he said flatly.

"Yes," she echoed, hands knotting together in her lap.

"The role of my new love interest."

She nearly tumbled from her chair. *"What?"*

She stared at him so hard his face blurred.

"It's a publicity stunt," Wolf said in the same flat, almost bored tone. "The position would last approximately four to six weeks. Of course, you'd be well compensated."

Shocked, mortified, Alexandra felt as though she'd burst into flames any moment. "But I—I…couldn't," she sputtered, reaching for her water glass even as a rivulet of perspiration slid down inside her gray linen jacket. She was broiling here on the terrace. She'd dressed far too warmly for lunch outside, and with the bright California sun beating down on her head she thought she'd melt any moment. "I don't date—" she broke off, swallowed convulsively "—actors."

Wolf's jaw shifted. A trace of amusement touched his features. "You don't have to. You just have to pretend to date me."

Him. Wolf Kerrick. International film star. Spanish-Irish heartthrob. Alexandra gulped more water. She was so hot she could barely think clearly. If only she'd dressed more appropriately. If only she'd thought to bring someone to the meeting with her. Her boss, Daniel deVoors, one of the industry's top directors, had sent her here today, telling her Wolf Kerrick had a proposition for her. She'd thought maybe Mr. Kerrick needed a personal assistant. It hadn't crossed her mind he'd be interviewing for a lover.

"Why?" she whispered.

"You're young, wholesome, ordinary, someone the public could relate to."

Young, wholesome and ordinary, Alexandra silently repeated, feeling her heart jump to lodge firmly in her throat. He didn't find her attractive even though she'd made such efforts today. Alexandra rarely wore makeup, but today she'd used a little mascara and a touch of lipstick, and obviously it'd made no difference. She was still wholesome and ordinary. She took a deep breath, suppressed the sting of his words. "But I still don't understand…."

"It's a PR move aimed at damage control." Wolf shifted in his seat so that his powerful body seemed to dwarf the table and the terrace and the day itself.

Alexandra's brows furrowed. She was finding it increasingly difficult to keep focused on what he was saying, disappointment washing through her in gigantic waves. She'd been so thrilled to meet Wolf Kerrick, to have this chance to interview with him. Last night she'd barely slept. Today she'd woken extra early and showered and dressed with such care....

But now...now she just felt hurt. Disappointed.

There was no job, just this ridiculous proposal.

Her temper stirred and she sat taller. "Damage control?" she repeated, trying to keep up with him. "Why would you need damage control...?" Her voice faded as it hit her, in one lucid swoop. *Joy Hughes.*

This was about Wolf's affair with Joy Hughes.

And looking across the table, it all came together. Mr. Kerrick didn't want to hire a love interest. He didn't want to be meeting her or sitting here in public having this conversation. He was doing this—speaking to her, asking her to play a part— to help repair his damaged reputation, and she knew who and what had damaged his reputation. His year-long affair with the very married film actress, Joy Hughes.

"Does this have to do with your...*affair?*" she asked awkwardly, torn between anger and shame that Daniel deVoors would even suggest her to Mr. Kerrick as a possible love interest.

Wolf Kerrick's lips suddenly pulled back in an almost wolflike snarl. "There was no affair."

Alexandra's heart jumped, but she didn't cower. "If there was no affair," she said huskily, fingers balling into fists, "you wouldn't need me, would you?"

Wolf leaned forward, dark eyes flashing, jaw jutting with anger. "There *was* no affair."

His dark eyes held hers, fierce, penetrating, and the stillness following his words was as dangerous as his tone of voice.

She felt the blister of his anger, as well as his underlying scorn. Yet she was angry, too. He must think she was stupid or naive to take everything he said at face value. And she might be naive, but she wasn't stupid. Alexandra met his gaze squarely. "Everyone knows you and Joy have been involved for the last year."

Wolf and Joy Hughes were both megastars. Bigger than film stars, larger than life, they personified Hollywood power and glamour. So much so that when they'd secretly linked up earlier in the year, their affair—Joy was still married to another Hollywood heavyweight—made headline news and had remained there for nearly six months.

Even now she remembered how their photos had been on every cover of every weekly tabloid—for months. "It's not exactly a secret," she added.

The planes of Wolf's face hardened, his high cheekbones growing more prominent. "The media fabricated the relationship. I thought the interest would die. I told Joy as much. It didn't."

He paused, considered his words. "The public's fickle. Today they're enthralled by rumors and gossip, tomorrow they're appalled. But the stories have gotten out of hand. The bad press will soon influence the box-office takings. I can't take that chance, not when it'll hurt every single person who works on my films."

He was right about that much, she agreed, biting her lower lip. She'd been in Hollywood four years, had worked for Paradise Pictures for nearly three and knew that a low-grossing film impacted everyone. A low-grossing film left an ugly black mark on everyone's résumé.

Rubbing at a tiny knot of tension throbbing in her temple, she tried to see her part in this. "But to generate new press by pretending to have a relationship with me? It's such an old Hollywood trick. I didn't think it was done anymore."

His long black lashes lifted and his dark gaze searched hers, his scrutiny so intense it left her feeling strangely exposed. "The studio wants proof that Joy and I aren't an item. Being seen with you would be the proof they need."

"Just by being seen with me?"

"That's how the tabloids work. They snap their photos, run their stories and publicly speculate about celebrities' happiness and future, often without interviewing one reliable source." His tone was rueful, his expression mocking. "After one week of being together in public, we'll be an item."

"That's all it takes?"

"Sometimes only one photo is necessary." His mouth

slanted. "But I should warn you, the pressure will be intense. The paparazzi are everywhere, photographers camp outside my door. Once reporters learn your name, they'll hunt down information on you—where you work, what you do, who you've dated—" He broke off, looked at her from beneath arched brows. "Do you have any scandals in your past, anything the press can dredge up?"

Stunned to silence, she shook her head.

"Old boyfriends with an axe to grind?" he persisted.

Again she shook her head. She'd hardly ever dated. Growing up on an isolated ranch, there hadn't been many chances to date, and moving to Los Angeles at nineteen had nipped her desire to date in the bud. The men she'd met in Los Angeles were often shallow, materialistic and crass, nothing like the men she'd been raised with, none revealing any of the male qualities she admired, like strength, courage, confidence, generosity.

Men in Los Angeles loved cars, tans and expensive restaurants. Oh, and women with fake breasts.

"There's nothing in my past worthy of tabloid interest," she said, briefly thinking of her mom who'd died when she was young and her oldest brother's wife who'd been killed in a car accident. But those weren't the kinds of things the gossip magazines would be interested in. Those were the personal heartbreaks that lay buried between the covers of photo albums, baby books and high school graduation diplomas.

But those personal heartbreaks were also one of the reasons she'd left Montana. Having grown up in the shadow of five older brothers, Alexandra needed space. Independence. She needed to be her own person and have control over her life.

Playing Wolf Kerrick's new love interest would strip her identity as well as her control.

She'd be followed, photographed, harassed.

"I'll make it worth your while," Wolf said quietly, as if able to read her mind, or the emotions flickering over her face. "I've met with Daniel and your studio. They're willing to offer you a significant promotion if you take the position. And when the assignment ends, you'll be offered an A.D. position with Daniel."

"Assistant director?" she repeated under her breath, dazed by the idea of really being involved in making pictures and not just taking coffee orders.

"Yes."

For the first time since Wolf had presented her with the proposal, she was tempted to accept, she really was. To escape from photocopy hell and actually do something on a film…to leave the office behind and go on location…to be involved with real decision making versus how much liquid sugar was needed to properly sweeten the lighting technician's double-shot iced coffee…

But looking at Wolf, she knew her decision wasn't quite so simple. Wolf was a man. An actor. A very popular actor as famous for his skills in the bedroom as his talent on-screen.

And maybe Wolf was notorious for bedding lots of women, but she couldn't do that—wouldn't do that. It's not who she was.

But what if Wolf expected that?

She shot an uncertain glance up into his face. "Mr. Kerrick, I think you should know right now, up front, that I don't do the casting-couch routine." Her heart raced as she considered his hard features, his firm, sensual mouth. "I won't do it. It's not how I was raised."

His lips curled up, a flicker of wry amusement touched his dark eyes before just as swiftly disappearing. "I've never needed to convince or pressure a woman into bed."

"Yes, I know," she said, pulse still pounding like mad. "But I wouldn't want you to think that later I'll do things—"

"Miss Shanahan, rest assured that there's no risk of that. Forgive my bluntness, but you're not my type."

Her face flooded with heat even as her blood turned to ice. Oh, God. How humiliating. But she'd practically asked for that, hadn't she?

Painfully embarrassed, Alexandra felt her insides curdle and cramp. Of course she wasn't his type. Of course he wouldn't want to take someone like her to bed. He could have any woman in the world, why would he want to be with her?

"I'm sorry," she said, voice noticeably husky, "but I don't

think this is going to work. I'm not who or what you need." She fumbled for her purse, finally finding it at her feet, next to her chair. "And I'm not about to try to change to please you or anyone else."

She rose to escape, but Wolf reached out, caught her hand, kept her from fleeing.

"That's where you're wrong." His deep voice, pitched low, vibrated inside her as his dark eyes, a glittering onyx, held her transfixed. "You're exactly what I want and need."

His words shook her, but it was his touch, that scalding press of skin on skin, that made her knees buckle. With his hand around her wrist, she felt electric, charged, different. "I know I'm no beauty queen, but there's no reason for you to be cruel—"

His fingers tightened around her wrist. "Cruel? I'm paying you a compliment. I've picked you to play the role of my lover." His voice deepened, betraying his Dublin roots. "I wouldn't ask just anyone—"

"And I'm to be flattered by that?"

"*Yes.*"

She tugged at her hand, hating the ruthless edge in his voice, that raw, hard, male quality that made him want to dominate her and everything else in his world. "That's where you're mistaken." Tears shimmered in her eyes. "Because I'm not flattered and I don't take it as a compliment that you've chosen me to fill a role in your life. I'm not an accessory, Mr. Kerrick. Not for you, not for anyone!"

She stole a quick breath, noticed the diners around them watching in rabid interest. "People are staring," she said softly, a faint catch in her voice. "Please release me and let me go."

"I'll release you, but I want you to sit down and finish this—"

"It *is* finished," she flashed furiously.

"No, it's not. Sit down. Now." He exhaled. "Please."

Alex slowly sank into her chair again, her purse falling limply to her lap.

Wolf leaned forward, his dark eyes never leaving hers. "Don't let your pride get in the way, Miss Shanahan. Your boss told me you're smart, ambitious. This is an opportunity to make a name for yourself."

Her nausea had returned, stronger than before. "Make a name for myself as what? Your fake girlfriend?" She stared at him incredulously. "You think I should jump at your proposal, be flattered because I'm a plain-Jane girl and don't get out much, is that it? And yes, I'm ambitious, but unfortunately not ambitious enough to date you. Not ambitious enough to pretend to be your girlfriend to get a promotion. I find it digusting that I'd gain industry status—respect—simply by being seen around town with you. That's not the way life should work—"

"Maybe it's not the way it should, but it's the way it does."

"And doesn't that strike you as immoral? Wrong?"

"No. It's practical."

"Of course it would seem so to you. You're the man that dates married women!" And with a violent jerk, she broke free and rose to rush from the table.

Fighting tears, Alexandra squeezed through the tables lining the terrace, wound her way down a pink painted hallway to the ladies' room even as his words rang in her head.

Perfect for the job. Damage control. Publicity stunt. Pretend to date me. Practical.

The tears fell even before she'd managed to lock herself inside the bathroom stall.

This was exactly why her father hadn't wanted her to come to California.

This was exactly what her brothers had predicted would happen.

They'd all said she was too young, too inexperienced to survive in a dog-eat-dog city like Los Angeles, and she'd been so determined to prove them wrong. So determined to make it on her own and do it right.

But playing Wolf Kerrick's girlfriend would be far from right.

The tears trickled down her face, and she scrubbed them away with a furious fist.

He'd pay her to be seen with him.

He'd make sure she was compensated.

Alexandra's throat squeezed closed. She felt as though she were gasping for air on the inside, fighting for calm and control.

And then it hit her. She didn't have to go back to the table. She didn't have to see Mr. Kerrick again or endure any more of his painful proposal.

She could just go. She could just leave and get her car and return to work.

It was as easy as that.

Calmer now, Alexandra exited the stall, rinsed off her face, patted her damp face and hands dry. The valet attendant had her car key. She had her purse with her. She'd just go now.

Alex left the bathroom but had only taken two steps when she froze, her body stiffening with horror.

Wolf Kerrick was waiting for her. And standing, he was even taller than she remembered.

She felt all her nerves tense, tighten. Even her heartbeat seemed to slow. "The men's restroom is on the other side," she said lowly.

"I know."

"The bar is the other direction—"

"You know I'm waiting for you."

Alexandra drew a quick, shallow breath. She was exhausted. Emotionally flattened. All her excitement, all her good feelings about meeting Wolf Kerrick were long gone. "There's no point. There's nothing more for either of us to say—"

"There's plenty. You can say yes."

My God, he was arrogant and insensitive. "I don't *want* to say yes."

"Why not?"

She flinched at his curt tone. It was clear he was used to getting his way and didn't like being thwarted. "I'd never sell myself—"

"This isn't slavery. I'm offering you a salary."

"And I want to make it in Hollywood my way."

"And what is your way?" he taunted. "Making copies? Answering phones? Getting coffee?"

Alexandra's cheeks flamed. "At least I have my self-respect!"

"You might respect yourself even more if you had a job that actually challenged you."

"My goodness but you're insufferable. You should fire your managers, Mr. Kerrick. They've got you believing your own PR, and that's a huge mistake."

He shocked her by bursting out laughing, eyes creasing with humor. "You really don't like me, Miss Shanahan, do you?"

"No."

"Why not?"

"It doesn't matter."

"It does to me."

"Why?" she retorted fiercely, spinning to face him, hands balled at her sides. "Does everyone have to be a fan? Do you want everyone lining up for your autograph?"

Still smiling, his dark eyes raked her. "No."

"Because I'd be lying if I said I liked you. Maybe once admired you, lined up to see your movies, but that was before I met you. Now I see who you really are and I don't like you or your chauvinistic, condescending attitude."

He jammed his hands into his trouser pockets, rocked back on his heels. "Your honesty's surprisingly refreshing."

"Were you ever nice?"

His lips pursed, black brows pulling as he mulled over her question. Reluctantly he shook his head. "No." Then the corner of his mouth tugged into a sardonic smile. "But you don't have to like me to date me."

"That's revolting."

"Alexandra, if you're not an actress and you don't date actors and you can't get yourself promoted out of the copy room at Paradise Pictures, why stay here in Hollywood? Why not just pack your bags and go home?"

She felt a pang inside her, the muscles around her heart tightening. She'd asked herself the very same question many times. "Because I still want to make pictures," she said softly. "I hope to one day be more involved, hope I can somehow make a difference."

He studied her a long moment, his expression closed, eyes

hooded. "You can make a difference," he said finally. "You can help make a picture—and save the jobs of dozens of people. We're to start filming *The Burning Shore* in a little over a month's time. Work with me. Let's get the film into production."

Alexandra bit down, pinched her lip between her teeth. She'd love to make a difference, do something positive, learn something new. She'd love to be challenged, too, but she didn't trust Wolf. "You think we could generate positive press together?"

He'd never looked so somber. "If I didn't, I wouldn't be here now."

CHAPTER TWO

WOLF ACCOMPANIED Alexandra to the front of the hotel, where she'd left her car with the valet attendant.

Lush purple bougainvillea covered the hotel's pink stucco entrance, and the fragrant blossoms of potted lemon and orange trees perfumed the air, but Wolf gave his surroundings scant attention.

Alexandra could feel the weight of Wolf's inspection as they waited for her car to appear.

The problem wasn't only the offer. And the issue wasn't just her morals or her values. It was her lack of experience.

She didn't know how to manage a man like Wolf Kerrick and couldn't imagine how one would even date a man like him.

But they won't be real dates, she reasoned. *They're pretend dates. It's not as if you'll really have to kiss him or touch him or be physically involved.*

Heat washed through her at the very idea of getting physically close. She really did need more experience. "If you gave me some time," she said after a moment, "allowed me a chance to think about your offer properly, I might say yes." She looked up, met his gaze before quickly looking away. "But I don't want to be pressured."

She drew another deep breath, flexed her fingers to ease her tension. "And if I did agree, how would this work?"

If he felt any elation or sensed that he'd won, none of it showed on his face. "We'd draw up a contract, include a generous financial compensation, as it's probable you'll miss some workdays due to events and premieres, and then begin going places together to be seen."

He made it sound so simple, she thought, and yet she wasn't a glamour girl, the sort to be invited to fancy parties or industry premieres. No, she was the girl raised by her dad, grandpa and five older brothers. There hadn't been a woman in the house, not since her mom died when Alexandra was five. Growing up, she was the original tomboy.

"And what makes you think people will believe you…and I…are together?" she asked, pushing thoughts of Montana and the Lazy L ranch from her mind. "I'm not your…usual choice in dates."

"Lots of stars date makeup artists, casting directors, the like."

She hesitated. "Some actors do, but not you."

"You can't believe everything you read in the tabloids."

Maybe, she thought, and maybe not, but she'd seen the pictures of the women he dated. He liked starlets and models, topless dancers and magazine centerfolds, his taste typically running toward women with more cleavage than brains. And Alex didn't even have to look down at her not-so-impressive chest to know her strength was not in her cup size.

Years ago, back in junior high school, she'd learned that there were only two avenues open for women: the one for pretty girls and the one for smart girls. Even in high school it had been one or the other—cheerleaders and beauty queens or bookworms and future librarians. Girls certainly couldn't be both. And since Alexandra knew she wasn't pom-pom-girl pretty, she'd decided then and there to be smart. Damn smart. "We both know I'm not pretty enough to be taken seriously as your new love interest."

"You could be if you tried to do something with yourself," Wolf answered with brutal candor. "Alexandra, you don't even try."

She bit down, not knowing where to look. "I don't try because I know already what I am and who I am. And I don't need makeup or fake hair or nails or a tan to make me something I'm not."

"Which is what?" he asked quietly.

"A bimbo. I'm not going to be a bimbo. I want to be respected. Taken seriously. And if I change myself—"

"You're changing your hairstyle, not your soul."

Her head jerked up.

"You're smart," he added. "Serious. And I'm sorry, but that eliminates the bimbo category for you."

She should have been flattered. Instead his words merely left her even more flustered.

Every time he looked at her she felt sparks on the inside, little bits of hot fire flaring here and there. It was like being a human sparkler, only worse because the heat didn't die.

"I just don't want to be laughed at," she said after a moment. "People can be unkind. I know the tabloids are famous for publishing unflattering photos and pointing out celebrities' flaws."

"Before we go public, you'll meet with stylists, receive wardrobe consultation. I have a team of professionals who will help ease you into the transition."

Alexandra was intrigued despite herself. "When would that happen?"

"As soon as you signed the contract."

Alexandra tried to imagine being groomed by top Hollywood stylists but couldn't. She might have lost twenty pounds since moving from Montana to California, but she still thought of herself as the sturdy country girl who'd worn cowboy boots before high heels. "A beautiful starlet would be far easier to introduce to the public," she said in a small voice.

"I'm not interested in squiring around a young actress desperate to make a name for herself—"

"But in real life—"

"This is real life, and I'm quite aware that I'm responsible for dozens of people's jobs. I just want to get *The Burning Shore* made and I want to do it without emotional complications."

She fell silent, digesting this. "You don't want anyone to fall in love with you."

His dark eyes creased, his mouth compressed. "That's exactly what I'm saying."

Thankfully her practical little blue Ford Escort appeared that moment in the famous hotel drive.

The uniformed valet climbed from the driver's seat and held the door for her.

Wolf walked her to the car. Alexandra slid behind the steering wheel. "I'll call you," she said.

"You've my number?"

She stared up into his dark eyes, seeing the hard, beautiful lines of his face, and her panic grew. No one had a face like Wolf. No one had his charisma either.

It'd be suicide to do this, she thought, absolute disaster—if not for him, then for her. She wasn't as sophisticated as he was, nor did she have his experience.

"I still have the card Daniel gave me. He wrote your cell number on the back."

Smiling faintly, Wolf closed her door and stepped away from the car. "Take your time, think about your options and call me when you're ready."

She hesitated and then leaned through the open window. "You think I'm going to say yes, don't you?"

His faint smile grew. "I know you will."

"Why?"

"Because you're a smart girl and you'll soon realize this is the opportunity of a lifetime."

The opportunity of a lifetime, she repeated over and over driving home, her hands shaking on the steering wheel and her insides doing nonstop flips.

The opportunity of a lifetime, she repeated yet again as she parked her car in the tiny garage adjacent to her California bungalow, one of the tiny nondescript row houses built in Culver City during the forties and fifties.

Her house was small, and until recently she'd shared it with another girl. But since the girl had a job transfer to Boston, Alexandra was now covering the rent by herself and it was tight. She'd considered getting another housemate but was so enjoying having the space all to herself that she hadn't gotten anybody yet.

And if she did sign the contract to play Wolf's new love interest, she wouldn't have to get a roommate, she'd be able to pay the entire rent herself.

Alexandra loved the thought of that.

Since moving to Los Angeles she'd really struggled, both financially and emotionally.

She'd taken a job waitressing and then a part-time job temping for an independent film studio, answering phones, handling mail, playing general office errand girl, which was mainly going to Starbucks and getting everyone's favorite espresso and latte.

Alex discovered that she liked being useful in the office. She was good in the office—quick, smart, agile, she could multi-task and never needed to be told anything twice.

After a year working for the independent film company, she answered a Paradise Pictures ad she saw in *Variety* and was hired to assist intense, brainy directors and producers with whatever needed to be done.

She'd worked for Paradise for nearly three years now and she thought she'd proven herself on more than one occasion, but the promotion had never come.

Why?

It wasn't as though she couldn't handle more responsibility. She actually needed the risk, craved change.

In the kitchen, Alexandra took out the business card Daniel had given her several days ago, the one with Wolf's private number. She tapped it on the counter, flipped it over to the personal cell number scribbled on the back and tried to imagine the next four weeks.

New clothes. Input from a stylist. Exciting parties.

Smiling nervously, she bit her lip. It'd be scary but also fun.

Then she thought of Wolf Kerrick and the whole concept of fun went out the window, leaving her unsure of herself all over again.

But it's an opportunity, she reminded herself sternly, *and that's what you want.*

Quickly she picked up the phone, dialed Wolf's number.

"It's Alexandra Shanahan," she said when he answered, dispensing with any preamble. "And I'll do it. But before anything else happens, I want the offer—and the studio's promise about the assistant director position—in writing."

"Of course."

She held the phone tighter. "And working on B-rate flicks doesn't count. I want to work on major studio films. Big-budget films."

"Certainly."

She folded one arm over her chest and pressed a knuckled fist to her rib cage. "I want to be clear that this is a job, and I'll treat it like a job. I'll do what I have to for the cameras, but I won't do anything inappropriate."

"And what is inappropriate?"

"Kissing, touching, sex."

"There's got to be a certain amount of intimacy for the camera."

"Only for the camera, then, okay?"

"Okay."

"I mean it, Mr. Kerrick."

"I've got it all down, Miss Shanahan. You'll get the contract tonight. It should be there by seven."

The contract did arrive at seven. But a courier service didn't deliver it. Instead Wolf Kerrick brought it himself.

She hadn't expected Wolf and she'd answered the door in her faded blue sweatpants, cropped yellow T-shirt and bare feet in dire need of a pedicure. Without her contacts, and in her glasses, with her hair in a messy knotted ponytail on top of her head, Alex knew she looked more like a librarian than the sex symbol required.

"Hi," she said awkwardly, tugging on her ponytail, trying to at least get her hair down even if she couldn't make the glasses vanish.

"Cleaning house, are you?" he asked.

"I didn't expect you."

"Mmm. But maybe I should come in. Two photographers tailed me. Red car on the right and the white car that hopped the curb. They're taking photos of both of us as we speak."

Alexandra opened the door so Wolf could enter.

As Wolf glanced around the house, she peeked out the living room curtain, and just as Wolf had said, the red car and the white car were out there, and both drivers held cameras with enormous telephoto lenses. "Those are some huge camera lenses," she said.

"I learned the hard way that you'll want to keep your curtains closed. Otherwise they'll get shots of you walking around."

She dropped the lace panel and faced him. "How did they know you were coming here?"

"There is always someone tailing me. Has been for years." He dropped onto her beige couch, extended his denim-clad legs so they rested on her oak coffee table and looked up at her with piercing dark eyes. "How long have you lived here?"

"Almost three years." The abruptness of his question was less disconcerting than the fact that Wolf Kerrick was stretched out in her living room, looking very relaxed-and comfortable—in a loose gray T-shirt, with his thick black hair tumbling across his forehead. "Why do you ask?"

"There's not much furniture."

"My former roommate took it all with her to Boston," she answered, thinking that even dressed down in jeans and a T-shirt, Wolf looked like a film star. It was his bone structure, coloring, the easy way he carried himself. He was more than beautiful, he was elegant and intense and physical. Sexy.

Alexandra exhaled in a painful rush.

That was really the problem. He was far too sexy for her and had been from the time she first laid eyes on him—which was in a movie, of course—eight years ago. In *Age of Valor,* just his second film, he'd played a soldier. And while he wasn't the lead in the film, his performance was so strong, he stole the show. Alexandra remembered sobbing when his character died in the film, dramatically blown to bits just before the movie's end. She'd liked him—the man, the actor, the character—so much she couldn't bear for the story to end without him still in it.

She had been fifteen at the time, just starting her sophomore year of high school, and of course she had known it was just a movie and he was just an actor, but she'd never forgotten his face or his name.

Wolf Kerrick.

Amused by the girl she'd once been, Alexandra took a seat

on the edge of the coffee table across from him. "Shall I sign the contract?"

Wolf's dark head tipped and his long black lashes dropped, brushing his high, strong cheekbones. "Think you can do this?"

Growing up, she'd been the ultimate tomboy. As the baby of the Shanahan clan, she'd stomped and swaggered around in her cowboy boots. But moving to Southern California had killed her confidence, and she was only just starting to realize how much she missed her old swagger.

She'd once been so brave, so full of bravado.

How had moving to California changed her so much? Was it Hollywood? The movie industry? What had made her feel so small, so insignificant, so less than?

"Yes. I know I can," she said forcibly, and strangely enough, she meant it. She was the girl who'd roped calves and ridden broncs and jumped off the barn roof just because her brothers said she couldn't. She was the girl who didn't take no for an answer. If she could ride a bull, she could date a wolf.

Alexandra's lips curved at her own feeble joke, but her smile faded as Wolf's black eyes met hers.

"Think you can handle me?" he murmured.

Her heart stuttered. She knew what he was asking. Like everyone else who read the tabloids, she knew he'd been arrested more than once for fighting and heard it didn't take much to bring out the street fighter in him.

She also knew that women found him irresistible, and having once been one of those giddy girls who threw themselves at him, knew she'd never behave so recklessly again.

"Yes," she answered equally firmly, ignoring the cold lash of adrenaline. "You won't be a problem. You might be a famous actor, but you're also just a man. Now give me the contract and let's get this over with."

He handed her the contract and a pen, and Alex spread the document on the table to read while she tapped the pen against her teeth. The form read correctly, all the terms were there, everything she asked for given.

With a confident flourish, Alexandra scrawled her name at

the space indicated. "There," she said, lifting her pen and handing the paper back to him. "Signed, sealed, delivered."

"My little lovebird," he mocked, taking the paper and folding it up.

Her cheeks heated. Her blue eyes locked with his. Her heart was pounding wildly, but she held his gaze, kept her chin up, refusing to show further weakness. "I won't be broken, Mr. Kerrick."

"Is that a challenge, Miss Shanahan?"

"No. I'm just stating a fact. I had some time to think about your offer, to look at the pros and cons, and I've agreed to do this not because it helps you but because it helps me. I know now what I want and I know what I need to do to get there. And you won't keep me from succeeding. There's too much at stake." And then she swallowed hard. "For both of us."

He studied her from across the table, his forearms resting against his knees, his eyebrows black slashes above bold dark eyes. "There will be pressure."

She rose to her feet. "I anticipate it."

"The attention will feel intrusive at times."

"I've considered that possibility, as well."

"You're truly prepared to take this all the way? Ready for the makeover, the new hair, the wardrobe and revamped image?"

"Yes."

He stood. "Tomorrow you'll pay a visit to the Juan Carlos Salon in Beverly Hills. The salon is expecting you. It'll be a long day. The car will be here at seven."

"I don't want a limo, Mr. Kerrick."

"It's part of the role, Miss Shanahan. And now that we've agreed to this little play, it's time we dropped the formalities. We're lovers now." He slowly moved toward her. "You're Alexandra and I'm Wolf and we're a very happy new couple."

He was standing so close to her now she could hardly breathe. "Right."

"Just follow my lead," he said.

"Your lead," she whispered, feeling the warmth of his body, his strength tangible and real. She tipped her head back, looked up into his face, with the strong cheekbones and high forehead, the piercing dark eyes.

"I'll make it easy for you."

"You're that good an actor?"

"I'm that good a lover."

She took an involuntary step backward. "You said there'd be no sex—"

"In public, it's my job to seduce you. To make the photographers sit up, take notice."

She inhaled hard, thinking he was the devil in the flesh. "In public, yes."

He leaned down and brushed the briefest kiss across her flushed cheek. "But in private, we're just friends, remember?"

She felt her stomach fall and her breath catch as his lips touched her cheek. The whisper of his warm breath sent fingers of fire racing through her veins.

Wolf headed for the door. "Don't forget to set your alarm clock. The limo will be here early."

Alexandra leaned against the door after Wolf closed it.

Her heart was still pounding and her tummy felt coiled in a new and aching tension.

This was not going to be easy. Pretending to be Wolf's girlfriend would be the hardest thing she'd ever done.

And then she pulled herself together. *No more negative thoughts,* she told herself. *No more running scared.* She'd signed the contract. She had to go for it now.

And she would go for it.

She'd been in Los Angeles four years and she was hungry. Really hungry. Hungry like one living on the streets, digging out of trash cans, looking for something to fill you up, get you by.

Because, God knew, she wanted to go somewhere. She was determined to go all the way, too, all the way up, to the top. Fame, fortune, power. She wanted the whole bit.

It was time to do what she'd left Bozeman, Montana, to do. Time to make Hollywood hers.

CHAPTER THREE

THEY WERE CUTTING HER hair off.

The next morning, covered in plastic drapes, Alexandra stared aghast as Juan Carlos lifted chunks of her waist-length hair and began to chop it off to shoulder length.

She'd had long hair—really long, down to her butt—since she was a little girl. Being the only daughter, her father had wanted her to be a princess and insisted she leave her hair long. Soon he'd learned her hair was the only thing he could control, as his princess preferred jeans, boots and playing with LEGO, blocks and army trucks.

Alexandra had kept her hair long for her dad and now she found herself fighting tears as it was whacked off.

"It'll be beautiful. You'll be beautiful," Juan Carlos reassured, catching sight of her tear-filmed eyes in his station's mirror. "Be patient. You'll see."

Alexandra wanted to believe him. And it was just hair, nothing more important than that. And if she couldn't handle getting her hair cut, how would she handle the other changes coming in the next few weeks?

With her long hair in pieces all over the floor, Juan Carlos patted her shoulders. "Now we change the color."

Thirty minutes later, Alexandra was still trying to get used to the smell of bleach and chemicals from the cream applied to her hair. They were doing a two-color process—overall color and highlights—and the smelly foils on her head made her want to gag. Did some women willingly do this?

Juan Carlos had told her he was giving her warm amber highlights and promised to make her a Hollywood golden girl.

Alex wasn't so sure about the golden part.

Squeezing her eyes shut, she battled her nerves, drew a deep breath and counted to ten.

At ten, she opened her eyes, caught a glimpse of her silver-wrapped alienlike self in the mirror and closed her eyes again.

This was not going to work.

Back at home five hours later, Alexandra looked in the mirror at the new, improved version of her. Her hair shimmered with a multitude of highlights, precision-cut to fall in thick, sexy waves around her face, playing up her black-lashed blue eyes and the strong cheekbones she didn't know she had.

The makeup artist had shown her how to use color and liner to subtly darken and define her lips, her brows, her eyes.

And studying the new, improved Alexandra, she thought she looked good. *Pretty*. Pretty in a way she'd never been before. Feminine but smart. And confident. Strong. And that's the thing she hadn't known she could be on the outside. On the inside, she liked to roughhouse with the best of them, riding bareback, helping in the roundups, slinging barbwire along with the ranch hands. She'd learned early that she had to keep up with her brothers or she'd be left behind, relegated to the kitchen and the laundry room at home, and if there was anything Alex didn't want, it was woman's work. Housework. Domestic chores that kept her locked inside when the sky was huge and blue beyond the windows of the house, where the land stretched endlessly, waiting for exploration and hours of adventure.

Alex's lips half curved, and she stared, fascinated, at the face of a woman she realized she barely knew.

She really was pretty, almost pretty like the girls in magazines. And maybe it was makeup and expensive hair color and a professional blow-dry, but she wasn't the fat girl she'd been at eleven and twelve and fifteen. She wasn't even the sturdy, healthy nineteen-year-old who'd arrived in Hollywood eager to make movies.

Reaching up, she touched the mirror, touching her reflection, the shimmering tawny lips, the dusty glow of cheeks and eyes that looked midnight-blue in the bathroom lights.

"Be confident," she whispered. "Be brave."

And with one last small, uncertain smile, she turned away from the mirror and left the bathroom, hitting the light switch on her way out.

In the living room she turned on the front porch light, and before she could decide if she should turn on the stereo or the TV or pick up a magazine to read, the doorbell rang.

Butterflies danced through her middle, spinning up and into her head.

God, she was nervous. Scared.

Why was she so scared? It wasn't as though she'd never been out with Wolf before. It's not as if she hadn't ever been alone with him either.

Hands pressed to her sides, she took a deep breath and reminded herself of all the reasons why she'd come to L.A. and all the things she wanted to learn, to do, to prove. Maybe Wolf Kerrick was way out of her league and maybe this was going to be a rocky couple of weeks, but doing this, playing this part, would help her succeed.

Wiping her damp hands on the side of her black trousers, she moved to the door and opened it.

And then he was there, even bigger than she remembered, taller, more intimidating. And twice as beautiful.

Maybe that's the part she found so disconcerting, too. Because she'd been around big men all her life. Brock was six-four, and Cormac a half an inch below that. But her brothers were more rugged—handsome but lacking the dark Latin sensuality that made Wolf's eyes just a little too dark and his lower lip a little too full and his black lashes a little too long. It'd be one thing if he didn't know his effect on women, but he did, and it only made him more dangerous. Wolf wasn't so much charming as lethal.

"I just need to get my purse," she said, opening the door wider and doing her best to hide her nerves. "Do you want to come in?"

"If you're just getting your handbag, I can wait here."

She silently disappeared, legs distinctly trembly as she went to the couch to scoop up the little evening bag she'd laid out earlier. The bag was so pretty, a small, black, handsome couture bag that looked simple but cost a fortune. Alexandra had seen the price tag when the stylist had presented it and gasped. The stylist had merely winked. "It's covered in your budget," she'd said.

Now Alexandra clutched the bag beneath her elbow, feeling briefly like a glamorous celebrity herself. She knew it was all hair and makeup and wardrobe, but still, it was such a treat, such a delight to feel genuinely pretty for a change.

"So what are we doing tonight?" she asked, returning to join Wolf at the door.

"Thought we'd have some drinks, get a bite to eat."

Alexandra nodded and closed the door behind her. She turned to head down the front steps, but Wolf hesitated and, reaching behind her, checked the door, giving the knob a twist, making sure it was locked.

She shot him a quick glance as they walked toward his Lamborghini. The fact that he'd double-check her door touched her, made her feel surprisingly safe.

She was still looking at him when his head turned and his dark eyes met hers. She shivered inwardly and amended her last thought. Make that as safe as one could feel with a wolf.

It was a warm night and the fog hadn't yet moved in. Wolf headed to Santa Monica, where he pulled in front of the luxurious Hotel Casa del Mar, which stood next door to its famous sister property, Shutters on the Beach.

The Casa Del Mar, built in 1926, was once the grandest of the opulent Santa Monica beach clubs and hotels, and a recent fifty-million-dollar renovation had returned the historic property to its former magnificence.

Although she'd never been there until tonight, Alexandra knew that the Veranda, the elegant lobby lounge, was famous for its literary crowd. Screenwriters and novelists hung out in the celebrated bar, with its enormous windows overlooking the sea and the plush velvet chaises and chairs scattered for comfortable seating.

The Veranda was packed when they entered, but miraculously an alcove opened up for Wolf and the cocktail waitress immediately took their drink orders.

Alexandra had thought the lounge was crowded when they walked in, buzzing with laughter and conversation, but the buzz seemed even louder now that Wolf had entered the room.

Everyone was looking their way, men and women alike watching Wolf, openly fascinated.

"I forgot. You're such a star," Alexandra said, sitting on the edge of her red velvet chair, afraid to relax and possibly ruin her artfully styled hair or carefully applied makeup.

"You forgot?"

"Well, I forgot it was like this." She pressed her hands against the chair's edge. "Everyone always looks at you. They watch everything you say and do. It's incredible. I guess that's what *star* means. You're the focus of everyone and everything."

He shrugged, unconcerned. "People are curious. They want to know if I'm as interesting as the characters I play."

"Are you?"

He laughed softly. "No." Reaching out, he took her hand, brought it to his lips. He kissed her fingertips and then curled her fingers over his and kissed the back of her hand, all while his gaze held her transfixed. "I'm sorry to say, I'm really quite boring."

She didn't believe him, not for a second.

Not when his eyes, glowing with an inner fire, belied his words, and Alexandra felt her belly clench as his lips moved across her skin.

He was not boring. Not now. Not ever.

Wolf tugged her hand, pulling her up and out of her chair, drawing her firmly toward him.

"Wolf," she whispered in protest.

He ignored her, pulling her down into his chair so that she sat awkwardly on his lap.

"*Wolf,*" she repeated fiercely, blood surging into her face, darkening her cheeks.

"You were too far away," he said.

She felt the hard heat of his lap through her thin black

trousers and it threw her, flustered her so that she tensed, going rigid in his arms. "And now I'm a little too close," she choked, her breath catching in her throat as his hand moved to the small of her back, holding her more securely.

"I think you're perfect."

"I feel ridiculous."

"Have I told you how much I like your hair?"

She felt as though everyone in the Veranda lounge must be looking at her. "Please let me off. People will talk."

"But isn't that the point? Don't we want them to?"

He was right, of course, but even knowing why she was on his lap didn't change the way she felt or how her body was responding—because it *was* responding. Her nerves were jumping and strange things were happening inside her, sharp hot streaks of sensation starting with the tight coil in her tummy and then racing to her breasts as well as lower, deeper, making her legs twitch and her mind wander.

"Stay here for our drink and then I'll let you off," he said, rubbing the small of her back as though it were perfectly ordinary for her to be on his lap with his strong hands casually caressing her, and maybe he could pretend ease, but Alexandra felt as though she'd pop out of her skin any moment.

His touch wasn't soothing and she wasn't relaxing. She couldn't relax, not when he was stirring dormant feelings and even more dormant nerve endings.

Her lower back was tingling, sizzling with heat and pressure, warming to life beneath the dizzying touch of his hand, and that burn was starting to make her ache in places she didn't want to ache. Her breasts were already growing fuller, more sensitive, and her belly was coiling hot and tight, making her think of escape. Relief.

She looked up into his face.

Had he had this effect on her four years ago? Somehow she didn't think so. She couldn't imagine it. Would she have very different feelings about him today if he had? "I think that's long enough," she whispered.

"Not even close." And then his hands were on her waist,

fingers sliding up toward her breasts, and she sucked in air, eyes widening in mute fascination.

He was turning her on. Really turning her on—and in public, too.

"*Wolf*. Let me go. Now."

"We're supposed to be lovers."

Her mouth was parched, her lips painfully dry, and she licked her lips, trying to moisten them. "I know, but does this have to be in public?"

"If it's not public, no one will know."

Alexandra thought she'd run to the bar and make her own drink if the cocktail waitress didn't return soon. "But may-be…maybe we can be one of those mysterious couples that don't really *do* PDAs."

"PDAs?" he asked, his head tipping back against the velvet chair as he watched her with lazy interest.

His hair was thick, glossy black, and he wore it a little long. And in a way it reminded her of a wolf pelt—thick, dense, male.

And Wolf was very male.

Alexandra struggled to swallow. She couldn't remember ever being this thirsty before. Her body was burning and her throat felt absolutely parched. She pressed her lips together, feeling her teeth beneath.

"PDAs?" he prompted again.

"Public displays of affection."

The corner of his mouth lifted. "But I've no problem with public displays of affection if I like my woman."

He'd trapped her in his eyes, and she gazed helplessly into the deep brown depths, a color somewhere between cocoa and black coffee, thinking they seemed endless, so dark, so deep, so alive with that unique fire of his.

One of his hands trailed up her spine, tracing her backbone and the little vertebrae between.

She shivered beneath the light caress, aroused despite her fierce desire not to be.

He had exactly the right touch, not too firm, not too delicate. And there was something about him, about his size and strength, about the tilt of his head and the mocking glint in his eyes that made her feel small and pretty and feminine. But not just feminine. Desirable. As though she were the only one in the room. The only woman in Los Angeles. California. Make that the planet.

Her pulse quickened and she found herself staring into his dark eyes, eyes that from far away were black but close like this had the smallest splinters of silver. Those shards of silver made her wonder if it was the lounge's soft light or the fire that burned within him that made his eyes glow, turning him into some fierce and beautiful work of art.

Fire and ice.

The words whispered through her head and wrapped uncomfortably tight around her heart.

Because that was really who he was, she realized, looking at his face, the hard but expressive sensual features, the glossy black hair, the equally strong black brows.

"Now you're staring," he teased, his hand sliding higher up her back to rub between her shoulder blades, finding the little knots and balls of fear and tension. And magically he smoothed the knots away, rubbing firmer and then lighter, heating her, melting that resistance within her.

She wasn't sure when she began to lean into him, seeking his touch, his warmth, but somehow his chest was where she wanted to be.

The cocktail waitress materialized with their drinks, and Wolf gestured for her to set them on the low table at his elbow. Smiling, she left the drinks and moved on, but not before giving Alexandra a brief inspection from beneath her lowered lashes.

Alexandra saw the look the waitress had given her and she wondered if everyone would look at her that way.

Wolf handed her martini glass to her before lifting his. They clinked glasses and Alexandra tilted her chocolate martini to her mouth, curious about a drink she'd heard of but never tried.

It was smooth, hot, strong, sweet, and she wrinkled her nose as she swallowed.

"Don't like it?" Wolf asked, watching her.

"It's different."

"I take it different is bad."

She smiled ruefully. "Different can be good. But in this case, different is just different."

"Mmm." His dark eyes glowed, and she felt, if not saw, the laughter within.

"You're not laughing at me, are you?"

"Actually I am."

And as she opened her mouth to protest, he caught the back of her head in his hand and pulled her close to cover her lips with his.

She inhaled at the sudden touch of his mouth on hers. It was a shock to her senses, his mouth so cool and firm, tasting of sweet chocolate and icy vodka. She shivered, her breasts peaking. At her shiver, his mouth hardened, the kiss deepening, the pressure parting her lips.

Her head spun, her senses swam, her body danced with pleasure that was as hot and sweet as it was electric.

The electric part dazzled her all over again, and blindly she leaned into him, searching for him, searching for more of the sensation and pleasure he offered.

Finally he lifted his head. She blinked, tried to focus, but she could only feel her mouth, soft, swollen, sensitive and it amazed her, this way he had of winning her over, taking her objections and melting them as surely as he'd just melted her.

Lifting her fingers to her mouth, Alex pressed down on her lips, feeling how the lower lip quivered and how her blood raced in her veins liquid-hot.

One kiss and she wanted more.

One kiss and she wanted to slide her hands into his thick ebony hair, twine her fingers through the glossy strands and hold tight, hold his face to hers so she could feel him, his beard and mouth, jaw and chin.

"You're looking a little more relaxed," he said, catching her hand in his and bringing it to his mouth, where he kissed the pulse beating frantically in her wrist.

"I think it's the chocolate martini," she said unsteadily.

His eyes creased. "I thought it was my kiss."

She lifted her glass to her mouth and took a greedy gulp to hide the fact that he was making her nervous all over again. Those butterflies in her stomach had returned, only this time they felt more like forks of jagged lightning.

The chocolate-flavored martini slid down her throat, cool and tantalizing but also empowering. The cocktail made her feel stronger, calmer than she would have otherwise.

By the time they headed for home, close to midnight, Alexandra was laughing and surprisingly at ease.

She didn't know if it was that first chocolate martini or Wolf making an effort to be charming, but she'd ended up having fun.

After drinks at the Casa Del Mar they'd driven to Houston's for steaks and salads and glasses of wine. Again everyone had stared when they'd entered the darkened brick building, and again the hostess had magically found them a table.

Wolf hadn't been the only celebrity dining at Houston's that night, though. There'd been several other well-known entertainers, and two of them, both men, had stopped by their table to say hello.

Now Wolf was walking her to her door. After she unlocked the door, she stepped inside, and he followed her in, closing the door behind him. For a moment she felt a spike in nerves again, nerves and anticipation. Would he kiss her again?

But instead of a kiss, he checked each room, made sure everything was as it should be before saying good-night, giving her a platonic peck on the forehead and returning to his car.

His brotherly kiss jolted her back to reality. The kiss on the forehead was a kiss in private, a kiss behind closed doors and an indication of how things really were.

She wasn't his love, wasn't his girlfriend. She wasn't even really his date. She was just a girl hired to play a part. Any kisses, any whispers, any sexy innuendos were for the public and the press, wherever the hidden photographers might be.

Alex leaned against the door and remembered the kisses

earlier. There'd been so much heat between them. When he'd kissed her, she'd felt unbelievable. Glamorous. Funny. Delicious.

"Delicious," Alex repeated, turning out the small hall light and heading for her bathroom, where she pulled her hair into a ponytail and washed her face, getting rid of the makeup.

In bed, Alex curled onto her side, covers pulled up high, so high that they covered her chin and the middle of her ear.

So you learned something important tonight, she told herself. *You learned that there's a difference between real and pretend, truth and fiction. Tonight was make-believe. And it's okay to enjoy the make-believe, but don't get it confused with reality.*

You're doing a job. That's it.

No emotions, no hopes, no feelings.

This, she reminded herself sternly, is business.

The next morning Alex was at work when the flowers arrived. Three dozen very long-stemmed pink roses in a stunning hand-blown glass vase. Oohing and aahing, the entire Paradise Pictures office staff broke away from their tasks to look over Alexandra's shoulder as she read the card.

Thank you for an unforgettable night. Looking forward to another. Wolf

Kristie, one of the other production assistants, snatched the card from Alexandra's hands. "Wolf?" she said, flashing the card at everyone. "There's only one Wolf I know of."

"Hmm," was all Alexandra said as she sat down in her chair and pushed the extravagant roses toward a corner of her desk to make some room to collate the scripts she'd just photocopied. It was one of the first jobs she did every morning. There were always script changes during the night, and the new, updated scenes had to be distributed to the cast and crew immediately.

But Kristie wasn't to be put off. She leaned across Alexandra's desk and held the small white florist card in front of Alexandra's eyes. "Wolf."

Alexandra looked up, her gaze meeting Kristie's. "I think that's what it does say."

"Wolf Kerrick?"

Alexandra suppressed a sigh. "What do you want me to say, Kristie?"

The young, bubbly production assistant from Duluth, Minnesota, arched her eyebrows. "You're seeing Wolf Kerrick?"

Alexandra shrugged as she reached for the next set of pages and stapled the corner. "I don't know if I'm seeing him. We went out last night. Had dinner and drinks—"

"Is that the first time?"

"Um, well, not exactly. We've had lunch. And then he's stopped by my house a couple times—"

"For real?"

Alexandra suppressed a smile. Kristie's expression was priceless. "We've only just met in the past week. Who knows where it'll go?"

But Kristie wasn't looking at the card anymore, she was studying Alexandra. "It's more than that. Something's going on. You're different, you know. You're…pretty."

Alexandra's eyebrows lifted. "I wasn't pretty before?"

"Not like this."

Rolling her eyes, Alexandra grabbed the florist card from Kristie and shoved it in her desk drawer. She tried to focus on the job in front of her, but Kristie hadn't budged and the other girls were still watching and waiting.

She knew she had to say something. They were desperate for a morsel of news, some juicy little tidbit, and isn't this what Alexandra had agreed to do? Play the part? Become Wolf's new love interest?

Shaking her head, Alexandra finally looked up. "If he proposes, I'll let you all know."

Three o'clock that afternoon, the studio's main number rang and the receptionist took the call and then buzzed Alexandra to let her know she had an incoming call from Wolf Kerrick. Unfortunately the receptionist chose to use the intercom to tell Alexandra of her call, instead of a private line.

With Kristie and the other girls staring in rabid fascination,

Alexandra picked up her phone and took the call off hold. "Alexandra Shanahan," she said as crisply as possible.

"Wolf Kerrick," the voice answered at the other end of the line. His voice was deep and husky and tinged with amusement.

Alexandra didn't know if it was the timbre of his voice, or the amusement in it, but it immediately set her teeth on edge. "Hello."

"Can I bring the coffee girl a coffee?"

Aware that Kristie was inching forward, Alexandra ducked her head, trying to avoid being overheard. "No, thank you."

"How about I take you for a coffee?"

"Wolf, I'm *working*."

"Not very hard."

"What does that mean?"

"It seems to me you're just sitting there, staring at your desk."

"How do you know?" Alexandra demanded before noticing the office had gone strangely silent. Lifting her head, she saw that Wolf, dressed in loose dark denims and a black linen shirt unbuttoned halfway down his chest, had entered the front doors and stood next to the receptionist's desk talking on his cell phone.

My God, he looked gorgeous. And sinful. "What are you doing?" she whispered urgently into the phone, trying to duck her head so he couldn't see her face or the telltale blush turning her cheeks a crimson pink.

"Watching you."

She squeezed her eyes shut. "Why?"

"Because I want to."

"Wolf."

"Can you just do that with a little more passion in your voice?"

"No!" Alexandra started to slam the phone down and then, remembering she had an audience, hung the receiver up more gently. Phone down, she watched Wolf slowly saunter toward her through the rows of desks.

She heard the girls whispering excitedly as he passed. Wolf had to have heard the whispers, too.

Reaching her desk, he stood over her, his linen shirt half open, giving her and everyone else a glimpse of burnished bronze skin and hard, toned muscles. His dark eyes half smiled down at her, and yet there was nothing sleepy about him. He had the silent, watchful air of a wolf before it attacked.

"I'm stealing you away," he said.

Alexandra hadn't expected to see Wolf for days. She'd thought maybe by the weekend he'd call her, contact her, set something up for the future, and yet here he was, at her desk, causing trouble.

And she wasn't ready for trouble. Didn't think she'd be ready for his kind of trouble for a long time. Last night had taken something out of her. Last night had been a tease, a torment. She'd had so much fun with him that she'd imagined he'd been enjoying her company just as much. Instead he'd been acting.

Acting.

Alexandra smiled her brightest, most confident smile to cover her trepidation. "I wish I could go. But I've so much work. I've a million things to do and Daniel—"

"Has already given you permission to take off early." Wolf smiled down at her, but the smile didn't quite reach his eyes. "So get your purse and let's go."

CHAPTER FOUR

IT WAS A GORGEOUS afternoon, hot, sunny, the sky a dazzling California blue. Wolf was driving a different car than he had last night, a gleaming red Ferrari that looked brand-new.

A studio head, just leaving his office and heading for his car, noticed the Ferrari, too, and wandered over to shake Wolf's hand and compliment him on the car.

"That's a Superamerica, isn't it?" he said to Wolf as he shook his hand. "Hardtop convertible."

Wolf opened the passenger-side door for Alexandra. "It is."

"I was reading about the car's revolving roof recently. Doesn't it open up in ten seconds?"

Wolf was heading to the driver's side now. "It does."

"What are they? Half mil?" he asked as Wolf settled behind the wheel.

Wolf put the key in the ignition, started the engine. "A little less than that," he said before putting the car into reverse.

The other man whistled. "Beautiful car."

Wolf nodded agreement and drove away. But Alexandra sat next to him, dumbfounded.

"This car is worth half a million dollars?"

Wolf shot her an amused glance. "It's not that much. It's closer to a third of a million. But I can see you don't approve."

She studied the car's interior. The steering wheel wasn't exactly normal. It had paddle shifters on the wheel, but other than that it looked like an ordinary—albeit very clean—sports car. "I don't understand why anyone would spend so much money on a car."

"I have the money."

"Yes, but—"

He was leaving Culver City behind and heading for Santa Monica. "But what?"

"But you could do a lot of good with that money. You could feed starving children and build houses for the homeless and things like that." She stopped talking, bit her lip, stared at her hands, inspecting the spa manicure she'd gotten at the salon yesterday. "I know it's none of my business. I just wish I had the means to help more people. I think we should all help more people."

Wolf looked at her for a long, silent moment. "I agree," he said quietly before returning his attention to the road.

They traveled in silence down Santa Monica Boulevard and then north on Highway 1 wrapping the coast toward Pacific Palisades and scenic, craggy Malibu.

Wolf drove well, fast but confidently, and with the cliffs to the right and the sea to the left, Alexandra felt as though she were part of a movie or some reality television show.

He had been unusually quiet since she made her comment about helping others, but she wasn't sorry for thinking people should help others and she wasn't sorry for thinking an expensive car like this was a waste of money. He could buy whatever he wanted and she could think whatever she wanted. They weren't really a couple. They didn't have to agree.

Finally Alexandra couldn't take the silence any longer. She made a pitiful stab at conversation by asking him, "Are you excited about the new film?"

"Excited?" Wolf repeated, his upper lip curling. "I wouldn't say I'm excited, but I will be glad to work again. Working distracts me. Keeps my mind off other things."

It wasn't the answer she'd expected. She'd imagined he enjoyed acting, thought he would have found a certain fizz factor from being one of the most highly acclaimed actors in the business. "What things?"

His eyebrow arched as he glanced at her. "We all have ghosts and demons."

"And you won't tell me yours."

"No."

Alexandra didn't know if it was his expression or the caustic curve of his sensual mouth, but she felt the strangest flutter inside her middle as though she were nothing but naked nerve endings.

"Do you ever go home?" she asked suddenly, not sure where the question came from but curious about him, curious about his past as well as those ghosts and demons he'd just mentioned.

He shot her a long, assessing glance from beneath his lashes. He knew what she was doing, too. "Ireland or Spain?"

"Which is home?"

"Both, I suppose. I'm bilingual and was raised in both countries."

"Your mother was Spanish."

"From Cadiz," he answered, slowing for the traffic light looming ahead. "I was born in Cadiz, but when I was twelve my parents divorced and I moved with my father to Dublin. Spain is home in ways Ireland could never be, but I'm comfortable in Ireland, I like the people."

"And yet now you're here, in America."

"It's what the career dictated."

Alexandra stole a glance at him from beneath her lashes. "Do you ever regret becoming an actor?"

He hesitated before answering, shifting gears down and then, after the light changed, accelerating until he pulled into the parking lot for the Malibu Coffeehouse.

Turning off the engine, he turned to look at her. "Every day," he said grimly.

After getting their coffee, Wolf drove to one of the scenic turnouts on Highway 1 and parked. Climbing from the car, they moved to the cliff's edge to savor the view.

Wolf drew a deep breath, breathing in the stinging salty air off the Pacific Ocean. He loved the ocean, loved the cliffs of Malibu and Pacific Palisades. This area reminded him of

Ireland's southern and western coasts, especially when the soupy fog rolled in, covering everything in a misty, mournful gray.

If it weren't for the ocean, Wolf didn't think he would have survived so many years in Southern California. He hated L.A. He hated the falseness, the superficiality, the attitude and airs. People in his business—like so many people in Los Angeles— were afraid to be real, human.

They were afraid of their bodies, their age, their flaws, their frailties. Women here went to ridiculous lengths to be beautiful: nipping, tucking, tightening, enlarging, enhancing, sucking, smoothing. They worked on themselves endlessly, refusing to age naturally, fixated on how they looked, how others perceived them, how attractive they were in comparison to other women.

God, he missed real women. He missed wit and banter, laughter and smiles that made the eyes crinkle and foreheads wrinkle instead of ghastly BOTOX-frozen faces. He'd love to share a drink with a girl who could tell a proper story, eat a bag of chips and not immediately worry about her thighs. Sometimes Dublin seemed too far away, and in those moments he missed his old life—the ordinary life before he'd become a celebrity—more than he could say.

Alexandra watched Wolf sip his coffee as they leaned against his half-a-million-dollar car. She felt wrong leaning against a car that cost so much, but he did it so she supposed it was okay for her to do it.

Ever since they'd left the Malibu Coffeehouse Wolf had been quiet, and his expression was unusually pensive now. Always enigmatic, he seemed even more distant than usual. Again she wondered why he didn't enjoy being an actor and why his success—and the accompanying fame—didn't mean more to him.

Was he really so spoiled? Was it arrogance that made him fail to appreciate his achievements? Or was it something else?

"There's nothing planned after this, is there?" she asked, wind blowing, tousling her hair. She tried tucking strands behind her ears, but they wouldn't stay there.

"We've a dinner tonight at Spago."

Any other time Alexandra would have been excited about the idea of eating at Spago. Wolfgang Puck's name and reputation spoke for itself. But she was tired—she hadn't been sleeping well lately—and after the tense afternoon she craved a quiet night at home. Alone. Preferably curled up on her couch with a good book.

"Do I have to go?" she asked in a small voice.

"Yes."

"Why?" she asked in an even smaller voice.

He glanced at her, expression blank. "It's Rye Priven's birthday."

Rye Priven was the newest heartthrob in Hollywood, a gorgeous Australian that had just co-starred in a film with Wolf. The film was in the editing stage now and was supposed to be released at Christmas, when all the big Academy Award contenders were released.

"But Rye Priven doesn't know me—"

"Everyone's coming as a couple," Wolf answered roughly. "You're supposed to be the other half of my couple."

She ducked her head, stared sightlessly at her cup. She was hating being part of the couple right now. Wolf was so intense. And unpredictable.

"Rye's hosting the party himself. He's keeping it low-key," Wolf added. "I think he's only invited six friends, so my absence would be conspicuous, particularly as I already told him I'd be there."

"I'm not saying you shouldn't go," she doggedly replied. "It's just that I don't feel like it."

He looked at her over the rim of his coffee as he took another sip. "You don't like me much, do you?"

"No," she blurted and then winced at her bluntness.

"Why not?" Wolf paused, waited for an answer. "It's a shame you can't be more articulate in naming my faults."

Alexandra shot him a swift assessing glance, but he didn't look the least bit injured. "Your morals and values are deplorable. You could be someone truly great, someone...heroic. But instead you just use people. Take advantage of them. I hate it."

"And you hate me, too."

"I—" she started to protest but then fell silent. She didn't want to start lying to him, because then the lies would never end. It was bad enough she'd agreed to do this, but to become as fake as her role? No. She wouldn't sell out. She couldn't. "*Hate* is a strong word," she conceded. "But I don't like you and I don't respect you. You just seem so bored and spoiled and arrogant. Selfish, too."

"You're a hard woman, Alexandra Shanahan."

She suddenly felt her anger start to melt. She didn't want to be angry, didn't like feeling angry. "You're just used to women falling all over you, desperate to impress you, please you. It's too bad, too, because you'll never know if people like you for you or because you're a famous movie star."

"Or if they like me for my body or my face."

Alexandra nearly choked on her sip of her now lukewarm coffee. "And that's exactly why I don't like you. You're so incredibly..." she drew a rough breath "...so..."

"Yes?"

"Conceited."

"Conceited," he repeated.

"You have so much—you've virtually everything—and you don't even appreciate it."

"And just what is everything?"

She gestured, her hand sweeping up and down. "This. You. Looks, wealth, fame, intelligence, success. You have it all, you have more than anyone else I know. But do you even feel grateful? Do you even have any idea how blessed you are? I don't think so."

"I hired you to play my girlfriend. I'm not paying you to be my conscience."

"I don't think you've even got a conscience!" Alexandra shrugged. "And you're right, none of this is my business. Just like who you pick up and take home isn't my business. Or the number of women you have in a week, that's not my concern either. You're free to take women and use them and abuse them, because as long as they give themselves over to you, you're not doing anything wrong."

"Right."

"Wrong!" Alexandra furiously tossed her cup into the trash bin and spun to face him. "Just because women will let you have them doesn't mean you should take them. Just because women get blinded by your good looks and fame, just because they hope a night of sex will turn into true love, doesn't mean it's okay for you to take advantage of them."

The corner of his mouth lifted. "Maybe I'm not taking advantage of these women. Maybe they're taking advantage of me. Maybe they know one night of sex is just that, one night of sex, and when they leave me in the morning they leave happy to have had one night with me. They've got bragging rights, a chance to talk big—"

"That's horrible."

"To you."

Her hands balled, nails pressing hard against tender skin. "Not just to me but to all women. It's a lack of respect, a lack of awareness of how women think and feel, of how making love makes them think they've fallen in love…"

"You're sounding as though this is pretty personal."

Her chest felt hot and tight, too hot and tight. She felt absolutely undone, beyond her own level of self-control. "Women aren't tissues, to be used and discarded."

"Have I somehow hurt you, Miss Shanahan?"

She turned away, stared out across the busy lights of the boulevard.

Yes.

Yes. Four years ago, you parked your fancy car and we kissed and made out. And then when I fumbled with your damn trousers and belt buckle, you realized I was inexperienced. You realized I didn't know how to touch you or give you pleasure and you got rid of me so fast afterward. If I couldn't give you what you wanted…

Tears filled her eyes and she squeezed her fists against her ribs, pressing hard against her sides, pressing skin to bone. "No," she whispered. "You've done nothing to me."

"Are you sure? Because it's almost as though you've some personal experience—"

"No."

"Good. Then you'll have no objections going to Rye's party tonight?"

Alexandra reached up and swiped away a tear before it could fall. "You still want me to go?"

"Want?" His shoulders lifted. "I don't know if it's want, but you did sign a contract, and regardless of your personal feelings—or even my own—you'll fulfill the contract."

"Even if I hate you," she whispered.

His mouth quirked, eyes dark and granite-hard. "Especially if you hate me. Fewer complications, remember?"

The party that night at Spago was less stressful than she'd feared.

The stylist had dropped off clothes for her to wear—a smart black cocktail dress that was both simple and sexy, very high stiletto heels and a pretty gold charm bracelet that was girlish and fun.

The stylist had shown Alexandra how to pile her hair on top of her head in a messy twist with loose tendrils falling here and there. With small gold studs in her ears and neutral makeup, she looked nothing like the office assistant she was.

Good, she thought, joining Wolf in the car. Because she wasn't going to be an office assistant or production assistant for long. She was going to learn how to direct. She was going to make movies.

Wolf was driving a different car again tonight. This one was a sleek pewter Ferrari from the '60s. Even she could see it was a classic that had been lovingly restored.

"I've seen three cars so far," she said, sliding into the passenger seat. "Are there more?"

Wolf waited for her to buckle her seat belt before driving off. "An entire warehouse full."

"A warehouse?"

"I collect cars." White teeth flashed, and Alexandra couldn't be sure if it was a smile or a snarl. "Something else for you to disapprove of."

Dinner was less tense than the drive to the restaurant. Nearly everyone attending the dinner was a celebrity. She counted four actors, two actresses, a comedian and an R & B singer, along with their respective dates. During dinner Wolf discussed politics with Rye and the R & B singer, and Alexandra was rather surprised by his depth of knowledge regarding world economics and the U.S. trade policy.

"Do I know you?" the man to her left asked when Alexandra turned from Wolf's conversation to her dinner salad.

She recognized the man—an actor named Will Cowell—but they'd never met before. "No," she answered, cutting the apple in her salad.

"Are you sure?"

She stabbed her fork into lettuce, apple, and blue cheese. "Quite sure."

"Hmm." Will studied her, elbow on the table, expression teasing. "Then I *should* know you."

She chewed her salad diligently, hoping he didn't see her blush. Swallowing, Alexandra wiped her mouth with her linen table napkin. "Why is that?"

"Because you don't look like a bimbo—and God knows I need a break from bimbos."

Alexandra laughed. She couldn't help it. "What makes you think I'm not a bimbo?"

"No fake boobs or collagen-plumped lips." He smiled charmingly. "I'm an expert in those things, you see."

Her eyebrows arched, but she took another bite of salad instead of replying. It seemed safer to eat the sweet-tart vinaigrette salad than discuss his expertise in fake breasts and lips.

"Can I have a word with you alone? In private?" Wolf suddenly growled into her ear.

She turned toward him, apple and cheese skewered on her fork. "Why?"

His dark eyes snapped with fire. "Alone," he repeated. "In private."

Wolf stood up, pushed his chair back and took her by the elbow.

With his hand on her lower back, he pressed her through the restaurant and down the hallway until he found a small alcove by the pay phones.

"What are you doing?" Wolf demanded, turning on her. "What game are you playing?"

Alexandra shook her head, nonplussed. "Game? There's no game. I was having dinner, talking to Will—"

"Will's pathological. He has to get in every woman's pants."

She jerked her head back as if slapped. "Well, he's not getting in mine, and we were just exchanging a few words. Pleasantries, that's all."

Wolf's features tightened. "He was looking at you as though he'd devour you any moment."

"If you didn't notice, *I* was devouring my salad."

"You're supposed to be devouring me."

Alexandra gasped with outrage and shock. Her jaw dropped, her eyes grew wide. And then she snapped her jaw closed and came out swinging. "Sorry, Wolf, but I'm afraid I don't have the experience!"

She gave him a shove, her hand connecting with his chest, and she'd pushed at him so hard her wrist did a painful little snap, but he didn't budge.

Wolf felt her hand hit his chest, but he didn't move a muscle. He couldn't. He was wound too tight.

No one and nothing got under his skin, not anymore. He wanted to believe that, but since meeting Alexandra Shanahan, she'd lived under his skin.

His gaze swept her face. "What do you mean that you haven't the experience?"

Her dark blue eyes snapped at him. "I mean that I'm not an actress and I haven't devoured lots of men and I can't do whatever it is you want me to do."

"Are we talking oral sex or intercourse?"

He watched, fascinated, as a wave of color stormed her cheeks.

"And that," she choked out, tendrils of hair falling around her face, "is none of your business."

"Just like my sex life is none of your business."

"That's because you have one and I don't!"

He leaned toward her, trapping her between the pay phone and the wall. "You could."

Another wave of color surged through her cheeks, darker, hotter than before. Her blue eyes shimmered. "It's not in our contract," she said through gritted teeth, nose in the air, cocky as a little girl in a denim skirt and cowboy boots.

"No," he muttered, "but this is." He closed the distance between them with one aggressive step.

Alexandra's heart thumped wildly and she pressed backward, her hands behind her, knuckles tight against the wall. He loomed over her, so tall, so big, so much more powerful, and it wasn't even his height that made him strong or his frame but the force inside him, that fire. He was alive and intense, engaged and aware.

She didn't want him to kiss her, didn't want him anywhere near her. But once his head dipped, it was like last night at Casa Del Mar's Veranda lounge.

Bolts of electricity shot through her, and that was even before his mouth completely covered hers.

And then when his lips did take hers, she felt the electricity again, hotter, brighter, sharper.

He felt good. He felt amazing. Unreal.

Her mouth softened. The pressure of his lips increased and her heart raced, fast, faster, as fire and hunger whipped through her.

She groaned as he parted her mouth with his tongue, groaned again as his tongue flicked the inside of her inner bottom lip, tasting her, teasing her, making her want more of him.

This wasn't a kiss, she realized, dazed. This was his first step in seducing her, taking her, and he intended to do it. Despite the contract.

But would that change when he realized she really was as inexperienced as she said?

Back at the table, Wolf sat with his arm draped over the back of Alexandra's chair. And her chair was close to his—so close that no one could mistake his actions for anything but a sign of possession.

He was claiming her, marking his territory, letting the other men know to stay away and letting other women know he was taken.

Alexandra, he noticed, didn't like it.

"You might as well put a Sold sign on me," she said through gritted teeth.

"That's not a bad idea," he answered, smiling faintly at her pink-cheeked indignation. He'd never met a woman who blushed so much—or made a simple blush so alluring.

Studying her profile, he found it hard to believe she was as inexperienced with men as she claimed. How could she be when she was so ridiculously pretty?

He looked at her thoughtfully, almost clinically, trying to understand what it was about her that made him want to put that Sold sign on her.

Maybe it was that leggy tomboy stride of hers, or her mouth that was endlessly expressive, sometimes set, sometimes pursed, sometimes smiling most beguilingly.

Wolf didn't know which he liked better—that full mouth with the tiny indentation in the bottom lip or the midnight-blue eyes set so wide beneath winged eyebrows.

Or her sharp mind and sassy tongue.

His sardonic smile stretched.

She was a breathtaking combination of girl and woman, funny, sensitive, proud, uncertain. Unlike the women in Los Angeles who pursued him, women who blatantly advertised their interest and availability, Alexandra didn't project her sexuality. It was hidden, secret, and yet when he kissed her, she became a different woman.

She became his woman.

It was as simple as that.

Later, as they drove from Spago back to Alexandra's house,

she sat as far as she could from Wolf in the snug sports car and kept her eyes firmly fixed out the passenger window.

Wolf had reached a whole new level of despicability. He'd shown his true colors, behaved like a member of the animal kingdom more than once.

"You're still upset about the kiss," Wolf said.

His nonchalance only antagonized her further. "Everyone noticed your behavior at dinner." She threw him a disgusted look. "You kept your arm on my shoulder throughout the meal as though you were afraid I'd bolt away any minute."

"I wasn't afraid you'd run away. Your heels are far too high—"

"Wolf, don't play the charming-Irishman card right now, okay?"

"And I like touching you," he continued smoothly as though she'd never interrupted. "You're my girlfriend. It's my prerogative."

"And that's how it felt, too. It was your prerogative to touch me. Your prerogative to kiss me. Your prerogative to do whatever you damn well pleased." She finally turned to face him. "Next time why don't you just pee all over me like an alpha wolf should."

He'd pulled up in front of her house, and turning off the engine, he flashed her a lazy white-toothed grin. "Hmm, kind of kinky for a girl without much experience, but if that's what you want—"

Alexandra threw the door open and jumped out of the car before she had to listen to another word.

And as she undressed for bed, peeling the smart, sexy black dress off, Alexandra wanted to scream with frustration. Spending time with Wolf was hard, far harder than she'd even imagined. It wasn't just one thing, it was everything. He wasn't just physically gorgeous, his personality was huge, his charisma larger than life.

He was far more than she could handle, and she'd known it, she'd known it from the beginning, but she wanted that promotion. She wanted it badly.

And unless you'd been a little girl who'd grown up outside

a small town, you didn't appreciate that for girls in small towns opportunity meant a job at Wal-Mart and success meant one day owning your own car free and clear. Unless you'd been the only girl in a family of overbearing brothers, you didn't understand the value of dreaming, and dreaming big.

Unless you'd listened to the sound of television late into the night, the canned laughter on TV shows and overly loud commercials the only sound in your house after everyone else had gone to bed, you didn't know the definition of *escape*.

You didn't know how important it was to get away and become someone else, something better, something more.

But Alexandra knew all these things, had lived all these things, and she decided years ago she'd have a different life than her mother, her father, her brothers. She'd do it differently than the people who seemed to just get swept along by life.

She wouldn't be swept along. She'd do the sweeping.

She wouldn't ever make anyone take care of her.

But Wolf Kerrick seemed determined to change all that. In fact, if she let herself really think about it, it felt as though Wolf Kerrick was sweeping *her*.

CHAPTER FIVE

ALEXANDRA'S FIRST thought on waking was that she needed to call Wolf immediately, before she lost her nerve.

"We need to talk," she said crisply, her tone no-nonsense when he answered the phone. "You hired me to make things better, not worse, and it's important we find a way to keep our public appearance positive."

If she'd caught him off guard, he gave no indication. "I agree," he said.

Alexandra couldn't read his inflection. "I can't help your image if we can't even communicate," she continued stiffly. "So I propose we work harder at creating clearer communication channels."

"Communication channels, yes."

She understood then that he was, without a doubt, mocking her. And Alexandra knew that she had a choice—she could call him on his attitude, thus detouring from the purpose of her call, or she could let his sarcasm slide. She chose to let his sarcasm slide. "Before we go out again," she persisted, "and before we make another appearance, we need to choreograph the evening."

Wolf cleared his throat. "Are we entering a dance competition, by chance?"

Alexandra chose to ignore this bit of sarcasm, too. "I need to know before we go places what you expect and how we're *both* to behave. I can't wing it anymore. I'm not an actress and I can't improvise the way you can."

There was silence on his end of the phone and the silence seemed to stretch endlessly.

Exasperated, she closed her eyes, counted to five. "Did you hear me?"

"What?" he asked innocently.

"This doesn't have to be difficult," she said through gritted teeth.

"You're right." And then his tone changed, his rough voice deepened. "So let me make this easier. We've a premiere Saturday afternoon. It's a matinee since it's a children's film. I did the voice for one of the characters and I've promised to be there. You'll attend and—" he broke off, hesitated as if searching for the right word "—pretend to enjoy me."

Alexandra flushed hotly. "That's not exactly the choreographed routine I was imagining. It sounds more like a set of military orders."

"But at least you know my expectations."

"And what about mine?" she flashed, furious that she was losing her temper yet again but unable to stop it. He had the most negative effect on her. From the beginning he'd annihilated her self-control.

"Well, you can expect to have your photograph taken, and expect to stand by my side and expect to be paid." He paused. "Is there anything else?"

"No," she choked out, hanging up.

The rest of the week passed too quickly for Alexandra's taste, knowing that on Saturday she'd be with Wolf again, attending the premiere.

She'd only been seeing him a few days, but already she was exhausted, worn out trying to juggle work responsibilities during the day and appearances with him.

Fortunately she was looking forward to the film. Even though it was only a matinee for *The Little Toy Solider,* the newest Pixar animation, Alexandra was looking forward to seeing exactly what happened at premieres.

She'd read about them for years in *People* magazine, seen

the photos of celebrities attending, and now she was finally going to one.

Even better, it was the premiere of an animated film—Alexandra's secret favorite. Back before her brother Brock had been widowed, she used to go into Bozeman, Montana, with his late wife Amy and their kids to see all the Disney films. In her mind, Saturday afternoons were made for movies, and she was glad to be going, eager to see just what kind of cartoon toy soldier Wolf'd be.

A stylist arrived at Alexandra's house early Saturday morning, bringing with her several wardrobe options. Jointly Alexandra and the stylist settled on the low-hipped sexy charcoal trousers cinched by a wide gray croc belt with an enormous round pewter studded buckle. On top she was wearing a burnout velvet tank in a color somewhere between lemon and mustard, topped by a fitted cropped coat of the same rich, saturated color.

She'd accessorized with sleek pewter heels and a chunky two-strand gray-and-white alabaster necklace. Her hair had been flatironed and it hung smooth and sleek past her shoulders. Makeup was even more subtle: pale foundation, lightly lined eyes in gray pencil, lots of mascara and a soft, neutral lip color called Naked for her mouth.

When Wolf arrived at one to pick her up, he was dressed casually elegant in jeans, a white dress shirt and a dark gray Armani jacket. He wasn't behind the wheel today. Instead he had a driver and a limo, important for the red-carpet arrivals.

He was cool and distant during the ride, and Alexandra sat opposite him, savoring the last bit of privacy before they stepped onto the red carpet and into the flash of a hundred camera strobes.

"I almost forgot," Wolf said, reaching into the limousine's side console. He handed her a clear glass tube the size of a rolling pin filled with gold confetti and a single sheet of rolled parchment paper.

She tipped the cylinder to watch gold glitter emerge from the sheer strips of shimmering confetti. "Not another invitation."

"With me, of all people."

She gave him a dark look and tipped the cylinder yet again but at a shallower angle, fascinated by the glitter clinging to the insides of the tube. "So what's this an invitation to?"

"It's for Matt Silverman's fiftieth birthday party."

"Ah." Matt Silverman was the most innovative director and producer in the business today, and everything he did—whether it was a futuristic sci-fi or a historical drama—became a blockbuster, guaranteed to garner a half dozen Academy Award nominations, including the coveted Best Picture. "When is it?"

"Thursday." Wolf glanced out the window. Traffic was slow through the 405 and 10 intersection. "It'll be a big party. Black-tie, live band, sit-down dinner in his Bel Air estate's garden. Nearly everyone in the business will be there." He leaned back against the seat, smiled crookedly if not a bit wearily. "But we've got to get through today's premiere and parties first."

She nodded, noticing the shadows under his eyes. "Do you ever get tired of the parties and events?"

The creases deepened at his eyes. His expression turned wry. "All the time."

"But…?"

"Every movie needs publicity, and publicity requires me being out there, doing the interviews, the talk shows, the premieres, the award shows, the parties and fund-raisers."

"And that doesn't even include making the films or the weeks on location," she added.

"You're right, it doesn't."

She'd never really thought about the life of a star like Wolf, imagining that fame, fortune and success made life easier, but she wasn't so sure anymore. "No wonder you're not in love with your career."

He shrugged. "It's a job, and I understand it's a job."

"You don't make it look like a job. You're incredibly talented."

His expression almost gentled. "You don't have to make points with me, Alexandra. I know how you really feel."

She waved her hand, batting away his comment. "If you made one less film a year, that would be less PR, fewer interviews and press junkets and parties, right?"

"One would hope."

"So do that. Make one less film. Or two. Find a way to have more time for yourself. I'm sure there are things you'd like to do."

The corner of his mouth lifted, but his dark eyes were deep, intense. "You're sounding an awful lot like you want to save me. But, love, I can't be saved."

"Yes, you can."

"This isn't a challenge, Alexandra."

She pressed her lips together, held tight to her opinion—and her temper—realizing now wasn't the time to debate him.

Instead she changed topics. "So what would you do if you had more free time? Would you pick up a hobby? Want to travel? Are there places you're anxious to go? What's top of your to-do list."

His eyes narrowed. "Ending world hunger."

Alexandra did a double take. Was he serious? She couldn't be sure, but he wasn't smiling, wasn't making light of his lofty ambition.

"Erasing Third World debt," he continued.

She simply stared at him.

"Stopping the spread of AIDS in Africa." His hard features softened, his expression turning rueful. "Sorry you asked?"

There was something in his face she'd never seen before, something behind the slightly bored, rather cynical mask he usually wore. Something fierce and raw and real. *Real.* For the first time she saw a man, not an actor or star.

Alexandra felt a tug inside her chest, a twinge of muscle that was almost pain. "No."

And then whatever fierce, raw emotion—passion—she'd seen disappeared, replaced by that public mask he wore to keep the world at bay.

With mask firmly in place, Wolf turned, glanced out the window and spotted the crowds lining the sidewalks. "We're here."

The morning after the premiere, Wolf flew to New York for a Monday-morning appearance on *Good Morning America* to promote *The Little Toy Soldier* and then an afternoon taping for the David Letterman show at the Ed Sullivan Theater on Broadway between Fifty-third and Fifty-fourth Streets. If things went well, he hoped to have dinner with friends Tuesday and then return to Los Angeles Wednesday morning.

He'd said maybe they'd have dinner Wednesday night—he'd let her know once he was back in town.

It was odd with Wolf out of town. Alexandra went to work Monday morning thinking she'd feel liberated, but instead she felt rather lost.

Wolf had been taking up so much time—physically and mentally—she didn't quite know what to do with herself now that he was gone for the next three days.

Alexandra tuned in to *Good Morning America* at the studio, caught the tail end of Wolf's interview—he looked so amazing on TV, it wasn't fair at all—and then turned the TV off once the interview ended to get back to work.

Tuesday she wondered if he'd call.

Wednesday she wondered if he'd caught his morning flight and was heading back to L.A.

Instead flowers arrived for her Wednesday noon, four dozen white roses with a stiff white embossed card that read, *Have been held up in NY, will pick you up tomorrow for party. Apologies. Wolf*

Alexandra hid the card before anyone else could see.

He wasn't coming back until tomorrow, until just before the party. And she didn't mind, not really, not until Kristie in the office casually dropped a newspaper on her desk, opened to the Entertainment section with the celebrity gossip column.

The VIP Room

Wolf Kerrick was seen having a cozy dinner Tuesday night with former flame, actress Joy Hughes, at Manhattan's celebrity favorite, Nobu. Are Wolf and Joy back together again?

Alexandra read the gossip item over and over again until her eyes began to burn and a lump formed in her throat. She felt almost…betrayed. Which was stupid since she and Wolf weren't a real couple, but still, they'd been spending so much time together lately that in some ways she did feel as if she was part of Wolf's life. Felt almost like Wolf's woman.

Quickly, before anyone could see, Alexandra wiped away tears, stood up, trashed the paper and went to make her third coffee run of the day.

Wolf picked her up in the limo fifteen minutes after the party officially started, but even then they were among the first arriving at Matt Silverman's fabulous Bel Air estate.

Although it was a private party and media hadn't been invited, dozens of photographers had still set up their cameras on tripods across the street from the Silverman mansion.

Walking through the gardens next to Wolf, Alexandra recognized nearly half the people there. And the other half were probably the really important people—the producers, directors, power agents like Benjamin Foster.

"Did you get my flowers?" Wolf asked as they stopped near the pool to take in the hundreds of floating water lilies illuminated by just as many floating candles.

Alexandra's stomach immediately knotted. "I did."

He turned his head, looked at her. "I'm sorry I was held up—"

"No apologies or explanations required."

She was trying to be poised, but the tartness of her answer gave her pain away.

"You saw the photograph of Joy and me at Nobu," Wolf said.

Had there been a photograph in another paper? Her heart felt strange. Tender. Almost fearful. "No. I just read a little blurb about your dinner in the local paper."

He was still looking at her. "There's nothing between us, Alexandra."

She nearly hung her head and then thought better of it. She was wearing vintage Armani tonight, an exquisite ivory pleated gown that the stylist had brought over yesterday. With the gold-heeled sandals on her feet and the gold band wrapped around

her arm she felt beautiful, like an Egyptian priestess or maybe
a princess, and she didn't want anything to ruin that.

"It's none of my business," she answered calmly.

"But it is, at least until our contract ends."

She managed a droll smile. "You're too good an actor."

"What does that mean?"

"It means we both know the truth. I'm not the kind of woman
you usually date. I'm serious, industrious. I like the quiet evenings
in and you—" she broke off and smiled brighter "—are the
bad-boy playboy, notorious for all-night parties."

He swore under his breath, a short, sharp, profane curse that
caught her by surprise.

Alexandra blinked at him. "I've never heard you curse before."

He took her chin in his hand, lifted it up. "I wish everything
was as simple as you make it out to be. I'd love for life to be
so black-and-white, but it's not. And you, sweetheart, don't
know me." His dark eyes burned into her, promising, punishing. "You know nothing about who I really am, and maybe
that's a good thing. Maybe it's better to let you remain sweet,
inexperienced, naive."

Alexandra didn't have time to answer or defend herself.
People were heading their way, flocking toward Wolf as though
he were a beacon of light.

Concealing her chaotic emotions, Alexandra quietly stood
next to him. Wolf appeared to have many industry friends. He'd
been a Hollywood force for nearly ten years, but it was only in
the last two years, since winning the Oscar for *Boys in Belfast*,
that he'd become viewed as a serious talent.

Waiters passed glasses of specialty cocktails on gilded wood
trays—cocktails like pomegranate martinis and Lemon Drop
shooters—and the crowd around Wolf grew louder and more
jovial as the drinks were consumed.

Alexandra tried not to wiggle while she stood for the first
hour at Wolf's side, but it was difficult not to feel self-conscious
given the amount of skin her cream Armani gown exposed.

Fortunately Wolf didn't forget her. Several times in that long hour he broke off his conversation to introduce her, point someone out or try to explain a reference, making sure he included her as much as he could. He even once reached out and touched her upper arm as he talked to yet another woman who'd come to congratulate him on his exceptional performance in his last film.

Two more young women were approaching Wolf now, both stunning, one very fair with straight waist-length blond hair and a figure that looked as though she could model for Victoria's Secret, and the other a sexy, sultry brunette that reminded Alexandra of Wolf's former flame, Joy Hughes.

As it turned out, the blonde *was* a model for Victoria's Secret and she introduced her friend, a former Miss Venezuela who'd come to Los Angeles to pursue an acting career.

Despite Alexandra's presence, the women flirted outrageously with Wolf, touching him, laughing, leaning seductively toward him, showing cleavage Alexandra would never have. But once again Wolf put his hand on her arm, rubbed it as if to reassure her, and some of Alexandra's tension eased. That was until Paige, the Victoria's Secret model, tripped and sent her red pomegranate martini flying—all across Alexandra's exquisite ivory Armani dress.

For a moment Alexandra just stood there, her bare shoulder wet and sticky, her breast and fitted bodice a splash of pale red, with little droplets of red staining the long straight skirt.

A seven-thousand-dollar vintage gown ruined.

She stared at Paige in shock, her gaze riveted to the model's empty glass. Empty because the cocktail was now all over her gown.

For a moment she could think of absolutely nothing to say— at least nothing polite, because on the inside she was livid, fuming. How could a model that pranced down a runway in four-inch heels and enormous white angel wings trip over nothing? And not just spill her drink but dump the entire contents over Alexandra and only Alexandra?

"Are you okay?" Wolf asked, his arm encircling her, bringing her closer to his side.

"I'm fine," she choked out. But she wasn't fine. She was

shaking, trembling in her heels. Her lovely dress was ruined and there would be no easy exit from the party, not with a stain like this.

Wolf flagged down a waiter and requested some soda water and a towel. "Soda water might help," he said.

She nodded, forcing a tight smile. "I'm fine, it's fine," she repeated, but her voice had grown husky. It was humiliating being Wolf's pretend girlfriend, humiliating playing a role and being ignored by everyone and pretending she didn't notice their condescension when Wolf introduced her.

But she understood their snubs, understood why they didn't care to meet her or remember her. Wolf had a reputation for dating and discarding young Hollywood starlets. And being young and reasonably pretty, people probably assumed that Alexandra—Wolf's newest plaything—would soon be gone. These people weren't going to try to impress someone or even be kind to someone who wasn't important.

And she wasn't important. Not to anyone here.

Shame filled her, shame at so many different levels. She shouldn't have signed the contract. Shouldn't have let her own ambition get before her morals. Shouldn't have allowed herself to be used.

Just because she wasn't an actress or a model or someone powerful in Hollywood didn't mean she wasn't valuable.

"I'm sorry." She struggled to maintain her composure. "This is so embarrassing."

"It's not at all." Wolf suddenly looked at Paige and Lulu and gave them such a dark, ferocious look that both women scuttled away. With Paige and Lulu gone, he drew her closer. "And you couldn't embarrass me, so don't say things like that."

Blinking back tears, she glanced up, and the depth of his concern made her see yet again that he did wear a public mask, a coolly amused mask, as though he were always laughing at life. Laughing at himself. But she was just beginning to realize that underneath the mask he wasn't laughing at all. "I should go before the entertainment reporters and photographers spot me looking like this."

She took a deep breath, straightened her shoulders. "Now let me just slip out now so no one can get pictures of us together. You stay here and do what you have to do."

"I'm not going to let you leave alone. If you want to go, we'll go together." Wolf reached inside his tuxedo for his mobile phone. "I'll call for the car."

She covered his hand with hers so he couldn't make the call. "You have to stay. Aren't you making one of the birthday toasts?"

He shrugged. "It's more of a roast than a toast."

"But still, you're wanted here, needed here."

He shook her hand off and punched in the number before putting the phone to his ear. "The speech is already typed up. I could have someone else do it."

The waiter returned at that moment with a small bottle of soda water and two clean white kitchen towels. Wolf hung up, reached into his pocket for a twenty-dollar bill to tip the waiter.

"Thank you, Mr. Kerrick," the waiter said, nodding appreciatively.

Alexandra took the soda water and towels from the waiter. "All right. I'll make you a deal. You stay here, and I'll go find a bathroom and see what I can do to salvage this dress. Okay?"

"Okay."

She nodded and forced a light note into her voice. "I'll be back soon."

Alexandra was heading to the house to look for a bathroom when she crossed paths with Jason Kirkpatrick, a young director she'd met earlier in the year when he'd dropped by Paradise Pictures to discuss directing a film for the studio. In the end, he wasn't hired, but Alexandra had enjoyed her brief conversation with him that morning and she smiled in recognition as he flagged her down.

"Alex! It's Alex, isn't it?" he said, hailing her.

"Yes, although I prefer Alexandra," she corrected. "And it's Jason, right?"

"Good memory." He rocked back on his heels. "So what happened to you?" he asked, lifting her hand that clutched the bottle of soda water to better see the vivid stain ruining her gown.

She'd nearly forgotten the catastrophe and grimaced now. "A famous lingerie model accidentally poured her drink on me."

"That's a lot of accident," he retorted, taking a step into the shrubbery and pulling her with him to let people pass behind them on the curving stone path.

She glanced down at the stain. "I'm thinking the pomegranate martinis are better in the glass."

He laughed. "You're funny."

"Thanks."

His laugh turned to a sympathetic smile. "Why don't you run home and change? The party hasn't even started. It's still only the cocktail hour."

"I'd go home if I could, but I don't want to make Wolf leave—"

"Why should Wolf have to leave? Zip home, change and come right back."

Alexandra's nose wrinkled. "I'd love to, but it's not that easy. I don't have a car and I didn't bring money for a cab. And Wolf—"

"Let me take you." Jason stretched his hands out. "My Porsche is right out front. Wolf's a friend of mine. I'd love to help him out."

"Oh, I don't know if that's a good idea." She glanced over her shoulder, struggling to see if she could find Wolf in the crowd, but the extensive garden was packed. "Wolf might not like it."

"It'll only take a moment and then—snap!—you'll be right back, pretty as a picture." Jason winked. "And trust me, you'll take a better picture in a new gown, if you get what I mean.

CHAPTER SIX

AT MATT SILVERMAN'S Bel Air estate, Wolf walked through the fancifully decorated gardens with the massive jacaranda trees festooned with twinkly lights, searching the clusters of party-goers and guests for Alexandra.

There were so many people—hundreds—that he was forced to look for splashes of cream and white fabric in the crowds to focus his search, and while he spotted several women in light-colored evening gowns, none were Alexandra.

As he headed back through the gardens to the estate's 1930s mansion, Wolf wondered if she had perhaps gone home. Maybe she couldn't get the red stain out of the dress and she hadn't wanted to make a scene.

He frowned as he neared the ornate fountain. Even if she was embarrassed by the stain, he couldn't imagine her just leaving without speaking to him.

And if she had left, how had she gotten home? Had she called a cab? Had a friend picked her up?

Not far from the fountain Wolf spotted his agent grabbing a couple of sushi appetizers from a tray one of the waiters held.

"How's it going?" Benjamin asked Wolf as he popped a bite of sashimi and wasabi into his mouth.

"Good." Wolf's brow furrowed, knowing it wasn't good. Nothing about tonight was good. In fact, nothing about this week was good. Dinner with Joy in Manhattan had been troubling and he'd been on edge since, waiting for another call, wondering if he'd need to hop on a plane. "You haven't seen Alexandra, by chance?"

"Lost your girlfriend?" Benjamin asked, dunking a slice of California roll into soy sauce.

"Paige poured her cocktail all over Alexandra's dress."

"Paige?" Benjamin repeated, chewing the seaweed-wrapped roll.

"Your client Paige. The model."

"Ah, Paige." Benjamin smiled. "She's hot, isn't she?" Then he remembered himself and glanced around. "Where is Alexandra?"

Wolf nearly reached out to grab Benjamin by the throat. "That's what I'm asking you."

The lighting director from Wolf's last film joined them and reached for a piece of yellowfin sushi. "You're looking for your girl?" he said to Wolf.

Wolf nodded. "She'd gone to clean up her gown."

"I saw her," the lighting director said. "She's wearing an off-white gown, right?"

"Yes."

"She left," the lighting director said, reaching for another piece of sushi. "With Jason. I figured you two had a fight."

Wolf's features hardened. His dark eyes glittered. "There was no fight." He inhaled sharply as he saw red. "But there will be now."

And as Wolf headed to the front circular driveway, he prayed he'd find Alexandra at home. Alone. Because if Jason was there…

Wolf shook his head, not even wanting to finish the thought. Because he knew exactly what he'd do and it wouldn't be pretty.

Across town, Alexandra stood swaying in her living room, having finished changing into the little black cocktail dress she'd worn to Rye's birthday party at Spago. Jason had offered to make drinks for them while she changed, and she'd agreed.

He'd been so nice about driving her all the way to Culver City and patiently waiting while she rummaged through her closet trying to find something elegant to wear. But the cocktail was doing funny things to her, and she grabbed the living room wall for support.

"My head," she whispered, her body going cold all over and alarmingly tingly.

"Have a headache, doll?"

She didn't like his tone or the way he was looking at her. But Alexandra didn't close her eyes until the room started to spin. "What's going on?" she demanded huskily as soon as she could open her eyes again.

Jason was standing in front of her. "Hi, big eyes." He reached up, pushed a long lock of hair from Alex's eyes. "How are you feeling?"

"Dizzy."

"Are you? Maybe we need to get you to your bedroom so you can lie down."

"No." She put out a hand and immediately thought she'd fall. She needed Wolf here. She shouldn't have left Wolf. "Call…call…Wo-Wolf." She forced the words out, squinting her eyes to try to slow the spinning, but it didn't help. Nothing was working right. She wasn't working right.

"You don't need Wolf," Jason answered, taking her hand, fingers wrapping around hers. "I can help you. I'll get you into bed, don't worry."

"I need a doc-doctor. Call doctor."

"No, no, you'll be fine. I'll just take you to bed, darling."

"Call Wolf," she repeated, struggling to resist him as he dragged her toward the bedroom.

"You'll feel better in bed. Trust me."

She felt stiff, sick, puppetlike, her legs and arms disjointed. *"No."*

In her room, Jason closed her bedroom door and Alexandra's legs gave out. Jason pulled her up, pressed her against the wall. "One kiss, baby," he crooned.

It was then she realized how drunk he was—or drugged he was—because this wasn't the Jason she'd met at the studio office a month ago and this wasn't the Jason who offered to drive her home from the party.

But now this Jason was trying to kiss her, and the more she struggled to escape, the more excited he became.

"Stop it. Let me go," she choked out, turning her head away from his wet mouth.

"Why? You like me. I know you like me."

"No, I don't like you." Alexandra sucked in a breath, fighting to stop her head from spinning, fighting to regain strength in her limbs.

"Don't be that way," he answered, leaning against her, holding her immobile. "I want you. I'm crazy about you."

"Get off—"

But he'd cut her words off with another hard kiss that repulsed her so much her stomach turned inside out. He'd pinned her to the wall, his body leveraged against her, his knee slammed between her legs, his hands groping over her.

"Jason." She choked, violently twisting. *"Stop."*

But her struggles only enticed him, her shuddering body inflaming his. "Come on, Alex, kiss me," he whispered, grabbing at her face. "Kiss me properly. You know how."

But she wouldn't, she couldn't, just as she couldn't find the strength she needed to break away.

Wolf was nearing the front porch of Alex's small house when he heard the scream.

Alexandra.

Heart pumping, he took the three steps at one time. He was prepared to break the door down but was relieved to discover it'd been left unlocked. With a shove of his shoulder he had the door open.

In the bedroom, Alexandra screamed as Jason's hands slid across her.

"Come on, baby," Jason crooned, shifting his weight, and suddenly she felt his bare legs against her own as he battled to part her thighs.

He'd dropped his trousers.

She tried to scream again, but before she could make a sound, his head dipped and his mouth covered hers once more, smashing her nose, her mouth, cutting off air. Frantic, she bit savagely into Jason's lip, felt him stiffen even as she tasted a spurt of blood.

Stunned, Jason lifted his head and then his fist, and Alex squeezed her eyes shut, preparing to be hit, when suddenly Jason was off her, being hauled away by a massive, shadowed shape.

Even though the room was dark and spinning, even though she could barely see, much less stand, she knew it was Wolf.

Somehow she had known he would come.

"Alexandra." He ground out her name in the dark, and in his voice she heard fury that turned her blood cold.

An icy shiver raced up and down her spine. Wolf sounded angry enough to commit murder. "I'm okay," she choked out, pressing her black dress down, trying to cover the length of her bare legs. It was so odd, so strange. Her body could have been anybody's body. Her body didn't even seem to recognize her. She couldn't move from the wall, couldn't walk, couldn't function.

What in God's name was wrong with her?

And as she heard Wolf speak, his voice low and harsh, his accent stronger than she'd ever heard it, Alexandra fell back, hit the wall and slid all the way down, passing out before she touched the ground.

Alexandra was having a nightmare and she couldn't wake up. Someone, something, was hurting her, jabbing something down her throat, shoving something down into her middle. She tried to pull away but couldn't. Hands held her still. There was no relief.

And then she was gagging, vomiting, and she wasn't sure if it was real or a dream. The pain felt real enough, but nothing seemed clear, nothing made sense. But finally the gagging stopped and she was left alone and she slept.

While Alexandra slept, sedated, Wolf paced next to her bed. The doctor had said the drugs were finally out of her system thanks to gastric lavage with activated charcoal.

As Wolf paced, he watched her sleep but was far from calm. She hadn't liked having her stomach pumped, and when she woke, she'd be confused. She wouldn't remember much of last night.

Wolf clenched his teeth in mute outrage.

What was she thinking, going home with Jason?

His gut churned. Burned. His temper felt lethal.

He continued to pace, battling to contain his anger when all he wanted to do was find Jason and annihilate him. He could, too. He could make Jason suffer—and more.

Many successful screen and television actors were short, even slight, and they'd learned to use the camera close-up to their advantage, the zoom lens capturing carved jaws and handsome clefted chins.

But Wolf wasn't small or slight. He had the size and height of the professional boxer he'd once been. He'd made a name for himself in Ireland as the Dublin Devil—a furious, fire-fisted street fighter who leveled all his opponents within just one round. He hit that hard. His blows were that accurate.

And now he wanted to do what he did best—fight.

On the inside, he wasn't an actor, he was still an athlete, a boxer. Hollywood had never been in Wolf's sights. Being half Irish, he was as steeped in the great Irish literary tradition as the next snot-nosed kid, knew the Irish playwrights and poets and had seen his share of theater by the time he turned sixteen. But be in a play? Put on makeup, learn lines, be fitted by a costume designer? Never.

It wasn't until an independent film company from America came calling, looking to cast an Irish boxer in a small role in an even smaller film, that Wolf got noticed.

The casting director loved him, but the film couldn't find proper funding and never opened in theaters, going straight instead to America's booming cable business. But it turned out Wolf didn't need a box-office hit to turn his fifteen minutes of fame into a huge career.

Anyone who had seen the film had come away with two impressions—the script was a convoluted mess and the tall, dark, brooding boxer, Wolf Kerrick, was unforgettable.

A year and one finished major motion picture later, critics were falling over themselves, gushing praise.

Fast forward ten-plus years and he was even more of a Hollywood heavyweight than anyone imagined he'd ever be.

He'd certainly surpassed anything he'd ever dreamed he'd be. But then, he'd never dreamed. He'd wanted little. Preferred even less.

Growing up, his parents had fought bitterly, and their divorce when he was twelve had been something of a relief. At least the long, drawn out screaming matches had ended. There'd been no more broken dishes or doors. At first Wolf's dad had disappeared. But then, when Wolf's mom hadn't been able to take care of Wolf or even keep a job, his dad had abruptly returned and moved Wolf back to Ireland with him.

Wolf knew his dad wasn't a bad man, but his dad wasn't a talker, and the changes, coupled with silence, made a confused kid angry. But Wolf soon discovered he liked being angry. Anger gave him power, anger made him strong, anger gave him a reason to go to bed at night and then wake up the next morning.

Being angry had filled his days, fueled his runs, helped him train.

Being angry had allowed him to take hits and, even more importantly, dish it out. Angry, he could pound his opponents, mash them. Punish them.

Which is what he'd do to Jason as soon as he knew Alexandra would be fine.

Hours later, Alexandra slowly opened her eyes, stared up at the lavender-tinted ceiling above her. It was lavender, wasn't it? But why lavender?

She narrowed her eyes, trying to figure out where she was and why the ceiling would be this color. She didn't know anyplace with a ceiling like this or walls papered in soft swirlies of lavender, cream, gold and gray.

What ugly paper.

Looking the other way, she saw the table next to her bed with the plastic water pitcher and plastic cup and straw jostling for prominence among vases of flowers and sprays of white orchids.

Hospital.

She was in the hospital.

Alex tried to swallow but stopped when it hurt like hell.

Her throat was unbelievably sore and her stomach felt just as bad. There was an IV taped to the back of her left hand, and a black paper had been taped over the window in her door.

Why was she here? What was going on?

Alex stirred, turning onto her side to find the call button, but before she could push it the door to her room opened. Wolf entered, carrying a cup of coffee.

He looked at her, one eyebrow lifting ever so slightly. "You live."

"Barely," she croaked, watching him close the door and then approach her side.

He said nothing, and for a long moment neither did she, lying there against the stiff hospital pillow feeling fragile and strangely broken. She hurt, her insides hurt, and not knowing what had happened and not having anyone here but Wolf made her feel even more defenseless.

"Look at me. I don't know what happened," Alex whispered, vocal cords bruised. "Jason gave me a ride home to change so I could return to the party. While I was changing, he made us a drink and then—" She broke off, bit her cracked lower lip. "He…he…got weird."

"You were screaming when I arrived," Wolf finished roughly.

"I was scared." She closed her eyes, drew a deep breath. "Thank you for coming to look for me." Opening her eyes, she reached out, caught Wolf's pinkie finger between two of hers. "You saved me."

He said nothing, his head averted, his narrowed gaze fixed on the wall.

She tugged on his hand, trying to persuade him to look at her. "Thank you, Wolf."

Slowly his head turned and he gazed down at her, a deep furrow between his thick brows, his dark eyes more black than brown. "What if I hadn't come? What if I hadn't left the party when I did?"

She stared up into his eyes. The black depths burned. But it wasn't just anger blazing in his eyes. It was fear.

"But you did," she whispered.

"If I'd been five minutes later—"

"But you weren't." She squeezed his hand. "Please, let's forget about it."

Wolf abruptly pulled away. He walked from the bed, went to the window, where he looked out. "Forget?"

"Yes, forget. Move on. There's so much more that's important—"

"Not to me." He glanced at her over his shoulder. "God, you're so innocent! So naive. You were drugged. Attacked. You had an allergic reaction to the pharmaceutical cocktail he put in your drink. *Alexandra*." His voice deepened, fell, vibrating with fury and outrage. "You could have *died* from the drugs alone."

Her heart thumped. She felt dizzy all over again. "I only had a drink with him, Wolf. I wouldn't take anything. I know it's dangerous."

"As we discovered."

"Please believe me."

He took a breath, his broad shoulders tensing, and then he exhaled in a slow, hard stream. "I believe you."

"You do?"

He nodded slowly, rubbed a hand over his eyes. "Jason likes to mix pills with his liquor—cocaine and temazepam are favorites of his." He fell silent a moment as he considered her. "Do you have family we should call? Someone I should contact?"

Her eyes widened. She shook her head. "There's no one," she whispered.

"You've no family?"

She stared up at him, terrified he'd discover the truth. No family? Alexandra had the most protective, overbearing family in the universe. "No."

"Do you want me to get you legal counsel then?"

"Legal counsel for what?"

"Because you'll want to press charges."

She was beginning to wish she hadn't woken up. This was too much, too overwhelming. "Do you want me to press charges?"

He exhaled in a harsh whoosh. "I don't know. I just want to beat the hell out of him. Want to make him—" He broke off, his beard-darkened jaw jutting tautly.

"Wolf, you could destroy him," breathed Alex. "And whatever he did, I don't want that."

He towered above her, his dark eyes frosted with ice, his features glacier-cold. "I would not be a man if I stood by and allowed him to go unpunished for hurting you."

"I won't let you! Someone has to think about your reputation. The press."

Wolf made a harsh sound in the back of his throat. "Press? You want to talk about press?" He laughed, but the sound was like fingernails down a chalkboard. "Alexandra, it's a little late to worry about bad press."

"What do you mean?"

"We're the topic of this morning's talk radio, and there was a blurb in the gossip section of the morning paper, too." He leaned over, kissed her forehead, his lips warm against the iciness of her skin. "And I can guarantee we'll be all over the news segments on the entertainment shows tonight," he murmured.

His words made her go numb all over. "What are they saying?"

"They're reporting that you were hospitalized for a drug overdose."

Her gaze lifted, found his. *"What?"*

"A photographer caught the ambulance wheeling you out of your house." He sighed. "The photo has me right there at your side."

"What is the paper saying?"

"You don't want to know."

She'd begun to tremble. "Tell me."

He hesitated so long she wasn't sure he would. And then he took her hand, lifted it to his mouth and kissed the backs of her fingers. "That you tried to kill yourself."

"Oh, my God."

His silence was deafening, and Alexandra closed her eyes, shrinking inwardly. All their joint efforts, everything they'd tried to do…gone.

Over.

"And this was in the paper?" she asked, imagining the reaction her family would have if they got word of this.

"Today's *Los Angeles Times.*"

She exhaled gradually, trying to calm herself. If it was just the *Los Angeles Times,* maybe none of her family would hear. None of her brothers lived in L.A. anymore.

"And *USA Today,*" Wolf added quietly.

Her stomach heaved. Her throat sealed closed. *USA Today* was a huge national paper. *"No."*

"No is right. Our publicity-stunt relationship has made headline news."

CHAPTER SEVEN

THEY KEPT ALEXANDRA for most of the day to give her sufficient opportunity to rest and recover. They would have kept her
overnight again but Wolf feared that the media frenzy outside
would only grow if she wasn't discharged.

The hospital administration, as fed up with the paparazzi
as Wolf, allowed Alexandra to exit the hospital late that
evening from a side door into the waiting limousine,
avoiding the main entrance where photographers and reporters still lurked.

"You're not taking me home?" Alexandra said as the limousine left UCLA's medical center, traveled down Wilshire Boulevard to the 405 Freeway on-ramp.

"Not with those vultures watching your house."

"But I need clothes, pajamas, a toothbrush at least."

"You can manage one night without all that."

She pressed her lips together to hold back the protest. She
didn't have a leg to stand on anyway. She'd gotten them into
this mess, and Wolf, considering the circumstances, was
braving the spate of bad press very well.

Wolf's home in Malibu was tucked among other celebrity
homes, each hidden behind massive walls, shrubbery and gates.
It wasn't until the limo passed through the gates and around one
of the tall white stucco walls that the house, lit by a spotlight,
came into view.

The house, a sprawling modern cube with enormous

windows that faced the sea, was as serene as the beach and blue watery horizon beyond.

Wolf unlocked the front door and swung it open before stepping back to let her enter.

The surfaces were sleek, glass, chrome. The couches were low and white, oversize and covered in white chenille. The cocktail table and end tables were equally huge, low thick slabs of exotic wood hand carved and crafted. Even the walls— where there were walls—were plastered white, and the artwork was selective, modern oil paintings by some of the contemporary masters of the day. One painting, more violet than purple, hung above the smooth stucco fireplace. Another vast gray-and-pewter canvas hung on the opposite wall, above a Brazilian-wood console.

"Your room," he said, opening the door to a guest room down the hall from his. "And you can sleep in this," he added, tossing a large gray T-shirt in her direction.

"You've done this before," she answered, clumsily catching the T-shirt.

He acted as though he hadn't heard. "A new toothbrush is on the counter in your bath. Toothpaste is in the drawer. Fresh towels are on the towel rack."

Alexandra headed into the bathroom and, stripping off her clothes, took a long hot shower and worked at peeling off the adhesive strips from the IV that still remained on her arm.

Once finished, she dried off, tugged Wolf's T-shirt over her head and brushed her teeth.

When she left the bathroom, she saw that his bedroom door was now closed and she could hear him talking in a low voice on the phone. She overheard bits of the conversation, phrases like *Soon I'll be there* and *There'll be lots of time in Africa.*

Joy.

He was talking to Joy about shooting the movie in Africa because soon he'd be there. Another couple of weeks and he'd be on location.

With Joy.

Alexandra swallowed the stab of jealousy. Wolf had said

there'd been no affair, he'd said they were only friends, but somehow Joy and Wolf's relationship made her feel insecure. Like an outsider. Wolf and Joy were both actors and celebrated and beautiful, while she was…

Ordinary.

Sighing, Alexandra returned to her room, shut the door and climbed into the guest bed. It was a huge bed for a guest room and she felt very small in it.

The small feeling only grew worse as she struggled to relax. Sleep was a long time coming. She'd spent too much time in bed the past twenty-four hours as it was.

And as she lay there, thoughts churning, stomach in knots, she realized she wasn't just upset about Joy. She was also really upset with herself for thinking she could compete with Joy, live in Wolf's world without getting hurt.

Alexandra felt a bittersweet ache inside her chest, a tug on her heartstrings. Sometimes Wolf reminded her of the cowboy of her girlish dreams. He was every bit as big, and handsome and strong. Capable of looking out for her without smothering her. Sure enough to let her be without trying to change who she was or what she dreamed.

If only he were that hero…

If only those happy Hollywood endings really came true. But she knew better. Once you visited Los Angeles you realized that Hollywood wasn't a place but an intersection of streets. You realized that the golden sun in California postcards was rarely seen due to a disgusting layer of smog. *It's not that happy endings aren't possible in Hollywood,* Alexandra told herself, pulling her pillow close to her cheek, *it's just that they're highly unlikely.*

Alexandra thrashed in bed much of the night but woke up to the smell of freshly ground coffee and felt almost like a new woman.

Unable to face putting her party dress back on, Alexandra dragged her hands through her hair and headed to the kitchen in the gray T-shirt. Fortunately it was long on her, hitting her midthigh, and it covered her better than any silky baby-doll pajamas would.

It was Wolf in the kitchen making coffee, and when Alexandra appeared in the doorway he offered her a cup.

"Please," she answered, watching him take another big white glazed mug down from the glass-fronted cabinet.

He filled her cup, and she added a spoon of sugar before clasping the mug between both hands and taking a sip. It was strong and very good. "Thanks."

"My pleasure."

She took another sip and covertly watched him as he sliced several oranges and squeezed fresh juice into two tumblers. Once he finished with the juice he turned his attention to making toast.

"Butter, marmalade, strawberry jam?" he asked, rummaging through his huge stainless-steel refrigerator.

"Just butter," she answered, wondering exactly what his timeline was for getting her home. She'd missed work yesterday and now today was Saturday, and although she hadn't anything planned, she felt a need to establish some control again. Get back to her usual routine.

He grabbed the newspaper from the kitchen counter. "I always have my coffee outside on the deck. Care to join me?"

Her eyes narrowed a fraction. He was being polite. Too polite. Something was up. "Only if you'll share some of the newspaper," she answered, suddenly on guard.

His mouth curved. It wasn't a friendly smile. "Depends on the section."

She was beginning to think that she'd woken to a potentially explosive situation. "I like Arts & Leisure," she said.

"Yours." He held the glass door for her, and as Alexandra stepped outside she blinked at the bright morning sunshine. Here in Malibu the sky was blue and the sun was shining and long, smooth bottle-green waves crashed on the white beach.

She took the seat he offered and he divided the newspaper, but unlike Wolf, she didn't start reading. She watched him for several minutes, curious that he could be so absorbed in the paper when life seemed so confusing. "Wolf."

"Hmm?"

"Are we going to talk about what happened?"

"No," he answered without looking up.

Seagulls swooped low overhead and her stomach thumped with nerves. "Why not?"

"Because there's nothing to discuss."

She pulled her section of the paper closer to her but still couldn't read. Sitting outside on the deck, drinking coffee, sharing the paper, watching the seagulls and listening to the waves break, they looked like a typical Malibu couple, and theirs was such a normal domestic scene, that Alexandra found herself hoping that maybe, just maybe, yesterday's headlines had already been forgotten.

That no one remembered her suicide attempt from a drug overdose.

She exhaled, the stream of air blowing a wisp of hair up and out of her eyes.

She hoped...until she glanced up from the paper and spotted a photographer on the beach with a camera focused in their direction. Her heart fell with a sickening thud. "There's a photographer on the beach."

"Really?" Wolf asked, turning the page in the paper. He didn't sound surprised or worried.

"You knew?" she demanded.

He folded the paper in half, glanced up at her, his expression shuttered. "There is always someone somewhere, lurking with a camera. You learn to get used to it, ignore the cameras as best as you can and get on with life."

She stared at him suspiciously. "You're sure we're not here for a photo op? A get-well shot for the paparazzi?"

He smiled grimly. "It's a nice idea. I wish I'd thought of it." He folded the paper yet again so it was a quarter of its original size. "As it happens, this is my house and this is the deck where I have breakfast every morning. And you, Alexandra, just happen to be here." He returned to his paper and resumed reading, but Alex couldn't read—or focus.

"They think I was distraught over Joy, don't they?" she whispered, holding her large ceramic mug between both hands.

"Mmm."

"But you weren't even with Joy at the party," Alexandra continued faintly, staring at the top of his head because that's all he'd give her.

"No," he answered, face still buried in the *Times*. "But getting the facts right isn't a priority for the tabloids. They're concerned with selling newspapers, not the truth—" He broke off as the phone began to ring in the house. "Let me grab that. It could be the studio. The producers are holding an emergency meeting this morning. They're discussing recasting the lead roles for the film. Sometime in the next hour we'll find out if it's me or Joy that's being replaced."

Alexandra's eyes widened with alarm. "Oh, Wolf—"

"Please don't." He paused in the doorway as the phone continued to ring. "It's too late for that, Alexandra. Let's just enjoy what's left of the morning, shall we?"

Alexandra watched Wolf hang up the phone and open the door and walk toward her where she still sat outside. "Bad news?" she asked quietly.

He didn't answer. He just stared down at her. "You're always so curious, so full of questions," he said thoughtfully. "Maybe it's time I got to know you better."

His expression filled her with unease. "What do you want to know?" she asked, trying to find a smile. He was acting strangely, had been acting strangely all morning, but the phone call had only heightened the tension another notch.

"Who you really are."

Her mouth opened to protest and then she snapped it closed. She owed him no explanations. They might have a contract, but it was going to end soon. Wolf would be leaving in two weeks for Africa, and once he was gone he'd be out of her life for good.

"Do I get to go home soon?" she asked, standing, wanting to put herself on more equal footing.

"Mmm…no."

"Why not?" she asked, trying to keep her tone reasonable. Maybe if she humored him, he'd finally send her back to her house.

"I've a lunch date and I'd very much like your company."

She glanced down at his gray T-shirt she was still wearing and then at her bare feet. "I have to go home to change. I've nothing here to wear."

"Benjamin is sending the stylist."

Alexandra stilled. "That was Benjamin on the phone?"

"Mmm."

Wolf's ambiguous answers were beginning to trouble her. "What's going on, Wolf?"

"Lunch."

"Why lunch?" she persisted, arms folding across her chest, pulling the T-shirt taut across her breasts.

His gaze dropped, sweeping slowly across the outline of her breasts and the pebbled nipples. He smiled, his cool, fierce, predatory smile. "I'm hungry," he answered. "And we need to do some damage control."

An hour and ten minutes later they were in Wolf's navy Lamborghini, a classic V12 sports car from the late '60s. It was the same car Wolf had originally picked her up in for their first official date as a couple at Casa Del Mar's Veranda lounge.

Alexandra had fun that night but somehow she didn't think she'd be having fun today.

As Wolf drove down Highway 1 south toward Los Angeles, Alexandra smoothed the snug skirt on her gray Michael Kors dress the stylist had brought her. The dress was fitted with thin spaghetti straps, a plunging sweetheart neckline and a beautiful black lace-and-satin-ribbon belt at the waist. Her heels were black, her clutch was black and her thick hair had been curled and left loose.

She looked great. Sexy. Polished. She should have been confident.

She wasn't.

"Where are we going to lunch?" she asked, fixing one of the delicate gold hoops at her ears. It'd twisted and caught in her hair.

"Asia de Cuba," he answered, briefly taking his eyes off the road.

Asia de Cuba, she silently repeated, crossing her legs and noting that her French pedicure could use a touch-up. "I don't know that place."

"It's a nice restaurant."

"Where is it?"

Wolf shot her a sideways glance. "My, you're curious today."

Alex shifted uncomfortably in the Lamborghini's low white leather seat and recrossed her legs the other way. "You're acting strange."

"Am I?"

Her jaw flexed as her gaze rested on him. Something was definitely up. "Secretive," she added.

"Really?"

She let the subject go for now. He obviously wasn't in a talkative mood and she didn't feel like playing games. Her lashes dropped, concealing her anxiety as the miles sped past. They were on the Santa Monica Freeway now, heading toward Hollywood.

"What are you not telling me?" she asked tersely. She didn't like Wolf like this, didn't like it when he played the famous actor card and made her feel like a walk-on part in his Broadway play. "You're acting as if you know something that I don't. Something that maybe I should."

"Indeed." Wolf shifted, accelerated, taking the steep curve of Sunset Boulevard fast. "And I've thought about telling you, but maybe I should just let you enjoy the surprise."

Surprise. So there was something about to happen. She exhaled, her nerves so on edge that she didn't think she'd be able to sit still another moment longer. "Why do I get the feeling this isn't going to be a good surprise?"

Wolf shrugged, glanced up into his rearview mirror to check the traffic behind him, including the police car that had settled behind them in their lane. "I suppose it all depends on how you feel about family get-togethers."

"Families are fine." Alexandra's stomach was back in free-fall form. "I didn't realize you had family in town."

"I don't."

She knew then, but she didn't want to know, didn't want to have her worst fears confirmed. "Then who?"

He pulled into the hotel drive which fronted the famous Sunset Strip. The Mondrian Hotel was within steps of some of the best restaurants, clubs and nightlife Los Angeles offered. He glanced at her as they approached the hotel, the Mondrian's entrance marked by a pair of massive decorative mahogany doors that soared thirty feet into the air. "Two men by the names of Troy and Trey."

Alexandra felt a shot of icy adrenaline shoot through her, pumping her veins full of cold silver liquid fear. Wolf couldn't have just said what he said. He couldn't know their names. There was no way...

Wolf heard her faint choking sound and gave her an appraising look. "Those names ring a bell, love?"

The hotel loomed closer; elegant, white and spare, it was said to be designed to remind guests of the famous Los Angeles fog that covered the city when the weather grew warm.

"Troy and Trey are my brothers," she said unsteadily. Her hands twisted in her lap even as she caught the lift of Wolf's eyebrow.

"The twins," she amended huskily.

"And just how many brothers do you have?"

"Five."

"Five," he echoed softly. "Out of how many kids?"

"Six."

"You're the only girl."

She nodded.

"And the youngest," he concluded.

She nodded again.

"So what was this about not having any family, Alexandra?" He'd pulled over to the hotel curb and shifted into park, but the engine still ran and he ignored the cream-suited valet attendant hovering outside.

She would have slunk down lower in her seat if she could. "You're an only child," she said hoarsely. "You wouldn't understand."

"Try me."

"There's five of them." She swallowed, pressed her hand over her stomach, feeling the nervous nausea start up again. She'd always had a weak stomach, everything used to make her queasy. She'd thought she'd beaten the childish impulse, but since meeting Wolf the feeling seemed to be back all the time. "And I don't know if you've met the twins yet, but they're all like that. Big, tough, no-nonsense, just like my dad and granddad."

"I haven't met the twins," Wolf answered, finally turning the key in the ignition. "But they're determined to see you. And me." He paused, considered her. "Apparently they're quite worried about you."

She tipped her head back against the buttery-soft leather seat and closed her eyes even as she gripped the door handle so tightly she felt as though the bones in her hand would break. "Don't make me go in there. Don't make me see them."

"They love you."

Alexandra heard Wolf open his door and she leaned forward, caught at his hand. "They love me too much," she said, holding tightly to his wrist. "And after Mom died it only got worse."

The valet attendant had opened her door and was standing beside her, waiting for her to step out, but neither she nor Wolf paid him any attention.

"They can't be bad brothers if they've flown here looking for you."

"Yes, they've rushed here." Her hand wrapped tighter around his wrist. "To bring me home."

"You don't know that."

"But I do," she insisted. Ever since she was little her brothers had been so protective that it'd suffocated her. They wouldn't let her do anything on her own. They hadn't wanted her to go away to college either. "I'm not going back." She lifted her head, met Wolf's dark gaze. "They can say what they want, do what they want. But I'm not going home. I'm staying here with you."

Wolf had heard a lot of ludicrous things in his life, touching things, too. At thirty-five, he thought he'd pretty much heard everything. But in all these years he'd never met anyone quite like Alexandra.

She was unique. An original.

"Why would you want to stay with me?" he teased. "You don't even like me."

Two pink spots burned high in her cheeks. "Maybe. But you're the only one I know who can stand up to them."

Wolf slipped out from her grasp and walked around to the passenger side, where he extended his hand to Alexandra. "A loving family like that only wants the best for you."

"Sure. I could go back to Montana and the Lazy L ranch and get married and have babies and wouldn't that be an exciting life?"

Wolf had to check his smile as he drew an extremely unwilling Alexandra to her feet. "Life on a ranch has to be a lot more interesting than that."

"Oh, yeah. Horses. Cows. It's just great."

"Benjamin said your brothers are big. Is that how they got their size? Chasing horses and cows around?"

It was her turn for the corners of her lips to curve. "All Shanahans are big."

Wolf took the car's claim check from the valet attendant before putting his arm around Alexandra to steer her through the huge mahogany doors and into the hotel's vast glossy white lobby. "So what happened to you?"

Her soft, husky laugh suddenly died as two enormous men stepped from the cool white sheer curtains floating everywhere.

Alexandra stiffened and froze. "Trey," she breathed unsteadily. "Troy."

CHAPTER EIGHT

THE BROTHERS SHANAHAN wasted no time getting to the point.

"We'd like a word alone with our sister," Trey said, and while his voice was quiet, his tone brooked no argument.

"I want Wolf to stay," Alexandra replied, reaching in panic for Wolf's hand.

"Alexandra, this is a matter for family," Troy said, shooting Wolf a far from friendly look.

"Yes, but Wolf is like family," she answered, holding his hand even tighter. She knew her brothers, knew they weren't the sort to mince words, and they weren't mincing any now.

Troy's expression became ever more suspicious as he stared Wolf down. "Then he should be protecting you, not hurting you," he said. "Because we don't like hearing you've been hospitalized any better than Dad or the others do."

Alexandra's hand was damp and it felt sticky clenching Wolf's hand, but she couldn't let go. "It's not what you think."

"No? Then explain it," Trey demanded.

She caught how Wolf's dark eyes flashed and his jaw clenched. He didn't like Trey's tone and he was fighting to control his temper.

Hotel guests glanced at them curiously as they crossed through the lobby, with its flutter of white curtains and the floating wall of elevators. The lobby, with its all-white surfaces, had a surreal beauty, reminding Alexandra more of an art gallery.

The slick and smooth white finishes and furnishings were designed to instill calm, but it wasn't working on anyone in their little group.

"Alexandra, we're worried about you," Troy said bluntly. "We've talked to Dad and we're here to take you home."

She wasn't surprised. This was how Shanahans handled things. They came, they conquered, they went.

"I'm not going home," she answered quietly, standing as tall she could manage considering that, as more than one person had said to her when she was growing up, the twins could pass for mountains.

"Well, I'm not leaving you here," Trey growled, his square jaw growing thicker by the second.

She gazed up at him and then at Troy, torn between admiration and exasperation. Her brothers were good-looking, damn good-looking, without an ounce of fat on them. They were made of hard, honed muscle that wrapped their arms and legs like steel and they were every bit as rigid.

Her smile was bittersweet. "Trey, you don't have a choice." She'd once enjoyed fighting with them, stirring her brothers up, trying to get a rise from them, but things were different now. The stakes were far higher. "This is my home—"

"That's absurd," Troy interrupted roughly. "Home is the Lazy L ranch, home is Dad, Brock, the kids."

She shook her head, aware of Wolf standing there, just behind her shoulder. She was grateful to have him with her and even more grateful he was letting her handle this her way. "Not anymore."

Trey cleared his throat, making a rough sound of disgust. "You're telling me the ranch isn't home?"

She looked from Trey to Troy and back. The twins had the same jaw, the same high cheekbones, the same blue eyes as clear as the Montana sky. "I'm sorry you've had a wasted trip. But tell Dad I'm fine. Tell him I'll try to come home for Christmas—"

"You'll come to Montana and tell him yourself," Troy interrupted brusquely, folding his arms, pulling the fabric of his white dress shirt even tauter. The snug fabric shaped the width of his chest and the thick biceps and triceps in his arms. "And while you're there, be sure to explain just how it was that you nearly died, because we know all about it. We know you were rushed to the hospital, had your stomach pumped and kept for a day under observation."

Alexandra felt Wolf's warmth and presence. She wasn't sure if he'd taken a step toward her or she'd taken a step back, but she could feel him there—his size, his strength, his fierce personality—and again it reassured her. All her life her brothers had trampled over her wishes, but this time having Wolf in her corner settled her. Gave her confidence. "What you heard, what you read in the paper was a mistake," she said carefully. "It's not what really happened."

"So you didn't try to kill yourself?" Troy demanded, voice dropping to a husky growl. "Because that nearly broke Dad's heart. He loves you more than the five of us boys put together."

Troy might as well have stabbed her with an ice pick, she thought, lips parting in silent protest as tears filled her eyes. The idea of her dad worrying about her, suffering because of her, was more than she could bear. "I'll call him," she said softly, her voice breaking. "I'll call him tonight."

Trey loomed over her. "You'll go home tonight and you'll talk to him in person. Properly. The way you should."

She felt rather than saw Trey's finger jabbing at her, emphasizing his disgust. She swiped away a tear, livid with him, both of them, realizing all over again why she'd left home. She loved her brothers and hated her brothers and couldn't understand how any relationship could be so complicated. They protected her and disciplined her and talked at her until she felt absolutely trapped.

She angrily wiped away another tear. "I never tried to kill myself. The media got it wrong. Somebody was being funny and put something in my drink."

Troy and Trey exchanged thunderous glances. "What kind of lifestyle is this?" Trey snapped. "You're too thin, too tan, too made-up. You're not Alex at all."

"I am," she protested.

"You're not," Troy said more gently. "You're some Hollywood paper doll. But that's not who Dad raised you to be, and Mom wouldn't be proud either."

Every word her brothers said hurt, but this last, this condemnation that her mother wouldn't have approved, cut her to the quick. She looked away, eyes closing, stunned by the depth of her pain.

She couldn't do this anymore, couldn't take this anymore. She turned to Wolf, put her hand on his forearm. "I want to go," she whispered. "Can we please just go?"

His narrowed gaze swept her tear-streaked face. "Of course. Whatever you want."

But before they could take two steps, Trey reached out, grabbed Alexandra's arm. "And what will I tell Dad?"

Wolf swiftly knocked Trey's hand from Alexandra's arm. His features contorted. "Don't touch her like that again. She's a woman, not one of your cows."

Trey's expression darkened. "She's my sister, and I love her and I want what's best for her."

"If you want what's best," Wolf answered evenly, "then tell your father she's happy and doing well in Los Angeles with me."

"With you," Troy repeated icily.

"And just who the hell are you to make decisions for Alexandra?" Trey asked, hands knuckling to fists.

Alexandra knew the twins were formidable opponents. Just like armored tanks, they rolled right over their opposition, and she sensed they were going to roll right now.

"Your sister's fiancé," Wolf answered quietly. "We're engaged to be married." He looked from one to the other. "Didn't you know?"

"Engaged?" Trey could barely get the word out, and Alexandra couldn't meet his eye, too shocked to think of a single thing to say.

Wolf, her fiancé? Engagement? Oh, how quickly this had escalated.

Troy pointed to her bare left hand. "There's no ring."

"It's still secret," Wolf said, smiling faintly. He seemed to have no problem with the story and looked downright amused by her brothers' sudden tailspin.

Alexandra struggled to think of something to say, but her mind was strangely blank. Everything had been fine until Paige spilled the drink on her gown, but that one spilled drink had consequences she couldn't have dreamed of.

Ruined dress. Lethal cocktail. Headline news. Now an engagement to Wolf. Amazing how fast one problem had snowballed into this!

"Secret," Troy was repeating, lower lip curling. He might have moved from Montana to Seattle and exchanged horses for fast cars, but he was still a very tough cowboy underneath. "What kind of bullshit is this about a secret engagement?" he demanded, rocking back on his heels. "Why keep it quiet? Are you ashamed of her?

"Where we come from, Shanahans are respected, and so Alexandra has always been respected," he continued. "Maybe this is Hollywood. Maybe you think you're so special you can treat Alexandra any way you want, but you've got another think coming. Alexandra's a good girl, the sweetest girl you'll ever meet, and she deserves to be treated right."

The entire time Troy was talking, Wolf was looking at Alexandra, one black eyebrow half cocked. She struggled to maintain a pinched, if not terrified, smile.

As Troy fell silent, the corner of Wolf's mouth tilted in a dry smile. "The only reason it's secret is that I haven't had a chance to ask your father for Alexandra's hand yet."

"You're going to ask him?" Troy asked bluntly.

"Yes," Wolf answered.

"When?"

Wolf's brows drew together. "That's really none of your business, is it?"

"I hope you're serious," Trey growled, "because Alexandra doesn't deserve to have her heart stepped on."

Alexandra would have laughed if the situation weren't so serious. It'd been four years since she left home, but Trey and Troy were still the same. They used to threaten the local guys if they came near her. Little Alexandra was too good to be touched. Little Alexandra was a nice girl, a sweet girl, a virgin. She shuddered inwardly, remembering.

If she didn't have any experience when she came to Los Angeles it was because her brothers had made sure that no man came near her. Apparently Dillon had put a bounty on the head of anybody who tried to get too friendly with his baby sister. And in her brother Dillon's mind, anything past first base was too friendly.

Trey reached into his pocket, drew out his wallet. "How much would it take to get rid of you? Five million? Ten? What do you want?"

Alexandra blanched, the blood draining from her face. *"Trey."*

"Name your price," Troy echoed.

"My price?" Wolf's hard, cynical expression bordered on incredulous. "You think I can be bought?"

"We're willing to try." Troy wasn't the least bit apologetic. "We want you gone."

"That's pretty obvious. But my relationship with Alexandra has nothing to do with you, and the only one who has a say in how we proceed with our engagement—" Wolf paused, looked pointedly at Alexandra "—is your sister."

They were all looking at her now, waiting for her to respond. Her mouth dried and she licked her lips, trying to find her voice. Maybe it didn't matter that she couldn't find her voice, because she didn't have the foggiest idea of what to say.

"Is it true?" Trey asked roughly. "Is this your dream man? This is who you want to marry?"

Alexandra's gaze clung to Wolf's. They'd find a way out of this one later—they'd have to—but for now she'd do anything to keep her brothers from dragging her back to Montana. Montana wasn't home anymore, hadn't been home for years. "Yes."

"So when's the wedding?" Troy persisted.

"Soon," Wolf replied, taking Alexandra's hand in his and kissing the back of her fingers. "We'd planned to elope, marry on location in Zambia."

"Zambia?" Troy spluttered.

"Marry Alexandra in Africa?" Trey thundered. "That's not going to happen. No way. Not a snowball's chance in hell."

Troy's square jaw hardened, his blue eyes splintering with cool shards of light. "If you're going to marry her, you marry her here, where her family can attend. Do you understand?"

Wolf's own jaw firmed, but wry amusement touched his eyes. "Hard not to. You have such a way with words."

Glancing down into Alexandra's pale face, he smiled a small, mocking smile. "It's a California wedding."

They never did have lunch, and Alexandra found the long drive back to Wolf's house nothing short of agonizing. Wolf was beyond quiet. He looked like the Grim Reaper at the wheel. She did her best to avoid looking at him, but even with the sun shining and the temperature outside in the seventies, Alexandra couldn't stop shivering.

Wolf had promised her brothers a California wedding.

In less than two weeks.

A wedding in less than two weeks. That was laughable. Hilarious. So why wasn't she laughing?

Why did she want to cry?

Alexandra squeezed her eyes shut as her teeth began to chatter. It was just the shock, she told herself. As soon as she and Wolf figured a way out of this mess, she'd be fine. They just needed to put their heads together and come up with a plan.

Fast.

"Take a hot bath when we get home," Wolf said, merging into traffic on Highway 1. They were probably just ten or fifteen minutes from his house now. "Or better yet, I can turn on the hot tub for you. It's just off the deck in the garden. Has a great view of the water. That might help your chill."

She bundled her arms across her chest. "We've got to think of a way out of this, something plausible, something that will keep my family out of Los Angeles and away from me."

Wolf gave her a peculiar look. "Were you not at the Mondrian with me? Did you not hear what I heard? Those brothers aren't going away until you're married. They're taking hotel rooms in town and camping out until the dirty deed is done."

And that just might be why she was violently shivering. She was doomed. Wolf, too.

"I'm sorry," she whispered. "I'm really sorry about all of this. If I'd just stayed at the party, none of this would have happened."

"Celebrity is a messy business."

Alex grimaced. Talk about cold comfort. "So what do we do now?"

"We get married."

"You mean *pretend* to get married."

Wolf shot her a darkly amused glance. "Your brothers don't strike me as the pretend type, and frankly pretending has gotten us into this mess. I think it's time we sorted things out properly. A real wedding with a real priest, real guests and real champagne."

Which meant real publicity, too, she thought, stifling a groan.

The PR game had completely taken over her life, and she didn't like it. She'd didn't even know who she was anymore, what with the stylists and designers and makeup artists constantly fixing her up, making her presentable. She was ready for the old Alexandra to return. The one that went to work every day on time, slept seven and a half hours every night and wore black, navy and gray because that way people might take her seriously.

Lately she'd actually begun to miss just being ordinary.

"I think this has gone far enough, Wolf, don't you?" she asked quietly.

"If I did, I wouldn't have just proposed."

She ground her teeth in mute irritation. "It wasn't much of a proposal."

"Apparently I am your dream man."

She could have screamed with vexation. "That was a mistake."

"One your brothers latched onto." He signaled a lane change as they neared the house. "I imagine they've already been in contact with your dad by now."

Alexandra pressed her fists against her eyes. She didn't want to hear any more, didn't want to picture her brothers on the phone with her dad. Because Wolf was right. That's exactly what Troy and Trey would have done. Called Dad. Then called Brock, Dillon and Cormac. They'd all be jumping on airplanes soon.

"If I got down on one knee, would you feel any better?" Wolf asked without the least bit of sympathy for her plight.

She lifted her head, glared at him. *"No."*

He shrugged and turned down the small green-hedge-lined lane leading to his beach house. "Exactly. So why bother with the theatrics?"

No two weeks had ever passed faster, and no elaborate, star-studded wedding had ever been planned so quickly. Wolf made a few calls to industry insiders, and within a day the wedding ceremony was set, the reception site booked. Within three days the myriad details—including guest list, bridal gown, colors, flowers, dinner menu and entertainment—had been addressed. And by the fourth day the hand-embossed wedding invitations were sent.

Alexandra laughed until she cried when she received an invitation to her own wedding.

It was all so horrible it was funny.

She, Alexandra Shanahan, who'd lost a lot of sleep at fifteen fantasizing about Wolf Kerrick, was now marrying him in Santa Barbara in little over a week.

Santa Barbara, a ninety-minute drive north of Los Angeles on Highway 1, perches snugly between the Santa Ynez Mountains and the gorgeous Pacific Ocean. The town, a mixture of red-tiled adobe homes, huge estates and historic landmarks, also has some of the best surfing in California. Little wonder that everyone from John Travolta to Oprah Winfrey has a second home there.

And now Alexandra was about to be married there.

Pacing her small dressing room at the Denzinger estate, she kept glancing at the little clock on her dressing room table. Just a half hour now until the ceremony began.

She trembled in her white satin beaded shoes.

She couldn't believe Wolf was insisting they go through with the wedding. There was no reason to get married. Wolf could just head to Africa and she could make excuses, claim cold feet, lack of compatibility. Anything but marriage!

Alexandra marched back across the carpet and stole yet another look at the clock. Twenty-five minutes.

Twenty-five minutes until she became his wife.

And Alexandra, who hated to cry, knew she was about to cry now. Not delicate tears but huge, depressed sobs.

Until now she had always thought of herself as the ultimate cynic, a bona fide nonromantic. She didn't believe in falling in love, had never felt an urge to marry or to be a mother for some guy's children. But now, confronted by a very public wedding to a man she still barely knew, Alexandra was aghast.

She couldn't believe she was marrying to seal a business deal, to propel herself higher up the ladder of success. Even for a cynic, this was a really big deal.

Even for a cynic, this was wrong.

She couldn't do this. Not for Wolf, not for her family, not for anyone. She needed to get out of here, escape before she made a fool of herself in front of every guest and every camera.

Alex stopped pacing, turned, pressed a knuckled fist to her mouth, forgetting her carefully applied lipstick.

She didn't like running away, but she didn't know how else to get out of this. Her family certainly wasn't going to listen. And Wolf…well, he was heading to Zambia day after tomorrow. He'd be fine.

Glancing down, she took in her full white gown, a fairy-tale dress for a fairy-tale wedding that she refused to let happen.

She reached for the back of her gown, tried to tug the hooks open, but there were too many—absolutely dozens—hidden in a satin-lined seam in her dress. She couldn't undress without assistance, and there was no one she could ask to help.

If she wanted to go, she'd have to leave like this.

Alexandra crossed to her travel tote bag tucked between the vanity and the corner of the room. She checked inside for her wallet. With a sigh of relief she saw it was there. Good. For a moment she'd feared all her cash and credit cards would be, with her luggage, already at the hotel.

Alex grabbed her wallet and left the rest.

She'd just buy what she needed whenever she got wherever she was going, because she certainly couldn't go back to her house in Culver City. She wasn't even sure she'd have a job waiting for her after she stood Wolf up at the altar. But those were problems she'd worry about later.

Alexandra left the changing room, slipping quietly down the mansion's long sunlit corridor, away from the spacious public rooms to the working quarters of kitchen, laundry and garage.

She passed several uniformed housemaids but didn't make eye contact, too intent on getting away before someone checked on her in the bridal dressing room and discovered her gone.

She turned one corner and then another, then spotted a severe-looking door at the end of this last hallway. With a push she was through the door, out, free.

The sky above was still bright blue with warm fingers of sunlight despite the late afternoon hour. In another hour the sun would be slipping toward the ocean, but for now everything was clear and warm and sunny, a picture-perfect California day.

Alex's fingers squeezed the wallet as her white satin heels crunched the pea gravel. An antique Rolls Royce waited, decorated with a lavish amount of white ribbon and a white floral display. The getaway car, she thought with a shudder, passing it so quickly her full starched skirts pressed against one shiny hub.

"Can I help you find something?" a dark, laconic voice drawled from behind her, and Alex stiffened, disbelief sweeping through her, turning her blood to ice.

Slowly, painfully she turned and faced Wolf where he leaned against the side of the brick building. Her throat worked. No words would come out. He was the last person she'd expected to see out here.

"Looking for a pay phone?" he asked, indicating her wallet.

She shook her head, the lace veil creeping forward to caress her cheek.

"Missing family? Your stylist? Makeup artist?" One black eyebrow arched as he supplied excuse after excuse.

She tensed, her insides already a fury of knots and misery. "I was looking for a cab."

He said nothing for a moment, intently studying her frozen expression. "Running away, are you?"

"I never *agreed* to marry you. I never—"

"You didn't deny it when I told your brothers we were engaged, that we were getting married. You told them—"

"I was scared!"

"As you should have been. In fact, you should have been scared weeks before when you agreed to sign a contract to play my lover. If you're such a nice, inexperienced girl, what in God's name are you doing with me?"

Her eyes grew rounder. She swallowed convulsively. Her hair, curled in long spirals, danced across her back.

He was bearing down on her, huge, powerful in the jet-black tuxedo with the starched white shirt and white tie. "But when your family arrives like some vengeful Celtic warlord, I am not going to forget my responsibility to you. I am not going to walk away from you."

He stood tall over her, so tall she had to tip her head back to see his dark, angry eyes. "And you, Alexandra, are not going to walk away from me."

CHAPTER NINE

THE RECEPTION, LIKE the wedding, was a blur of lavender and rose and gold, of helicopters droning overheard and the sea crashing on rocks below. The wind kept catching at Alexandra's veil, blowing it up and down.

Now that the ceremony was over, she was glad she hadn't been able to hear the minister. It helped lessen the impact of his words, helped her focus instead on the future, the far distant future when she'd be someone—not because she'd married someone powerful, influential, but because she herself was powerful. Influential.

The guests kept flocking to meet her during the dinner reception. Being Wolf Kerrick's new blushing bride suddenly catapulted her to a position of importance. Whereas at Spago and the Silverman birthday party she'd been no one worth noting, now everyone wanted to greet her, and she air-kissed celebs, hugged actresses she'd never met and took dozens of smiling photographs with the industry's top execs.

It's a shame she hadn't won everyone over on her own merit, but at least the crowd's warmth and enthusiasm reassured the Shanahan men that their only girl had done okay for herself.

In fact, by the time Alexandra danced with her father, the men in her family had become Wolf Kerrick's newest, biggest fans.

Something Alexandra found painful as well as annoying.

The reception, like the ceremony, was held in the Denzinger garden, and the colors of the wedding were the same colors of the blue horizon, where the setting sun painted the ocean shades of lavender, rose and gold. A perfect Hollywood set for a perfect Hollywood film. But this was real.

The reception swept past her in a kaleidoscope of toasts and kisses, hugs and best wishes. There was dinner and then that nerve-racking first dance, the cake and the tossing of the garter. All the traditional things one did at an American wedding.

Wolf was now drawing her back onto the dance floor. He'd just been in conversation with her father—again.

"You and Dad seem to have found a lot in common," she said through gritted teeth as Wolf spun her around the floor in a grand Strauss waltz.

"He's fascinating," Wolf said.

"Maybe you're just trying to make points."

"Maybe," he agreed, twirling her around. "And you should smile, because he's watching right now and he really wants his little girl to be happy."

Alexandra stepped intentionally on his toe. "Oops!"

His hand settled lower on her back. "I didn't realize my love was quite so clumsy."

She offered him another dazzling but vacant smile. "I guess you don't really know me either."

The orchestra was playing with great gusto as they only had one more number before they ended their set, giving way to the R & B band.

"You understand this is for the cameras only, right?" Alexandra made sure everyone could see her teeth in her wide smile. "I'm playing a part, a role, and getting paid for it. Don't think for a moment that I'm actually attracted to you."

His smile revealed amusement. "But you are."

"No."

"You were."

"No."

"Love, I'm an actor, not stupid."

Alexandra tried to hold herself apart and aloof from him, but the strength in his grip made it increasingly difficult.

"We've met before," he added, spinning her around the floor, thoroughly enjoying the waltz. "Remember?"

She stared at his chin, afraid to look higher.

"It was about four years ago," he continued. "We met at the Beverly Hills Hotel in the Polo Lounge. You were with friends and—"

"I don't remember," she interrupted tersely, glancing wildly up, meeting his mocking dark gaze before glancing even more swiftly away.

"We passed each other in the hallway. I was just coming from the men's room and you were on your way to the ladies' room—"

"I don't remember," she interrupted breathlessly.

His lips curved ever so slightly. "We left the hotel together."

"No—"

"Went to the Ivy for dinner."

Her body felt cold all over and she'd stopped protesting now.

"After dinner we parked high up in the Hollywood Hills with a view of the entire valley."

Alexandra stared. He'd known. He'd known who she was all along. He'd known this entire time.

His dark gaze found hers, held. "How could you think I wouldn't remember you?"

Wordlessly she searched his face, trying to understand what he'd been thinking. "But I was heavier by nearly twenty pounds."

"I don't remember that."

Again she searched his eyes. "What do you remember?"

"Your sweetness, your intelligence, your humor—" he broke off, assessed the impact his words were having on her "—and your incredible inexperience."

When she couldn't manage to even squeak a protest, he dropped his head, kissed the curve of her ear and whispered, "A girl who didn't even know how to unzip a man's pants, give a hand job or perform oral sex. Now that's a girl to take home to meet Mom."

Alexandra shoved hard on his chest, abruptly ending the waltz. "You *remember*."

Grooves bracketed his firm lips. His lips curved, but it wasn't a tender smile. He reached for her, pulling her back into his arms and dipping his head. He kissed below her ear, in the small, delicate hollow where a pulse beat wildly, erratically. "Of course I remember."

His voice dropped even lower, so husky, so sensual it hummed all the way through her. "You couldn't possibly think that I'd marry just any woman. Could you, Alexandra?"

It was well after midnight before they were finally able to break away from the reception, which had turned into the party of the year. The wedding planners had arranged surprise appearances by several of the guests who happened to be top *Billboard* recording artists performing their hit songs, and everyone was dancing, including Alexandra, who suddenly felt as if she were the most popular girl in America.

But by the time she climbed into the waiting Rolls Royce, her satin beaded shoes had blistered nearly every toe on her feet and rubbed her heels raw. She'd tried taking her shoes off, but her full wedding gown was too long and she'd ended up tripping so many times she'd inadvertently pulled the bustled raw silk train down.

There was no traffic at such a late hour, and the drive from the Denzinger estate to the historic Four Seasons Biltmore, the premier hotel in Santa Barbara nestled in the exclusive Montecito enclave, was short. So short that Alexandra didn't even have a chance to get her head around the fact that tonight she and Wolf were sharing a room.

Despite the late hour, the hotel manager was there in person to greet them when the Rolls Royce purred to a stop in front of the Biltmore. The hotel, with its soaring archways and Spanish-colonial detail, had been a mecca for the Hollywood elite since the 1920s when Greta Garbo and Errol Flynn helped put it on the map.

The hotel manager personally escorted them to their suite, the Odell Cottage, the resort's premier accommodation. The luxury cottage, built in 1904, had three bedrooms, a large salon with fireplace, a fireplace in the master bedroom and an exquisite private patio larger than Alexandra's whole house in Culver City.

Bottles of chilled champagne and a stocked refrigerator in the cottage's kitchen came compliments of the hotel. There were plush robes in the marble bathrooms. Any need they had would be met. And then the manager was gone and Alexandra and Wolf were alone.

"I thought he'd never leave," Wolf said, tugging on his white silk bow tie.

Funny how two people could have such different interpretations. Alexandra had wanted the manager never to leave. She wandered through the enormous cottage, thinking only in California would a house this size be called a cottage. The flat beamed ceiling, painted a glossy white, reflected the firelight from the salon's and master bedroom's fireplaces. Votive candles had been lit on the mantel. More candles flickered in the bathroom on the marble ledge beneath the mirror. And then she noticed the dresser in the master bedroom.

Oh, God. She turned away from the dresser groaning beneath the dozens of vivid red, passion-red roses, her stomach heaving up and down as though she were doing jumping jacks. What was she doing here?

"You can't avoid me forever," Wolf drawled from the doorway, startling her. She nervously glanced at him over her shoulder, suddenly feeling as though he were a complete stranger.

In ways he was.

She'd seen him in countless movies, had kissed him and been escorted around town by him, but she didn't know him, didn't know what he really thought about anything, much less her.

"I'm not trying to avoid you," she said defensively, watching him pull his bow tie from around his collar and toss the silk onto the table near the bed. She heard the anxious note in her voice and moved past him to return to the cottage's stylish living room.

The warm fire drew her, and she crouched in her full white bridal gown in front of the hearth, hands outstretched.

"You're running away from me," Wolf said with certainty, turning to watch her.

A lump filled her throat and she curled her fingers against the fire's heat. He wasn't far off the mark. She was scared.

Scared of what would happen next. But she couldn't tell him that she was still as inexperienced as she had been four years ago, that she still didn't know how to pleasure a man or…be pleasured by a man.

Jerkily Alexandra pulled the Italian lace veil from her head and folded it into a neat square before rising. "Why should I avoid you?" she said, keeping her voice even, battling to keep her fear at bay. "This is just a studio stunt, a media ploy that will soon be resolved—"

"No," he interrupted, still standing in the doorway, his coat now off, his shirt partway unbuttoned. "Wrong."

Her heart stuttered. She was glad he was far away, glad he couldn't see how she'd begun to shake. Give her a wild horse and she'd ride it, but give her a man like Wolf…

Alexandra licked her upper lip, her nerves making her mouth dry. During the reception she'd done everything in her power to keep from being alone with him, had done everything she could to pretend she wasn't married to him, but it was awfully hard now that they were here, in the bridal suite, alone.

His dark eyes narrowed fractionally. "As I said while we were dancing, I wouldn't marry just anyone. I certainly wouldn't marry someone for publicity or for my career. I married you because I want you."

Wolf's voice was deep, thick, like honey in sunlight, and it drugged her senses almost as much as his heady, dizzying kisses.

"I want you," he repeated again, quieter, deeper, his voice hypnotic.

Alexandra looked across the room at him and her brain felt slow, thoughts scattered, fuzzy. With Wolf's dark hair falling forward on his brow he looked as wild and untamable as his namesake. "You don't know me. You said so yourself."

He stretched out his hands, the shirt pulling wider, revealing his chest and the bronzed plane of muscle. "Then this is where we start."

He was a man, a beautiful, primitive, masculine man, and the idea that he wanted her, that he desired her, filled her with fear and nerves and curiosity.

He wasn't even touching her, just looking at her, and yet she felt as though he'd already taken her in his arms, run his hands down the length of her. She felt edgy, taut, physical, aware of her skin, her face and lips, her body where it curved, her legs where they joined. She felt all her fingers and toes. The indentation of her waist. The fullness of her hips and breasts.

He made her aware that she was a woman.

But that was the thing—what did a man do with a woman? Oh, she knew the mechanics—how could a farm girl not know?—but the scenes from films, the love scenes and the heat and the passion and the desperation…

And what would a woman do with a man?

Wolf was unbuttoning the rest of his dress shirt now, and she stared at him, watching the way he moved, his hands, the corded muscles of his arms. She watched his eyes, the focus, the intensity, the flare of heat in his dark eyes.

He was waking something in her, stirring her as much as if she'd been on his lap, his hand on her belly, covering her, warming her, making her feel the hunger only he had ever made her feel.

Shirt off, he reached for the button on his trousers. Alexandra's eyes grew wider, her mouth drier. Her heart thumped as she watched him undo the button. "We can't," she finally choked out. "*I* can't."

"Why not?"

"It'd be wrong—"

He started walking toward her. "We're married."

"In a fake ceremony with a fake minister and fake guests!"

"The minister and guests were real," he said mildly, watching her take a step away from the fire, behind the couch, doing her best to avoid him, "which means the ceremony was real, too."

She pressed her hands to the back of the elegant sofa. "But you know this is over as soon as your film wraps."

She felt cornered, caught, as though he'd been a real wolf tracking her. And now he had her where he wanted her to be. A shudder coursed through her, a shudder of fear, a shudder of desire. "This is just temporary," she insisted breathlessly, knowing she couldn't manage him. Or this.

He suddenly moved so fast she didn't have a chance to escape, and he was there at her side, circling her wrists with his hands. "I don't think I ever said that," he said, the pads of his thumbs caressing her frantic pulse.

But I did, she thought, trying to keep from losing her head. "But I did. I do—"

"And the film," he continued, interrupting her, "might never wrap. It's a cursed film, has been from the start." And then he tugged her toward him, one resistant inch at a time until she could feel the heat of his body scorch hers through the silk bodice of her wedding gown.

"You're my wife," he said, tugging her even more firmly, pulling her off balance so that she fell helplessly against him.

She inhaled sharply as his knees parted and she tumbled into his arms, his hips cradling hers, her breasts crushed against his chest. And then his head descended, and his mouth covered hers, stifling her gasp, catching her breath.

She was lost again, she thought, the pressure of his mouth on hers turning her inside out, making her lose track of all thought, all reason.

No wonder all his costars fell so hard for him. He kissed them senseless, kissed them into surrender and submission.

She gripped his shirt, desperate to find some center, some sanity, but his tongue was teasing the inside of her lip and she was shivering, burning from the inside out. Something about his mouth on hers made her want to open herself, open her mouth and body for him.

And the more she wanted him, the more certain she was that this was wrong, these feelings were wrong, and panicked, she now pressed at his chest. She'd intended to push away, but the sinewy planes of his chest felt shockingly good.

His body was warm and hard, his muscle dense and smooth beneath the palm of her hand.

He felt too good. This all felt too good. Anything this good had to be…

Wrong.

"Stop," she choked out against his mouth.

His hand reached up, tangled in her hair. "Why?"

"This is crazy. It doesn't make sense."

She felt his chest lift, fall, as if filled with silent laughter.

"Passion doesn't have to make sense," he answered before drawing her closer again, his hand sliding from her hair, down her back, to rest on her hips. Despite the full skirt she felt him, his strength and hunger, as well as his hand as it curved over her backside, shaping her against him.

And as he pressed her to him, he lifted her skirt, found her thighs encased in silk, and with a snap he unhooked the garter belt from the top of each thigh-high stocking.

With her skirt still lifted, he pulled her back against him, rubbed her hips against his so she could feel him, the hard length of him barely restrained by his thin trousers.

She gasped as her belly clenched tight and heat washed through her, filling her, making her insides feel warm and liquid.

He rubbed her against him again and her breath caught in her throat. His erection was long, hard, thick, and yet when the tip brushed against the apex of her legs, she felt little shock waves rush through her.

Felt muscles she didn't even know she had, start to squeeze.

Felt as though she were melting inside, hot cream, and when he slid his hand beneath her panties her legs wobbled.

No one had ever touched her there, and yet his touch was better than good, his touch made her feel wild, brazen, and she wanted more, wanting him to explore her and soothe all the sensitive nerves that throbbed right now.

"You feel amazing." His voice was deep, passion-rough. "So smooth and soft and slick."

Overwhelmed, she buried her face against his chest, her arms around him, her hands fists in his lower back.

"Wet," he added, his voice a velvet sandpaper on her senses. "You're wet for me."

He was still touching her, lightly, delicately, the curls, the lips, the wildly sensitive hardened nub, and she was wet and growing wetter. And then when he slid a finger inside her, she bucked at his touch, amazed at how much she felt, at the heady sensation of being explored by him.

Her response nearly pushed him over the edge, and he turned her around, tugged and ripped at the back of the dress until the tiny jeweled straps fell from her shoulders and the fitted bodice opened and tumbled forward, revealing her high, round breasts.

"You are beyond beautiful," he said, hands covering her breasts, feeling her nipples stiffen, harden beneath his hands.

Self-control nearly shattered, Wolf stretched her out in front of the fire, and for a moment he just looked at her, rose-tipped breasts bare, skirts tangled around her legs and the glow of the fire warming her skin.

He unzipped his pants as he watched her face. "I want you." His voice was hoarse and his dark eyes burned with barely leashed hunger.

She nodded once, her heart pounding too hard for her to actually answer.

His sculptured features were taut. His eyes smoldered. Again he struck her as fire and ice, ancient Celtic myth twined with a thousand years of Spanish passion.

Alexandra felt a stirring inside her, a whisper in her heart, something infinitely special and rare, something magical that not everyone might know.

She loved him.

Emotion surged through her, fierce and unexpected. She wanted this man, she wanted him completely.

"I don't know how to do this," she said as he moved between her legs, his erection pressing urgently between her thighs, the tip of his shaft silky against her dampness.

He'd started to enter her, but now he stopped. He'd felt the resistance inside her, too. His weight on his forearms, he looked down at her, searched her eyes. "You've never—"

"No," she whispered, aware of his stomach and hips and thighs covering hers. It was so intimate and dominant she shook, her thighs quivering from tension.

"I'm the first?" he asked.

The tears weren't far off, but they weren't tears of fear. They were pure emotion.

It was so surreal being here like this, married to Wolf, making love for the first time as his bride. His *wife*. "Yes," she answered huskily.

He kissed her deeply.

"I don't want to hurt you," he murmured against her mouth even as she felt the heat of his body throb inside her. He hadn't broken her hymen yet. He was uncertain, too, she realized. He was afraid of giving her pain.

Her eyes burned hotter. His body felt like lava inside her. But it was nothing compared to the tenderness in her heart. Wolf would be her first lover, and if fate was good, hopefully her last.

He stroked the side of her face, wiping away the one tear trickling over her cheekbone. "You're crying."

"It's a big night."

"It is," he agreed and he'd never sounded more Irish.

His dark eyes met hers and held, and there was suddenly no mask, no wall up between them, nothing but a beautiful fire in his eyes, a passion and hunger that spoke of dreams unfulfilled and hope he still cherished. Wolf might be the world's most beloved star, but he was also a man still searching for love. And a home.

"Take me," she said, sliding her hands down his back to his narrow hips, hard with sinewy muscle. "Don't be afraid. I'm not."

And then he was kissing her again, kissing her as if she were the last woman on earth and this the last kiss ever. He pressed forward as he kissed her, pressing against the resistance, and then she felt him, full and hard, filling her, deeper and deeper still.

It did hurt, but at the same time it was wondrous, new, sacred. Sacred because felt right. Sacred because somehow she knew she'd always been waiting for him. Even that one painful night four years ago had just been a detour until they finally got to where they were supposed to go.

Here.

Right here, together, like this.

His hips rocked, thrusting into her, and she felt the hot fire start to give way to a different sensation, one of warmth and fullness and even pleasure.

As he stroked her, moving in and out, she instinctively squeezed down on him, savoring his hardness, his strength, the feel of him taking her, making her his in front of the fire while she still wore her wedding gown, the full skirts and stiff petticoat ruched around her hips, the garter belt around her waist, the white silk stockings rolled down to her knees.

When his tempo increased, the pleasure did, too. Her hands slid across his back and she whimpered at the building tension, the way everything was tightening, turning, both maddening and exciting.

She'd been shy before they made love, but now that they were here, like this, in this together, she wanted whatever it was he could give her. She wanted all of what this could be, all of what they could be.

As the tension built, Alexandra felt more frantic, her hips rising to meet his, pressing against him.

"You can come," he whispered against her throat, his lips warm, his teeth nipping at the column of her neck. "Let go. Come for me."

And then as he drove into her harder, faster, pushing her ever closer to that point of no return, she was suddenly, spectacularly there, exploding in waves of intense pleasure, the rhythmic contractions electric blue and silver shock waves that rippled through her one after another. The pleasure was unlike anything she'd known before, and her body still shuddered with exquisite sensitivity when Wolf came, too, pumping even deeper into her, and as he filled her body, he filled her heart.

I love him, she thought, wrapping her arms around his neck and pressing her face to his shoulder. *I love this man.*

CHAPTER TEN

SHE WAS STILL WRAPPED in Wolf's arms, her body not yet cool, when he lifted his head, kissed her once and then pulled away.

Standing, he gazed down at her where she lay half-naked in her crumpled, stained bridal gown, her pale breasts bare, the white skirts hiked high around her hips. "Yet another ruined gown," he said.

He was referring to her vintage Armani gown, and she smiled faintly. "I don't mind this time."

"I should have undressed you completely."

She tucked a tendril of hair back, away from her eyes. "I'm glad you didn't. It was more exciting this way."

"You are a Hollywood girl after all," he said, scooping her into his arms and carrying her into the bathroom, where he stripped her and walked her into the shower with him.

He lathered her beneath the steaming shower spray, rubbing the suds across her breasts, down over her stomach, her hips, her bottom and then gently between her tender thighs. "Sore?" he asked as, shivering with pleasure, she leaned against him.

If she thought about it, she was sore, but it wasn't bad, not like the terrible violation she'd feared. In fact, making love with Wolf had made her body feel better, made *her* feel better. Made her feel…complete, although she wasn't sure how that worked.

"I'm good," she murmured as he bathed her with the handheld shower head, washing the bubbles from her now pink breasts and then lower to rinse the suds from the cleft in her bottom and her bottom itself.

She gasped as he continued to rinse her from behind, the jetted spray caressing the backs of her thighs and then between. He'd angled the showerhead so that the tingling spray struck her sensitive folds and the small peaked nub at the top of her inner lips.

She clutched at his arm, torn between pleasure and shame.

"Does this hurt?" he asked, his voice passion-rough.

"No." She blushed. "I'm just…shy."

"Close your eyes then."

She was beginning to pant at the erotic beating of water on her tender skin. "Is this right?"

"There's nothing wrong with me giving you pleasure," he said, gently widening her legs with his knee and bringing the showerhead closer to her. "You're mine now and I want you to feel good."

Her legs quivered beneath her, and she clung to Wolf's arm, her hand wrapped around his tight bicep as the warm water teased her, tormented her, bringing her closer to another orgasm.

"Wolf," she choked out, the heat inside her building, rising. "I don't want…I can't…come—"

"Don't worry, love. You can come. You won't be alone."

And, opening her eyes, she looked down. While he was pleasuring her with the showerhead in his right hand, he was stroking himself with his left.

Pulse racing, senses enflamed, she felt the warm water caress her even as she watched Wolf stroke his erection.

His shaft was huge, hard, the head a perfect smooth cap tinged with pink, and as his hand rode the length, she felt overcome not by shyness but wonder. He was beautiful, the way he was made was beautiful, and as he stroked himself, the muscles in his abdomen knotted and his bicep clenched.

She heard him groan, a deep, guttural groan, and it was primitive and raw and the sexiest thing she'd ever heard.

He was close to coming, and that's when Alexandra stopped fighting her orgasm, opening her legs just a little wider, rocking forward on her toes so the water pressure was right where she wanted it most. And then she was there, a gasp, a muffled cry, and then with a louder cry she climaxed with him.

A few minutes later, dry and wrapped in the hotel's plush robe, a rosy-cheeked Alexandra joined Wolf in raiding the cottage's stocked refrigerator.

Famished, they sampled the platter of cheese and crackers, then Wolf fed Alexandra bites of chocolate-covered strawberries between fizzy sips of delicate gold champagne.

Finally they found their way into the bedroom and, with robes discarded, lay close together beneath the fluffiest feather duvet Alexandra had ever encountered.

The wedding had been terrifying. The reception overwhelming. And the lovemaking mind-blowing.

She smiled into the crook of her arm and blushed remembering everything she and Wolf had just done.

My God, he did it for her. In every way. And finally, finally all the questions about sex had been answered and her curiosity put to rest.

Making love with Wolf was better than anything she'd ever imagined, and waiting to make love with him was worth all the sleepless nights, the impossible fantasies, the sharp, relentless craving she'd felt when he touched her, kissed her, aroused the dormant fire in her.

Snuggling close to him, she felt his arm wrap more snugly around her and pull her back until her bottom rested against his hips and his hand covered her breast. Even though she was exhausted, she felt a flare of heat all over again, desire licking at her, through her, tightening her nipples until they pebbled beneath Wolf's hand.

He laughed softly behind her, his breath tickling the back of her neck. "Go to sleep," he said, his voice vibrating through her, low, husky, sexy. Amused. "Or you'll be too sore to enjoy it again tomorrow."

They did make love again in the morning, a slow, sensual coming together that made Alexandra feel utterly fulfilled and extremely lazy. But the warm, languid mood evaporated as soon as Wolf told her the plans for the rest of the day.

"We're leaving for Africa this afternoon?" She rolled away and sat up, clutching the duvet to her chest. "On the first day of our honeymoon?"

"You knew we were going—"

"I knew *you* were going." She sat back, wrapped the covers around her, leaving Wolf naked. But that was fine—he didn't have a modest bone in his body. "And I didn't think you were going until tomorrow."

He shrugged and left the bed. "There must have been some miscommunication."

She sat there watching as he headed for the shower. *"Wolf."*

He reached into the glass shower, turned the handles, adjusted the water's temperature. "You've known all along I'm going on location," he said before climbing in.

That was one way of ending a discussion, she thought irritably, waiting for him to finish. And when she heard the water turn off, she was at the shower door, waiting for him to step out.

"Yes, I know *you* need to go away," she said, resuming the discussion where they'd left off, "but we never discussed me going with you."

He rubbed the white towel over his wet hair and face before mopping his chest and wrapping the towel snugly around his lean hips. "If you weren't joining me, Alexandra, why did we have you apply for a passport?" When she didn't answer, he shrugged and reached for his shave cream and razor. "Hop into the shower. It's a British Airways flight this afternoon. We can't be late."

One second they were still on the runway in Los Angeles and the next they were off.

Zambia. Africa.

Alex curled her fingers into her palm, hiding the sudden tremor in her veins. She knew Wolf's next picture—an adaptation of the novel *The Burning Shore*—was to be filmed there, but she'd never been to Africa, had never been to

Europe. And except for trips into neighboring Canada with her family when she was a little girl, she'd never been out of the United States.

It was a long flight but comfortable, as they were flying first class on British Airways and everyone on board, from the captain to the purser to the newest wide-eyed flight attendant, personally welcomed Wolf on board.

After the five-course dinner, the wide leather seats actually turned into flat, surprisingly comfortable beds.

Alexandra woke to breakfast, coffee and news that they'd be landing in a little over two hours.

But by the time they arrived in Lusaka, Zambia's biggest city as well as airport, Alexandra was ready to stretch her legs and move around.

Unfortunately their journey wasn't over yet, as the plane that had been chartered to ferry Wolf and Alexandra to the set wasn't at the airport. Wolf made a few calls and put the alternatives before Alexandra: they could either overnight in Lusaka and hope the plane would be available tomorrow or hire one of the safari services to drive them to the lodge in Kafue National Park.

Alexandra opted for hiring a driver. It was only a four hour drive and she'd had enough flying for one day.

She'd seen plenty of Land Rovers in Los Angeles—the celebrity crowd liked driving them—but as their cases were transferred into the roofless four-by-four vehicle, she realized that Land Rovers in Africa were actually utilitarian jeeps.

The driver, a safari guide who'd once been a poacher before serving time behind bars, was now an ardent conservationist and eager to share his love for Zambia's country and culture.

Kafue, he told them, was Zambia's oldest park and the largest. Established in 1950, it was the second largest national park in the world and about the size of Wales.

Their lodge and encampment was situated on the banks of the Kafue River in the Namwala West area.

The farther they traveled from Lusaka and the highway, the more primitive conditions got, with the road sometimes disappearing for miles at a time. Alexandra clung to a handrail on the side of the Land Rover as the blue-gray vehicle bumped and shuddered over the grassy, rocky and pothole-scarred terrain.

Some of the bumps were small and others were bone-jarring. As a small airplane flew overhead, Alexandra glanced up, wishing now they'd maybe waited for the charter flight. That had to be easier on the joints than this.

By late afternoon they were traveling through the brachystegia woodland broken by fantastically shaped kopjes. The scenery was spectacular, the colors of the landscape every shade of green and gold. They passed enormous herds of impala and hartebeest and then later a herd of puku grazing with zebra while a lone puku buck stood off to the side, head up, alert, on guard to protect the others.

"Are there big game animals here?" Alexandra asked as flocks of colorful birds lifted from a nearby tree.

"Lions, leopards, cheetahs, elephants," he counted on his fingers. "Hippo at the river, and where you're staying there are quite a few."

Alexandra glanced excitedly at Wolf. "We're on the river?"

"Your lodge has a deck overhanging the riverbanks. At twilight you'll see many of the animals come to drink."

And then suddenly they were there, on the banks of the deep blue Kafue River. The lodge stood two stories tall, dominating the camp with its steep thatched roof and pale-yellow-pigmented mud-and-plaster walls.

A dozen smaller thatched bungalows bordered the wide river. Those, Alexandra discovered, were reserved for the principal actors, directors and senior production staff, while the rest of the film crew would be billeted in the dozen new tent cabins just recently pitched.

As Tom and Alice Stewart, owners of the Kafue Lodge, came out to greet Wolf, they spotted their Zambian driver, a man who over the years had become a great friend. As everyone talked and caught up on news, Alexandra walked along the wooden deck toward the river to stretch her legs and get her bearings.

Africa.

Africa. Zambia. Kafue. Silently she repeated the exotic

names as she faced the river, basking in the sun as the late, long rays of light painted the opposite riverbank copper and jade.

"Sorry you came?" Wolf asked, standing a little ways behind her.

She wasn't entirely surprised to hear his voice. She'd felt him near, watching her, protecting her.

"No." She turned, smiled at him over her shoulder. "This is amazing. We're honeymooning in Africa."

He walked toward her, hands in his pockets, his handsome jaw shadowed with a day's growth of beard. "I've always loved Africa. It's why I wanted to do this movie. It was a chance to bring the country I love to the screen."

He was gazing out across the river, eyes narrowed, dense black lashes fanning his high cheekbones, and Alexandra flashed to their wedding night and the wonderful and wicked things they'd done together.

Biting her lip, she fought to suppress the flush already creeping up her cheeks.

Wolf caught the blush anyway. "You're not thinking about Africa."

Her blush deepened, her cheeks now scarlet. "No."

"Penny for your thoughts?"

"Oh, no."

He reached out, caught her by the back of her neck, pulled her against him. "That's okay," he murmured mockingly, dark eyes drinking her in. "I know what you're thinking and I want it, too."

And then he was kissing her, turning her world upside down with that dizzying, maddening, knee-melting kiss of his. Her hands crept up to clasp his shirt and then she wound one arm higher, to wrap around his neck. She felt desperate—starved and parched, as though she couldn't get enough.

She couldn't get enough.

It was Wolf who finally ended the kiss, and lifting his head, his black eyebrows rose. "I don't think you're as sweet as your brothers think."

Her lips parted to protest indignantly, but instead she

laughed, a great big belly laugh that had tears smarting her eyes. "I think you're finally starting to get to know me."

Wolf was being hailed by one of the film crew standing at the lodge, but he didn't immediately go. Instead he stroked her cheek with his thumb. "There's a lot more I'd like to know, too. And that discovery, love, will continue tonight."

Wolf didn't forget his promise either. That evening after a rowdy dinner with the crew that had assembled—Joy, Alexandra noticed, hadn't yet arrived—she found herself relaxing with the predominantly male crew. Having grown up in an all-male household, she was comfortable with men, knew how they talked, understood that they didn't share feelings.

During dinner she good-naturedly endured the teasing, taunts and challenges thrown Wolf's way. As a brand-new husband, the cast and crew were lamenting the end of Wolf's freedom along with his bachelor days.

Wolf was the one who grew weary of the jests. As the moon rose higher in the sky and the crew started in on yet another round of beer and wine, Wolf told Alexandra that they were leaving and calling it a night. "Bring your glass," he said, indicating her empty wine goblet.

"Where are we going?" she asked.

"Back to our room. I've had enough of these blokes. I'd rather be alone with you."

He picked up a bottle of wine and a glass, and with her hand tucked into his they walked away from the lodge and down the flattened grass path to their *rondavel*.

Inside, he set the wine on the nightstand, taking her glass from her and placing it beside the bottle. But once Wolf took Alexandra into his arms, his mouth covering hers and turning her into a slave of her own senses, the wine was forgotten.

Joy didn't arrive the next day either, causing considerable consternation in camp. Alexandra noticed the director and key staff engaging in several serious conversations at the open-air *boma* that overlooked the bend in the river. It was early spring and the tropical climate was temperate, with mornings and evenings decidedly cool while midday was sunny and extremely pleasant. However, the rainy season was just six weeks away and every day on location was precious. They couldn't afford wasted days and yet there was little they could do without Joy, as she was in virtually every scene in the movie.

Late afternoon Daniel called for a read-through of the script and asked Alexandra if she'd mind reading Joy's lines to allow the rest of the cast a chance to go through the script together.

She was embarrassed at first, but Daniel insisted, and as Alexandra took a seat at the long table in the lodge, Wolf gave her an encouraging nod. After a while she was so engrossed in the plot and story she lost her self-consciousness and enjoyed the read-through.

It was nearly dinner by the time they finished. Alice appeared as they were ending the read-through to invite everyone to the river *boma* for appetizers and cocktails.

"We've a bartender pouring drinks," she said. "And if you're lucky, you'll see some of our famous wildlife—and no, I'm not just talking about my husband Tom."

Wolf waited for Alexandra while she returned Joy's script to Daniel and together they headed for the river bar. The sun was setting on the horizon, and as the deep lavender shadows stretched along the river, game began to appear.

Standing on the elevated rosewood deck, Wolf drew her in front of him and wrapped his arm around her shoulders. He felt so good, so warm and strong and solid. She reached up, covered his forearm with her hands, held him to her. She felt so safe standing together like this, absolutely secure. If only she could always feel this way.

Folding chairs covered in zebra and gemsbok dotted the deck and gradually they filled with the cast and crew. In the distance a lion roared, and Alexandra jumped, still not used to having real lions so close. Last night she'd woken to use the en suite bathroom and a deep huffing sound outside their *rondavel* had scared her—enough to wake Wolf as she'd scampered back into bed. Turned out the huffing had been a lioness walking through camp, trying to attract the attention of her mate.

Alexandra ended up getting the attention of her mate, too.

Wolf must have remembered last night's middle-of-the-night seduction because he suddenly bent his head and nipped at the side of her neck, hardening her nipples and sending goose bumps up and down her arms.

"Not here," she whispered, voice husky.

"Then let's have a drink and excuse ourselves," he said even as he slipped a hand between them to caress her backside.

It was getting hotter and harder to breathe, and as much as Alexandra liked the film crew, she didn't think making love in front of them was such a good idea. Taking a quick step, she broke out of his arms. "Wait there. I'll get the drinks."

"You have two minutes or I'm dragging you back to the bungalow minus refreshments."

She laughed, wagged her finger reprovingly at him. "We can't go to our bungalow yet. Everyone will talk. We should at least wait until after dinner."

"I can't wait."

"Yes you can."

His dark eyes flashed a warning. "Fine. I'll just make you pay later."

She laughed again because when Wolf was like this he made her feel good, reminding her of the days at home when she used to challenge her brothers. She didn't used to be afraid of anything.

As Alexandra waited her turn in line, she looked out at the river, now growing murky as dusk gave way to night. She liked it here in the "bush," as their hosts Tom and Alice called it. She liked the smell, the feel, the pattern of the days.

Life was very communal, with everyone coming together at the lodge for meals, but then once the sun went down, the fire pit became the hub of social activity.

In the evenings the fireplace was surrounded by folding canvas chairs where the guests—in this case the crew and cast—relaxed, sipping cold vodkas, drinking beer and exchanging stories late into the night.

Being in camp at Kafue was almost like being in Montana on the ranch.

Just then a lion growled, louder, closer, and Alexandra shivered and grinned. Well, *almost* like Montana. Not quite.

During dinner Daniel deVoors drew Wolf into a discussion with the lighting director about setting up the cameras for the first scene they wanted to shoot. The lighting director had been watching the way the sun moved through the sky the past few days and the quality of light.

Alexandra leaned back in her chair and listened without really paying attention. The truth was she only had eyes for Wolf.

Spanish-Irish Wolf Kerrick with his savage beauty. Dark-haired, dark-eyed, with soul and sin carved into his features.

He knew the effect he had on women, she thought, knew how he could lay waste to an entire continent with a lift of a brow, the curve of his lip.

He'd possessed her imagination the very same way. She hadn't wanted to want him, had been sure this time she could, she would, resist him.

She'd been wrong.

As if he could feel her long scrutiny, Wolf turned his head, looked at her, meeting her gaze. Their eyes locked, held.

Desire flared, hot and tangible.

Abruptly Wolf pushed back his chair, murmured something unintelligible to the others, but before he could completely break away, a laughing female voice called to them in the darkness.

"Now did you all really think I wasn't coming?"

Alexandra froze, heart still thumping even though the blood began to chill in her veins.

Joy Hughes had just arrived.

CHAPTER ELEVEN

WHERE WAS HE?

Wolf still hadn't come to bed yet and now it was after midnight.

Alexandra had spent the past three hours waiting for him, two and a half of those hours in bed. Two and a half hours where every minute felt endless, where she jumped at every creak outside, where she waited nervously, anxiously, stomach churning, imagination worked overtime.

Where was he? What was he doing? Who was he with?

Some questions were more easily answered than others. She knew he was here in the camp. A sixth sense told her Wolf was with Joy. And as to what they were doing, Alexandra didn't even want to imagine that…

If only he'd return. Or if she could only fall asleep and escape her crazy, punishing thoughts.

Instead she lay restless in the big bed beneath the thatched roof with the white gauzy mosquito netting draped around the mattress.

Why *had* Wolf married her? Why had he thought it necessary to go through with the wedding? Was it really about the lethal cocktail she'd ingested and the fallout of publicity and her family's outrage? Or was the wedding an attempt to cover something else?

To cover for someone else?

A stunt to distract everyone from what was really happening…

What *was* really happening?

Tears stung her eyes. She rolled over onto her stomach, pressed her face into her pillow, hoping to make the tears stop.

Alexandra woke much later to the mattress sagging beneath Wolf's weight as he slid into bed. Her heart thumped as she felt him adjust the covers. She wondered if he'd reach for her, hold her or even say something. But he didn't come near her. And lying there in the dark, she listened as he sighed a deep gut-wrenching sigh. The sound was so heavy, so sorrowful that Alexandra's heart fell, tumbling all the way down.

Now that Joy had arrived, nothing was going to be the same.

The next morning the cast sat down with Daniel for a second read-through. Daniel again asked Alexandra to join them, not to read anyone's lines this time but to listen and learn. "You're the one who wants to be a director," he said, offering her a chair to his left.

Wolf was already seated at the table, four chairs down from Daniel. When Joy arrived with her cup of hot tea, she grabbed a chair next to Wolf, sliding in with a conspiratorial wink.

"You've already done a read-through," Joy said, getting comfortable before lifting and blowing on her tea. "But who played me?"

It was quiet for a moment and then Wolf answered, "Alex did."

Joy took a tiny sip of her tea, her dark-winged eyebrows arching higher. "Alex who?"

There was another odd moment of silence as various cast members glanced at Wolf and Alexandra. Wolf cleared his throat, gestured to Alex, who was sitting with Daniel. "Alexandra. My wife."

Joy hesitated ever so slightly and then laughed, a light tinkling laugh to fill the strained silence. But she never once looked at Alex or acknowledged her directly. "That's right. You're married now. I forgot. Silly me."

Alexandra stared at Joy for a long moment, even as one of the vervet monkeys who'd decided to make Kafue Lodge home tossed pieces of grass down on the table. Alexandra seethed on the inside. How could Joy have forgotten that Wolf was married?

Or did Joy just intend to pretend that Wolf was still single? That everything between them was still the same?

Temper boiling, Alexandra leaned forward. "Did your husband come with you, Joy?"

Joy looked almost startled by Alexandra's question, and Wolf looked furious.

Joy forced a tight smile, shook her head. "No."

Daniel intervened at that moment, crisply directing everyone to open their scripts to the first scene, and Alexandra opened her notebook but not before she saw the look Wolf was giving her. He looked stunned. And furious. There was, Alexandra thought shakily, her bravado giving way, going to be hell to pay later.

She was right. As everyone took a break for lunch, Wolf immediately made a beeline for Alexandra. "Let's take a walk," he said tersely.

She'd been standing next to Daniel at the time, and the director gave her an apologetic look before disappearing.

"I don't feel like a walk right now," she answered, trying to hang on to her anger, trying to find the courage she'd felt earlier. Wolf was her husband. She had a right to stand up for herself. She had a right to tell other women to back off, too, especially if the other woman happened to be Wolf's former lover.

"It's not really an option." Wolf's tone was clipped, grim. "We need to talk."

What Wolf really meant was that he needed to talk and Alexandra needed to listen. As they crossed from the lodge, the raised wood deck gave way to a dirt path, and they followed the path a short distance along the river while the peering eyes of half-submerged hippos followed them.

"What was that back there?" Wolf demanded, stopping beneath one of the many large evergreen waterberry trees shadowing the riverbank.

Alexandra knew she couldn't feign ignorance. She knew why he was upset, but maybe it was time he discovered how she felt. "You insisted we get married, Wolf. You said you had a responsibility to me."

Monkeys chattered above them in the tree, dropping bits of leaves and fruit stems on their heads.

"I'm perfectly aware of my responsibilities."

"Then why do I feel like you'd rather be Joy's husband than mine?"

"Don't be absurd."

"I'm not." Her voice throbbed with outrage. "You're the one that didn't come to bed last night until two in the morning—"

"You were awake?"

"I waited for you."

He sighed impatiently, brushed a stem off his shoulder. "Alexandra, you know Joy's a close friend of mine. She'd just arrived in camp. It's a long trip here, she'd had a series of misadventures—"

"Then she should bring her own husband, not use mine!"

Wolf took a step back, jaw dropping. He lifted a hand to his mouth, giving her a look that wasn't hard to decipher. He thought she was childish, beyond childish. He loathed her right now. "Don't be petty or unkind," he said quietly. "It doesn't suit you."

Then he turned and walked off, heading back to the lodge.

Everyone was eating lunch outside, scattered around the cold fire pit or on the deck with views of the river. Tom had pointed out the family of crocodiles sunning themselves on the opposite side of the river, and everyone passed binoculars as they ate the African barbecue lunch of *borewors*—grilled sausages.

Alexandra ate with a couple of the lighting technicians since Wolf was deep in discussion with Daniel and Joy. He didn't look at her once during lunch, and his cool dismissal stung.

After lunch everyone returned to meetings and Alexandra pulled a book from her carry-on travel bag and found a chair at the deserted *boma* at the river.

She was still sitting there two hours later when Daniel deVoors appeared. He hadn't shaved in days and the gold-brown bristles on his face glinted in the sunlight. "Beautiful here, isn't it?" he commented.

She nodded, put down her book. "I love it. Reminds me of Montana."

He laughed, pulled up a chair. "Reminds me of South Africa. I grew up there until I was sixteen and then my family moved to Australia and then the States." He dragged another chair toward them, put his feet on the seat. "Wolf is a total beast today. What's going on?"

Daniel had been there at the very beginning. He and Benjamin had helped set up the meeting with Wolf. "We got in a fight," she said lowly. "About Joy."

"Joy's beautiful."

Alexandra nodded. "I guess I'm jealous."

Daniel cocked his head. "Wolf married you."

"Because Joy was already married."

"What does Wolf say?"

"That I'm being petty."

"What do you think?"

She looked up at him, expression serious. "I think she's a threat. I think Wolf still has feelings for her."

"And I think Wolf always will. Wolf's the most loyal person I know. He takes care of his friends."

She made a rough sound, hating the rush of emotion. "So what do I do?"

"Be nice to Joy?"

She said nothing, and after a moment Daniel leaned forward, patted her knee. "If they really wanted to be together, they'd be together, Alexandra. It's easy to get a divorce." He gave her an encouraging smile. "Chin up and don't let things you can't control get you down."

She and Wolf still weren't speaking as they both washed and dressed for dinner—which meant Wolf put on a clean shirt and she added a sweater over her knit top.

Outside, around the fire, Alexandra's spirits continued to sink. Wolf was sitting near her, but he could have been anyone as he didn't acknowledge her.

Alexandra had never felt like such an outsider. Or a failure.

Four years in Los Angeles. Four years and now this.

She'd moved to Los Angeles with high hopes. She'd wanted to succeed, she'd wanted to be respected, she'd wanted to be important. *Valued.* And playing Wolf's love interest and then marrying him had gotten her recognition but not respect.

Certainly not self-respect.

Hyenas laughed hysterically in the dark and Alexandra crossed her arms over her chest, suppressing a shiver, thinking the hyenas tonight could be laughing at her.

They should be laughing at her.

Alexandra had wanted to prove herself, had wanted to show her family that she was smart, independent, savvy. Instead she'd discovered she was just as naive as they'd feared. Instead of succeeding on her own merit, she'd made a name for herself dating a famous actor.

Marrying a famous actor.

She glanced at Wolf and realized with a jolt he was looking at her. His dark eyes were shuttered. She couldn't tell what he was thinking, but she wondered if tonight he was as full of regrets as she was.

Wolf brusquely stood. "I'm going to bed," he announced, saying good-night to everyone. "See you tomorrow."

Alexandra watched him turn to leave, again without speaking to her, filling her with hurt and then indignation. Was he just going to ignore her forever?

And while he ignored her, what did he expect her to do? They were camped in the middle of the African bush. The next safari lodge was a two-hour drive away. She had no one but him and the crew to talk to.

Although Alexandra dreaded being confrontational, she jumped up from her chair and went after Wolf.

"This isn't working," she said, following Wolf's steps as he climbed the stairs to their elevated *rondavel.*

"No," he agreed, pivoting on the deck, "it's not."

"So what happens now?" she asked. "Do I go home? Do we get a divorce—"

"A divorce?" he interrupted incredulously, his profile bathed in moonlight. "I'm Irish-Spanish."

"So?"

"I don't believe in divorce and I won't accept that as a satisfactory solution."

Silence stretched and Alexandra wasn't sure where to look, what to do. She could hear a splash in the river and wondered if it was a hippo or a crocodile, wondered if the old male hippo that Tom had nicknamed Alfred would come foraging through camp tonight as he had last night.

Sighing, she pushed back a thick handful of hair from her face. "You know, you're not the kind of man I ever planned to settle down with."

"No?"

She shook her head slowly. "No."

"Why not?"

"I guess I wanted someone like my dad. He loved my mom so much." Alexandra's voice suddenly thickened with emotion. "She was diagnosed with cancer when I was four, and my dad fought for her with everything he had. He was not going to lose her." Blinking, she prayed he wouldn't see her tears. "And that's what I wanted when I grew up. A man who'd fight for me."

"And that's why you were still a virgin at twenty-three? You were holding out for a hero?"

She hated his mocking tone, hated that he'd laugh at her when she was sharing something so deeply personal, so incredibly painful. Anger rushed through her and she clamped her jaw tight.

The river and surrounding reserve were alive with wildlife tonight. In the distance a lion growled, and much closer monkeys shrieked in the cluster of palm and waterberry trees lining the river.

"Not a hero," she said finally, breaking the silence, "but a man who has grown up. A man who knows what's important. A man who'd honor his commitment to me."

Wolf didn't answer and Alexandra turned to look at him. He was leaning on the deck rail, watching her, his face partially shadowed.

His silence unnerved her. His silence made her feel small and ridiculous and insignificant all over again. Steeling herself,

Alex forced a cool, careless smile. "You think I'm childish and immature. Overly sensitive and too emotional, right?"

Again he didn't answer. Not immediately. Then he shook his head. "No," he said quietly. "I don't."

Her heart thumped painfully hard, and she waited, hoping he'd say more, hoping he'd explain himself, his actions and silences, his irritation and distance, but he didn't.

If only she understood him better. If only she knew what motivated him and what was important to him and why.

"It's late," he said, pushing off the rail. "I'm tired, going to bed—"

"Wolf?"

"Yes?"

She searched his face, trying to see something that would help her, trying to learn what she needed to learn. "What kind of woman would you marry?"

He groaned. "Oh, Alexandra."

Shame burned her cheeks, and before she could defend herself he shook his head and added, "The woman I did."

For a moment she didn't understand and she stared at him, confused as well as shy.

"Alexandra, you're the woman I wanted to marry." He reached for her, pulled her to him. "So I did."

He made love to her with an almost ferocious passion, his hunger driven as much by emotion as it was by physical desire. Pinning her arms down above her head, his hands gripped around her wrists, he took her, claiming her, surging into her with fierce, deep thrusts. Alexandra welcomed the intensity, needing the intensity, needing an outlet for her own tangled feelings. But just before she came, he released her wrists and his hands slid over hers, palm to palm, fingers linking.

And, hands locked tightly, head dipped, mouth covering hers, he pushed her to the pinnacle of pleasure and didn't stop, even when she started climaxing. Kissing her, he sucked on her tongue while she exploded around him, her body rippling with pleasure as she held him deep and tight inside her.

The sex was unbelievable, she thought sleepily, curled in his arms afterward, but great sex wasn't going to be enough. She needed his heart.

She needed all of it.

Alexandra woke alone, and as she rolled over inside the mosquito-net tent, she winced at the bright sunlight flooding the *rondavel*. Wolf or one of the housekeepers had opened the wood shutters.

Alexandra hadn't been wearing a watch since it had seemed rather pointless here in the bush, so after taking a fast shower—very fast, as all the hot water was already gone—she dressed in cargo pants and a blue-gray T-shirt and went in search of coffee.

The cast and crew were all busy packing up the Land Rovers and checking the big four-by-four truck that held the cameras. Several Zambian bush guides were on hand this morning to get them to the location they wanted to film as well as to keep an eye out for potential dangers.

Like elephants, Alexandra silently noted. Black rhinos. Lions. Leopards. Cheetahs. Warthogs. And those were just a few, she concluded, taking a sip of the strong, hot coffee she'd sweetened with a smidge of the tinned sweetened condensed milk they used here and another liberal teaspoon of sugar.

And while she savored her coffee, she began to hear bits and pieces of a conversation taking place around the lodge's corner.

"I thought I was going."

It was Joy, Alexandra realized, and she was far from happy.

"I will take you sometime, but you're needed here."

"But, Wolf, you can't go alone. Why don't you wait until I can go with you?"

Stiffening, Alexandra held the hot cup to her lips but didn't drink.

"I'm not going alone," he answered. "Alexandra's going with me."

"But she can't fly and I can! I've always been your copilot. Wait a few days and I'll have a break from shooting and we can go together."

Joy paused and Alexandra had to strain to hear Joy's next

words. "Besides, Wolf, you don't even know *if* she'll go. She might be terrified of small planes, and face it, that little Piper Tri-Pacer isn't the prettiest of aircraft."

"It flies," Wolf said.

"On a wing and a prayer," Joy retorted with a laugh.

Wolf said something in reply that Alexandra didn't catch as Wolf and Joy had begun walking again, heading away from the lodge to the Land Rovers and trucks.

Alexandra was still trying to sort out the meaning of the conversation she'd overheard when Wolf appeared, alone.

"Good morning," he said, bending over to drop a kiss on her lips. And even though his lips just brushed hers, her insides jumped as though she'd been given an electric shock.

"Morning," she answered huskily, making herself take a sip from her cup. "How are you?"

"Good." He dropped into a chair next to hers and propped one boot on top of the other. "I slept great." He looked at her, grinned lazily, teeth flashing. "And you?"

"Good." She took another quick sip, looking at him from beneath lowered lashes. He'd shaved this morning and his hair was thick and glossy black, reflecting the morning sun.

Wolf was studying her just as carefully. "I've got an errand to run today. Feel like coming along?"

This is what Wolf and Joy had been discussing. And Wolf's errand included flying, with Wolf at the controls.

Alexandra wasn't afraid of flying. Three of her five brothers were pilots and they had an airstrip at the Lazy L ranch so her brothers could fly in and out, avoiding the lengthy trip into Bozeman for short hops. But her brothers were expert pilots and their aircraft were always new and scrupulously maintained.

God only knew the maintenance history of the Piper Joy had mentioned.

But then there was Joy, and she'd wanted to make this trip with Wolf and suggested that Alexandra wouldn't want to go and might be afraid to fly. Alexandra was competitive enough not to let Joy win or, in this case, be right.

"I'd love to go," she said cheerfully.

"We're flying."

"Great."

If he questioned her enthusiasm, he gave no indication. "I'll be flying us."

"You're the pilot," she agreed.

One of his eyebrows lifted ever so slightly. "It's a Piper Tri-Pacer."

"A two-seater?"

"Four."

She swallowed around the lump filling her throat. She didn't even know what a Piper Tri-Pacer was. "Let's do it."

He turned his head, looked at her hard. "No questions? Concerns? You're not worried?"

Not worried? She was panicking like mad. Wolf was smart, gorgeous, and while he was amazing in bed, she wasn't sure about his skills as a pilot. And they were flying in a dilapidated plane over the African bush. "My brothers fly," she said airily. "I'm used to little planes."

"Great." Wolf gave her an approving smile. "Let's grab the picnic lunch the kitchen packed and head on out. Big Red's waiting."

"Big Red?"

"The Tri-Pacer."

"Right."

Wrong, Alexandra thought ten minutes later as she stood in front of the saddest excuse for a plane she ever saw.

What must have once been a jaunty red-and-white paint job was now old, chipped, scarred, peeling and faded. The nose looked dinged, the propeller as though it'd tangled with a wildebeest, the tail as if it'd housed a family of baboons. And later Alexandra discovered it had.

On her toes, she peered into the interior, which was nearly all red. Cracked red leather seats with bits of hard yellow foam protruding.

"That's the original leather," Wolf said, tossing their lunch and a huge knapsack into the back of the plane.

As if she hadn't noticed. "Mmm."

"Great little plane."

She stared at the red cockpit with its black instrument panels, the radio and the headphones dangling from the yoke. It was definitely snug inside. And while Wolf had called it a four-seater, she couldn't imagine squeezing two people in the very cramped backseat.

Belted in next to Wolf, she saw him wave to Tom, who'd come down to the primitive airstrip to see them off.

"We'll be back before dark," Wolf shouted.

Tom gave them a thumbs-up sign.

"We're off."

But they weren't exactly off, Alexandra thought, heart pounding as the plane lurched and lumbered down the rough airstrip. They weren't going to make it off the ground. They were going to just roll their way to Lusaka or wherever they were going.

But just when Alexandra feared they'd never lift, the little red-and-white Piper went airborne—not high but gaining speed and altitude.

Alexandra's hands were damp as she clutched the sides of her cracked leather seat. Her heart was still racing but not as frantically. It'd been scary taking off, and yet now, thousands of feet above the bush, she had such an incredible view of the landscape below that Alexandra laughed, her fear replaced by exhilaration.

This was unreal. By far the most adventurous thing she'd ever done.

"This trip just keeps getting better and better," she said.

Wolf looked at her, dark eyes creased. "I love flying but especially here." He suddenly pointed. "Look. Elephants." And there they were, a huge herd clustered around a grove of waterberry trees.

Alexandra's eyes opened wide. "There must be twenty or thirty of them."

"This is their home."

Their real home, she thought, *their native habitat. Where they belonged.*

As they flew north, Wolf pointed out more game. The giraffes and zebras traveling together. What looked like a lone black rhino. Hundreds of grazing hartebeest and sable.

They'd been traveling for over an hour when Alexandra reached into the backseat to retrieve the water canteen. She was screwing off the top when Wolf silently swore.

She took a quick drink, replaced the cap. "What's wrong?"

"Mmm." He wasn't relaxed anymore and his gaze was fixed on the control panel in front of him.

It was then she realized they were losing altitude. Rapidly.

She glanced at the controls, watched as he clicked the fuel button to the left, the right. She looked up to the fuel gauge. The gauge showed empty. But the tank had been full when they'd left. She saw the gauge, saw him check, knew they'd refueled the plane just this morning.

"Wolf."

"We're going to be landing," he said calmly, as if his announcement was nothing out of the ordinary. "Lock down the canteen and anything loose. Make sure you have nothing sharp in your pockets. Then secure your seat belt. We're about to land."

She shot him another frantic glance as the grassy African plain loomed closer. She couldn't believe this was happening. "You mean *crash.*"

He lightly drew on the yoke, keeping the Piper's nose up. "No," he contradicted her coolly, "I mean land."

CHAPTER TWELVE

CONSIDERING IT WAS A crash landing, Wolf did admirably well trying to keep the wreck of a plane in one piece.

They hit hard, bounced up, came down again. They were rolling, bouncing across the rough terrain, when a huge out-cropping of rock threatened to shear them in two.

Wolf slammed on the brakes, pulling hard to the right, and they avoided the rocks but ended up flipping the plane.

Despite bracing herself, Alexandra slammed against the plane's frame as they flipped and then once against the cockpit controls and then finally she dangled in her seat upside down.

"Alexandra," Wolf snapped urgently.

Disoriented, she turned to look at him. Blood trickled down his temple. "I'm okay." She swallowed, dazed.

"You're sure?"

She wiggled her fingers, her ankles, her toes. "Yes." She frowned at him. "But you're bleeding."

"Just a scratch." The urgency had faded from his voice and he worked now to undo his seat belt. It took him just a moment, and then he braced himself, putting a foot and an arm out as he turned himself over and around. Once he was right up, he undid her belt and lifted her out.

Stumbling from the cockpit, Alexandra staggered a few steps on legs that promised to give out. She squinted against the bright sunlight, lifting a weak hand to shield her eyes as she looked to her left and then her right. The savannah stretched in every direction. "Where are we?"

"Based on the plane's compass, I'd say South Luangwa."

"South Luangwa," she repeated numbly, beginning to shiver. It was just shock; she knew it was shock, because she wasn't cold. Not when it had to be at least eighty degrees right now. "Is that a province?"

"It's another national park."

Her head jerked around. "As in, another animal park?"

"Animals don't have parks. They have protected land."

Wolf reached into the back of the plane, retrieved the huge duffel bag as well as the knapsack with their lunch and beverages. "We're actually invading their space."

"It's not the invasion I'm worried about. It's personal safety."

"We should be fine. If anything gets too close, we can take shelter in the plane."

She shot the upside down plane a dubious glance. "It's forty years old and covered in fabric. Will it really stop a rhino? Or an elephant?"

"Probably not a charging rhino." He knelt next to the knapsack, found a transmitter radio. "Or an angry elephant bull for that matter." He looked up at her. "But the likelihood of us getting attacked is next to none. This is a six-thousand-acre park. The crash was loud. The animals are running the opposite direction right now."

She compressed her lips. Maybe the impalas and zebras were, but the lions were probably thinking *Yum, yum, fresh meat*. "Does that radio work?"

"I'm going to try to get a signal."

For nearly twenty minutes he worked with the radio, and Alexandra sat next to him, periodically holding her breath, hoping against hope that something miraculous would happen.

Unfortunately they seemed to have run out of miracles for the rest of the day.

Not knowing how long it would be before they were found, Alexandra and Wolf agreed to eat only a fraction of the generous lunch packed. They were already rationing water.

"Where were we going?" Alexandra finally thought to ask as she finished the corner of her meat pie.

"A village north of here." Wolf returned the water canteen to the plane, where it'd stay cooler in the shade. "It's one of the villages I adopted several years ago."

She perched on the red leather bench seat Wolf had taken out of the back of the plane. "How did you adopt a village?"

"Well, some people help sponsor a child in a developing country. I chose to sponsor a village."

She wrapped her arms around her knees, fascinated. "What do you do?"

He shrugged as he dropped onto the ground near her. It was blistering hot out, but they were both trying to take refuge in the shade adjacent to the plane. "Build schools, wells, dig irrigation ditches, develop sanitation facilities, establish medical clinics, provide vaccines, educate about AIDS." He sighed, shook his head. "I'll do whatever I can."

"I had no idea." She felt a wave of tenderness. "That's wonderful. How long have you been doing this?"

"Almost ten years."

"How many villages do you sponsor?"

Uncomfortable, he looked away, dark lashes dropping, concealing his expression. "Not enough," he said at last.

"Tell me—you have to have an idea. Three? Five? Seven?"

"More than twenty. Not quite thirty."

"Thirty villages," she repeated in awe.

His features tightened. He looked pained. "A little money goes a long way out here. There's so much more I want to do, so much more we need to do."

"I think people try, but Africa's a big continent," she said softly. "It's far away, too, and people at home or abroad probably don't know what you know. They haven't seen what you've seen."

"They've an idea," he flashed roughly. "It's all over *Time* and *Newsweek* magazines. The news is always doing segments on children starving and dying—" He broke off, got to his feet. "I'm going to take a short walk. Don't worry, I won't go far."

She watched him set off, his stride long, impatient, angry.

He was gone maybe a half hour, and during the time he was away she sat close to the plane, just in case. But as she sat there, her nervousness gave way to calm.

It was peaceful here, beautiful and golden and serene.

The African savannah was more like Montana than anything she'd ever seen, and it wasn't necessarily the trees and climate as much as the sense of size and openness, the feeling that land and sky stretched endlessly.

She was glad when Wolf returned. His shirt clung wetly to his skin and his hat was damp and dark on his brow. "You look hot," she said.

"I am," he answered, peeling off his shirt and tossing it onto one of the plane's damaged wheels. "Were you scared while I was gone?"

"Not very," she answered, admiring the planes of his chest and his tight, hard abs. He had a gorgeous body, and it was hers. Her husband. She smiled on the inside, happy despite everything. "I like it here."

"In the middle of nowhere?"

"It's not nowhere. It's Africa. Zambia."

The corner of his mouth lifted. "You're a funny girl." He reached into the tail of the plane, muscles rippling and contracting as he rummaged around the back before finding what he was looking for—a battered wood box.

"What's that for?"

"Kindling for tonight's fire," he said, back to rummaging in the tail.

"Wolf, if you quit acting, would you want to direct? Write? Produce?"

"None of the above. I'd be done."

"For a while? A vacation?"

"Forever." He turned from the plane, shot her a dry glance. "I'm sick of L.A., sick of Hollywood, sick of the fake people and fake talk. I want out."

"Where would you go? Dublin?"

"I have a house on the west coast of Ireland. Galway. But I

don't know if I'd move there. Maybe I won't move anywhere. Maybe I'll just bum around, village to village, doing what I can to help."

"You'd sell your house? Your cars—that huge collection?"

"The cars will soon be sold anyway. I buy them, fix them up, sell them at a profit and all proceeds go to one of my charities."

"You've charities, too?"

He nodded yes.

She looked at him for a long time. "Are you really going to leave Los Angeles?"

"Soon. I have to," he said. "It's time. Time to become a real person again. Time to leave the craziness behind."

She leaned forward on the red bench seat, hands balled together. "Wouldn't you miss Hollywood?"

He didn't even hesitate. "No."

Alexandra struggled to think of something to say but nothing came. She couldn't imagine Wolf walking away from Hollywood completely, couldn't imagine him never making another film, never starring in another role. He was too good. Too talented. People enjoyed him so much. "Hollywood would miss you," she said softly.

His laugh was low, cynical. "Only because I make them money."

She shook her head, not thinking about the money or the business but of his talent. He had the rare ability to bring the most complex and disparate characters to life. There were times she used to tell herself Wolf was famous because of his face— his eyes, his mouth, his sex appeal—but not even the most beautiful man could achieve what Wolf had without that rare ability to become another, to become the character, sliding into the skin, feeling the emotions, thinking the thoughts and making even the most vile mortal compelling, fascinating, even sympathetic.

Alex felt a strange tug inside her. Sorrow. Gratitude. Even if he never acted in another film, she'd always be a huge fan. "People will miss you."

He made a rough sound before dragging his hands through

his thick black hair, rifling it on end. "Nothing lasts forever. No one lives forever. All things—even good things—end."

Tears started to her eyes, and Alex turned her head, closed her eyes, willing the tears not to fall. And yet it was a battle, a battle when her chest burned hot, thick with bittersweet emotion. She suddenly pictured the ranch and where she'd been the moment she'd learned her mother had cancer. "So why haven't you walked before?"

Wolf lifted his hands. "I've tried. But the studios…"

He didn't have to finish the explanation. She knew already. The studios wouldn't let him. The studios had too much invested in him.

There would be his agent who wanted his twenty percent. The manager who took another hefty chunk. The publicist and the personal assistants.

The directors who'd already cast him in future films.

The studios themselves who paid bills on the backs of their superstars.

"How long have you felt this way?" she asked, struggling to take it all in, struggling to believe that Wolf really meant what he said.

"Four years. Five."

Five? She swallowed. "And they know this?"

He made a hoarse sound even as the corner of his mouth lifted. "Oh, they know."

"And what do they say?"

His mouth twisted yet again. "What do you think?"

"One more film," she answered softly.

His head inclined. "One more film, just one more, just help us with this, don't let us down, we need you, we need you now, our careers, our lives depend on you."

He snorted, his dark eyes flashing with scorn. "*Their* lives. Talk about greed. People all over the world are dying of hunger, dying for lack of medicine, shelter, lack of the most essential things, and then you have the fat cats in Hollywood talking about *their* lives. It blows me away."

"Not everyone in the industry is loaded. Lots of people—

most of those that actually work on your films—struggle to get by just like everyone else," she said gently.

Some of the tension at his mouth eased. "I know. And that's one of the reasons I continue to work. I know I support a lot of people. But I also know if I stopped acting, they'd find other films, other jobs."

She leaned forward. "If you stopped acting tomorrow, what would you do?"

He didn't even hesitate. "What I'm doing now. I'd help the villages. I'd work with UNICEF, raise more money, raise awareness, become an activist and help anywhere I could."

The sun was just beginning to set when Wolf took a crowbar to the wooden crate, splintering it into medium pieces. Together they gathered some twigs and small branches from a tree near the rocky outcropping.

They put off starting the fire until it was late, eating a half sandwich each and a little of the fruit. And just as Wolf was about to strike the match to light the fire, he looked up and saw Alexandra crouched right next to him, calm, trusting, and he felt as though someone had reached into his chest and ripped his heart out with a violent yank.

What if they couldn't get out of here? What if they ran out of water? Food?

His gaze searched her face, and yet there was no panic in her eyes, no anger or resentment anywhere in her beautiful face. She was more than a good sport. He loved her adventurous attitude almost as much as he loved how genuine she was. How real. She was, he thought, reaching for her, that girl he'd been looking for, the one that reminded him of home.

Wolf cupped her cheek and Alexandra closed her eyes. Just that one touch melted her. Just that one touch made her want incredible things.

She opened her eyes and looked up at him. His eyes were just as endless as the sky above them and even darker.

He wanted her. She felt his desire, felt the need. It was basic and raw. And yet she waited, waiting for him to make the first move.

He touched her mouth with the tip of his finger, gently, lightly stroking down so that her lips burned and tingled, now so sensitive.

Down his fingertip went, over her lower lip to trail down her chin. He traced her jaw and then up to her right earlobe and back across the flushed curve of her cheek.

She was trembling as she stood there, trembling beneath his slow, unhurried touch. She wanted to be caught in his arms, dragged close and kissed until her head spun but he had a different script in mind.

"Kiss me," she breathed, unable to stand it.

"So impatient," he mocked, lowering his head and dropping a brief kiss against her mouth, catching the corner of her lips and the swell of her upper lip.

The brush of his mouth against hers made her belly flip, sending rivulets of fire and ice through her veins.

Shivering, she took a step toward him. "Kiss me again," she urged.

Lifting her up, he carried her to the door of the plane, where he stripped off her clothes and then his and made love to her on what was left of the plane.

Afterward, they stayed inside the plane, and Wolf used some of the blankets from the stash he'd been taking to the village—one for a bed, another for a pillow and the last to cover them.

She lay sleepily against his chest, thinking his body fit hers perfectly. He was hard and strong where she was soft. Stifling a yawn, she thought there'd be no one else, no one that would ever make her feel like this.

Alexandra woke to the feel of Wolf's lips and beard-roughened jaw kissing the back of her neck.

"Good morning," he said.

Sighing contentedly, she scooted closer. "Good morning."

But he wasn't staying in bed. He was getting up. "I'm going to try the radio again. Somebody's got to find us soon."

It was harder to pass the time the second day, at least until Wolf remembered the books, paper, small chalkboards and chalk in the supplies he'd been flying to the village.

With the chalkboards and chalk they began their own version of Twenty Questions. They took turns writing questions down for each other and then they'd turn their chalkboard over and the other would have to answer. Some of the questions were random—what's your favorite color, what's your Chinese zodiac sign, what size shoe do you wear—while others were far more revealing.

"How did you get the name Wolf?" she asked, flashing him her chalkboard. "It's not Spanish or Irish."

"If you were a true fan, you'd know the answer."

She rolled her eyes. "Members of your fan club get the details in a newsletter?"

He laughed appreciatively. "It's a shortened version of my name. I was christened Tynan Wolfe Kerrick. A casting director convinced me to drop Tynan and then the *e* off Wolfe."

"What did your dad call you, then?"

"Tynan."

"And your mom?" she persisted.

The corners of his mouth tilted, and he smiled mockingly up at her from beneath his dense black lashes. "Trouble."

They both laughed and then he held up his board. *Why Hollywood?* it read.

"I've always loved movies," she said. "I was crazy about them as a kid. And not just a little bit but wildly, passionately. It's one of the ways my family helped me cope with losing Mom. They took me to movies every weekend in Bozeman. We didn't have a lot of theatres, so sometimes we'd see the same movie four or five times."

"You have a good family," he said gently.

She nodded thoughtfully. "I do."

"Do you remember your first movie?"

"Disney's *The Little Mermaid*." She smiled shyly. "I remember I cried for Ariel when she lost her voice. And then I cried again at the end, when she and Prince Eric got married—" She broke off, remembering not just that day but all the movies, all the trips to the theater. The way you crunched popcorn and stepped in sticky soda on the way to your seat. The dramatic darkening of the theater as the lights went out. The swish of the curtains opening. The clicking sound the projector made as the movie ended.

She lifted her eyebrows. "I even remember the first movie I saw you in. I was fifteen. You were playing a soldier and you died—" she took a quick breath "—and I cried then, too. And now look at us, stranded here in the middle of nowhere!"

"It's not nowhere," he answered gravely, mimicking her response from yesterday. "It's Zambia. Africa."

She sat nestled in his arms as the sun set, the savannah painted a stunning blood-red, and then the sun disappeared and the horizon turned dark. Not long after, a lion roared in the distance.

Alexandra scrambled to her feet. "I think it's time to light that fire."

"I agree."

Later, as the fire burned, they played their Twenty Questions again, this time without chalkboards since it would be too hard to see. "How old were you when your mom died?" he asked.

Alex leaned forward, pressed her chest against her knees. "Five."

"Are you like her?"

She shook her head. "My brothers say no. They said Mom was sweet—" She broke off, laughed and then took a quick, sharp breath. "I miss her. Being the only girl in my family was hard."

Wolf leaned against one of the red seats from the cockpit and watched her face as she talked. Her face was so expressive in the firelight. Her eyes shone and her mouth curved, twitched, moved, and he thought she just might be the most beautiful woman he'd ever met.

"Mothers are special, aren't they?" he said, grabbing a stalk of dry grass and breaking it off. He rubbed the tall brittle grass between his thumb and finger, twirling it around as though it'd soon take flight.

"I wish I'd been older. Wish I knew her better. Sometimes I'm angry with my brothers because they had so much more time with her. Brock was a senior in high school. Practically an adult." Her eyes filled with tears. She blinked and quickly pushed away the tear. "I was just starting kindergarten. And—" she pushed away another tear "—I don't really remember her. I remember *The Little Mermaid,* but I don't remember her. How's that fair?"

"It's not," he said gently.

"Sometimes I think everything would be so different if my mom were alive today."

He heard the wistfulness in her voice. "How?"

She shrugged. "Maybe I'd be a different person."

"But why would you want to be different? You wouldn't be you—and you're perfect as you are."

Her head ducked and she stared at the fire and then she lifted her head, smiled shyly. "Thank you."

"My pleasure." His gaze held hers, and as the tears dried in her eyes, he knew he hated seeing her cry. He'd do anything to keep her from crying. "So what makes you happy?"

She wrinkled her nose, laughed. "Snow," she whispered. "It reminds me of the movies. It changes everything. Makes simple things beautiful."

And maybe that was her magic, Wolf thought, standing up and holding a hand out to her. She made simple things beautiful, too.

Alexandra was so hungry that night she had a hard time falling asleep. Every time she'd start to doze off, her stomach growled. It was a relief when she did fall into a proper sleep, a deep sleep with a good dream, and she was still in that dream, a place of muted color and muffled sound, when she felt a gust of cold air blow over her.

"Hey, Sleeping Beauty, time to wake up."

Slowly, sleepily she opened her eyes, struggling to focus. "Wolf?"

He was standing outside the plane and he was smiling broadly. "Help has finally arrived."

She sat up so fast she banged her head on the side of the plane. "Seriously?" she demanded, moving to her knees to peek around Wolf. And there was help. A Luangwa park warden in a dusty Land Rover.

She let out a cheer. "We're saved!"

The Luangwa warden had been authorized to drive them to Lusaka, where a massive search-and-rescue party was being organized. They stopped at one of the lodges en route, where they both showered and had a quick meal before continuing on to the capital city.

It took over half the day to get there, and by the time they reached the hotel in downtown, the press had already gathered, their cameras and microphones set up.

As they stepped from the warden's Land Rover there was a cheer, and Daniel was among the first to rush toward them, welcoming them back.

Daniel hugged both. "This is a miracle," he said, wrapping an arm around Alexandra and facing Wolf. "This is better than the best possible scenario." He grinned, but you could see the fatigue etched in deep lines near his eyes. "I don't think I've ever prayed that much in my life."

Wolf clapped a hand on Daniel's back. "We're good, we're fine. Alexandra was a champ."

Daniel shook his head, still overcome. "Joy was hysterical when you didn't return. She feared the worst, but I was sure that you'd make it through somehow. Thank God I was right."

Daniel turned to Wolf, clapped him hard on the back. "My God, am I glad to see you. You can't imagine the chaos or the media frenzy. The studio in Hollywood has been overwhelmed with calls from media all over the world. Reporters and photographers have been rushing to Lusaka from nearly every continent. It's been utter chaos."

Wolf nodded. "Then let's get this press conference over and done with. We're hungry and thirsty and Alexandra's going to want to call her family soon."

Daniel nodded agreement and the three of them approached the makeshift podium where dozens of microphones had been set up. As Daniel made a brief introduction, Alexandra stood behind Wolf, her gaze skimming the crowd of journalists and cameramen.

Then it was Wolf's turn to talk, and he told them about the plane and what he believed caused the crash. He described their two and a half days roughing it in the South Luangwa National Park before being discovered earlier that morning by one of the park wardens.

While Wolf gave them dry details about their stay, information about survival and practical details about food, water and shelter, she recalled something entirely different.

She remembered the deepness of the night, the vastness of the velvet-black sky, the glitter of stars overhead.

She remembered the warmth of Wolf sleeping next to her, his arm curved protectively around her.

She remembered the feel of his hard body on hers, covering her, filling her.

She remembered tenderness. Hunger. Peace.

She remembered love.

Alexandra swallowed around the thickness lodging in her throat.

She'd fallen *in* love with him before they'd ever arrived in Africa, but there, in the South Luangwa National Park, she'd *loved* him. The depth of her feelings for him stunned her, terrified her, left her breathless, speechless. Somehow she'd become his real wife.

Wolf finished speaking, and the crowd of reporters erupted into a frenzy of sound, each journalist shouting to be heard over the other.

"Wolf, did you encounter any animals?"

"What exactly did you eat, Mr. Kerrick?"

"How did you and Mrs. Kerrick manage the extreme heat in the middle of the day?"

"A question for your bride, Wolf. Will you let her speak?"

Wolf turned to Alexandra, extended a hand, encouraging her to join him at the microphones.

Nervously she took his hand and moved to stand beside him. She was trembling—nerves, relief, exhaustion—as she stepped next to Wolf and she feared doing something foolish, embarrassing them both somehow.

But then his arm circled her, his hand resting lightly on her hip, and she was immediately reassured. Calmed. He applied no pressure to her hip, but his touch, his skin was warm and it soothed her. Just being near him she knew that everything would be okay.

But that's how he'd always made her feel.

Even in the beginning. She hadn't wanted to pretend, but Wolf was so magnetic, so compelling, so reassuring that she'd agreed to the part, agreed to the deal.

Crazy. Ridiculous. Miraculous.

She glanced up, looked into his face, seeing the beautifully savage features that made him the world's favorite star. But he wasn't an actor to her. Wasn't a film star or matinee idol. He was just Wolf.

"Are you okay?" he asked, his voice a delicious Irish murmur of sound.

She nodded and, biting her lower lip, realized she meant it. She was okay. Wolf made everything okay.

"How did Wolf handle the crisis, Alexandra?" a reporter shouted.

She looked at Wolf, smiled. "Fine. Better than I did."

"And what did you eat?"

She leaned toward the microphones. "The lodge had sent us with a picnic lunch. It was pretty hearty and we rationed that over the next couple of days."

"Did you plan this, Wolf? Honeymooning on location, plane crash with new bride? Great media news story…"

Wolf laughed wearily. "No. I almost wish I had. It's a good one, isn't it?"

"But that's not exactly true, Wolf." It was Joy who interrupted. Her voice carried, immediately quieting the crowd. Everyone turned to look at her. She'd found a microphone and was standing off to the side. "Meeting and marrying Alexandra Shanahan was a publicity stunt. He did it to end speculation about our relationship."

"Joy." Wolf shook his head, issuing a warning. "No."

She gave him a small, sad smile. "This has to be told, Wolf, it's the only way. The only way you can ever hope to be free." Tears glittered in her eyes. "He never intended to marry Alexandra. He never imagined it'd get that far. But when she got sick, Wolf's such a gentleman he did what he thought was the right thing. He married her. But, Wolf, it's not a real marriage. I know you don't love her. I know you just did this for me."

CHAPTER THIRTEEN

THE PRESS HAD A FIELD day with that one. Talk about tabloid news. Photos were snapped and headlines scribbled and captions created…all while Alexandra stood at the podium, staring aghast at Wolf.

Was Joy right? Was what she'd just said true?

Even as reporters erupted in shouts, Wolf grabbed Alexandra's hand and hustled her away from the pandemonium and into the hotel, where a suite had been reserved for them.

It was the royal suite, the hotel day manager said, handing them the keys, in honor of their esteemed guests. But Wolf barely answered and Alexandra was downright catatonic.

On the top floor, in their room, Wolf made Alexandra sit. "Listen to me," he said roughly. "I will tell you this one time and I need you to listen and believe me." His accent deepened, growing more pronounced with his exhaustion and stress.

"There is nothing between Joy and me. We're friends," he continued. "Only friends. People have always made it out to be more, but that's because people have an insatiable need for scandal."

"But Joy said—"

"I don't care what Joy said. I'm telling you the truth. And it's me you need to believe. I'm your husband. I'm the one you turn to when you need something, when you doubt, when you question sanity. It's me. Understand?"

Her lower lip trembled and she bit into it ruthlessly, biting down so hard she tasted blood.

"Joy's not a happy person," Wolf continued. "She's struggled for years with booze and pills and bouts of depression. Try to realize she's suffering right now and anything she says or does is because she's in pain."

Alexandra covered her face to keep him from seeing how his words hurt. She knew he thought he was helping. She knew he thought he was making everything clear. But he didn't realize a woman wanted more than a sexually faithful husband. A woman needed her man to be emotionally faithful, too.

Wolf crouched in front of her and pulled her hands away from her face. "Why are you crying?"

"Because I'm afraid."

His dark eyes were tormented. "Of what? Me?"

And then the tears fell. Because she wasn't afraid of him, not physically, but she was afraid he'd never give her what she needed most. "I can't compete for you."

"You don't have to."

"But I feel like I do. I feel like I could lose you any moment."

He let her go then and slowly stood. "If you feel that way, you'll make it happen. You will lose me because you'll think it into reality."

She reached out for him, hands up, pleading. "Am I not here? Am I not saying Wolf, help me make this work?"

"Listen to me, Alexandra. I am here and I want to make this work, too." He returned to her, pulled her up into his arms and stroked her wet cheeks with his thumbs. "You're not alone in this." His voice fell, deepened. He touched his mouth to hers. "I want to be with you."

And when they made love, it was so good and so tender and so raw and real it hurt.

Wolf was right for her in so many ways. Wolf was everything she'd ever wanted in a man. But still a small part of her was afraid. She could fight Joy when it was the two of them, Alexandra and Wolf. But when Wolf went through the door, he was out there on his own.

And maybe that's what she feared. His judgment. His inability to take a stand, a side.

Her side.

Lying next to Wolf, she watched him sleep, his impossibly thick lashes like ebony crescents on his cheeks.

Tomorrow he'd go back to work, and then what?

But they woke the next day to even more bad news.

The producers pulled the plug on the film. They were ordering all crew and cast back home.

There'd been problems with the project from the beginning, but Joy's highly televised outburst was the final straw. Alexandra tried to talk about it with Wolf, but he just shook his head, unable to communicate.

They spent the afternoon killing time, sightseeing in Lusaka. And then the next morning Alexandra and Wolf boarded the British Airways jet and headed home.

Back in California they returned to Wolf's Malibu house. After Africa, the house felt strange, too big, too new, too modern. But they hadn't been home even a day before Joy started calling.

Alexandra told herself they were just phone calls. She told herself to let it go, not to care. She remembered Wolf's explanations, remembered how he'd seemed sincere, and it worked. At first.

But the phone calls didn't stop. She'd phone him on his mobile or at the house and she'd be crying. She'd be inconsolable. Wolf would take the phone into his office at the back of the house and have endless conversations with her.

Wolf told Alexandra that Joy was upset about the film being shelved. She was worried she'd alienated them. She worried that the public blamed her for any problems in Wolf and Alexandra's marriage.

It was always on the tip of Alexandra's tongue to say, "Yes, she does cause problems." But she knew it'd only antagonize Wolf, so she bit her tongue and didn't complain.

But the weeks passed and the calls continued and Wolf grew more distracted. They still made love, but in some ways Wolf wasn't quite there anymore. It wasn't that the pleasure was gone, but the emotional intensity had changed. Faded.

And it tormented her, it really did.

After making love one night, Wolf fell into an immediate deep sleep, and after lying there sleepless, Alexandra finally got up. She went to the kitchen to get something to eat, and Wolf's mobile phone was there on the counter. She hated this phone, she thought. It might as well be Joy's phone.

Glancing down, she saw he had a missed call.

Joy, probably.

And suddenly desperate to know just how bad this was, Alexandra clicked on his phone's call list and scanned through the incoming calls from just today. New York, New York, New York, all the same number. Joy's number.

She scrolled down through the entire in-box. Joy. Joy. Joy. Joy. She clicked on his out-box, checked numbers dialed.

Joy. Joy. Joy. Joy.

Covering her mouth, she sat down on a stool at the counter and tried to keep her scream from coming out.

She was losing him. She was losing him and she couldn't seem to stop it, change it, do anything about it.

"Alexandra." It was Wolf standing in the kitchen doorway.

She couldn't even turn to look at him or he'd see the suffering in her face. "I think we're in trouble here, Wolf. Things aren't going so well."

"Want to talk about it?"

She shook her head and pushed his phone back and forth on the counter. "Talking's not helping. In fact, when you and I talk, things just seem to get worse."

He cleared his throat. "In bed, earlier, everything was fine."

She almost laughed. In bed. Of course a man would think that way. And then she closed her eyes to keep the hurt in. "I'm running out of steam, Wolf. I'm thinking this isn't going the way it needs to go." She swallowed around the lump filling her throat. "Not for me. Nor you."

"It has been hard, Alex. But it'll get easier soon."

"Why? Is Joy seeing a doctor? Taking a new antidepressant? What makes you think any of this will ever change?"

"She's working to fix her problems, yes."

Alexandra slammed her hands onto the counter. "But aren't we all? My God, Wolf, what about me? Can't you see I'm having problems? Can't you see I'm hurt? Can't you see I need you, too? Maybe even need you more?"

"Alex."

"No." She dashed away the tears. "Please, please don't do that anymore. Don't sigh like I'm the difficult one. Don't make me feel like I'm being unreasonable to want to have my husband's attention."

"How many times do I have to tell you, you have me?"

"All right, then answer me this." She balled her fist against the cool counter. "If Joy called you tomorrow and said she needed you, you'd go." She lifted her head, looked at him. "Wouldn't you?"

"I'd help any friend that needed me."

"Then help me," she whispered, her gaze holding his. "Pick me."

He'd frozen in place. She hadn't said the actual words yet, hadn't even planned on saying the words, but suddenly it was there, the nuance.

She was about to draw the battle lines. Demand his loyalty. Define the boundaries.

"What are you saying?" he asked, expression shuttered.

What was she saying? she wondered. Did she really know what she was saying? Her thoughts spun. She struggled to gain control before the situation got out of hand. She was tired, worn down, emotional. Did she really want to do this now?

"Alexandra?" he prompted.

"Maybe it's time we settled things once and for all," she said, so cold on the inside that she felt like a puppet, oddly detached. "Maybe we should just say what needs to be said."

His expression grew increasingly wary. "And what needs to be said?"

Her eyes burned. She swallowed. "Who do you want? Joy or me?"

"Alexandra…"

"Wolf, I need to know. If you were to pick only one of us, would it be her or me?"

"It doesn't work like that," he said impatiently. "You're my wife. And Joy, she's…she's a friend and troubled, and the situation's complicated."

Complicated?

Why was his love so complicated? How could it be so complicated? Love wasn't complicated for her. She knew who she loved and she knew why she loved and she knew that as long as Wolf was in her life he was her priority. It was as complicated—or simple—as that.

"I've put you first," she said flatly. "From the beginning I've put you first. Now do the same for me—"

"Alexandra."

"Wolf, I can't handle this anymore."

He looked at her so long she felt her heart slow and her insides gel. He looked at her with pain and exhaustion, sorrow and frustration. And she realized he wasn't going to give her what she wanted. Wasn't going to give her what she needed.

"I'll pack my things," he said quietly. "I have a trip to Venice in a few days. I'll just leave early."

"So that's your decision?" she choked out, chilled.

"I'm sick of the pressure, Alexandra. I can't be who or what you want me to be and I'm worn out from trying, too."

Wolf drew a suitcase out from the walk-in closet and began to pack. She watched him in stunned silence. He was packing so fast he was almost throwing clothes into the bag.

"You're really going to go?" she whispered, sinking down onto the foot of the bed. She could barely breathe as she watched him pack. Her pulse raced and her heart squeezed up into her throat.

He shoved his leather wash kit into the bag. "I didn't get to where I am by playing nice and lining up straight and following rules. But at the same time, I'm loyal and honorable and I protect those I love."

"Do you love Joy?"

Wolf paused, head lifting, dark eyes finding hers. "What is it with you and Joy? She's a bloody alcoholic. Alcoholism is a disease and you're damn lucky not to have it."

His words only made her ache more. She swallowed the lump in her throat, swallowed back the hurt. He was packing shoes now, a belt, and he'd pulled his tuxedo out and was slipping that into a hanging garment bag.

"Wolf."

"What?" he snapped, zipping the garment bag closed.

She blinked back the tears threatening to fall. She wished he'd turn around, wished he'd at least look at her. He didn't.

She slid off the bed and gently, lightly, put her hand on his back, feeling the taut muscles, the tension in his spine. "I'm sorry."

"I'm not so sure you are," he said coldly as he grabbed his bag and walked away.

She watched him in disbelief. He was leaving. Like that. No kiss, no touch, nothing warm or reassuring.

What the hell had happened? Since Zambia Wolf had been different. Changed.

Alexandra hurried after Wolf, trailing him down the staircase to the hall below. "Is it over then?" Alexandra cried as he reached to open the garage door. "Are we finished?"

Wolf stopped. His broad shoulders nearly filled the door frame, casting a long, dark shadow behind him. "I don't know."

She pressed a hand to her chest, her heart beating so hard it hurt. "Do you want a divorce?"

He said nothing, choosing to remain silent, and his silence was worse than any words. Rage and pain and heartbreak filled her.

"Wolf?" she demanded, even though she already knew the answer. But she wanted to hear it from him, wanted him to finally speak the truth.

Slowly his head turned. She could just glimpse the hard line of his cheekbone, the curve of his ear. "I don't know. I need time. I need to think."

The words broke what was left of her heart. Hot, furious emotion rushed through her. The emotions were wild, the pain extreme. He'd made her feel safe. He'd made her feel loved. He'd made her believe he'd be there for her and with her and that it was okay to love him. It was okay to fall in love with him. It was okay to imagine a life together. But it was all a lie. He'd lied. He'd pretended. He'd *acted*.

"You tricked me," she choked out, taking a step toward him. "You deceived me."

He said nothing.

Her hands balled convulsively. Tears blinded her. Hysteria, rage, grief bubbled, boiled. "If you go and leave me, Wolf, I won't be here when you return."

And still he said nothing.

The pain and his silence whipped at her, tormenting her. *"Wolf."*

"I hear you, Alexandra. You don't have to shout."

She was wiping the tears away, one after the other. "If you go to Venice now, I won't be here when you come back," she repeated in a whisper. "I won't."

He nodded. And then he left.

Alexandra crawled into bed after he left, carrying the house phone and the mobile phone with her, just in case Wolf changed his mind. Just in case he called.

She didn't leave the house in case he changed his mind.

But night came, and the Europe flights were all gone. And when she turned on the television the next morning there was a story about the Venice Film Festival and the glittering guest list, with Wolf Kerrick and Joy Hughes making their first appearance together since the dramatic plane crash and rescue in Zambia.

And then suddenly there they were, Wolf and Joy, arriving at the Venice airport, filmed amid a blinding strobe of flashes. Joy wore an enormous mink coat over her jeans and turtleneck sweater, while Wolf was in his favorite jeans and a T-shirt topped with a wool coat. They looked gorgeous together, Alexandra thought, the way a celebrity couple should look.

Turning off the television, Alexandra knew it was time to pack, find a place of her own, return to work and move on.

* * *

In the first month after separating from Wolf, Alexandra was so overwhelmed trying to adjust to a different life, settling into her new home—a condo close to downtown Los Angeles in a new development filled with artists, writers and trendy business executives—and learning the ropes of her new job that she didn't really let herself think about the end of their relationship.

But later, as the newness wore off and the pattern of her days emerged, her work became more routine and she grew comfortable reading scripts, meeting with studio heads and acting as the intermediary between directors, actors and producers. People took her seriously. Her opinions were respected. And before long her name was added to the credits of her first film as an assistant director. It was a huge personal moment for Alexandra. She wasn't just a coffee girl anymore but a valuable member of a studio making major motion pictures.

That night she took Kristie and some of the other girls from the studio's front office out to dinner at the Ivy and they celebrated. Alexandra promised Kristie and the others that if they wanted to get out of copy-room hell, she'd do everything she could to help them, and she meant it.

It was a lovely dinner, warm, happy, full of laughter and enthusiasm. After four and a half years in Los Angeles, Alexandra finally felt as though she belonged. She'd made it. She could live here, survive here and be happy here.

Even without Wolf.

But back home later that night, after Alexandra entered her dimly lit condo, she walked to the enormous plate-glass window in the living room with its view of downtown. The skyscrapers were lit and the streets below were dotted with yellow lights. She felt a pang of such sorrow and loss it nearly doubled her.

She realized she'd never really accepted that the relationship was over. In the back of her mind she'd secretly thought that maybe, just maybe, it could be saved. But it hadn't worked out that way.

After Wolf's Venice trip, he went to London for six weeks, where he filled in for an actor in a West End play. When the play closed, he engaged in a series of meetings with the producers of *The Burning Shore* and eventually, by promising to put up his own money and coming onto the picture as a coproducer, he got the studio to agree to finish the film. Wolf had gone back to Africa.

Alexandra sank down on the arm of her sofa, her stomach falling along with her heart.

Until now she'd hoped, secretly hoped, it would just be a matter of time before Wolf returned to her. She'd thought that after he finished in Zambia he'd call or come see her. She'd imagined that being in Zambia would remind him of her, of the experiences they'd shared, and he'd realize he missed her. Loved her. And wanted her.

But it'd been months since the filming had wrapped, and instead of returning to California, Wolf had sold his Malibu home and bought a house in the outskirts of Dublin.

Sitting on the arm of her sofa, Alexandra was forced to confront the reality that Wolf was never coming back. At least not for her. And despite her best efforts to put on a brave face, focus on her career and begin to move forward, she'd only managed to do the above because she'd thought soon she and Wolf would be together again and everything would eventually be fine.

But Wolf wasn't coming back and they weren't going to be together again and somehow, she thought, reaching up to catch a tear before it fell, she had to believe that everything would still be fine.

But to make everything truly finished, she had to take the next step, the step she dreaded, the one that would legally separate them. Neither had taken any action to dissolve their marriage, and Alexandra had thought it was because Wolf still loved her. But maybe it wasn't love that kept them legally bound but public relations.

Maybe he was waiting for her to be the one to file, to initiate the divorce proceedings, to preserve his image. His precious reputation.

If she filed, she'd be the bad girl and he'd remain the hero.

Eyes hot and gritty, Alexandra moved to the computer at the desk in her kitchen nook. She pulled the keyboard out on the granite counter and clicked on her e-mail account and then Wolf's e-mail address.

Wolf, she typed quickly, I wanted you to be the first to know that I'm filing for divorce tomorrow. I'm not asking for spousal support or a settlement. I wish you well always. Alexandra

She read and reread her brief message, hoping it sounded relatively cordial. She wanted to be fair and calm and nonemotional. Twice she went to add another line, something more personal and then less personal, but eventually she just gave up and pressed send, whisking the message from her out-box to his in-box.

The next day she used her lunch break to drive to the county courthouse, where she filled out the necessary paperwork. After signing her name, she submitted the forms to the clerk. The clerk stamped her paperwork and gave her a receipt.

"If it's uncontested," the clerk said, "in six months you'll receive a letter confirming the dissolution."

Alexandra nodded, thanked the clerk and turned away.

And that, she said silently, a massive lump swelling in her throat, is *the end of that.*

Two weeks later, Alexandra had been invited to attend an industry party, one of those gala events she'd been so in awe of a year ago. After her brief marriage to Wolf and her new position at Paradise Pictures, industry parties felt normal.

As she stepped from the limo—the studio always sent a limo for her when she attended events and she'd wondered more than once if that was Wolf's doing—camera flashes briefly blinded her. She stood next to the car for a moment in her snug deep blue satin evening gown and smiled, the deep plunging V neckline showing off the creamy skin between her breasts, the neckline accented with a romantic satin ruffle that caught the light and shimmered like midnight with a full moon.

She'd started to move on when photographers shouted out, pleading with her for just another picture, so Alexandra paused again, shoulders squared, stomach pulled in flat, and forced another smile, the firm, confident smile she'd seen countless celebrities do. As she held her position, she realized Wolf had been right. She'd become a celebrity by virtue of association. Once she'd married him, she'd earned an elite Hollywood status. And although they now lived on separate continents, she was still Mrs. Wolf Kerrick around town.

And there were nights like tonight when, despite the physical distance between them, Alexandra almost believed that Wolf was near. It was as though he were still part of her life, aware of her world and the things she was doing.

Or maybe that was just wishful thinking, she thought, clutching her black handbag—the same one she'd carried that very first night she and Wolf had gone out together for drinks at the Casa Del Mar—and headed in.

Inside the hotel's ballroom doors, she was handed a flute of champagne. As she moved through the crowd, she heard bits and pieces of peoples' conversations. It was mid-June and the big summer blockbusters were just starting to be released. Everyone had something to say about the summer films as well as the need to get box-office revenue up again. For the fourth year in a row attendance was down and industry insiders were worried. People just weren't going to movies the way they used to despite the increasing number of choices. What would it take to get people back to theaters again?

Across the ballroom she spotted Daniel deVoors at the same time he saw her. He lifted his flute in acknowledgment. She smiled and planned to cross the enormous room in a little bit to visit with him.

Like Wolf, Daniel had returned to Africa to finish filming *The Burning Shore*. The film was in postproduction now, slated as a Christmas release. The heavyweight films, the ones considered to be Oscar contenders, were usually released in December and January in order to be fresh in Academy members' minds at nomination time. Wolf, it was rumored, would be up for another Academy Award as best actor. Daniel would be up for best director, and it was said that Joy would probably earn her first nomination for best actress.

Moving through the crowded ballroom toward Daniel,

Alexandra knew that even though she found it painful to think about Wolf, she was happy for him—as well as the cast and crew—that the picture had finally come together. It wasn't even his financial investment she cared about. Rather, she knew how much he loved Africa and the story and the people there. She was proud that he'd made something so problematic work. He'd really fought for the film, and it'd paid off.

Daniel shifted in the crowd, and as he moved to one side, she felt an icy shaft of pain and heartbreak.

Wolf. He was here.

Pulse leaping, she drank him in—tall, darkly handsome, dressed in a black tuxedo with a black dress shirt and no bow tie, of course. His hair was longer—considerably longer, nearly down to his shoulders—and the style made him look even more fierce and primitive and male. Then he reached out and drew the woman next to him closer to his side.

Joy.

Her heart squeezed into a tattered ball and then fell, a dramatic free fall all the way to the tips of her navy satin pumps.

He was here. With Joy.

She couldn't move, couldn't take another step, and for the first time since arriving at the hotel she felt grateful for the crowd surging around her. She needed them, all these people, to buffer her, keep her from falling, fainting, weeping.

Instead she stood there, rooted to her spot, and felt pain roll. Pain and loss and rejection. The emotions were so intense she knew they had to show on her face. She wasn't an actress, couldn't hide her feelings, not feelings this strong, and she prayed no one saw how once again her heart was breaking.

Seeing Wolf and Joy together tonight was nothing short of excruciating. She'd never heard back from Wolf after she'd filed the divorce papers, but the media had somehow managed to get a copy of the paperwork and *People* magazine had run a color copy of the front page of the form. There in an enormous picture was her request to end her marriage. The headline to the accompanying article was every bit as salacious as she'd feared. And still no word from Wolf.

But now here he was, a dozen yards away, with Joy. And even if she believed that Joy and Wolf had never been lovers, the fact that Wolf still saw Joy and spent time with her cut, and cut deeply.

Alexandra envied Joy and Wolf's bond. It was obvious they had a special connection, and standing there, watching them, Alexandra had never felt like such an outsider as she did just then.

Someone bumped her from behind and she finally forced herself to move, slipping as quickly through the crowd as she could.

With a frozen smile fixed to her face she prayed no one could see how much she was hurting. Cameras were everywhere. The last thing she wanted was photos in tomorrow's paper showing her leaving the fund-raiser in tears.

And yet, as she slid into the backseat of the limo, her frozen smile shattered and tears filled her eyes.

She'd loved him. Trusted him. And it'd broken her heart.

CHAPTER FOURTEEN

IT WAS A LONG, ENDLESS, sleepless night. She cried off and on, getting up once to wash her face, and by the time her alarm finally went off, Alexandra felt as though she'd gone thirteen rounds in a heavyweight fight.

After dressing and downing a cup of strong black coffee, she dragged herself to work feeling half-alive.

Even though she felt like hell, the front office was buzzing with excitement. Apparently Wolf had been in there early for a brief meeting with one of the studio's heads. Kristie had seen Wolf on her way in—he'd just been leaving—and she was telling the other girls that he'd looked even more gorgeous than usual.

"His hair's long now," she whispered dramatically. "And it makes him look wicked and unbelievably sexy."

Alexandra carried her mug of herbal tea past the giggling office staff to her desk in the back. Her promotion had meant a private office, and it wasn't big but it was at least quiet with the door shut.

Taking a seat at her desk, she turned on her computer, checked e-mail, answered the ones requiring an immediate response and then got busy reading the script needing her attention first.

She didn't know how long she'd been reading when she felt the oddest shivery sensation, like that of a feather being trailed across her skin. Reaching up, she rubbed at her nape, where the skin felt most sensitive. All the hairs on her arms were standing up, as well.

It was then she realized she wasn't alone. Wolf was standing just inside her door.

For a long moment she simply stared at him. He looked like a pirate with his long black hair and his dark, shadowed jaw.

"Your hair's so long," she said almost absently.

"It's for my next role. Blackbeard."

"He was vile."

Creases fanned at his eyes. "Brilliant."

"Cruel."

"Practical."

"Insensitive."

"Legendary."

Alexandra fell silent. She wasn't going to win. Wolf was Wolf. He'd always be smarter, faster, stronger, richer, more beautiful.

His jaw jutted at an angle and his dark lashes dropped, concealing his eyes. "You left quickly last night, before we could speak."

Her heart ached fiercely. "There was no reason for us to speak."

He didn't move, and yet she felt his physical presence grow, his anger and leashed tension filling the room. "There's our marriage."

"Divorce," she corrected.

"I've contested the divorce."

Alexandra grabbed at the edge of her desk, reeling. "You what?"

"I'm Irish and Spanish. I don't believe in divorce."

"But this is California."

"And you married me. And maybe I'm vile and cruel and insensitive, but I view marriage as a holy union—"

"Really? Then where the hell have you been?" She slapped her hands on her desktop, hitting the surface so hard her tea sloshed a little in the white ceramic mug. "I certainly wouldn't say you've been doing anything to try to save the marriage."

"You gave me an ultimatum," he said unapologetically.

"So you leave and never contact me again?"

He shrugged. "I was giving you time."

"To hate you!"

His dark eyes flashed. Lines etched at his mouth. "Hate's a sister emotion to love."

She shook her head. She couldn't do this, not now, not here, not like this. She hadn't gotten any sleep last night. Her head ached from crying.

For the past months she'd done everything she could to stabilize herself, to make her new world okay. And to do that, she'd had to minimize Wolf, reduce his influence and the impact he had on her.

When his name was mentioned on television or she came across one of his movies on cable, she turned the channel. When the papers printed an interview, she skipped it. When people at parties mentioned him, she moved to another group gathered. It wasn't that she was bitter, it was just that everything to do with him—them—still hurt. Even after the end of their relationship, even after filing for divorce, her heart still felt broken.

Leaving the party last night she'd felt destroyed. She'd felt empty. Different. Changed. And she didn't like these feelings at all, didn't like the helplessness they entailed. "This isn't the time, Wolf," she said woodenly. "I'm working—"

"And work is more important than us? Than our marriage, our family?"

She drew a rough breath. "We were never a family."

"We could have been. We could have had a good life, a great life—"

"How? With you on the road? Movie after movie, always setting out, going on location, playing the lead against another Hollywood ingenue?"

His mouth tightened and deep grooves shaped his lips while finer lines creased his eyes. "So this isn't really about Joy, is it? It was never as much Joy as your own insecurity."

Alexandra just looked at him, eyes dry, head throbbing, heart in pieces.

"I've spent the past months analyzing what the hell happened," he added. "And I never really understood where it fell apart or why it had to. I loved you. I would have done anything for you—"

"You chose Joy over me!"

"I chose to stand by Joy while she struggled with a brutal disease that could have destroyed her career the same way it destroyed her marriage."

"But you should have stood by me."

His expression turned furious. "I did. I'm here. I contested the divorce." He slugged his fist against the door frame. "Why are you so bloody insecure? Because that's the real issue, isn't it? It's not me making films or traveling and going on location, but you're afraid of other women. You're so afraid I'll fall for another woman that you're shutting me out, not even giving us a chance to succeed."

Her eyes opened wide. Her stomach rose, up into her throat.

My God, he knew her. He knew her too well.

He knew exactly what she was afraid of, and that knowledge knocked her off balance.

With trembling fingers Alexandra pushed her mug across her desk. She couldn't look at him, couldn't face him now. "It would kill me if I found out through the newspapers or tabloids that you'd found someone else. And, Wolf, it'd happen. Sooner or later. It's bound to happen—"

"*Why?*"

"Because I'm ordinary. I'm not like you."

She felt rather than heard him leave. And his abrupt departure created an even more violent loss than what she'd felt before.

Alexandra was still sitting numbly at her desk when her phone rang. Dazed, she picked it up.

Her brother Troy was at the other end of the line. "Alexandra, Dad's had a heart attack. Please come home."

Troy sent his jet for her and she boarded the plane in Burbank, at the executive terminal there. It was a two-and-a-half-hour flight to Bozeman, Montana, and her oldest brother, Brock, was waiting for her at the Bozeman airport to drive her to the hospital where her father was in ICU.

Brock wrapped her in a huge bear hug and kissed her cheek. "We've missed you, little girl," he said, stepping back to look her over.

She nodded around the lump in her throat. "I've missed you, too." Alexandra pushed a long wave of hair back from her face. "How's Dad?"

Brock shrugged as he lifted her bag. "As good as can be hoped."

She knew from Brock's tone that Dad wasn't doing well. They were walking to Brock's truck now and she had to practically run to keep up with his long strides. "And the kids?" she asked, referring to his children, fraternal twins Molly and Mack.

"They'll be thrilled to see you." He shot her a hard look. "You know, it was hard for them losing you and their mom so close together."

"Brock, they were babies when I left. And you weren't even living at the ranch anymore. You and Amy had your own place then."

He shrugged again. "I'm just saying."

She knew what he was saying. He wasn't any different from Troy or Trey or Dillon or Cormac. She was the girl in the family. It had been her responsibility to keep things together. And Alexandra hadn't wanted that responsibility. She was the youngest. She hardly even knew who she was, and being the only woman nearly smothered her at times.

At the hospital, Alexandra leaned over her father's bed. He had an oxygen tent around him and tubes and wires running every which way. "Daddy," she whispered, covering his hand with hers. "Daddy, I'm here."

For a moment she thought he hadn't heard her, but then his eyes briefly opened and he looked at her for a second. "Good," he sighed heavily. "I'm glad you're home."

Alexandra sat by his side until twilight, when Dillon, the youngest of her brothers, appeared and told her Brock was waiting downstairs to take her back to the ranch. "I'll stay with Dad until midnight. That's when Cormac will come," he added, giving her a quick hug and a peck on the forehead. "Now go see your niece and nephew. They're desperate to see Aunt Alex."

Brock wasn't the only one in the truck. Molly and Mack were there, too, and they wiggled like puppies as she climbed in the passenger seat.

"How's Grandpa?" Molly asked, big-eyed in the backseat. "Is he talking yet?"

Alexandra managed a small smile. "Not a lot yet, but he knows we're there."

It was a forty-minute drive back to the ranch and dark by the time they reached the two-story stone-and-wood house. Cormac was waiting on the front steps when the truck appeared in the long, dusty drive.

As Alexandra stepped from the truck, he scooped her in another Shanahan death-grip hug. The Shanahans were Black Irish, all tall, dark and rugged, but Cormac was the exception. He was the only blonde one in the batch, and it was Cormac her friends all used to have crushes on.

The housekeeper had dinner waiting. And after dinner, with six-year-old Molly sitting on her lap, Alexandra played Mack—Cormac's namesake—in a game of checkers. Mack at six could already trounce her, and like a true Shanahan, he crowed with pleasure. Molly looked at Alexandra and made a face. "Boys," she said with six-year-old disgust.

Alexandra winked. "I agree."

After she read to the kids and put them to bed, she returned downstairs and walked in on a conversation she obviously wasn't supposed to hear as Cormac and Brock both went quiet.

"What?" she said, looking from one to the other. "What's wrong? Is it Dad? Has he gotten worse?"

Cormac shook his head. "No. Dad's stable. It's Wolf." He hesitated. "He's on the way."

Alexandra's forehead furrowed. *Wolf? On his way here? To the ranch?* "That's a mistake. How did you hear this? Who told you? Was this in a paper or something?"

"I just talked to him on the phone," Brock said. "He called to check on Dad."

Alexandra couldn't believe it. She looked from Brock to Cormac. "But that doesn't mean he's coming here."

Brock shrugged. "He said he was."

"When?"

"I don't know." He looked at her more closely. "Why? Is there a problem? Wolf said everything was all patched up."

"All patched up?" Alexandra felt like weeping with frustration. "That's what he said?"

"That's what he said."

In her old bedroom, Alexandra tried dialing Wolf's cell number, but he didn't pick up. Each time she called she got his voice mail. "Wolf," she said on the fifth call, "it's Alexandra. Brock said you're coming here. I don't think that's a good idea. Please call me back."

But he didn't call back, and Alexandra knew that was not good.

She was still sitting on her bed in the dark, clutching her phone, when Brock knocked on the door on his way to bed.

"Did you reach him?" Brock asked gruffly, standing in her bedroom door.

"No." She cleared her throat. She didn't want him to know she'd been crying. "I just kept getting his voice mail."

"He might already be on his way."

That's exactly what she was afraid of.

"You're lucky," her brother said bluntly. "He still cares about you. He wouldn't be coming here if he didn't."

"It's not that easy," she answered, feeling defensive.

"That's pride talking, little girl. It's time you did some forgiving and forgetting. He's just a man, and all men make mistakes."

Chilled on the inside, she wrapped her arms around her knees, trying to get warm. "But he's not just any man. He's a star, a huge star, and gorgeous. And I'm nothing like him and I can't keep up with him or compete with the women who throw themselves at him—"

"So you're just going to quit your marriage? Just like that?" A contemptuous note had entered his voice.

"It hurts!" She blinked back fresh tears. "And being afraid and worried hurts, too. I hate that feeling. I hate not knowing—"

"But you do know. You know he loves you and you know he wants to be married to you. And, little girl, I hate to disappoint you, but there are no real guarantees in life. There's just our hearts and our hopes and learning to live one day at a time." His voice dropped, roughened. "If I'd known Amy was going to die two years after our wedding, do you think I would have married her? If I'd known we'd have two babies who would grow up without a mother, do you think I would have conceived them?"

Even in the dark she heard and felt Brock's grief. It was still there, five and a half years after Amy's death. He'd loved her since he'd first laid eyes on her.

"Yes," she whispered, wiping away a tear in the dark. "She was made for you."

Brock didn't speak, and she saw his head bow, his silhouette filling the doorway.

"Yes," he agreed, "she was made for me. Just like your Wolf was made for you." Brock reached for the doorknob, started to pull the door closed but stopped partway.

"There's worse things than being afraid, Alex. There's losing your heart altogether." And then he stepped into the hall and quietly, gently, closed her bedroom door behind him.

Wolf had a hell of a time finding the Lazy L ranch. Everyone knew the Shanahans, but that didn't make locating the property entrance easy. He'd called Brock last night to check on Alexandra's father and get directions, and while Brock hadn't told him not to come, he certainly hadn't been encouraging.

But Brock's lack of enthusiasm didn't stop Wolf from flying up first thing the next morning.

Now he was parking in front of the huge split-logs-and-stone house, and as he climbed from the four-by-four Jeep, the front door of the house opened and out trooped three of Alexandra's brothers. Brock, Cormac and Dillon.

They weren't, Wolf noted, catching sight of their grim faces, very welcoming either.

"I'm here for Alexandra," he said, letting the Jeep door slam behind him.

"She's with Dad," Brock answered. "In Bozeman, at the hospital."

Wolf shrugged. "I'll wait for her here then."

"She doesn't want to see you," Dillon said flatly.

Wolf shrugged. "I'm still waiting."

Cormac folded his arms across his chest. "Maybe you should wait in Los Angeles. She knows where to find you there, doesn't she?"

"No, actually. I don't live in Los Angeles anymore. So if it's all right with you—" and his smile was predatory, antagonistic "—I'll just wait here until she returns."

Cormac's eyes narrowed. "Maybe you didn't hear me. She's not here. And even if she were, she doesn't want to see you. I suggest you get back in your car and go home."

Wolf drew a deep breath. It'd been a long morning. It was going to be a long afternoon and night. "I'll wait for Alexandra."

The front door of the house opened again and this time Troy and Trey appeared. The twins had come home to the Lazy L ranch, too. Their dad must be very sick for all five brothers to have returned now, especially when three of them lived out of state in metropolitan places like New York, San Francisco and Seattle.

"You're still here?" Troy drawled, moving to stand next to his brothers. "I thought you were told to leave."

Any other time Wolf would have admired their family loyalty. Right now he just wanted to see Alexandra. "Your dad's sick. This isn't the time for this—"

"You should have thought of that before you broke Alexandra's heart," Trey said coldly.

Wolf shook his head. He wasn't going to get anywhere with the Shanahan brothers using words. "I want to talk to Alexandra and you don't want me to. What do I have to do to get a few minutes alone with her?"

"Nothing," Dillon said. "It's not happening. Not unless you go through me."

"And me," Brock added.

Trey stepped forward. "Count me in. That's three."

"Four," Troy chimed.

Wolf looked drily at Cormac. "What about you? Thinking about joining my side, evening up the odds a little?"

Cormac checked his smile, shook his head. "Sorry, Kerrick, I'm with them. That makes five."

Wolf studied the lineup of Shanahan brothers. "You don't really mean to keep your sister from me."

Troy jammed his hands into his jean pockets. "We do."

Wolf nodded once, slow and thoughtful. "Let me get this right. If I fight all of you, you'll give me a few minutes alone with my wife?"

"You fight all five of us and you'll get five minutes."

Wolf glanced from one brother to another. "So where are we going to do this? Outside or in the barn?"

Brock sighed. "The barn will work just fine."

As soon as Alexandra spotted the silver rental Jeep parked in front of the house, her stomach tightened up, a flurry of nerves, hope and fear. Wolf. He'd arrived. For a brief moment she considered turning around and heading straight back to Bozeman. Instead she parked. And as she turned off the ignition she thought of her dad—widowed young with six kids, one just entering kindergarten—and her brother Brock who at thirty became a single father to twin infants overnight.

She'd experienced enough loss in her own family to know there weren't any guarantees, and yet that's exactly what she'd been wanting: a promise from Wolf that he'd never leave her, couldn't forget her, wouldn't hurt her. But that wasn't realistic or fair. Love didn't make one impervious, but it did help with the bumps and bruises meted out by fate.

Alexandra also knew it was time to silence that insecure voice inside her head, the one that moved in with her when she'd relocated to L.A. Because that frightened, insecure voice was wrong. Beautiful women with great bodies were not more valuable than smart women with kind hearts. The outsides didn't matter more than the insides, and maybe she'd finally believe that Wolf loved her if she learned to love and accept herself.

She owed Wolf an apology. Hoped he'd forgive her and

hoped he still loved her enough to give them and their marriage one more shot.

Pocketing her car keys, Alexandra stepped from the car and took a deep breath for courage. Time to fix this. Time to make things right.

As the car door shut behind her, she heard a crash in the barn. The loud crash was followed by a hollow thud and then a metallic-sounding bang.

What in God's name was that?

She glanced around, searching for signs of life. But the house was dark and, except for the crash and slam sounds coming from the barn, everything was quiet. Too quiet.

Where was everyone? Cormac had said the twins were flying in today, which would mean all five brothers should be here. Where were they? Where was even one?

And for that matter, where was Wolf?

And then, as another thud and bang came from the barn, Alexandra's skin prickled with that sick sixth sense that told her all her questions would be answered once she reached the barn.

Before she'd even gotten the barn door open, she knew from the grunts and groans of pain coming from inside that her brothers were fighting. And with a horrific wave of dread she knew exactly whom they were fighting.

The grunts and groans grew considerably louder as she flung the wide red door open.

"What in God's name are you doing?" she shouted, watching even as one of her brothers—Dillon?—took a hard swing at Wolf.

Wolf had turned to look at her and he took the blow to the side of the head.

Alexandra heard the crack of a knuckled fist against her husband's head, and furious tears started to her eyes. "Stop this! Stop it right now. Wolf. Brock. All of you. Stop it."

And miraculously it did stop. Dillon fell back, bits of straw in his black hair, while Wolf swayed, bloodied, in his place. The others simply looked at her, their faces revealing various bumps and bruises.

"How long has this been going on?" she demanded, entering the barn to circle her brothers before ending in front of Wolf. "Hours?"

"Not hours," Brock answered roughly, the corner of his mouth split and speckled with dried blood. "Maybe an hour." He paused, touched his tongue to his cracked lip. "Maybe two."

She couldn't even look at Wolf. She could already see he'd taken the brunt of the beating. "How? Why?"

Dillon dragged a hand through his hair, knocking the bits of straw out. "It was his idea," he said, nodding at Wolf. "He said he'd fight us—"

"No," Cormac interrupted, glancing down at his right hand and gingerly flexing his fingers into a tender fist. "You were the one that said Wolf had to fight each of us to talk to Alexandra."

"What?" she croaked, taking a step closer to Wolf and staring aghast at her brothers. "You all fought him?" They didn't answer and that was answer enough. She shook her head in disbelief. "Five against one? For one, maybe two hours?"

"It wasn't quite like that," Trey said, grimacing at her description. "We took turns."

"You took turns?" she whispered, livid beyond measure. Her brothers were fighters, she knew that. Nearly every one had been kicked out of school at one point for roughhousing. But they weren't kids anymore, they were men. *Men.* And they'd spent the last hour or so beating up her husband while their father lay in the hospital in an oxygen tent. "If Dad knew what you're doing…" Her voice faded and she looked at them again. "My God, you're all out of your minds."

Dillon made a face. "We did it for you, Alex—"

"Get out!" she snapped, pointing to the barn door. "Get out before I beat each of you—and I won't use my fist, I'll use a shovel or a pitchfork!"

Her brothers quickly trooped out and Alexandra slowly turned to face Wolf, who had a black eye, a bloody nose, swollen lip, bruised cheekbone and a big ugly mark at his temple.

"What were you thinking?" she whispered.

Wolf shrugged wearily. "I wanted to be with you," he said,

swaying on his feet. "I wanted to be here—" he drew a breath and reached up to wipe away blood trickling from a cut in his cheekbone "—for you."

"For me?"

He wiped the blood on the back of his jeans. "You must be worried sick about your dad. If it were my dad, I would be."

"And that's why you're here?"

"Alexandra, I said I'd be there for you anytime you needed me. And so I'm here."

She blinked back tears. He looked as if he'd been run over by a truck. "Getting ambushed by my brothers."

"I was doing okay."

Her lips pursed. "Let's get you to the kitchen and get some ice on those bumps and bruises."

In the kitchen, she directed Wolf to a chair at the scarred pine farm table while she made him an ice pack out of a plastic bag and some ice cubes inside a clean dish towel.

She studied him, ice pack in hand. Blood continued to trickle from a cut in his cheekbone—he might need stitches for that one—and more blood dried at the corner of his lip. His forehead was shadowed with pink and purple. His hair was long, definitely not combed. He hadn't shaved in God knew how long and circles were etched deeply beneath his famous smoldering eyes.

"Wolf, I'm worried some of these cuts will end up in scars."

"I don't care."

"*I* do," she said, pressing the ice pack to his temple, furious all over again.

"Alexandra, I'd fight a hundred men for you. I'd slay dragons, too."

She saw him wince as she shifted the ice pack around on his head. "Wolf, when I said fight for me, I didn't mean literally."

His laugh was low and self-mocking. "I might be too old to box professionally, but I wasn't going to lose you, Alexandra. You're mine. You've been mine from the very beginning."

"When you called me 'ordinary'?" she replied.

He reached up to wrap his hand around her wrist as she held the ice to his temple. "Ordinary's a good thing, love. After ten years of Hollywood nonsense, I welcomed you like a breath of fresh air. It didn't take me long to realize that I might be far from home but you were exactly what I needed. Wanted. Loved."

Alexandra's hand trembled as she clutched the ice pack. Wolf was her undoing. "I don't stand a chance against you, do I?" she murmured.

He tipped his head back, smiled up at her, dark eyes hot, wicked. "No."

And he just kept on melting her heart.

It wasn't fair. She couldn't resist him. And God knew she'd tried.

Wolf's hand warmed hers, and once her trembling stopped, he pulled her hand away, discarded the ice pack and drew her down onto his lap. "Come home, lady," he said, dropping his head to kiss her throat. "Come home with me. Start a family with me."

She leaned against him as his arms went around her. "You forgive me then?"

"There's nothing to forgive. I'm as much at fault as you. I can see now I didn't handle Joy's illness well. I thought I was doing the right thing, but in retrospect I see I only made the problem worse."

"She's better now?"

Wolf's shoulders lifted. "She was in Arizona in rehab for three months. She swears she's done drinking, but it's not my battle anymore. It's hers. We both know it."

Her forehead furrowed with concern. "You were really worried about her."

"I thought she'd die," he answered simply.

Alexandra twisted on his knee to better see his face. *"Die?"*

"My mom was an alcoholic, too." Wolf rubbed his hand over his jaw, and for a moment a shadow of the old torment was back, darkening his eyes. "That's why my father took me away from her when I was twelve. She died less than a year later—alcohol poisoning—and I've always blamed my father. And myself. I hated that we just left her, didn't help her. I thought we might as well have killed her ourselves."

"That's why you couldn't turn your back on Joy," Alexandra concluded softly.

The corner of his mouth lifted, but he still looked tortured. "Those are those ghosts and demons I mentioned." He let out a half sigh. "But trying to help Joy when she didn't want to give up drinking taught me invaluable lessons. We can't help someone that doesn't want to be helped, and in the end, our first responsibility is to ourselves."

She leaned forward, wrapped her arms around his neck, felt his warm, hard chest crush her breasts. And it was a delicious sensation, familiar as well as exciting. "I love you."

"I should have been there for you more, Alexandra. I should have listened to you better—listened with my heart, not my head."

"But you were."

"No—"

"Yes," she whispered, cutting his protest off with a slow and very tender kiss. "I love you, Wolf," she said against his mouth. "I love you more than you'll ever know. I'm just so grateful you're here and that you waited for me and fought for me and didn't give up on me."

He made a rough sound in the back of his throat and stroked her hair back from her face and then along her cheek. "I will always fight for you."

"Even when I get scared and do foolish things?"

"Especially then," he answered soberly.

Alexandra dashed away fresh tears. "I've learned lessons, too. And I know now why I didn't feel loved enough. It wasn't anything you were doing. It was me. I didn't love me enough to believe that you could love me, too."

"How could anyone not love you, Alexandra? Your family dotes on you. Your brothers would go to the ends of the earth for you. And I know this—I will never love anyone the way I love you. I couldn't. You were made for me and I've spent years traveling the world to find you."

Swallowing a soft cry, she dragged her hands through Wolf's

hair, fingers twining in the black, inky length. "So that's how an Irish Spaniard ends up in Los Angeles."

"I came to find my heart."

She blinked even as a tear trickled down her cheek. "I promise you'll never have to search for it again."

Wolf cupped her wet face in his hands. "And I'm going to hold you to that promise," he said roughly before kissing her absolutely senseless.

And maybe, Alexandra thought hours later as she lay snuggled in her husband's strong arms in her rather small childhood bed, those Hollywood happy endings really do come true.

PURE PRINCESS,
BARTERED BRIDE

CAITLIN CREWS

Caitlin Crews discovered her first romance novel at the age of twelve. It involved swashbuckling pirates, grand adventures, a heroine with rustling skirts and a mind of her own, and a seriously mouth-watering and masterful hero. The book (the title of which remains lost in the mists of time) made a serious impression. Caitlin was immediately smitten with romances and romance heroes, to the detriment of her middle school social life. And so began her life-long love affair with romance novels, many of which she insists on keeping near her at all times.

Caitlin has made her home in places as far-flung as York, England, and Atlanta, Georgia. She was raised near New York City and fell in love with London on her first visit when she was a teenager. She has backpacked in Zimbabwe, been on safari in Botswana and visited tiny villages in Namibia. She has, while visiting the place in question, declared her intention to live in Prague, Dublin, Paris, Athens, Nice, the Greek islands, Rome, Venice, and/or any of the Hawaiian islands. Writing about exotic places seems like the next best thing to moving there.

She currently lives in California, with her animator/comic book artist husband and their menagerie of ridiculous animals.

To Jane Porter: inspiration, mentor, and the big sister I always wanted.

Thank you, for everything.

PROLOGUE

LUC GARNIER did not believe in love.

Love was madness. Agony, despair and crockery hurled against walls. Luc believed in facts. In proof. In ironclad contracts and the implacable truth of money. He had been relentless and focused all his life and as a result, wildly successful. He did not believe this was a matter of luck or chance. Emotion played no part in it.

Just as emotion played no part in picking out his future bride.

The Côte d'Azur preened itself in the warm afternoon sun as Luc strode down a side street in Nice, headed for the Promenade des Anglais, where the famously luxurious Hotel Negresco sat in gracious Victorian splendor, looking out onto the sparkling blue waters of the Baie des Anges and the Mediterranean Sea beyond. The Hotel Negresco was one of Luc's favorite hotels in France, and thus the world, overflowing as it was with museum-quality art and a famously accommodating staff—but he had a far more pressing reason for visiting Nice's landmark hotel today.

Luc had flown in that morning from his Paris headquarters, determined to see for himself if the latest potential bride—who looked so good on paper—looked even half as good in person. But then, they all looked good on paper, as they had to be of a noble family to so much as make his list.

The last woman he had considered for the position had seemed like a perfect match on paper—but a few days spent tailing Lady Emma around her London society life had quickly revealed that the young noblewoman had a secret penchant for late nights with rough gentlemen.

It wasn't that Luc necessarily minded that his wife might have a past—he simply preferred that, whatever the past was, it had involved the sort of people who would not make interesting headlines should the tabloids catch wind of them. *Lady Emma Prefers Goths to Garnier.* He could imagine it all too well.

"That's the way modern women are these days," his number two man had told him, after Luc had discovered Lady Emma's late-night bar-crawling. Alessandro was the closest thing Luc had to a friend, but even so, he'd thrown his hands up in the air when Luc had glared at him across his opulent Paris office.

"Modern women may be as loose as they like," he'd snapped. "But my wife will not be. Is this so much to ask?"

"This is not all you ask!" Alessandro had replied with a laugh. He'd begun to tick off the necessary items on his fingers. "She must be noble, if not royal, to honor your bloodline. She must be pure in word and deed. She must never have been young or stupid, as no scandal can ever have touched her." He'd shaken his head sadly. "I do not think this woman exists."

"She may not," Luc had agreed, closing the dossier he had compiled on Lady Emma and setting it aside with distaste. "My mother taught me long ago that beauty is too often a mask for dishonor and betrayal. One cannot depend on it—only on an irreproachable reputation." He had smiled at Alessandro. "If she does exist, I will find her."

"And what if this paragon does not wish to marry you when you have hunted her down?" Alessandro had asked dryly. "What then?"

Luc had laughed. "Please." He'd sat back in his chair and

gazed at his friend, crooking his brow in amusement. "That is not very likely, is it? What woman would not benefit from becoming my wife? What can any woman possibly want that I cannot give her? I will place all of my wealth and power at the disposal of whatever woman can fill the position."

Alessandro had sighed heavily, his romantic Italian soul no doubt mortally wounded at the prospect of *filling the position* of wife. "Women like romance and fairy tales," he'd said. Luc rather thought Alessandro was the one who preferred such fripperies, but had not said so. "They do not want marriage to be conducted as a business proposition."

"But that is what it is," Luc had said, shrugging again. "The correct woman must understand this as well."

"I fear you will be looking for a very long time, my friend," Alessandro had said, shaking his head.

But Luc had never been afraid of hard, seemingly fruitless work, he reflected as he turned the corner and saw the famous façade of the Hotel Negresco before him. In fact, he thrived on it. His famous parents had died when he was barely twenty-three, and he had had to make his own way in the world in their considerable shadows. Even before their deaths in a boating accident he had been more or less on his own—his parents having been far more interested in each other and their endless romantic complications than in their son.

Luc could not bring himself to regret his unorthodox up-bringing, no matter how many people seemed to think it pointed to some lack in him—something no one had dared say to his face in some time. Growing up in such a way, sur-rounded by so much heightened emotion mixed with jealousy and betrayal and avid outside interest, had stripped him of many of the needs that ruled other men. It had also made him that much more successful, which was all he cared about— for what else was there? He did not need the emotions that other men did. He was not interested in love, and all the upheaval and agony it brought. He wanted a wife in the most traditional sense, for the most traditional reasons. He was nearing forty now, and it was time he created a family to carry on his legacy and his mother's royal Italian bloodline. The wife he chose would have to be from an equally august bloodline—noble for centuries, at the very least, as his family was. It was tradition. It was his duty.

He needed a wife who knew her duty.

He strode into the elegant old hotel, past the white-gloved doormen, and did not bother to gape like a tourist at the sparkling lobby that emanated old French charm and elegance all around him. He had seen it many times before. The Hotel Negresco prided itself on its luxuriousness. Luc made his way toward the Salon Royal, with its Gustave Eiffel-designed dome and Baccarat chandeliers sparkling over a crowd of some of the world's foremost philanthropists. He ignored the well-dressed and genteel throng, as well as the priceless art that graced the walls. He searched the room until his eyes fell on the woman he'd been looking for—Princess Gabrielle of Miravakia.

She stood out from the crowd in a good way, he was pleased to note. She did not call attention to herself. She did not display her chest in an inappropriate manner or hang all over the men who competed for her attention. She seemed cool and elegant, refined and royal, as she stood in the center of a knot of extremely well-dressed patrons.

She was lovely—but then, she should be. She was a royal princess, after all—the heir to her country's throne. He ignored her looks and concentrated on the way she presented herself: her public persona, which was by all accounts completely without blemish.

Her hair was swept back into an elegant knot at the nape of her neck, and she wore a simple cocktail dress with restrained hints of jewelry at her ears and one wrist. Nothing flashy or gauche. She was all sophistication and class, presiding over this great reception for one of her pet charities with all the grace for which she was known. She was every inch the perfect princess.

He liked what he saw. But he couldn't trust what she showed the world at a reception for six hundred. Could a woman really be as above reproach as this one appeared to be?

Luc signaled a passing waiter and requested a drink, then moved to the outskirts of the crowd, from where he could watch her without being observed in return. She was in Nice for the week, he knew, and was expected to make a number of appearances—which interested him less than what she got up to in her free time.

He was sure that, like Lady Emma before her, Princess Gabrielle would eventually show herself to him. He had only to wait, and watch.

But as Luc watched the perfect-looking princess make her rounds, he allowed himself a moment of cautious optimism as he sampled his drink.

If she proved to be as perfect as she looked, he had done it. He had finally found his bride.

CHAPTER ONE

"Do your duty," her father ordered her only moments before the organ burst into life—his version of an encouraging speech. He frowned at her. "Make me proud."

That was the entirety of his fatherly pre-wedding advice.

The words swam in Princess Gabrielle's head even as the heavy weight of her silk taffeta wedding gown tugged at her and slowed her down. The long train swept back from her dress, extending almost ten feet behind her as befitted a royal princess on her wedding day. Gabrielle only knew that it was hard to walk with ten feet of fabric to pull along with her, though she kept her spine erect and her head high—as always.

Thank God for the veil that covered her face, hiding the expression she was afraid she couldn't control for the first time in her twenty-five years—to say nothing of the prickly heat flooding her eyes.

She could not cry. Not here. Not now.

Not as she walked down the aisle of her kingdom's holiest of cathedrals, holding fast to her father's arm. Her father— King Josef of Miravakia. The man she had spent her life trying—and failing—to please.

Even at university she had been too determined to win her father's elusive approval to do anything but study hard. While her peers had partied and explored all that London had to offer,

Gabrielle had lost herself in her books and her research. After university, despite the degree she'd obtained in Economics, she had dedicated herself to charity work, according to her father's expectations of the Crown Princess of Miravakia.

Anything and everything to curry her father's favor. It was the mantra of Gabrielle's life.

Even this. Marriage to a perfect stranger of his choosing.

Why was she going through with this? Hers was not some ancient feudal kingdom—and she was no chattel. But if there was a way to go against her father's wishes without incurring his wrath she did not know what it was. She knew that she could have said no. Couldn't she? Or was she simply too desperate to prove to her father that she was worthy of his approval—even when the stakes were so high?

"I have accepted a marriage proposal," King Josef had told her one morning, barely three months ago, jolting Gabrielle from her contemplation of the day's schedule. He had not glanced up from his breakfast as he spoke. It had surprised Gabrielle that he'd spoken at all—he generally preferred to breakfast in silence, with only his newspapers spread around him, though he insisted that she join him every morning.

"A marriage proposal?" Gabrielle had been amazed—her father had shown no interest in remarrying, not in all the long years since Gabrielle's mother had died of cancer when Gabrielle was barely five.

"I found the combination of a royal bloodline and near-limitless wealth sufficiently attractive," the King had said, almost thoughtfully. "And it will certainly bolster the standing of the Miravakian throne."

It had been as if he was discussing the purchase of a vehicle. But Gabrielle's thoughts had raced ahead anyway. Was she really to have a stepmother? She rather thought it might be fun to have someone else around the *palazzo*. Much as she loved her father and tried to please him, he was not an easy man.

"There will be no tedious long engagement," he had continued, touching his thin, disapproving lips with his linen napkin and signaling one of the hovering footmen for more coffee. Finally, he'd looked at her. "I've no patience for such things."

"No, of course not," Gabrielle had agreed. Her mind had been racing wildly. Who on earth could possibly meet her father's high standards? He had a universally low opinion of almost every woman he'd ever encountered, as far as she knew—and then again, as King of Miravakia, he would only consider a bride from a select class of royals. *And how like him to keep his intentions a secret*, she'd thought, almost amused.

"I expect you to conduct yourself well," he'd said, sipping at his coffee. "None of the hysterics that seem to afflict your sex when they come into contact with a wedding ceremony, thank you."

Gabrielle had known better than to respond to that.

He'd sniffed. "I have confidence that you can put everything together quickly and efficiently, with as little disruption as possible."

"Of course, Father," Gabrielle had said at once. She had never planned a wedding before, but how different could it be from the state events she'd put together in the past? She had a marvelous staff whom she already knew could perform miracles. And who knew? Perhaps a new wife would bring out the softer side of her stern father. She'd give quite a bit to see that.

Lost in her reverie, she had been startled when her father had pushed back his chair and stood. He'd moved toward the door without another word—the subject closed. Gabrielle had almost laughed. How typical of him. She'd felt a surge of affection for his brusque ways—because clearly something romantic lurked beneath the cold exterior.

"Father," she had called, stopping him before he quit the room. He'd turned back to face her, a slight frown between his eyebrows.

"What is it?" he had asked impatiently.

"Am I to know the bride's name?" she had asked, biting back an indulgent smile.

He'd stared at her. "You need to pay closer attention, Gabrielle, if you are to succeed me without running this country into the ground," he'd snapped, his arctic tone making her wince. His frown had deepened as he'd glared at her. "*You*, obviously, are the bride."

And then he'd turned on his heel and strode from the room, without a backward glance.

In the cathedral, Gabrielle felt her breath catch in her throat as the memory of that morning washed over her, while her pulse fluttered wildly. Panic was setting in, as heavy around her as the veil she wore and the train she trailed behind her. She fought to pull air into her lungs—ordered herself to stay calm.

Her father would never forgive her if she made a scene. If she showed anything but docile acceptance—even gratitude— for the way he'd chosen to manage her affairs. Her life.

Her marriage.

Gabrielle felt the crisp, heavy sleeve of her father's ornamental coat beneath her trembling fingers as he led her down the long aisle, his measured steps bringing her closer and closer to her fate.

She couldn't think of it. Couldn't think of *him*—her groom. Soon to be her husband. A man she had never even met, and yet he would be her spouse. Her mate. King of her people when she became their queen. Gabrielle's lips parted on a sound that was far too close to a sob—though it was thankfully hidden in the swirl of music that surrounded her.

She could not. Not here. Not now. It was too late.

The cathedral was packed to capacity on all sides, filled with Europe's royals and assorted nobles. Political allies and strategic partners of her father's. The music soared toward the stained glass heights, filling the space and caressing the carved marble statues. Outside, she knew, the people of Miravakia were celebrating their princess's wedding day as a national holiday. There would be rejoicing in the streets, the papers claimed, now that their Gabrielle had found her husband. Their future king.

A man she did not know and had never seen—not in person. Not face-to-face.

Her husband-to-be was a man who had won his wife through contracts—meetings with her father, bargains struck and approved without her knowledge or consent. Her father had not asked Gabrielle for her input—he had not considered her feelings at all. He had decided that it was time she married, and he had produced the bridegroom of his choice.

And Gabrielle never argued with her father. Never rebelled, never contradicted. Gabrielle was good. Obedient. Respectful to a fault. In the hope that her father would one day respect her back. Love her, maybe—just a little.

Instead, he'd sold her off to the highest bidder.

Luc felt triumph surge through him as he watched the woman—*soon to be his wife*—walk toward him down the long ceremonial aisle. He barely noticed the arching stained glass above him as he stood at the altar, or the hunched statues of gargoyles peering down at him—his attention was focused entirely on her.

Finally.

Luc's mouth pressed into a thin line as he thought of his reckless, thoughtless mother and the destruction she had wrought with her rebellions. Her "passions." But Luc was not his temperamental, easily manipulated father. He would not stand for such behavior—not from *his* wife.

She must be above reproach. She must be practical—as this was to be a marriage on paper first and flesh afterward. But most of all she must be trustworthy. Because Luc, unlike many of his station, would not tolerate disloyalty. There would be no *discreet affairs* in this marriage. He would accept nothing less than one hundred percent obedience. There would be no tabloid speculation, no scandals for the voyeurs to pick over. *Never again.*

He'd searched for years. He'd rejected untold numbers of women before arriving at near misses like Lady Emma. As with everything in his life, from his business to the personal life he guarded ferociously, Luc's refusal to compromise had first isolated, then rewarded him.

Because he had not compromised, because he did not know the meaning of the word, he had exactly what he wanted. The perfect princess. At last.

Princess Gabrielle was biddable. Docile—as evidenced by her presence in the cathedral today, calmly walking down the aisle into an arranged marriage because her father had ordered her to do so. *So far, so good*, he thought with deep satisfaction as he watched her slow, sure approach.

He remembered the sun-drenched days when he'd followed her in Nice, her seemingly effortless poise, no matter how many clamored for her attention. She had never caused a single scandal in her life. She was known for her serenity and her complete lack of tabloid presence. When she made the papers it was in recognition of her charity work. Never for her exploits. Compared to the other royals who debauched themselves all over Europe, she might be a saint. Which suited Luc just fine.

Luc Garnier had built an empire based on his perfectionist streak. If it was not perfect, it would not carry his name.

His wife would be no different.

He had left nothing to chance. He had had others collect the initial information, but then he had made the final decision—as he always did, no matter the acquisition in question. He had followed her personally, because he knew that he could not trust anyone's opinion but his own. Not when it came to a matter of such importance. Others might make mistakes, or overlook seemingly small details that would later prove to be of importance—but not Luc. He would never have approached her father if he had not been absolutely satisfied that Princess Gabrielle was not just the best choice, but the only choice for his bride.

Luc had met with King Josef to settle the final contracts in the King's sumptuous suite at the Hotel le Bristol in Paris, with its stunning view of the great Sacré-Coeur basilica that rose, gleaming white, and towered above the city from Montmartre.

"You do not wish to meet her?" the older man had asked when the business was done, settling back in his chair to enjoy his port.

"It is not necessary," Luc had replied. He had inclined his head. "Unless you wish it?"

"What is it to me?" the King had asked, letting out a puff of air through his nose. "She will marry you whether you meet her or not."

"You are certain?" Luc had asked lightly, though he had not in truth been concerned. Arrangements would never have reached this stage if the King had not been sure of his daughter's obedience. "Ours is an unusual settlement in this day and age. A princess and a kingdom in exchange for wealth and business interests—I am told this sounds like something out of a history book."

The King had made a dismissive noise. "My daughter was raised to do the right thing regarding her country. I have always insisted that Gabrielle understands her position necessitates a certain dignity." The King had swirled his port in its tumbler. He had frowned. "And great responsibility."

"She appears to have taken it to heart," Luc had said, looking at his own drink. "I have never heard her mentioned without reference to her grace and composure."

"Of course." The King had seemed almost taken aback. "She has known all her life that her role as princess would come before any more personal considerations. She will be a good queen one day—though she requires a firm hand to guide her." He'd sniffed. "You will have no trouble with her."

No trouble, Luc had thought with deep satisfaction, would suit him perfectly.

The King had waved his hand, seeming perturbed that they had spoken so long about something he found far beneath his notice. "But enough of that. Let us drink to the future of Miravakia." He had raised his glass.

"To the future of Miravakia," Luc had murmured in response. She would be his wife, and finally, *finally*, he would prove to himself and to the world that he was not cut from the same histrionic cloth as his late parents. Finally he would prove that he, Luc Garnier, was above reproach as well.

"Yes, yes," King Josef had said, and then raised a brow at Luc, as if sharing a confidence. "And to women who know their place."

As she moved closer now, down the cathedral's long aisle, Luc let himself smile, though he did not relax.

She was perfect. He had made sure of it. And now she was his.

Gabrielle could see him now, from beneath her veil, as she finally approached the altar. He stood straight and tall at the front of the cathedral, his gaze seeming to command her even as she walked toward him. Toward their future.

Luc Garnier. Her groom. Gabrielle had never met him— but she had researched him in the months since her father had announced his name. He was descended from centuries of Italian royalty on his mother's side, with a French billionaire father whose fortunes he had doubled before he turned twenty-five. His parents' tumultuous love affair had made headlines while Luc was still young. They had perished in a boating accident when Luc was still in his early twenties, which many claimed was the reason he was so driven, so determined. She fancied she could see his ruthlessness in the line of his jaw, the gleam of his dark eyes.

I can't do this—

But she was doing it.

She had no choice—she had given herself no choice—but she didn't have to watch it happen. She kept her eyes lowered. She didn't want to look at this man—this stranger who would soon be her husband—but she could feel him next to her, above her, as her father handed her off. Luc's large hands took her trembling fingers between his, and guided her the final few steps toward the bishop.

Gabrielle's senses went into overload. Her heart pounded against her ribs while tears of anger and something else, something darker, pooled behind her eyes and threatened to blind her.

He was so masculine, so unyielding. Next to her, his big body seemed to dwarf hers. His body radiated power and menace like heat, surging from their clasped hands through Gabrielle's veins—making her limbs feel dangerously weak.

This is just another panic attack. She ordered herself to breathe. To get a hold of herself and the riot of confusion that made her tremble against the man at her side.

The stranger her father had sold her to.

If Gabrielle closed her eyes she could imagine herself out in the sunshine, basking in the cool winds that swept down from the Alps on the mainland and scrubbed the island clean and cool even at the height of summer. Black pines and red roofs spread across the hilly island, cascading to the rocky beaches that lined the shore. Gabrielle's tiny country was a fiercely independent island in the Adriatic Sea, closer to the rugged Croatian coastline to the east than Italy to the west, and she loved it.

For her country, her father, she would do anything.

Even this.

But she kept her eyes closed and imagined herself anywhere but here.

Anywhere at all…

"Open your eyes," Luc ordered her under his breath, as the wizened bishop performed the ceremony before them. The silly creature had gone stiff next to him, and he could see her eyes squeezed shut beneath her veil—so tight that her mouth puckered slightly.

He felt her start, her delicate hands trembling against his. Her fingers were cold and pale. Her features were indistinct behind the ornate veil, but he could see the fabric move with each breath she took.

"How…?" Her voice was the slightest whisper of sound, but still it tickled his senses. Luc's gaze traveled over the elegant line of her neck, exposed beneath the translucent shimmer of her veil. She was made of fine lines and gentle curves, and he wanted to put his mouth on every one of them.

The rush of desire surprised him. He'd known that she was beautiful, and had anticipated that he would enjoy marital relations with her. But this was something more than *enjoyment*. He was aware of the tension in her shoulders, the ragged edge to her breathing. He was *aware* of her, and he could hardly see her face through the veil. He felt lust pool in his groin and radiate outward, so that even the touch of her fingers at an altar three feet from the bishop sent heat washing through him.

Then he realized that she was shaking. Perhaps she was not quite as sanguine about this wedding as he'd supposed.

Luc almost laughed. There he was, imagining their wedding night in vivid, languorous detail, while his bride was awash in nerves. He couldn't blame her—he knew that many found him intimidating. Why shouldn't she?

"We will suit each other well," he whispered, trying to sound reassuring. An impulse entirely foreign to him—as alien as the urge to protect her that followed it.

He felt the shiver that snaked through her then, and he squeezed his fingers tighter around hers.

She was his, and he took care of what was his.

Even if he was what had made her nervous in the first place.

Gabrielle forced herself to open her eyes and to take part in her own wedding, even though the stranger's—*her husband's*—voice sent spasms of uneasiness throughout her body. His hand was too hot against hers. He was too close.

Thank God she still had her veil to hide behind.

The bishop intoned the old, sacred words, and Gabrielle had the sensation that everything was moving too fast. It was as if she was both present and far-distant, and out of control either way. She felt Luc's strong hands on hers as he slid the platinum ring onto her finger. She marveled at the size and power of his hand, in contrast to the cool metal she held as she did the same. She heard his voice again when he repeated his vows, this time confident and loud, connecting hard with something deep in her belly.

But nothing could prepare her for the moment when he pulled back her veil, exposing her face to his uncompromising gaze. Gabrielle's mouth went dry. *Fear*, she told herself, though another part of her scoffed at that idea. She could feel him in her pores, surrounding her, claiming her. Something in her wanted it—wanted him—even though he seemed so overwhelming. Even though he was a stranger.

The cathedral fell away. It was as if the two of them stood alone, Gabrielle naked and vulnerable before him. She had known that he was darkly, disturbingly handsome—that women on several continents vied for his attentions. So close, Gabrielle could see why.

His thick dark hair brushed the top of his stiff white collar. The traditional dove-gray morning suit he wore emphasized the breadth of his shoulders and the hard planes of his chest. His features were hewn from stone. There were creases at the corners of his eyes, though she could not imagine this man laughing. He looked harsh, beautiful in the way that the mountains were, and equally remote. His dark gray eyes looked almost black in the light from above, beneath his dark brows. His mouth was set in a firm, flat, resolute line.

He was her husband.

He was a stranger.

More than this, he was a man. And so intensely masculine that Gabrielle could not breathe as he regarded her for a searing moment. As if she was prey and he the dangerous predator. That odd part of her that she'd never felt before thrilled to the idea.

Luc stepped closer, filling Gabrielle's vision. She could smell the hint of his expensive cologne, could see the faint challenge in his gaze. Her lips parted as an unfamiliar sensation coursed through her—something having to do with the accelerated kick of her heart, the disturbing heaviness creeping through her limbs.

One big hand molded to the curve of her cheek. Anchoring her. Holding her. Gabrielle dared not move. She barely breathed. She locked her knees beneath her, suddenly afraid she would topple over.

The heat from his open palm was shocking. It ignited a fire that streaked through her body, confusing her even as something sweet and hot pooled deep inside. Her stomach clenched, and then began to ache. Her breath came in shallow bursts.

Luc did not look away. He tilted her face toward her as he moved even closer, and then he settled his firm mouth against hers.

It was no kiss. It was an act of possession. A hard, hot brand of his ownership.

Luc pulled back, his gaze penetrating, then returned his attention to the bishop—as if Gabrielle had ceased to be of interest to him the moment he'd claimed her.

Gabrielle wanted to scream. She felt the need for it churning inside her, clamoring against the back of her throat.

He was just like her father. He could—and would, she felt certain, in a rush of intuition and fear—dictate her every move. She would be expected to produce heirs. To be naked in front of a man who made her *feel* naked already—even dressed in all her layers of white taffeta, embroidery, pearls.

She could not do this. Why had she agreed to do this? Why had she not said no to her father, as any sane woman would have?

Luc took her hand again, turning Gabrielle to face the congregation. Her attendants moved behind her, moving the great train as the couple began the long walk down the length of the cathedral.

They were man and wife. She was married. Gabrielle's head spun. Luc placed her small hand on his arm and led her down the aisle.

She could feel the power he held tightly leashed in his body as he walked next to her.

Everything inside Gabrielle rose up in protest, making her knees wobble beneath her and her eyes glaze with tears.

This was a terrible mistake.

How could she have let this happen?

CHAPTER TWO

His bride was afraid of him.

"I make you anxious," Luc said in an undertone, his attention trained on her as they stood together in the receiving line after the ceremony.

She smiled, she greeted, she introduced—she was the perfect hostess. And the look she sent him was guarded.

"Of course not," she murmured, smiling, and then turned her attention to one of her cousins, the Baron something-or-other.

Luc expected nothing less from a princess so renowned for her perfect manners, her propriety. Much unlike her royal contemporaries—including the cousin whose hand she clasped now. Luc's mouth twisted as he thought of them, his supposed peers. Paparazzi fodder, like his parents had been— living out their private dramas in full, headline-shrieking view of the voyeuristic world, no matter that it humiliated their only son.

"Congratulations," the cousin said effusively, shaking Luc's hand—his own far too soft and fleshy. Luc eyed him with a distaste he did not bother to hide, and the man's smile toppled from his mouth.

Luc had vowed years ago that he would never live such a useless, empty life. He had vowed that he would never marry until he found a woman as private as he was—as dedicated to not just the appearance of propriety, but of serenity. At nearly forty, he had been waiting a long time.

"Thank you," he said to the Baron with the barest civility. The other man hurried away. Next to him, Luc felt his new wife tense. Perhaps she was not afraid of him, as she'd said. Perhaps it was only a certain wariness. While Luc could not blame her, when grown men quaked before him, it would not do. A healthy respect was one thing, but he did not want her *skittish*.

He gazed at her. Princess Gabrielle was the real deal. More than simply lovely—as he'd thought before—she was beautiful as a princess should be. Her glorious blue-green eyes were said to be the very color of the Adriatic. Standing next to her in her father's *palazzo*, high on the hill overlooking the sea, Luc believed it.

Her masses of honey-blond hair were swept up today, the better to anchor the tiara she wore. Jewels glinted at her ears and throat, emphasizing the long, graceful line of her neck. Her mouth, curved now in the polite smile he suspected she could produce by rote, was soft and full. She was delicate and elegant. And, more than all these things, he knew that she was virtuous as well. She was like a confection in her wedding finery—and she was *his*.

But he had seen the sheen of tears in her eyes back in the cathedral. He had seen the panic, the confusion. Once again, that odd protective urge flared to life within him. He normally did not care whether people respected or feared him, so long as they either did his bidding or got out of his way—but somehow he did not want that reaction from her. She was his wife. And, even though he thought her reaction was more to do with nerves and their new reality as a wedded couple than with any real fear, he felt compelled to reassure her.

"Come," he said, when the last of their guests had moved through the line. Without waiting for her reply, he took her arm and steered her across the marble floor and out to the sweeping veranda that circled the *palazzo*, offering stunning views from the heights of Miravakia's hills to the craggy coastline far below.

"But the meal—" she began. Her voice was musical. Lovely like the rest of her. She did not look at him as she spoke. Instead, she stared at her arm, at the place where his palm wrapped around her elbow, skin to skin.

Luc could see her reaction to his touch in the slight tremor that shook her. He smiled.

"They'll wait for us, I think."

Outside, the ocean breezes swelled around them. Bells rang out in the villages, celebrating them. Their wedding. Their future—the future Luc had worked so hard to make sure he obtained, exactly as he'd pictured it.

But his bride—his *wife*—was still not looking at him. She tilted her chin up and gazed at the sea, as if she could see the Italian coast far off in the distance.

"You must look at me," Luc said. His tone was gentle, but serious.

It took her a long moment, but she complied, biting down on her bottom lip as she did so. Luc felt a stab of desire in his gut. He wanted to lean over and lick that full lip of hers— soothe the bite. But he would take this slowly. Allow her to get used to him.

"See?" His lips curved. "It is not so bad, is it?"

"I am married to a perfect stranger," she said, her gaze wary though her tone was polite.

"I am a stranger today," Luc agreed. "But I won't be to-morrow. Don't worry. I know the transition may be...difficult."

"'Difficult,'" she repeated, and looked away. She let out a small sound that Luc thought was almost a laugh. She smoothed her palms down the front of her gown—a nervous gesture. "I suppose that's one word for it."

"You are afraid of me." It wasn't a question.

When she did not respond, he reached over and took her chin his hand, gently swinging her face toward his. She was several inches shorter than his six feet, and had to tilt her head back to look up at him.

Desire pooled within him, heavy and hot. She was his. From the sparkling tiara on her head, to those wary blue eyes, to the tips of her royal toes. *His*. At last.

"I don't know you well enough to be afraid of you," she told him, her voice barely above a whisper.

His touch obviously distressed her, but Luc couldn't bring himself to let her go. As in the cathedral, every touch sent fire raging through his blood. It had surprised him, but now he found he welcomed it. He stroked the side of her face and ran his thumb across her full lips.

Gabrielle gasped and jerked away from him, her color rising. "I don't know you at all," she managed to say, her voice shaking.

"You are well-known, Your Royal Highness, for always doing your duty, are you not?" he asked.

"I…I try to respect my father's wishes, yes," she said.

Her eyes widened as he gazed down at her.

"I am a man who keeps my promises. That's all you need to know about me today. The rest will come."

She stepped back, and he let her go. He watched, fascinated, as her gaze fell away from his. Yet he could see the flutter of her pulse at her throat, and he knew that she felt the same fire, the same desire he did.

Though he suspected it scared the hell out of her. And that kind of fear Luc could handle.

In fact, he thought, with purely male satisfaction as she turned and headed back toward the reception with only a single, scared look over her shoulder, he looked forward to handling it.

He couldn't wait.

* * *

The wedding meal was torture.

Gabrielle felt as if her skin was alive—she wanted to scratch wildly, to squirm, to tear it off in strips and throw it away. She couldn't sit still in her seat at the high table in the great ballroom. She shifted, desperate to put more space between her body and Luc's right next to her, all the while conscious that they were being watched, observed, commented upon. It wouldn't do to be seen fidgeting in her chair like a child. But she couldn't seem to escape Luc's knowing, confounding gaze, no matter how far away from him she tried to get, and the longer it went on the more agitated she became. He merely watched her, amused.

"What made you decide to get married?" she asked him finally, frantic to divert her attention from the restless agitation that was eating her alive. If the silence continued to stretch between them, *she* might be what snapped.

"I beg your pardon?" he asked.

She was sure that he had heard her. How could he not? Every time she shifted away from him he filled the space she created. His arm, his hard thigh, his shoulder brushed against her. A light pressure here, the faintest brush of his sleeve there. He was crowding her, making it hard for her to take a full breath. She was light-headed.

"Why now?" she asked, determined to break this strange, breathless spell that had her in such a panic. She had never been prone to flights of fancy before—she prided herself on being rational, in fact—but this situation was bringing it out in her. *Which is perfectly normal*, she soothed herself. *Completely rational*. This situation—being married to a perfect stranger like a medieval spoil of war—was what was not normal. Anyone would be beside herself. Though she couldn't help thinking anyone else would have refused to be in this situation in the first place—refused to be married off so cold-bloodedly.

Married. The word echoed in her head, sounding more and more like doom each time. *Married. Married. Married—*

"I was looking for you," he said, in that deep, sure voice of his that sent spirals of reaction arrowing deep into her bones. "The perfect, proper princess. No one else would do."

Gabrielle glanced quickly at him, then away. "Of course," she said politely, to restrain the rising hysteria she was afraid might choke her. "And yet you never met me until today."

"There was no need."

She felt more than saw the arrogant shrug. Temper twined with her distress and she felt her blood pump, hot and angry. *No need?*

"Naturally," she agreed, in the most polite and iciest tone she could manage. "Why meet your bride? How modern of me."

She felt the force of that dark gray gaze and dared herself to meet it. The contact burned. She felt a deep shuddering inside, and had to remind herself to inhale. To blink. To get a hold of herself.

"I am a traditional man," he said. One dark brow rose, challenging her. "Once my mind is made up, that is sufficient." On another man she might have thought there was a hint of a smile at the corner of his hard mouth. But his expression was so forbidding, his eyes so gray. She swallowed.

"I see. You decided it was time to get married, and I fit the bill," she said carefully.

She was like a horse, or a dog—only her bloodline was considered relevant to the proceedings. Had he considered a selection of princesses before deciding she would do? She could feel hysteria rising again, and tried to stave it off by grabbing for her champagne glass. She gulped some of the fizzy liquid before continuing.

"Were there certain requirements to fulfill? A checklist of some kind?" she asked, her voice rising. But was she really surprised? Men like her husband—like her father—thought the feelings of those around them, *her* feelings, were beneath their notice. Irrelevant.

She thought she might be going mad.

"Gabrielle."

She stilled at the unexpected sound of her name on his lips. Her fingers clenched tight around the delicate stem of her glass, but the way he said her name was like a bell ringing somewhere deep inside her—even though his tone was firm.

She didn't understand it. He hadn't even bothered to meet her before their wedding. And yet he spoke her name and she did his bidding at once, like the purebred dog he thought she was.

"Forgive me," she said crisply, setting her glass down very precisely next to her plate, piled high with food she had yet to touch. "I think the emotion of the day is going to my head."

"Perhaps you should eat," he suggested smoothly, indicating her plate with a nod. Again, the ghost of a smile flirted with his hard mouth. "You must keep up your strength."

Gabrielle's eyes flew to his, then dropped to her plate. He could not mean what she thought he did, could he? Surely he couldn't expect…?

"You look as if you might cry at any moment," he said from beside her, his voice hard as he leaned closer. She could feel the heat of him pressed against the gossamer-thin sleeve of her dress, burning her, and ordered herself not to jerk away. "The guests will imagine you are having second thoughts."

There was no missing the sardonic inflection that time. Gabrielle forced herself to smile prettily for the benefit of whoever might be watching.

"Heaven forbid," she murmured, not realizing she'd spoken aloud until she saw he was watching her, those dark brows raised.

"Eat," he suggested again.

She did not mistake the undercurrent of steel in his voice, and found herself reaching for her fork. Her body obeyed him without thought even as her mind reeled at his arrogance. What if she was not hungry? Would he force-feed her?

She shied away from that thought immediately, afraid to follow it through. He was…too much. Gabrielle took a bite of the fresh-grilled fish on her plate and tried to imagine what life with this man would be like. She tried to imagine an ordinary Tuesday afternoon. A forgettable Saturday morning. But she could not. She could only imagine his dark eyes flashing and his hands strong and demanding on her. She could only picture tangled limbs and his hot skin sliding against hers.

He was too much.

"Please excuse me," she murmured, setting her fork down abruptly and presenting him with her most demure smile— as if her body was not undergoing a full-scale riot even as she spoke. She had to stop it. "I'll be right back."

"Of course," Luc said, in the same polite tone. He rose as she rose, pulling back her chair and summoning one of the hovering servants to aid her with her voluminous skirts, courteous in word and deed. He looked like the perfect gentleman, the perfect husband.

And if she had not seen the knowing gleam in his dark gaze she might have been tempted to believe it herself.

CHAPTER THREE

Luc paid only slight attention to the speech King Josef was making.

"Today Miravakia welcomes its future king," his father-in-law intoned, standing in his full regalia at the head of the long table covered in gleaming silver and white linen, his voice pitched to carry throughout the great room. "But may that day be far off in the future."

Luc was far more interested in his bride at the moment than stale jokes about royal succession, though the guests laughed heartily—as they were expected to do. It was only polite.

Gabrielle, however, did not laugh with the rest. The color was high on her soft cheeks, and she had been sitting far too still beside him since she'd returned from the powder room, her long skirts rustling as she attempted to angle her body away from him. He preferred her attempts at sparring with him, he thought, amused.

"And what about you?" he asked, picking up their conversation from before as if she had not run away in the middle of it. He wondered idly if she believed she'd fooled him—if she believed he was unaware she had made an excuse to escape him. He dismissed the thought. Let her believe it if it made her feel better about her situation.

She threw a cautious look his way, her eyes more blue than

green in the dim glow of the ballroom. She vibrated with tension—and, he thought, awareness. Though Luc considered the possibility that she was too innocent to realize it. It seemed impossible in this day and age, but then Luc was used to achieving the impossible. It was one of his chief defining characteristics.

"Me?" she repeated.

"Why did you choose to marry now?" he asked. Once again, he found himself trying to put her at ease, and was amazed at himself. He had stopped trying to charm women when he was little more than a boy. He didn't need it. No matter how he behaved, they adored him and begged for more. But none of them had mattered until this one. For her, he would be charming. Her perfection deserved nothing less.

"Choose?" She echoed him again—and then smiled, though this was not her usual gracious smile, the one that she had been wearing all day, beaming around the room. This one was tighter and aimed at her lap, where she clasped her hands in the folds of her wedding dress. "My father expected me to do my duty. And so I have."

"You are twenty-five." He watched her closely as he spoke, attuned to the way she worried her full lower lip with her teeth. "Other girls your age live in flats with friends from university. They prefer nightlife and the party circuit to marriage or talk of duty."

"I am not other girls," Gabrielle said.

Luc watched, fascinated, as the pulse in the hollow of her neck fluttered wildly. In her lap, her fingers dug into each other. She betrayed no other sign of her agitation.

"My mother died when I was quite young and I was raised to be my father's hostess." She expelled a breath. "I will be Queen. I have responsibilities."

As she spoke, she kept her eyes fixed on her father, who had said something very similar, if Luc recalled correctly.

Luc followed her gaze, not at all surprised to see that the King had retaken his seat, without any words specifically directed to his daughter. Evidently this bothered Gabrielle, though she fought to conceal it. Luc could see the sheen of emotion in her eyes, could read her agitation as clearly as if it was in school-boy Italian.

Luc detested emotion. He loathed the way people blamed their emotions for all manner of sins—as if emotions were separate, ungovernable entities. As if one did not possess a will, a mind.

But Gabrielle, for all the emotion he had sensed in her today, was not letting it rule her. She did not inflict her emotions, her passions, on everyone around her. She did not cause any scenes. She simply sat in her seat, smiling, and handled herself like the queen she would be someday. *His* queen.

Luc approved. He reminded himself that her finer sensibilities were one of the reasons he had chosen her. Her charity and her empathy could not exist in a vacuum. Perhaps emotion was the price.

He decided it was a small one. He decided that he, Luc Garnier, who prided himself on a life lived free of the cloying perfume of emotions, could tolerate hers. Even indulge them on occasion.

"You have made him proud," he told her, nodding at her father, feeling benevolent. "You are the jewel of his kingdom."

Finally she turned her head and met his gaze. The shine of tears was gone, and her sea-colored eyes were clear and grave as she regarded him.

"Some jewels are prized for their sentimental value," she said, her musical voice pitched low, but not low enough to hide the faint tremor in it. "And others for their monetary value."

"You are invaluable," he told her, assuming that would be the end of it. Didn't women love such compliments? He'd never bothered to give them before. But Gabrielle shrugged, her mouth tightening.

"Who is to say what my father values?" she asked, her light tone unconvincing. "I would be the last to know."

"But I know," he said.

"Yes." Again that grave sea-green gaze. "I am invaluable—a jewel without price." She looked away. "And yet somehow contracts were drawn up, a price agreed upon, and here we are."

There was the taint of bitterness to her words. Luc frowned. He should not have indulged her—he regretted the impulse. This was what happened when emotions were given rein. Was she so foolish? How had she imagined the courtship of a royal princess, next in line to her country's throne, would proceed?

"Tell me, Your Royal Highness," he said, leaning close, enjoying the way her eyes widened. Though she did not back away from him. He liked her show of courage, but he wanted to make his point perfectly clear. "What was your expectation? You are not, as you say, other girls. Did you expect to find your king in the online personals? How did you think it would work?"

Her head reared back, and she straightened her already near-perfect posture.

"I... Of course I didn't—"

"Perhaps you thought you should have a gap year from your duties," he continued in the same tone. Low and lethal. "A vacation from the real you, as so many of your royal peers have had—to the delight of the press. Perhaps you could have traveled around the world with a selection of low-born reckless friends? Taken drugs in some dirty club in Berlin? Had anonymous sex on an Argentine beach? Is that how you thought you would best serve your country?"

If he'd thought she was in the grip of emotion before, that had been nothing. Her face was pale now, with hectic color high on her cheeks and in her eyes. Yet again she did not crack or crumble. Someone sitting further away would not have seen the difference in her expression at all.

"I have never done any of those things," she said in a tight, controlled voice. "I have always thought of Miravakia first!"

"Do not speak to me of contracts and prices in this way, as if you are the victim of some subterfuge," he ordered her harshly. "You insult us both."

Her gaze flew to his, and he read the crackling temper there. It intrigued him as much as it annoyed him—but either way he could not allow it. There could be no rebellion, no bitterness, no intrigue in this marriage. There could only be his will and her surrender.

He remembered where they were only because the band chose that moment to begin playing. He sat back in his chair, away from her. *She is not merely a business acquisition*, he told himself, once more grappling with the urge to protect her—safeguard her. *She is not a hotel or a company.*

She was his wife. He could allow her more leeway than he would allow the other things he controlled. At least today.

"No more of this," he said, rising to his feet. She looked at him warily. He extended his hand to her and smiled. He could be charming if he chose. "I believe it is time for me to dance with my wife."

His smile was devastating.

Gabrielle gulped back her reaction to it, suddenly worried that she might scream, or weep, or some appalling combination of the two. Anything to release the pressure building inside her, restless and intense all at once. But that smile—

It changed him. It took stone and forbidding mountain and softened it, illuminating his features—making him magic. He was, she realized with a delicate shiver of foreboding, a dangerously attractive man.

Dangerous to her, specifically.

For she was helpless before him. He held out his hand and she placed hers within it. Without comment, without thought. Meekly. Obediently. Despite the fact she'd been trying to keep from touching him for hours now. Was she losing her mind?

But she did not dare disobey him. Had anyone ever disobeyed him? And lived to tell the tale?

His smile might have made him momentarily beautiful. His hand was firm around hers, brooking no argument, allowing her no concession as he led her from the high table. The faces of the wedding guests blurred, becoming as indistinct as the flickering candles. She wondered briefly—in a kind of panic—what he would do if she pulled back, tried to move away as she wished. Would he simply tow her along beside him? Or would her body refuse the order and follow his lead without consulting her? She did not think that now—in public, on a dance floor in front of so many onlookers—was the time to test the theory.

He was no playboy, like the few other suitors her father had considered since Gabrielle had reached her majority. This man did not flirt or cajole. There were no pretty words. Only that brief, glorious smile that had jolted through her like an electric shock. Everything else he would demand. Or he would simply take.

He led her to the center of the dance floor. Gabrielle's heavy dress clung to her hips, her legs—made her feel as if she waded through honey. Luc pulled her close, one lean and muscled arm banding around her back, holding her. Caging her.

It had been hard enough to sit next to him throughout the meal. But this—this was agony.

In his arms, there was nowhere to hide. Face-to-face with him, she felt exposed, vulnerable. Trapped. Her breasts felt heavy and tight against the brocaded bodice of her gown. It took her long, panicked moments to register the fact that she was not having a dizzy spell, that he was moving them around the ballroom with an easy grace and consummate skill, never releasing her from that commanding gray gaze that seemed to see into her very core.

She felt as if she were made of glass and might shatter into pieces at any moment.

"I always wondered what couples talk about," she blurted out, desperate to lessen the tension between them, to divert her attention from that hard mouth now so breathlessly, intimidatingly close to hers, "when they dance at their weddings." She laughed nervously. "But then we are not like most couples, I suppose."

"Again, you forget yourself," he said dismissively, though his gray eyes seemed to darken as she stared up at him. "You are surrounded by a collection of aristocrats, some with ancient family names and kingdoms at their disposal. Do you imagine they are all passionately in love with their politically expedient spouses?"

Infuriating, pompous, *rude* man. How could he speak to her so condescendingly? How could he be her husband?

"I've never thought about it," she flared back at him. "I've hardly had time to adjust to my own 'politically expedient' marriage, much less critique anyone else's!"

His expression did not change, though the arm around her back tightened just a fraction—just enough to make Gabrielle gasp, but not enough to make her miss her step as their dance continued. She was suddenly certain that she did not want to hear whatever he might say next.

"Have you been married before?" she asked hurriedly, hoping to fend him off.

"Never." His brows arched, making him seem both regal and inaccessible at once. Gabrielle swallowed nervously.

"You must have had long-term relationships," she continued. She had no idea what she was saying. "You are forty, are you not?"

"Is this a blind date, Gabrielle?" he asked, his voice dangerously low. "Do you plan to sort out my character through a series of inane questions?"

"I'm trying to get to know you," she replied evenly, raising her chin in defiance. "It seems a reasonable thing to do, under the circumstances. What else should we talk about? The weather?"

"You have the rest of your life to get to know me," he said, with a Gallic sort of shrug. The ultimate dismissal. "Or do you think knowing the way I take my coffee will give you insight? Will it make you more comfortable? The end result is the same. I am your husband."

He was hateful. And his derisive tone ignited the temper she'd worked her whole life to keep under wraps.

"I think you must be the one who is afraid," she declared, anger making her brave. "Why else react so strongly to simple questions?"

She expected him to lash back at her—to try to cow her with his dark gaze or that sharp edge in his voice.

But instead he threw back his head and laughed. It was not long, or loud, but it was real. His gray eyes gleamed almost silver for a moment, and she saw an indentation in his lean jaw—far too masculine to be called a dimple. His eyes crinkled in the corners, and he was once again magical and irresistible.

Suddenly Gabrielle had the sensation that she was standing on a ledge at the edge of some vast cavern, and the ground beneath her feet was shaky. Again that restless tension swelled inside her, terrifying her. Her skin was too small, too sensitive. He filled her senses. And when he looked down at her again, his expression sobering, she felt something shift inside her. It felt irrevocable. Or possibly insane.

Nerves, she thought, desperately trying to maintain her calm. *Nothing but nerves—and too much champagne on an empty stomach.*

CHAPTER FOUR

ALONE at last in the sumptuous chamber that served as her dressing room, with the reception carrying on below her, Gabrielle stared at herself in the mirror and told herself she was being ridiculous. First, no man could possibly be as intense or overwhelming as Luc Garnier seemed to be. She was letting her imagination run away with her, her emotions heightened by the events of the day. Second, she was forgetting that the tight corset of her dress was probably responsible for her breathless, dizzy reaction to him. He was no magician—able to command her body like some kind of snake charmer. Her gown was simply too uncomfortable—she'd been in it all day.

She had convinced herself, more or less, and started to remove her heavy diamond and pearl earrings when the door opened behind her and he stepped into the room.

Gabrielle froze.

The cathedral and the ballroom had not prepared her—both were so large, so vast. The dressing room was tiny in comparison and Luc seemed to fill it, pushing all the air out the room as he closed the door behind him.

Gabrielle was still unable to move. She stared at him through the mirror as his dark eyes flicked along her spine, then met hers. She felt his gaze like fire, licking into her bones, searing her skin.

"I…" She didn't know what she meant to say, only that she was pleading with him. She put her earrings down on the vanity table in front of her, and twisted around to face him. He had not moved—he still filled the doorway with his rangy, muscled frame—and yet she felt his closeness as if he held her. "I cannot…"

She couldn't say it.

Sex seemed to crowd into the room then, like a thick fog. It was that hot, hard light in his eyes. It was the way he looked at her—as if he owned her, body and soul. It was the parade of images in her head. All of them decadent and disturbing. All of them involving that unyielding mouth of his and those cool, assessing, knowing eyes.

She couldn't bear it.

"Surely you don't…?"

She thought she might burst into tears, but he moved then, and once again she could do nothing but gape at him. He stalked toward her like something wild, untamed. Something fierce and uncompromising came and went across his face, and she knew in a flash that he wanted her—and that she could not survive it.

She could not survive *him*.

"What are you doing?" she asked him, her voice barely a thread of sound, weak to her own ears. He continued toward her, towering above her, forcing her to tilt her head back so she could stare up at him across the great expanse of his rock-hard torso, showed to perfection in his crisp white dress shirt.

Her mind raced. He had said he was traditional—how traditional? Surely he couldn't expect that she would fall into bed with a man she had only met hours before? So what if it was the marital bed?

Could he?

He did not speak. His eyes were shuttered as he gazed down at her, and then he moved, his big hands catching her around the waist and lifting her to her feet.

He was incredibly, panic-inducingly strong. Gabrielle's world tilted and whirled, and then she was in his arms again—but this time they were not on a dance floor, surrounded by witnesses. This time they were all alone, and he pulled her much too close, until she sprawled against him, her breasts flattened against the wall of his chest. They ached. Gabrielle moaned—whether in protest or terror, she did not know.

"I will not attempt to claim any marital rights tonight, if that's what you're afraid of," he said then, his breath fanning over her face.

"I… Thank you…" Gabrielle said formally, and was then furious with herself. As if it was *his* decision to make! As if *she* did not exist!

"We will grow into each other, you and I," he told her. His mouth was so close, and it both tempted and terrified her in equal measure. She remembered the feel of his mouth against hers in the cathedral. Brutal. Territorial. She didn't know why it made her knees tremble and her core melt.

"But our wedding night should be commemorated, should it not?" he asked.

"I don't—"

But he wasn't really asking.

His mouth came down on hers, as uncompromising and hard as she remembered—as he had been since she'd met him so few hours before. This time he tasted her lips only briefly, before moving across her jaw, her temple, learning the shape of her. His mouth was hot. Gabrielle felt her own fall open in shock—in response. She felt feverish. Outside herself.

Something in her thrilled to it—to him—even as the rest of her balked at such a naked display of ownership. Her hands flew to his shoulders, though it was like pushing against stone.

Then, as suddenly, he set her away from him, a very masculine triumph written across his face.

"You are mine," he said. Claiming her. He reached over and

smoothed an errant strand of her hair back into place, the tenderness of the gesture at odds with the harshness of his words, his expression. "Change into your traveling clothes and meet me outside the ballroom, Gabrielle. We will stay on the other side of the island tonight." He paused. "Wife."

She stood frozen in place for a long time after he left. The air rushed back into the room with his departure. Her heartbeat slowly returned to normal. Her hands eventually stopped shaking.

But inside her a new resolve hardened, and turned into steel.

She could not survive him, she had thought in a moment of panic. But she was not panicked now, and she knew that it was true. It was not simply that Luc Garnier was another man like her single-minded father—though she knew that he was. It was not even that he clearly wanted things entirely his own way—what man in his position, having bartered for a royal wife and his own eventual kingdom, would not? It was that she was so detestably weak.

Weakness had led her here, to this sham of a wedding night. She was married to a man who terrified her on a fundamental level and she had walked calmly to her own slaughter. Her father had not had to coerce her—he had only announced his intentions and Gabrielle had acquiesced, as she always did, because she'd thought that somehow her doing so would impress him. Instead, it had only made him less inclined to consider her feelings at all.

What a thing to realize now—far too late.

Gabrielle blew out a shaky breath and knew, on some level, that acquiescing to Luc Garnier would be far more damaging and permanent. She would not survive it intact—not as the Gabrielle she was now. She could not handle his heat or his darkness—and she would not be recognizable to herself if she tried. She would go mad—lose her mind.

She thought of his fierce gaze, his resolute expression, and felt as if she already had.

She had never stood up for herself. She had let her father order her around her entire life. Now her husband would do the same. Worse. He would demand even more from her. Suddenly Gabrielle could see her life stretch out before her—one decision made by her husband after another until she ceased to exist. Until she was completely absorbed into him, lost in him. A man like Luc Garnier would accept nothing less than her complete surrender.

She took a deep breath, then released it. She looked around the chamber as if she'd never seen it before. Perhaps she had simply never realized until now that it was a prison cell.

And it was past time to escape.

Luc's body shouted at him to turn around, return to the dressing room and finish what he'd started.

He was hard, ready. His blood was pumping and it had nearly killed him to take his hands off of her soft skin.

Her taste was addictive. Sweet, with an underlying kick.

He paused in the long corridor outside her door. He wanted to bury himself in her—in his wife—and make them both delirious with need and release. Again and again until they were exhausted from it. It was a complication he hadn't foreseen—and he had been so sure he'd covered all the angles.

Tonight he could allow himself some amusement on that score. It was not very often that Luc Garnier was taken by surprise. He had expected to desire her—she was a beautiful woman and he had long had a taste for classic beauty. Who did not? But the need raking through him and tempting him to charge back through the door and claim what was his—that was unexpected.

Perhaps it was not a complication. Perhaps it was merely a side benefit—confirmation that he'd made the correct choice. The fact that he knew very few men in his position who lusted after their wives meant nothing. When had Luc been at all like other men?

He forced himself to walk away from her door, to leave her in peace. For tonight, at least.

They had their whole lives to explore this combustible chemistry. He could allow her one night to come to terms with it.

His mouth curved at the idea of behaving benevolently—for any reason. It was a new sensation, and not entirely pleasant. He was not a man who denied his appetites.

But it was only for tonight.

In the morning he would continue her education. He would touch her until she welcomed it, until she begged him for more.

And then all bets were off.

It had been so easy, Gabrielle marveled almost a week later, looking out over the endless sea of lights below her. Los Angeles gleamed and beckoned, sprawled out before her, seeming seductive and immense from Gabrielle's spot high in the Hollywood Hills.

Gabrielle couldn't believe *how* easy it had been—it made her wonder why she had waited so long to do something simply because she wanted to do it, without worrying about the feelings or opinions or wishes of anyone else.

Gabrielle had left the *palazzo* after a quick change of clothes, driven down to the docks, boarded a ferry—and been in Italy by morning. Once she'd made her way to Rome she had booked herself into a hotel for the night and called an old friend from university. Cassandra had not missed a beat, despite the fact she and Gabrielle had not seen each other in ages. She had apologized for the fact that she could not be in California to greet Gabrielle because she was filming in Vancouver, but she had offered Gabrielle the use of her house. Gabrielle had boarded a flight the next morning, had a brief stopover in London, and had been in Los Angeles by early afternoon.

Not bad for an obedient princess who had never lifted a finger in protest her whole adult life.

Tonight Gabrielle stood out on Cassandra's deck and sipped at a glass of white wine. Hollywood was splayed out before her, sparkling into the warm night, the lights and sounds wafting up from the famous Sunset Strip far below. She loved California—what little she'd seen of it in her jet-lagged and emotional haze. She loved the eucalyptus and rosemary-scented hills, with columns of cyprus trees scattered here and there. She loved the coyote howls at night and the warm sun during the day. She loved the red-topped houses that reminded her of home, and the hints of the Mediterranean throughout the landscape—houses clinging to the hilltops in clusters and the sea far below.

Gabrielle felt rebellious: American. She had helped herself to her friend's closet, as Cassandra had urged her to do. She wore denim jeans and a silk blouse tonight, and had left her feet bare. She curled her toes into the sun-bleached wood beneath her and reveled in the freedom of even so small an action. Her hair swirled around her shoulders in the warm night air. The outfit was light years away from the way she dressed normally—the pathologically proper Princess wore Chanel suits in soothing pastels and kept her hair in a smooth French twist.

And Gabrielle never wore jeans. Never. Her father believed jeans were "common," and out of deference to him Gabrielle hadn't worn a pair since her days at university. Tonight she decided she loved them. She liked the feel of the denim against her skin, defining every inch of her thighs and smoothing down her calves to tease her toes. They felt decadent and disobedient—two things Gabrielle wanted very much to be herself.

How had she let this happen? she wondered again, as despair moved through her body like a wave. How had she allowed her life to get so far from her own control? How had she *handed* it to someone else with so little thought? She balked at the idea that she would go so far to please someone—but facts were facts. She *had* handed over her life. First to her father, and then to her brand-new, terrifying stranger of a husband.

Behind her, the doorbell echoed through the pretty California Craftsman house, built like an expanded bungalow. Gabrielle smiled. That would be the housekeeper—the efficient and helpful Uma, who had promised to return with groceries for Gabrielle so she need not venture out into the hair-raising traffic on the Los Angeles streets.

Gabrielle padded to the front door, her bare feet making the faintest whisper of sound against the dark wood floor.

"You're a lifesaver—" she began, throwing the door open.

But it was not Uma who stood there.

It was Luc.

CHAPTER FIVE

LUC. Her husband. On the doorstep in front of her.

A kind of fire exploded through Gabrielle's body, heating her skin and raising the fine hairs on the back of her neck. Her mouth went dry.

If she could have moved she would have run for it, bare feet and all—she would have scrabbled up the hillside and run until she collapsed. Anything to put space between them.

But she was paralyzed by the fury in his dark gaze, the rigid set of his muscular shoulders, the power emanating from his strong frame. He was no less imposing in a cotton sweater and dark trousers than he had been in a morning suit on their wedding day.

In fact, the ferocious masculinity he trumpeted from every pore was even more intense than she remembered—with the California night behind him, and that hot banked rage she could practically taste simmering in his nearly black gaze.

She had been wary of him a week ago. But she could see— instantly—that the Luc Garnier she had met on her wedding day had been tame and sweet next to the one who now stood, incensed, on the doorstep before her.

You should have kept running, a little voice inside her insisted. *You should never have stopped.*

"Hello, Gabrielle." His voice was rich, dark and mocking.

Gabrielle flinched. "I think you forgot something in your haste to get away," he continued, looming over her on the front step.

His shoulders blocked out everything else—or perhaps it only seemed that way through the tears of reaction she fought to hold back.

"I—forgot something…?" she stammered.

His mouth twisted. "Your husband."

And then Luc walked inside, ignoring the wineglass that fell from her bloodless fingers, stepping over the shattered glass and the pool of liquid that spread across the floor—and never once taking his eyes off of her.

How dared she stare at him like that? When she had humiliated him on their wedding day—and run off across the planet! After all the leeway he had granted her—a mistake he would never make again.

How could he have been so wrong? How could he have mistaken her character like this? If one of his subordinates had been responsible for an error of this magnitude Luc would have fired and destroyed him. Had he only believed what he'd wanted to believe? Had he succumbed to the lie of her charms like any other, lesser man?

Luc bit back the bellow of rage and betrayal that threatened to spill out. He would remain in control. He would not sink to her level. Though it cost him, and he felt himself snarl with the effort of controlling his temper.

His eyes raked over her—his recalcitrant princess. Not perfect at all, but a lie. A lie who was now his wife.

Tonight she did not look like the obedient, biddable Princess Gabrielle he had chosen so carefully. It was as if that woman did not exist. *That woman had never existed!* Her thick tresses flowed around her, free and wild and the color of honey. She smelled sweet and fresh, like the scent of jasmine outside, rising up from the hills. And she pulled away from him as he stepped over the threshold and closed the door behind him—closing them inside.

Her feet were bare. Tight blue jeans showcased the curve of her hips and the long, slender length of her legs. Luc imagined those legs wrapped around his neck and felt himself harden immediately. He wanted her.

He hated that he wanted her. When she had played him for a fool. When she had managed to deceive him—he who prided himself on his immunity to such deceptions. He should never have believed the lie of her wide eyes, her trembling lips. Her supposed charity. Her proclaimed innocence. Moreover, he should have claimed what was his immediately, and to hell with her feelings.

So much for his urge to protect her. He would never indulge it again.

"What are you doing here?" Gabrielle asked into the tense silence, her eyes huge, as if she could read his mind.

She backed away as he approached, keeping a good two strides between them. She danced backward into the living room, and then moved to the back of the nearest sofa—as if a piece of furniture would provide a barrier. As if she would need some kind of barrier.

Luc might have found her amusing in other circumstances. But not much had amused him since he'd realized that she'd not only abandoned him, but had done so at a moment calculated to cause the most gossip, the most speculation. He thought he might hate her for that. He stopped in the center of the room and crossed his arms over his chest, to keep himself from doing anything he might regret.

"What am I doing here?" He smiled without humor. "I couldn't allow my bride to spend our honeymoon alone, could I?"

"Honeymoon?" She shook her head. "I don't understand."

"What did you think I would tell them, Gabrielle?" Luc

asked softly. "Did you consider it at all? What exactly did you think of as you abandoned me in the middle of our wedding reception, surrounded by our guests?"

"I'm sorry," she said, almost helplessly.

She clasped her hands in front of her. Perhaps she did not know that the movement pushed her breasts forward, drawing his attention to them and creating an intriguing shadow beneath her blouse. But he suspected she did. He suspected that everything about her was calculated.

And he'd fallen for it. Hook, line and sinker. He who had never lost control with a woman in his life, who had gone to such lengths to prevent exactly this scenario, had been well and truly played. He took a step closer.

"Sorry?" he repeated. He kept his tone mild. "That's all you have to say?"

"I…I had to leave," she said, that musical voice low. Pleading. "I can't do this—don't you see?"

He did not see. He felt. A churning mess of sex, fury, bitterness and possession that flared whenever he thought of her and was like wildfire now that she was in the same room. Even though he hated what she was—what she'd done to him. Because of it, perhaps.

"Why don't you tell me?" he said, moving toward the fireplace. He leaned casually against the mantel, though he did not feel in the least bit casual tonight. "I see my wife. The woman I married in a cathedral packed full of most of Europe. Tell me what you see that I do not."

"You're a stranger!" Frustration made her voice shake. Color was high on her cheeks, accentuating her classic bone structure and the perfection of her full mouth. "You… I met you at the altar!"

"So?" He straightened from the mantel. "This is your objection? This caused you to race across the world to get away from me?"

"Are you insane?" She let out a short laugh. "We don't live in the Middle Ages. Normal people get to know each other before they get married."

"But you and I are not normal people," Luc said, with an edge in his voice, closing the distance between them. Hadn't they already discussed this? Was she truly so naïve? He somehow doubted it after the past week. He watched as she fought against her urge to run from him as he rounded the couch. It was written across her face. Yet she stood firm. "You are the Crown Princess of Miravakia."

She held her hands out, warding him off.

"This is my fault," she said desperately.

"Then we agree," he bit out.

"I should have objected sooner," she continued, wary. "I've spent the days since the wedding asking myself how I could have let things get so far. My only excuse is I…I am not used to denying my father's wishes."

"Yes," Luc said bitterly. "The obedient, demure Princess Gabrielle, of whom I have heard so much. It was first assumed that you were kidnapped, you understand. Because no one could imagine the biddable, dependable Princess disappearing in such a public, humiliating way *deliberately*."

She flinched. "I am so sorry." Her eyes searched his. "You must believe me! I didn't know what else to do."

"You are my wife, Gabrielle." His voice was cold. Bitter. "That means something to me even if it does not mean anything to you."

Her color deepened. "I can't tell you—"

"And let me make something clear." He reached over and took her upper arms in his hands, forcing her to stand still, to look up at him.

Her skin was like satin. He wanted to strip her clothes from her body and explore it. He wanted to punish her. Or both at the same time. He should have done it from the start.

He should have taken her in that dressing room of hers, with her wedding dress still on. He should never have played at the courteous gentleman—a role he knew nothing about and never would.

"Please—" she started.

"I do not believe in bloodless faked marriages of convenience," he told her with finality. "It will not happen with us."

"What? What do you mean?" She blinked. "There must be—"

"I mean exactly what I said." He drew her closer, so that her panicked breath caused her firm breasts to brush against his chest. "You made vows. I expect you to honor those vows in word and deed. Do I make myself clear?"

"But—but—" Gabrielle shook her head, trying to clear it. But Luc was so close—his hands burning into her flesh. She couldn't seem to catch a breath. "You can't be serious! We don't even know each other!"

"I think I've gotten to know you well enough over the past week," he said, his voice almost tender, at odds with the darkness in his eyes, the hard set of his jaw. "As I chased you across the planet, the scorned and humiliated husband you abandoned so cavalierly. What more do I need to know?"

"No!" She was trembling, her eyes glazed with frustration or fear, but he no longer believed her. Or cared. "I didn't— I never—"

"Tell me, Gabrielle—when did you decide to deceive me? Or was this your plan all along?" His voice was harsh. So close, his hard features seemed made of stone.

"Of course not!" she cried. "Why can't you understand? I made a mistake!"

"Yes," he hissed. "You did."

Something sparked then, in the dark depths of his gaze— something hot and wild, bitter and lethal.

She knew what he was going to do in the split second

before he did it—and she thought she screamed. She thought she cast him away from her with the force of that scream. But she didn't make a sound. She didn't move at all.

His merciless mouth came down on hers and she was lost.

Luc's mouth was hard—and inexpressibly delicious. Gabrielle's head fell back as her mind spun out, leaving her dizzy and weak. He held her jaw in his strong hand—guiding her lips with his.

He did not seduce, caress. He took. He demanded. He possessed.

And Gabrielle's body burst into flame after flame of sensation. It was as if her body spoke to his in its own ancient language, and Gabrielle could neither control it nor understand it. She felt hot, and then cold. Luc deepened the kiss, playing with her tongue, her lips. Her hands crept up to the warm soft cotton of his sweater, then pressed against the planes of his chest. He made a slight sound of encouragement, or passion, as his powerful arm wrapped around her hips and dragged her up against the length of his body.

She could feel him from head to toe, pressed hard against her, imprinting himself, his taste, into her senses.

She was insane with the feel of him—the glory and the terror.

"Kiss me back, damn you," he growled, breaking away for only a moment.

Gabrielle stared at him, dazed. And then once again his mouth took hers, slanting to get a better, sweeter fit, and Gabrielle ached. Her breasts ached as she pressed against the implacable strength of his chest. Her belly ached, and she pulsed with heat between her legs.

Gabrielle felt the glass of the sliding door behind her, the coolness sharp against her overheated skin. She hadn't noticed that Luc had backed her into the door until he pressed her back against the glass. He moved his fingers into her hair, fisting his hand in the silky mass.

Once again he pulled his mouth away from hers. His face seemed harsh, dangerous. Gabrielle shivered. His dark eyes bored into her, and she had the irrational thought that he could *see* what his kisses had done to her—could see the almost painful throbbing low in her belly, in the molten core of her.

She opened her mouth to speak—perhaps to beg him to take her, to ease her agony, to let her go. She would never know.

The doorbell rang again, echoing through the house.

Luc glared. "Are you expecting someone? Is that why you ran to California—to meet your lover?"

"My…" Gabrielle shook her head, reeling. She couldn't make sense of his words, or the suspicion that glittered in his dark eyes. "It's the housekeeper," she said, her voice no more than a whisper, and huskier than it should have been. She looked down and saw that her hands had curled into fists. "She's come to bring groceries."

Her voice trailed away into nothing. She looked up, and the full force of his angry gaze slammed into her.

His eyes glittered. "There will be no more lies, Gabrielle. No more betrayal. Do you understand me?"

"Yes," she said, although she had no idea what he was talking about. But he was so elemental, so terrifying. How could she say anything else?

You are weak, she told herself bitterly. *And he is your greatest weakness of all.*

"Somehow," he said softly, though nothing else about him gentled at all, "I don't believe you." His hard mouth twisted. "Wait here."

CHAPTER SIX

THANK God for this distraction, Gabrielle thought in a daze, sinking gratefully into the leather couch.

She could hear Luc's low, commanding voice from the kitchen, and Uma's happy chatter in return, but what she noticed most of all was Luc's absence.

Breathing room. Space. As if the room had expanded when he left it.

Her lips still trembled, her knees felt suspiciously weak, and she could *taste* him in her mouth. A rich wine against her tongue, sending out little thrills of response through her limbs. She could feel his hard body against her skin as if he was still touching her. As if she wished he was still touching her. As if he had marked her, somehow.

Gabrielle couldn't seem to stop the riot in her mind, the chaotic surge of emotions and impressions that flooded through her veins and left her feeling electrified. Altered. Scared. And dangerously, absurdly excited.

How could she respond like that? How could she find him so intoxicating that even his anger couldn't dissuade her? Her body didn't care if he was angry, if he overwhelmed her, if his expressions or his words were cruel.

Her body craved his touch. Even now. Still.

Gabrielle blinked and gazed down at herself, as if she was

looking at a stranger. She had never spent much time thinking about her body. She knew that she was considered beautiful, of course; her father had insisted upon it, demanded she tend to her beauty as she tended to any other royal duty. She was to be beautiful, but never flashy. Hers was a quiet sort of beauty that lent itself to charitable work and her role as her father's hostess, and her thoughts about her appearance tended to focus entirely on how best to utilize it.

Tonight, however, she felt vivid. Alive. Wild and untamed. Not quiet or capable, but loud and crazy with need. How had he done that? How had he turned her body against itself without so much as asking her permission?

He would not ask. She knew that on some elemental level. He would not ask for what he could take. He would simply take it—as if it was his due.

She inhaled sharply against the riot of images that conjured up.

And then her eyes clapped to his—as if she'd sensed him there in the wide archway, watching her with that impenetrable gray gaze. As if she'd summoned him.

She felt a tickle along the nape of her neck and wondered almost helplessly if he had some kind of beacon, something that emanated from him and announced his presence. Shouted it before he entered the room.

Behind him, the front door slammed shut.

They were alone. Again.

Gabrielle felt her mouth run dry. She ran her palms along her thighs, trying to settle herself. She felt jittery beneath her own hands—silly with a need she only half understood.

"So quiet," Luc said, his dark voice mocking.

Gabrielle didn't know if it was defiance or fear, but she felt something move through her then. She knew it was related to the feeling that had compelled her to leave the palace—to escape. This time it brought an angry flush to her cheeks as she tossed her head back.

"What's the point in speaking if you continue to cut me off?" she asked, for all the world as if she felt as bold and careless as he seemed to be. She eyed him. "You're quite rude, you know."

She was startled by the flash of his teeth and the sound of his sudden laughter. That same dent in his jaw glinted for a moment—the one that had mesmerized her on their wedding day. It fascinated her anew.

She hadn't meant to amuse him. Had she? But she felt a warmth course through her anyway, suggesting that some part of her wanted to please him, to amuse him. Maybe more of her than she wanted to admit.

Why should she want to please this man, when he had done nothing but scare and overwhelm her? What did that say about the kind of person she was?

But had she ever been anyone else?

Once again, she despaired of her own weakness.

"I am rude, yes," Luc agreed, closing the distance between them with sure strides. "And ruthless. And arrogant. And whatever else you need to call me. Does it make you feel better to say it out loud?"

"Better?" Now it was Gabrielle's turn to laugh, as if he wasn't bearing down on her with so much barely leashed, alarming purpose. "Why would it make me feel better to find myself shackled to such a man?"

"Shackled." His dark eyes gleamed as he stopped before her, forcing her to crane her head back, looking up the long, solid length of his spectacular body—the one she had now felt crushed against her own, from her neck to her calves. "Now, there's an idea."

Gabrielle felt her lips part as the vision he'd intended rushed at her. Her arms bound. Her naked flesh open and inviting, and Luc so dark and powerful above her. She shivered. His mouth flattened.

"An idea you like, I think. Somehow I am not surprised."

"I...I don't know what you mean."

But she lied. And he knew it.

He reached down and took her hand into his bigger one. She did not resist as he pulled her to her feet—she couldn't seem to summon the will to do anything but stare at him. She thought of her hands bound, tied against the four-poster bed in the master bedroom that she'd been sleeping in so restlessly. Their bodies writhing together. Once again she was paralyzed. Was it fear, she thought, or something else?

Longing, something more honest whispered in the back of her mind.

She thought he would kiss her again when he brought her in close—near enough to feel the heat of his body, to smell the scent of his skin.

But instead he traced unknowable shapes across her cheek and down to her collarbone, tested the length of one thick strand of her hair, and then stepped back.

"Put on your shoes," he ordered her, curt and sure. "We're going out."

"Out?" Was that her voice? So breathy and insubstantial? Why did he turn her brain to cotton and fire?

"To dinner," he clarified and then smirked, as if she were simple.

"Dinner," she repeated, and was furious with herself when his smirk sharpened. She was not usually so stupid and dull-witted—yet from the moment she'd met him, from almost their first words, she had done nothing to show him that she was anything else. What must he think? That her father had sold off his idiot daughter?

"Surely the concept cannot alarm you?" Luc said, in that

intensely sardonic tone. "I feel certain you must have had dinner before."

Sarcasm. How delightful.

"Not with you," she snapped at him. "And not in this city. But, yes, thank you—I have had dinner before. How good of you to point it out to me." He was not the only one who could be sarcastic, she thought defiantly. But he ignored it.

"How interesting that you would choose to run away to a place you know nothing about."

She couldn't help but notice that he didn't look interested at all. He looked furious.

"I came here because my friend lives here," Gabrielle said, with a helpless sort of gesture around Cassandra's living room, ignoring the words *run away*. It was harder to ignore the dark look he had trained on her. "I knew I would be safe here."

"Safety is relative, Gabrielle," Luc murmured, his gaze almost feral. "And transient."

She eased away from him, feeling the sofa at the backs of her knees. She edged her way along its length—away from him.

She was all too aware that he had let her go.

"Happily, there are any number of excellent restaurants in this city," Luc told her, as if they were discussing nothing more than dinner plans. "And several that suit my purposes completely."

"I'm surprised you want to go out in public," she shot at him—emboldened by the distance she'd put between them. Whole strides and a glass table. "You'll have to behave, you know. No browbeating or threats in front of witnesses."

She was pleased with her own daring—so uncharacteristic—and she couldn't regret the words once they left her mouth, despite the way Luc's brows snapped together. But then, impossibly, he let out another laugh.

"Look at you," he said, that deep voice turning to silk. "So proud of yourself for standing up to me. Do you know *why* we're going out, Gabrielle?"

"Because you're hungry, I imagine." She sniffed, as if it was of no matter to her.

"Because your little stunt has resulted in our being splashed across every European tabloid imaginable," Luc corrected her, still in that almost soft tone.

The hair rose on her arms and her neck, and she understood on a deep, physical level that he was more furious than she'd seen him. That she was in more danger from this Luc than the louder, more obviously angry Luc she'd seen before.

"'Luc's Luck Runs Out.' 'Runaway Princess Bride.'" His hands clenched at his sides convulsively as his eyes bored into her. "You have made me the laughingstock of Europe."

"I…" She didn't know what to say, or why she felt the strangest urge to go to him, to try and soothe him. "I'm sorry," she said. "The tabloids have never paid any attention to me before. I never gave them a thought."

"Clearly." He let out a derisive sound. "But now, my darling bride, you will think of nothing else. You will smile and make eyes at me, do everything in your power to convince the world that we are nothing but a couple in love—do you understand?"

"I'm not an actress—" she began, frowning.

"Are you not?" His words cut into her, delivered with so much irony—so much disbelief.

What must he think of her? She blinked away the sudden heat across her face, behind her eyes. One of her hands flew to her throat, where she could feel the agitation in her pulse as well as her skin. She realized what she must look like and forced the hand back to her side.

"I don't see the purpose of this." Gabrielle took another step back, trying to ward off the unexpected pain. Why should she care if he thought ill of her? It only proved how little they knew each other. And yet…

"You do not have to see the purpose of it," he told her. "You need only to put on your shoes—and suitable trousers. My tastes do not run to barefoot brides cavorting in vulgar displays for the world to see. You will be Queen one day. I remember this, even if you do not."

"We cannot pretend that this marriage is anything but a farce, bare feet or not," Gabrielle protested, stung by his words. "Why would you want to parade it in front of cameras?"

"Listen carefully," he ordered her, closing the distance between them with such dizzying speed that Gabrielle gasped, faced with the unwelcome knowledge that he'd been toying with her. *Letting her* think she was getting the space from him she so desperately wanted.

He reached over and took her head between his hands, forcing her to be still, to look at him. Holding her suspended in his grasp.

It should not have made that mad heat punch into life in her belly. But it did. She felt ashamed of herself. And as if she'd been set on sweet, deadly fire.

"This marriage is no farce," he whispered, his mouth too close, his eyes burning with dark fury. "This marriage is real. I do not believe in divorce, even from deceivers like you. We do not have to like each other. But you have made this relationship into a matter of public scorn and ridicule and I will not have it. I will not allow it."

"I've never deceived you!" Gabrielle felt her eyes swim, whether from hurt or desire she was afraid to discover. Her lungs felt constricted, contained, as if he held them between his powerful hands as well.

"Everything about you is a lie," Luc gritted out. But his hands were gentle—holding her, not hurting her. He bit off an oath. "Especially this," he muttered thickly, and took her mouth with his.

Once again that piercing pleasure, all fire and need. Once again the roar of response charged through her. Gabrielle felt her nipples harden even while she shuddered and her body readied itself for him. She forgot to breathe, to think, as his lips demanded her response and then took it, again and again.

He set her away from him, his gaze shuttered. Gabrielle felt weak. Loose. Dangerously softened. Her hand moved to her lips, as if she could still feel the mark of him—his possession.

"Gabrielle." He said her name as if he hated the sound of it, but then his cruel mouth twitched into something not quite a smile. "Put on your shoes."

CHAPTER SEVEN

Luc watched Gabrielle closely from across the small table at the famous Ivy restaurant in Beverly Hills, drumming his fingers against the white linen tabletop. He tried to keep his temper under control, but he could feel it bubbling up, threatening to erupt.

He could not allow that. Not in a place he had chosen because it was so public, so exposed. He kept a lid on his fury.

Barely.

She had done as he asked. She'd smiled for the scrum of photographers who camped out in front of the Los Angeles landmark, and had even laughed with every indication of delight when Luc had kissed her in a shower of flashbulbs.

So calculated, he thought now. Though another part of him argued that she had only done what he'd told her to do.

Now she sat facing him, her mysterious calm smile locked across her mouth, looking as if she was having a marvelous time trying to pick out celebrities from the crowd around them on the outdoor patio.

He found it infuriating.

He wanted to mess up her perfection, wreck that serene countenance—see what boiled underneath all that bland politeness. Because he'd already had a taste of it, and it had sent a dark need raging through his blood.

"It appears you are quite an actress after all," he said, pitching his voice low enough to reach her ears but go no further. He watched her stiffen, though her smile did not falter. Just as she'd done at their wedding reception, she managed to avoid broadcasting even the slightest hint of any internal discomfort.

"If you mean that I know how to behave in public, then, yes, I am," she said. Her voice was smooth, though her chin rose slightly in challenge. "I always assumed that was a result of good breeding."

"The same good breeding that inspired you to abandon your own wedding reception?" he asked smoothly. "How proud your father was of *that* display."

He could see her response in the quiver of her lips and the tense stillness of her body—but, even so, to the untrained eye she might have been discussing the perfect California night that held them both in its soft, warm cocoon.

"That was an aberration," she said. Through her teeth.

"Lucky me."

"Tell me," she invited him, leaning close so he could see the storm in her sea-colored eyes, which pleased him more than it should have, "what would you have done in my position?"

"I would have honored my promises," he replied at once, harshly.

"How easy for you to say." She took a ragged breath. "How easy for you to criticize something you know nothing about."

"Then tell me about it," he suggested, sitting back in his chair. "We have an entire dinner to get through, Gabrielle, and then the rest of our lives. If there is something you feel I should know, you have all the time in the world to explain it to me. Who knows?" He smiled slightly. Coolly. "I might even see your point of view."

"You will never see my point of view," she snapped back at him, surprising him. "You have no interest in why I left—

you only care that it injured your pride. Your image! What explanation could possibly soothe the wounded pride of a powerful man?"

Luc definitely did not care for the sarcastic tone she used. But he watched her until she glanced away, one hand moving to her throat.

"You will never know unless you try," he said. Daring her.

"My father has had very specific expectations of me ever since I was a girl," she told him after a moment. Reluctantly. "He was—is—a hard man to please, but I tried. I got only top marks at university. I bowed to his wishes and became active on the charity circuit, supporting the causes he thought best instead of using my degree to help him run our country. He did not want his Crown Princess involved in matters of state unless it was to plan events or throw parties. Whatever he wished, I did."

"Go on," he urged when she paused again. He tried to picture a young, motherless Gabrielle, growing up in the shadow of her grim, humorless father, and found he did not like the image he conjured up. He wasn't sure he believed it, either. Surely the obedient child she described would not have run off the way she had?

"It's not such an interesting story, really," she said, refolding the napkin on her lap. "I tried my best to please my father up until the day he married me off to a man I'd never met without so much as asking me my opinion on the match." Her shoulders squared. She looked at him, bravely, and then away. "I felt as if the world was closing in on me. Trapping me. I didn't mean to leave you like that—but I had to go or be swallowed whole."

"And you couldn't speak to me about it." He tried to keep his voice light, but she glanced at him nervously and he knew he'd failed. "You couldn't ask for my help."

"Ask for your help?" She looked mystified by the very idea.

She actually let out a startled laugh. "I wouldn't…" She shook her head. "You were a stranger," she said, frowning. "How could I explain this to you when it wasn't personal at all, and yet involved you all the same?"

Part of him wanted to rage at her—to demand that she acknowledge that she should have run *to* him, not *from* him—but he clamped down on it. Why was he so quick to believe this story? Poor little lost princess, desperate to please her autocratic father. It was the story of every rich, entitled noble he'd ever met in one form or another, and yet somehow Gabrielle had found a way to splash them both across a thousand glossy tabloids—something no other woman had managed in a very long time. She claimed it had been unconsciously done on her part—he thought it far more likely a deliberate act. Her first chance for a full-scale rebellion, for all the world to see. Maybe the perfect princess had indeed chafed against her role—but not in the way she claimed tonight. Perhaps the tabloids had been the best weapon she could come up with, and he the best victim.

"I am your husband," he said, as mildly as he could, his gaze trained on her face. "It is my duty to protect you."

"Even from yourself?" she asked wryly.

He did not respond—he only watched her reach for her wineglass, tracking the slight tremor in her hand. She pressed the glass to her lips. Luc wondered how he could find such a simple gesture so erotic when he wasn't sure a single word she spoke was the truth. She was a liar—she had deceived him and made a mockery of him in front of the world—and still he wanted her.

He wanted her—needed her—with a fury he could neither explain nor deny. It had started as he'd watched her smile her way through a week in Nice, had simmered as she'd walked toward him down the aisle in Miravakia, and had only been stoked to an inferno in her absence. Now that he had tracked

her down she was so close to him—just across the tiny table—
and he burned.

"I am no threat to you," he told her, though he knew he
made himself a liar as he said it. He didn't care.

Her eyes met his, large and knowing across the table.

"You'll forgive me, I think," she said, with that same wry
twist of her mouth, turning his own words back on him, "if
somehow I cannot quite believe you."

The dinner passed in a strange, tense bubble. Gabrielle was
aware of far too much—the scrape of her blouse against her
overheated skin, the swell of her breasts against the silky
material of her bra, the rush of warm, fragrant air into her
lungs, and always Luc's inflexible, brooding presence that she
was convinced she could *feel*. He was too big for the table—
he overwhelmed it, his long legs brushing up against hers at
odd, shocking intervals, his body seeming to block out the
night. She could see, taste, only Luc. She barely touched her
plate of grilled shrimp, and was startled when the waiter
brought them both coffee.

"You don't care for coffee?" Luc asked, in that smooth voice
that sounded so polite and yet set off every alarm in her body.

She kept herself from squirming in her seat only with the
most iron control.

"What makes you say that?" she asked, stalling. She picked
up her cup and blew on the hot liquid, wishing she could cool
herself as easily.

"You made a face," he said. "Or I should say you *almost*
made a face? You are, of course, too well trained to make one
in public."

"I don't think I did anything of the kind," she said stiffly,
aware that he was toying with her, yet unable to do anything
but respond as he intended. It made her feel annoyed at
herself. As if she was a mouse too close to the claws of a cat.

"I am beginning to understand the intricacies of your public face," he told her, eyeing her over his own coffee. His gaze was neither kind nor cutting, but it made Gabrielle shiver slightly. She decided to blame the slight breeze. "Soon enough I will be able to read you, and what will you do then?"

"If you could read me," she replied lightly, "you would not have to wonder if I was lying to you."

"There is that."

"Then I hope you're a quick study," she threw at him, riding the wave of emotion that flashed through her.

"Oh, I am," he promised her, his dark voice hinting at things she was sure she didn't want to understand. Their eyes met and her breath caught—and then his gaze traveled over her mouth, pointedly.

Gabrielle swallowed and put her coffee down.

"Are you finished?" he nearly purred, raising a hand to signal the waiter. He never looked away from her face. "We can head home whenever you like."

Head home? she repeated to herself. *Together?*

That was impossible. Surely he didn't expect…?

"Home?" she echoed nervously. "You mean Cassandra's house?"

"Is that her name?" He sounded bored. And also amused.

"Surely you have a hotel somewhere?" she said.

His lips twitched. "I own a number of hotels," he said. "Most of them in Asia—though there are a few in France and Italy as well. None in this country."

"That's not what I mean," she said crossly. "You can't stay at Cassandra's house with—with—" She cut herself off. Flustered.

"With you?" He finished for her, his gaze enigmatic. "Can't I?"

"Of course not. That's ridiculous. We are not…" She looked down at her lap and saw her hands had curled into fists. Resolutely, she unclenched them both and placed them before her on the table, like a civilized person. "And you can't think that we—"

"I meant what I said earlier," Luc said—so unbending, so resolute. His gaze serious. "I expect you to be my wife—in every sense of the term."

"You're insane!" she whispered, too overwrought to scream as she wanted to do. Though she felt the force of it as if she had made enough noise to tear at her throat. Or perhaps that was the other part of her—the part that was fascinated by him? The part that secretly wanted to be his wife, *in every sense of the term*, just as he'd said. She drew in a jagged breath.

"Tell yourself whatever you need to tell yourself, Gabrielle," he threw back at her, his dark eyes glittering. He leaned forward, seeming to loom over the table, dwarfing her before him. "You play the offended innocent so well, but you're fooling no one."

"I have no idea what you're talking about," she blustered, with all the bravado she could summon.

"All I have to do is touch you," Luc murmured, reaching over and capturing her hand with his. He laced his fingers with hers—the contact shocking, intimate. Flesh against flesh. Electricity leapt between them, igniting her blood—making her gasp. Her breasts felt heavy, and once more she felt that hot, wet need between her legs.

His dark eyes shone with a hard, masculine triumph.

"And again," he said quietly, with an intense satisfaction that she couldn't mistake, "you are made a liar."

Outside the restaurant, Gabrielle fought for composure while Luc called for his driver.

She wanted to rage at Luc—for his high-handedness, for his ruthlessness, but most of all because she feared that he knew things about her body, about *her*, that she was afraid to discover.

She knew she could not survive this. Him. No matter how

loudly her body clamored, no matter the searing ache radiating out from her core. He would change her, mark her. She couldn't let it happen—and yet, as he had proved, all he had to do was lay his fingers against hers and her body betrayed her in an instant.

She was desperate.

But she had to keep her plastic, perfect smile on her face, no matter what. She had to act delighted when Luc returned to her side, and she had to gaze at him adoringly as they waited for the car. All of which she executed flawlessly, as if she really was the carefree new bride he wanted her to be.

What would it be like if I was that blissful new bride? a traitorous voice whispered. If she had not run—if she had stayed with him that evening—where would they be now?

Gabrielle shook the disturbing questions away, and concentrated on maintaining her composure. Luc accused her of being an actress, as if it was something shameful, but he was lucky she'd had the training she'd had. Without it she might have shattered into pieces right there on the street and left it to the photographers to clean up the mess.

"Finally," Luc said, much closer than she'd expected, as his sleek black car approached the curb.

His lips barely touched the delicate shell of her ear, and yet she felt the hot lash of desire spike in her belly and then flood through her body. She hated that he affected her this way. She hated that her knees weakened at the thought of the night to come, even when her mind balked.

There would be no *night to come*. She barely knew the man! She'd been in his company for all of six hours in total—including their wedding! He was delusional if he thought she would leap into bed with him—no matter if he was, technically, her husband. No matter if her own body seemed to want him in ways she was afraid to explore.

She knew that she would be burned without recognition—

forever altered—if he got his way, and she could not allow it to happen. She had to hold on to what little sense of self she'd somehow wrested from the ruins of the last week—from her whole previous life as a dutiful, controlled princess. It was as if she'd finally woken up from a very long bad dream, and here was a nightmare in human form, threatening to suck her back down under.

But she kept her smile firmly in place as Luc handed her into the backseat of the luxurious sedan. She opened her mouth to thank him, but his attention was caught by one of the men standing in the pack of photographers jostling for position around the car.

Luc stiffened almost imperceptibly, and the harsh curve of his mouth went glacial. It was frightening to watch—though Gabrielle allowed herself a quick moment of relief that he was not looking at *her* that way. As if he would like to tear the man apart with his bare hands, and was strongly considering doing so.

"Silvio—what a delightful surprise," Luc said in deeply sardonic Italian. "What brings you to California? A vacation?"

However angry he had been with her—and was still—Gabrielle knew he had never used that horribly cold, vicious tone before. Not on her. Not yet. She shivered. The other man, obviously a paparazzo if the camera slung across his neck was any indication, seemed oblivious. He even smiled at Luc, a bland and casual smile that drew attention to his cold eyes, as if he could not sense the danger.

"Where my prince goes, I follow," he replied in the same language, his mockery all too evident. "How's married life treating you, Luc? Is it all you dreamed now that you've finally run her to ground?"

"And more," Luc said, baring his teeth. "I'm sure I'll see you around."

"You can count on it," Silvio shot back.

"I always do," Luc retorted, that feral smile in place.

Then, much worse, he climbed into the car next to Gabrielle, closed the door, and turned all that icy ferocity on her.

CHAPTER EIGHT

Luc was silent as the sleek car hugged the twists and turns that led up into the hills—but it was a kind of silence that was much worse, Gabrielle thought with mounting trepidation, than anything he might have said.

She could *feel* him. Without looking at him—because she didn't dare—she could sense the way he lounged against the butter-soft leather seat, his indolent posture at odds with the dark power that seemed to hum through him like a live wire. She could feel anger come off of him in waves, like heat. The way his dark eyes consumed her sent terrified shivers down her spine. He seemed to fill the entire car with his presence— crowding her, pressing against her, cornering her—though he was not touching her at all.

How could he do such a thing? How could he seem to possess her without so much as lifting a finger?

She called her reaction terror, but some deep feminine knowledge inside her knew better and whispered the truth. Her breasts felt swollen, surging against the confines of her bra, her blouse. Her breath came too fast, too shallow. Her legs felt restless, and a kind of panic made her want to squirm, to run, to scream. It clawed at her throat and teased at her eyes, and she didn't know what she would do if the pressure grew stronger. Would she burst? Explode?

The car pulled up in front of Cassandra's house, and Gabrielle stared at the pretty Craftsman façade—though she did not see it. She was aware only of his quiet, brooding presence behind her as she stepped from the car. She could feel only her own body's panicked response in the staccato beat of her heart, the heat that suffused her, and the tell-tale dampness between her legs.

How could this be happening? When he seemed so angry—so furious with her? Had she no self-respect at all?

But then she already knew that she did not—could not have. A woman with self-respect would surely not have found herself married to a stranger. She would not have married him, and if she had she would not have abandoned him at their wedding, only to be pursued across the world like some runaway bride. Whether she called it weakness or a lack of self-respect, it worked out to the same thing in the end—didn't it?

"Come," Luc said, taking her hand with his in a dictatorial gesture that pulled her closer to his body—too close. His dark gaze seemed to glitter in the dark night, and his mouth pulled into a merciless line. "It is time to stop playing these games."

She did not exactly *run*. She opened the door and then hurried away from him. Luc watched her move with a quiet satisfaction, knowing she walked far too quickly for someone unaffected.

He knew better. He'd seen the high color on that gorgeous face of hers. He'd watched her growing agitation on the drive home.

Seeing Silvio—that gutter-swine—had only solidified the rage he'd been carrying around ever since the humiliating moment he'd realized that his perfect, proper princess had in fact *done a runner* and left him to face the consequences of her choices. Silvio was the worst of the paparazzi who had hounded Luc for years. And he'd been after a story like this for ages—ever since Luc had lost his temper in what seemed now like another life, and blackened the lowlife's eyes at his parents' funeral.

That had been the last time Luc had been splashed across so many tabloids—the last time he'd excited so much scandalous comment. Since then there had been the odd photograph, depending on who he happened to be dating, and the usual complaint that he was "notoriously reclusive." When in truth he simply did not wish to fund Silvio's parasitic existence.

Damn Gabrielle for playing right into Silvio's hands. Damn his *wife* for giving scum like Silvio ammunition.

But Luc knew exactly how to make her pay.

His gaze lingered on the sway of her hips, the twitch of her hair against her shapely back. He smiled—hard.

He was looking forward to it.

Inside the house, Gabrielle fled across the living room and found herself face-to-face with her reflection in the sliding doors. She placed her palms against the cool glass, surprised when her hands didn't sizzle with all the heat she was sure she was letting off.

Luc did not turn on the lights when he came in behind her. A streetlight from outside spilled into the room, lengthening the shadows he stalked through, as quiet and as dangerous as some lethal jungle cat.

She was his prey. She could feel it in a primal way, down into her bones.

"There is nowhere left to run, Gabrielle." His voice was so low. Menacing. It seemed to vibrate against her spine, sending waves of reaction radiating out and consuming her.

"I'm not running," she said, tilting her chin up. She hated how childish she sounded. So pointlessly defiant. He laughed. It sent a new chill through her.

"You should have known how this would end," he continued, as if she hadn't spoken. "You should have known better."

"I don't know you at all," she said—but it came out as little more than a whisper.

And it was a lie. She knew things she would prefer to ignore. Her body knew him better than she wanted to admit— and it cried out for him in the darkened room, no matter how she longed to deny it.

"You are mine." Possession and finality rang in his voice.

"You do not own me," she breathed at him, bracing herself against the glass door and straightening her back against him. "No one can *own* another person!"

"Does it make you feel safer to think so?" he asked, mocking her. "Do you think political correctness will help you tonight?"

She didn't know what she thought—she only knew he was too close, and every cell in her body screamed at her to flee. To do anything and everything she could to escape what was coming as surely as day followed night. To hold on to herself—because he would raze her to ashes in his wake, and who knew what she might be when he was finished?

Luc stopped behind her. His hands came up to hold her shoulders. He traced the shape of her arms beneath his palms. The reflection in the glass blurred his features slightly—made him seem more approachable, somehow, less remote.

Or maybe it was the way he touched her that made her blood sing his name, and washed away any half-formed thoughts she might have had left of escaping him.

She felt the warmth of his skin through the thin fabric of her blouse. She felt the surprising hardness of his palms as they moved along the lines of her body.

As if he was testing her. Training her. The thought made her belly clench.

She shuddered, and felt herself weaken. She who was already so weak where he was concerned. A delicious, terri- fying languor stole through her, moving like fire in the wake of his hands, daring her to ease back against the hard, solid length of his body, as if she could no longer hold her head high of her own volition. She felt him against every inch of her back—too hot to the touch.

She should say something. She should remind him that they were strangers. She should try to put him off somehow. It was too soon—it would always be too soon. She should refuse to do whatever it was he was planning to do—was already doing.

She knew that there would be no turning back.

But she couldn't seem to move.

He used his mouth then—heat and breath against her temple, her neck, the fine bones and hollows near her collarbone.

She had the impression of fire—flames licking from his mouth to ravage her body—and then he was turning her to face him, tilting her head back. She saw his dark and troubled gaze before his mouth fastened to hers, and then she could think of nothing but the way he kissed her.

She was lost. Again and again and again.

His mouth plundered hers, taking control and molding her mouth to his will. This time Gabrielle knew how to kiss him back, but she could do little more than that as he took her mouth with the same ruthlessness as he'd done everything else.

It was as if a storm raged through her—crushing and incinerating everything in its path. Gabrielle felt the power and strength of his mouth against hers, and everything else was part of the inferno that swept through her. Fire. Awe. Panic.

She pulled away from him—wanting to wrench herself out of his arms, but managing only to put the barest breath of space between them.

She would be lost forever if she let this happen. Something powerful and old inside her had been telling her this since she'd laid eyes on him, and she could feel the truth of it resonate through her, sending aftershocks through her skin, her blood, her mind. Her lips burned. And—most treacherous of all—she yearned for him. For more.

She searched his dark eyes, his implacable face, but found only stone. Iron.

She felt dizzy, suddenly—overwhelmed. He was so remote, too powerful, and she knew that she could not emerge from this the same as she was now. He would alter her, change her, forever marking her life into *before* and *after*—and she was terrified that *after* would mean the end of her, of who she was, of who she wanted to be. He would reduce her, dominate her, and she had no idea what would become of her. Gabrielle felt her lips part on a half-formed protest, or perhaps a plea—anything to stop the storm that was Luc Garnier, anything to put more space between what remained hers and what he would take.

But he stopped her with another kiss, this one even more frightening for all it was gentle. Gabrielle felt herself shake against him.

"Enough," he said quietly against her mouth. "The time for talking is over."

She went straight to his head, far more potent than any alcohol he'd ever tasted.

Luc kissed her again and again, bending her backward over his arm, holding her firmly against him so he could roam freely across her mouth, her neck. She tasted like nothing he had ever imagined before—sweet, addictive, and so hot it burned to touch her. It burned worse when he stopped.

She kissed like an innocent. Like the lies she'd told.

Tasting her, Luc wanted to believe every last one of them.

He groaned and swung her around, pulling her down with him onto the sofa and settling her across his lap, her knees on either side of him. He sucked in a breath as their hips made contact. He surged against her softness and made her moan in response.

Luc's hands roamed over the curves he'd longed to possess since he'd first laid eyes on her. He pressed his open mouth against her neck, and thrilled to hear the low keening sound she made in the back of her throat. Impatient to see more of her, he pulled the silky blouse over her head, baring her breasts to his view.

"Please…" she said, her voice deep and husky, cascading over him. With a single, sure motion, Luc released the clasp of her bra and tossed the filmy piece of lingerie aside.

Her breasts jutted before him, firm and proud, her nipples standing to attention at eye level. He could no more resist taking one tender bud into his mouth than he could resist his next breath. He covered the other breast with his hand, testing her shape, learning her curves.

Braced above him, trapped between his hardness and the heat of his mouth, Gabrielle swayed in his arms. Her thick, luxuriant hair fell around them in wild waves, smelling of flowers and musk, cocooning them together.

When her moans grew throaty, Luc switched his mouth to the other nipple, laving the tight peak with his tongue while his hand explored the breast he'd left behind.

"Luc—" She gasped out his name and he liked it. He liked the desperation in her tone, the blind need on her face.

She was his. He would never let her forget it again.

"Please," she cried. "I don't—I don't know—"

He sucked her nipple into his mouth, hard, moved his hips against hers, and she exploded in his arms.

Her head fell back, exposing her throat as the shudders racked her slender body. Triumph and a dark, keening sort of need ignited Luc's blood. He wanted to be inside her. He wanted to personally investigate every last lie her trim body with its surprising lushness wanted to tell. He wanted to explore them all, with his mouth hot against her and himself deep within her, until the only truth she knew was him.

She lifted her head as if it was far too heavy, and blinked at him, dazed.

The worst part was that he no longer cared what she was lying about, how she had deceived him. As long as he could touch her, he didn't care about a damned thing.

It made him mean.

"Are you always so responsive?" he asked acidly. "Or is this a show for my benefit?"

She shook her head slightly, a faraway look on her lovely face and then a slight frown between her eyes. She shifted position, still straddling him, and Luc bit back a groan as the movement ground her harder against him.

"Why would I put on a show for you?" she asked.

"Touché," he muttered, and claimed her mouth once more.

Only as he explored her mouth, wondering if he would ever get used to the kick of it, did it occur to him that she had sounded bewildered instead of spiteful.

He thrust the thought aside.

He had to get inside this woman—his wife—or go insane. *Now.*

CHAPTER NINE

GABRIELLE had to be dreaming.

She could almost convince herself of it—a foreign country, a strange house, the compelling and dangerous man who held her in his strong arms and reduced her to a shivering wreck. Aftershocks still skated along her limbs, so much concentrated pleasure making the air feel heavy around her. But Luc's skin was warm next to hers, his kisses drugging and irresistible.

She knew she was awake—more awake, perhaps, than she had ever been before.

"Luc…" She tested his name, tested whether or not she was dreaming.

"Hush." His mouth came down on hers, a tidal wave of sensation crashing over her. If she could have gasped or screamed—but he was everywhere, crowding her and holding her, molding her body to his.

He swept her up into his arms then, breaking from another scorching kiss to haul her tight against his hard chest. He rose from the sofa in a single, effortless movement, not trumpeting his lean, whipcord strength but using it without thought—which made it that much more shocking. Breathtaking. Gabrielle felt a flutter of reaction steal through her. His dark eyes gleamed in the shadows, her throat felt dry, and she worried that she had lost the ability to speak.

She could only stare at the uncompromising planes of his face as he moved through the house, holding her in this parody of lovers on a wedding night. The wedding night she had run away from. Would he have carried her this way a week ago, in the dressing room of her father's *palazzo*? Or later that night, in the suite of rooms he'd reserved across the island? Would she have felt this same way, as if she was under his spell, enchanted, helpless to look away from him for even a moment? She could remember too well how commanding and overbearing he had seemed in his morning coat—his shoulders so broad, his torso so lean and muscled, his eyes a darker gray than his coat. He was even more disconcerting tonight, bothering her, *troubling* her in every sense of the word. A deep shudder moved through her then, starting deep inside and working its way out. She was afraid. So deeply afraid.

But Gabrielle had to be honest with herself, and the truth was stripped bare and evident as she looked at him, caught in his gaze as surely as a fly in a spiderweb. She felt the steel bands of his strong arms hold her easily—the heat of him soaking into her, surrounding her, while leftover pleasure still hummed through her body.

It was not fear that warmed her blood, that made her feel so feverish and out of control. It was not fear that made her crave more of his hot mouth, his clever tongue, his masterful hands.

It was desire.

Gabrielle might not have felt it before—not like this—but she knew what it was. She knew what the ache between her thighs meant. What the tightness of her nipples meant. She thought she knew exactly what it all meant, and even while it terrified her she could admit that something in her thrilled to the battery of new sensation. Welcomed it. Wanted it.

The same old doubts and fears crowded into her head then, louder and more insistent. She blinked and closed her eyes against him, as if that could block him out, even as she clung to him—even as he moved with that same inexorable force through Cassandra's home.

She did not know this man. This marriage was a horrible mistake, foisted upon her by her father. She had spent twenty-five years in blind obedience, but she was blind no longer, and she knew without a shadow of a doubt that marriage to Luc Garnier would destroy whatever burgeoning independence she'd discovered in the short week since she'd found the courage to stand up for herself.

He would take her over completely, and it started here. It had already started—the moment he'd appeared at the door. She would disappear into him, drown completely.

It was already happening—every time he touched her.

"Luc—" she said again, pulling back from him, suddenly aware of how helpless she was, held high against his chest this way. How clearly it underscored his power and her lack of it. Never in a lifetime of powerlessness had she seen it so starkly, so clearly.

His eyes gleamed, and then everything tilted wildly. Gabrielle gasped even as she registered that he'd tossed her onto the wide four-poster bed in the master bedroom as if she weighed no more than a feather. She bounced once, and then his hard body sprawled across hers, pinning her to the mattress. Gabrielle froze, while her heart beat wildly within her chest.

Sensation fed into sensation—his hands roamed from her hips to her shoulders, then around her waist to test the shape of her bottom and trace the indentation of her spine—until Gabrielle could hardly tell the difference between them. There was only this fire, this need. He was heavy and hard all over. He crushed her into the mattress, pinning her, stealing the breath from her body…and she gloried in it. She felt electri-fied from each point of contact, from the dark addiction that was his clever, cruel mouth against hers, from the wall of his chest above her, from the hard muscled thigh that pressed intimately against her own. Her breasts throbbed and she felt herself melt, hot and wet beneath him. Her body was ready for him—ready and desperate and *now*.

He braced himself on his hands, and Gabrielle fumbled with the buttons on his shirt, the material as soft as a cloud beneath her fingers. She had to put her hands on his skin—to see if she was the only one feverish with this need, to see if she could feel the same relentless desire in him. Muttering a curse, he twisted until he could rip the shirt from his torso, then tossed it to the floor. And then there was nothing between her breasts and his muscles, hard-packed beneath his tight, smooth flesh. Only her skin against his skin.

The delicious slide of it, the textures and the feel of so much strength so close against her, made her mouth go dry.

Her hands trembled as she ran them across the fascinating planes of his chest, through the dusting of dark hair between his hard pectoral muscles and arrowing down his taut abdomen, the differences between them making her shiver and want. She throbbed everywhere. She could feel her pulse pound in her head, her heart and between her legs. Remembering the joy of it when he'd done it to her, she leaned closer and placed her open mouth on the tight male nipple she discovered. He groaned, and she turned her attention to the other nipple.

"No more," he muttered in Italian, dark and gruff into the crook of her neck.

The same place on his body tasted of salt and something else—something that reminded her of Cypress trees and Adriatic breezes.

"Do not tease me."

With deft, sure hands, he stripped the rest of his clothes from his body, and then did the same for Gabrielle, lifting her hips as if she weighed no more than one of the down pillows she lay against, pulling off her trousers with ruthless efficiency.

Then he laid his naked body against hers, making Gabrielle gasp. She felt the crisp hair on his thighs press against her own smoother ones. His hard chest rubbed deliciously against her nipples. She could feel his erection strain against her softness, making her dizzy with want. Need. *Luc.*

He braced himself on his hands above her, and looked down at her. The frank hunger in his gaze excited her almost more than she could bear.

She felt wanton. Powerful.

"Don't tease me," she whispered, daring to throw his own words back at him.

His mouth curved, but it was less a smile than something purely male and sexual. It connected with something deep inside Gabrielle and made her ache.

Everywhere.

"Your wish is my command, Your Royal Highness," he murmured.

And then, without any warning, he twisted his hips and thrust into her.

He came up hard against her, hearing her cry out as he did so. It was so unexpected—so surprising—that Luc stopped moving, his breath scraping in and out of his chest as he stared down at her in shock.

"You are a virgin." It was not a question.

Her eyes swam with surprised tears as she looked up at him, her small hands braced against his chest as if holding him off.

"You should have told me—" But he cut himself off. She had told him in every way she could. Her wariness of him, though she had looked at him with such sensual curiosity at their wedding reception. Her artless kisses. The innocence he had first wanted to honor, and then had cynically believed she was faking. When exactly should she have explained that she was an untouched virgin? When he was having a temper tantrum over that piece of filth paparazzo? He hadn't wanted to believe the evidence before him.

But he hadn't meant to hurt her.

"Yes," she said after a moment, squirming against him. He thought she was trying to get away from him, little realizing that her movements had quite the opposite effect. He was deep inside her, all the way to the hilt, and yet she kept wriggling, drawing him in even further. It was torture. Sweet, delicious torture.

"Of course I'm a virgin!" Again she moved restlessly, crossly, beneath him. "What does it matter?"

He searched her face. She was flushed as much from anger as passion, but he knew her body now. He knew how she responded. He moved experimentally, just a roll of his hips, and she gasped again, the color on her cheeks deepening. Confusion washed across her face, and she bit down on her full lower lip.

"Did that hurt?" he asked quietly. He did it again, and her breath came out in a rush.

"I…I don't know…" she stammered, her gaze almost troubled.

"I would not have hurt you if I'd known," he told her. He traced the curve of her neck with his fingertips, down to her perfect breasts. Regret seared into him, and he kissed one proud crest, then the other. An apology of sorts.

"If you'd known…?" she repeated. She blinked. "Because you thought…?" She didn't finish the sentence, but stared up at him in sudden outrage. Her hands balled up into fists against his chest.

"Yes, I *thought*." He rolled his hips again, pleased to see her outrage fade into a tiny sigh, her hands unclenching and sliding down toward his hips. "You are not fresh from the convent. I did not negotiate our marriage with your Mother Superior. You are a grown woman."

He did not say *I thought you were a liar.*

He felt her softness and her heat surround him. She cradled him between her thighs.

"No," she said, her voice breathy, "I was not in a convent. Not technically. But of course there was no… I could never—" She broke off, her cheeks turning a deep shade of rose.

Inside his chest, something stirred to life and expanded, triumphant.

Mine, he thought. He wanted to roar it. No other man had ever touched her. No other man ever would. She was his. More completely than before.

"For all intents and purposes you might as well have been in a convent," he murmured. "I understand."

He exulted in it.

"Luc…"

His name on her lips excited him. He kissed her deeply. He moved against her slowly, carefully. Deliberately.

"Trust me," he whispered, sinking deep into her, sheathing himself completely in her hot depths.

He built the fire with long, slow kisses. He fanned each and every flame that he could think of, kissing the elegant line of her neck, reaching around to hold her bottom on the shelf of his hands. He set an easy, unhurried pace—encouraging her to do more than simply accept his thrusts. Soon she moved to meet him, her hips rising of their own accord, as if she couldn't help herself. Her legs moved restlessly, then found their way to rest on the back of his. His hands caressed her and guided her, reaching between them and stroking her in her most sensitive place until her breath came in short, hot pants and her head thrashed from side to side against the pillows.

Mine, he thought.

When she flew apart, he followed.

* * *

A long time later, Gabrielle woke with a start.

At first she didn't know what could have woken her. But then, almost immediately, she recognized Luc's hard body against her own, sprawling across the bed with one arm carelessly thrown out over her. Had that been what pulled her from sleep? She had never shared a bed with someone else before. It felt strange and almost invasive to have so much big male animal crowding into her space, taking up so much real estate on the mattress that had seemed vast to her before. Tonight it seemed woefully inadequate. He was so *large*.

The events of the long night teased at her, vivid images chasing each other through her head, each one connected to sensations she could still feel in her limbs. She felt used in a way she never had before. She felt like a woman. As if she had finally discovered the purpose of her breasts, her hips. As if she'd been created to give him pleasure, and as if she should glory in it.

Gabrielle looked at Luc as he slept, his firm, cruel mouth soft and almost sweet in slumber, making him appear much more approachable. Younger and smoother. She smiled to herself. It wasn't that he looked boyish—she couldn't imagine Luc as a boy; the harsh lines of his face forbade it somehow— but he seemed so much *less* in sleep. More easily contained, maybe. Less frightening. Less overwhelming. Not so edgy and abrasive. Easier, somehow, to contend with.

She shivered, though she was not cold, and turned, so her back faced him and she could stare into the darkness. Was she changed, as she'd feared? Altered forever? How could she tell? She hadn't expected it to be so…*physical*. She hadn't expected to feel him so deep inside her body, or that having someone invade her in that way would make her feel so small and yet so strong all at the same time. It was so confusing even now. She had known the mechanics of the act, of course, but the execution had been so…*Luc*.

He was like a force of nature. He had hurt her, and then he

had made her feel nearly wrung out from the pleasure he could give her. Even now, wide awake and tormenting herself in the night with questions she wasn't sure she wanted answered, she wanted *him*. His very nearness made her nervous—made her body hum in yearning, even though she could feel aches in various places from new and unusual activity. Even after everything that had already happened she wanted him. Was that more of her abominable weakness? Or was he simply that powerful?

"You are thinking so loudly that no one can sleep," Luc said then, making her flinch away from him in surprise. When she turned over to face him he was watching her, those dark eyes bottomless in the dark of the bedroom.

"I'm sorry," she said automatically. Then wondered why she should apologize for something so ridiculous as his claim that he could hear her *thinking*. He was not supernatural. No matter how he might appear sometimes. "You must be a very light sleeper."

He reached over and traced the frown between her eyes, smoothing it away with his strong fingers. She leaned into his touch the way plants leaned toward the sun, and with as little conscious thought.

"You do not need to worry," he told her in that commanding voice. "I will take care of you."

It sounded like a vow. All his rage from earlier in the evening seemed to have left him. All that ferocity and anger. Though he was no less imposing a figure, lying there so dark and masculine against the sheets, his well-sculpted shoulders broad enough to block out the rest of the room from her view. Gabrielle discovered she was holding her breath and let it go—only to catch it again when his fingers moved to drag across her lips in an unmistakably sensual gesture.

But, "Sleep," he said.

"I don't know what woke me," she whispered. She felt that

speaking in her normal voice would be like talking too loudly in a church. She could sense that a great storm had passed in him—the one that had taken them both over, the one she was still not certain she had survived intact—but she didn't know why. She was afraid to upset the delicate balance that seemed to hover between them. She wanted his eyes to remain so clear and very nearly soft as he looked at her—she wanted his mouth to curve as it did now.

She didn't know why she should want any of those things. Was this what she had feared? Was this how the losing of herself began? Or had it already started—was it already too late?

In the dark room, so late at night, Gabrielle wasn't sure she cared.

"Perhaps I have created a monster," he said, sliding one strong hand around to cup the back of her neck and draw her close to kiss her. "Perhaps you can only rest for a short amount of time before you require me again."

Was he teasing her? In a good-natured way? Gabrielle found this possibility shocking—but no more shocking than her body's immediate response to the feel of his mouth against hers. Her nipples hardened, and she felt herself soften for him. On command. At the slightest touch. Even the faint soreness between her legs failed to keep the desire from coiling in her middle. She slid her hands into his thick black hair, reveling in the texture of it, the shape of his head, his hard body once again moving over hers, crushing her so deliciously beneath him.

But she only whispered, "Perhaps," and lost herself in him once again.

CHAPTER TEN

WHEN Gabrielle woke again, late morning sunshine spilled into the room, disorienting her as she sat up in the big bed.

She knew immediately that Luc was gone—from the bed, from the room—knew even before she looked around to confirm it. His presence was too elemental, too disturbing—she knew she would have sensed it if he was near.

Gabrielle pushed the heavy mass of her hair back from her face, stretched, and took a moment to catalog the various twinges and aches in interesting places in her body. She felt herself flush as she remembered all the ways she'd moved, all the things she'd done, all the things he'd taught her in one short night.

Not that she had been a prude, exactly, before this strange marriage. She might not have done as much with the opposite sex as her contemporaries had. Or, truthfully, anything at all. Her knowledge of men might have been more theoretical than practical. But she'd dreamed, and her dreams had never been particularly tame. She had assumed her imagination filled in the blanks adequately enough. But she had dreamed about sex the way she'd dreamed about love—all so vague and hidden in soft focus.

Nothing about Luc Garnier was in soft focus. He was vivid and challenging and shockingly physical.

Gabrielle swung out of bed and pulled on the silk robe she'd left draped over the plush armchair near the dark mahogany armoire. She tiptoed over to the bedroom door. It was open a crack, and she stood near it, straining to hear. From far off she heard the unmistakable deep tones of Luc's voice. She eased the door shut and realized that her breathing had gone shallow—her flush deepened and spread. What had he done to her? And how could she possibly face him now, knowing what it had been like between them in the dark—in the bed?

Pressing her hands against her cheeks, as if that could calm her, Gabrielle turned and headed for the *en suite* master bathroom. She was, apparently, no longer able to control herself, but she could certainly control how she looked. Best not to appear before him half-naked and wanton, with her hair in disarray. Gabrielle might not have known what to do about the intimidating man who had suddenly become so intimate with her, but she certainly knew how to dress herself to hide her emotional state. It was one of her gifts.

After a shower—which she knew she drew out longer than she should have, so anxious was she about this morning after—Gabrielle blew her hair dry and then took care to dress like the princess she was. Not the Americanized version of herself Luc had been so displeased with the day before.

She chose a pair of cream-colored linen trousers made especially for her by the Miravakian designer she had hired to oversee her official wardrobe, and paired them with a whisper-soft cashmere sweater in a champagne hue. Then she arranged her hair into its usual French twist, smooth and elegant. She added the slightest dab of scent behind each ear, and put on a pair of pearl studs that announced their pedigree—and hers—with an understated gleam. She chose her makeup with care, deciding that Luc was the kind of man who, like her father, preferred the fantasy of the bare face—little realizing the amount of work and skill it took to produce such a look.

But understated elegance was what Gabrielle was known for and what Luc had signed on for—the pinnacle of her personal achievement to date, she thought then, her mouth twisting into a wry smile.

Casting her thoughts aside, since they did her no good, Gabrielle eyed herself critically in the full-length mirror on the back of the closet door. She would do. Gone was last night's wild creature, with her uninhibited hair and bare feet. In her place was the Princess Gabrielle she had always been. Muted. Pastel. *Soothing.*

It was her armor.

Luc looked up when she walked out through the sliding glass doors onto the deck, where he was taking one in a series of business calls that had started early in the morning. He murmured a few closing remarks in French, then ordered his assistants to fax him the relevant documents before hanging up and giving his wife his full attention.

The bright California sunshine spilled over her, highlighting the fine elegance of her features. She looked every inch the well-bred, well-behaved Miravakian princess he had originally believed her to be—from the smooth hair swept back from her face to the quietly sophisticated apparel. This woman standing before him was the one he'd seen in Nice—not a hair out of place, oozing composure.

She nodded at him, her cultivated social smile at the ready. "I'm sorry that I slept so long this morning," she said. "I hope I haven't kept you waiting."

So polite. As if she had not spent a long, sweaty night in his arms. But, much as Luc wanted to remind her of what had happened between them, he was also relieved to see this version of her. It proved he had not been delusional in Nice— that this *had* been the woman he'd thought he was marrying. And he preferred that the world see only this: the capable, elegant princess, a credit to her country. And, of course, to her husband.

He would be the only one who knew the other side of her. His own, private, uninhibited princess behind closed doors. He nearly smiled at the thought.

"The rest suits you," he replied, rising and beckoning her closer, to take the seat opposite him at a small wrought-iron table. The housekeeper had prepared a tray—a selection of ripe, inviting Californian fruits and fresh-baked pastries. "Come. Do you take coffee in the morning?"

"Please," Gabrielle replied, settling herself into the chair with an unstudied grace that Luc found mesmerizing. She nodded her thanks when he poured her a cup of steaming black liquid from the carafe in the center of the table, and cradled the cup in her hands.

"It's a lovely morning," she remarked, and then talked for a few moments about the differences in temperature between Miravakia and Los Angeles, and her delight in the unexpected similarities between the two places—all in that same well-modulated, polite tone.

Luc recognized the fact that she was handling him with consummate skill—as if they were complete strangers seated next to each other at a formal dinner. Acting the perfect hostess, making perfect small talk to ease any possible awkwardness, smoothing her way into their shared morning with bright words and an easy tone.

She was a natural at it, he thought in satisfaction and some amusement.

He wondered if it was difficult for her—particularly today, when so much had happened between them the night before. He wondered how she felt—and then had to check a laugh at the notion that he, Luc Garnier, was concerned about a woman's feelings.

The last woman whose feelings had interested him at all

had been his mother, and that had been an issue of survival rather than concern. Vittoria Giacinta Garnier had been as histrionic as her name suggested. She had tyrannized the household with her ever-shifting moods, making her feelings the centerpiece not only of her own life but of her husband's and her son's as well. Her gravitational pull had been like a black hole, sucking them all in.

"Does that amuse you?" Gabrielle asked, jolting him out the past. She placed her cup back on the table and folded her hands neatly in her lap. "I assure you I would not like to live so far from Miravakia, but I'm surprised to discover that Los Angeles is not as barbaric as I had been led to believe."

"And what of your husband?" Luc asked. He had promised himself that he would go easy on her, having misjudged her so severely. Yet the words seemed to come out anyway, despite what he'd decided. "Is *he* as barbaric as you expected?" He imagined she thought so, and yet somehow he could not bring himself to regret the events of the previous night, or her surprising innocence. Which was his now, to cultivate as he chose.

Color bloomed high on her cheekbones, making Luc toy with the notion that she could read his suddenly graphic thoughts. He rather thought her flush would be significantly more pronounced if she could.

"I had no such expectation," she said quietly. Then, with every appearance of serenity save her flushed skin, she adroitly changed the subject.

"You do that so well," Luc said. She raised her brows in question. Even that was faultlessly polite. "Divert the conversation from subjects you do not wish to discuss."

Genuine humor warmed her face then, making him realize he had not seen it before—which was, he thought, a terrible shame. She was beautiful. Stunning, with that smile—an authentic one, warm and real.

"A necessary skill for someone in my position, I think," she said. "It's often helpful to talk of anything and everything save the one thing the person you're talking to would most like to discuss." She swept her eyes down. "I believe that when men excel at it, they call it diplomacy."

"Do you enjoy your position?" he asked, not sure where the question came from and ignoring that last little dig. He was trying to merge the different versions of Gabrielle together into one: the perfect bride, nervous and skittish; the runaway paparazzi-baiting liar; the wild, excited woman who had trembled beneath him; and this gracious, elegant woman who laughed on the one hand and yet looked as if a tornado could not ruffle her composure. He was not sure how all of them could be the same woman. She fascinated him.

Like any other puzzle, he assured himself. He would figure her out, too, and then lose the knife's-edge intensity of his current interest in her. It was only a matter of time.

"I have been my father's hostess since I was quite young," Gabrielle said. She picked up her coffee cup again, and took a delicate sip. She tilted her head slightly, considering. "I have always been aware that we represent not just ourselves, but our country. I enjoy that." She looked at him for a moment, then returned her eyes to her coffee. "Do you do a great deal of entertaining? I imagine you must, as head of such a vast empire."

"No." Luc wished he had not spoken so quickly, so matter-of-factly, when he saw her stiffen almost imperceptibly in her chair. "But it is not only your life that has altered with this marriage, Gabrielle. Mine has as well. It is time I recognized some of the responsibilities that I have ignored until now."

"I would not have thought you were the sort of man who ignored responsibilities of any kind," she replied after a moment. He did not know what to do with the odd sensation that gripped him then, at her easy assumption that he was a responsible sort of man—and that she believed this with such casual certainty and so dismissed it.

"You must understand that when my parents died I was only twenty-three," Luc said, shrugging. "I had to seize control of my father's company or allow all that he had worked for to fall into the hands of others." He had no intention of telling her the truth of that battle—how many had betrayed him, how many lifelong so-called friends he had been forced to jettison. But Luc was not a man who looked back. He smiled. "I became quite focused."

"Yes," she said. "You are known for it. It is impressive. Even threatening, I imagine." She smiled, as if to lessen the sting of her words.

"I consider that a compliment," Luc said, lounging in his chair. "I have worked hard to be considered a threat."

"And you have achieved your goal," she said dryly.

She reached over to the table, putting her cup down and picking up a bright red strawberry—which drove any thought he might have had of responding to her dry tone out of his head. Luc watched her pop the dark red berry between her decadent lips, and felt himself harden in response. But he had decided that he could not use the powerful sexuality between them as a weapon against her—she was far too innocent for those sorts of sensual games. He had decided, as he fielded the usual barrage of phone calls from his office and enjoyed his morning coffee, that he needed to court his wife. Reel her in. Charm and please her. That had been his initial intention—until she'd run off from the reception. He was resolved that it was still the right thing to do, no matter how desperately, in that moment, he wanted to exchange that strawberry in her mouth for something he would find far more satisfying.

"No one believed I could manage the company…my father's holdings," he continued, trying to bury the urge to turn this breakfast into something far more sensual. "I was just out of university." His eyes connected with hers, and her obvious interest in what he was saying seemed to collide into his gut with the force of a blow. He shrugged again, expansively. "I do not like being told what I can and cannot do."

Only twenty-three back then, Gabrielle thought, *and already so formidable*. She frowned slightly when he stopped talking.

"I'm so sorry," she said. She searched his hard face and imagined she saw something there—something that hinted at the pain he must have felt. Though it was entirely possible she was projecting—*wanting* him to have a softness somewhere that she could relate to, to make it easier for her. There was no visible sign of softness anywhere on the body he maintained at the level of a warrior's physique. She swallowed, and continued. "Twenty-three is still very young. It must have been devastating to lose your parents like that."

"You lost your mother, too, did you not?" he asked, his eyes dark as he looked at her. He was so forbidding, and yet she was not as terrified of him as she had been before. What was this new, strange spell that made her relax slightly around him? She had not the slightest doubt that he was even more dangerous now than he had been before—it was her damned body again, making decisions without consulting her brain. Her body was relaxed—it simply wanted him near. Her brain was far more conflicted.

"Yes," she said finally, jerking her gaze away from his. Gabrielle remembered so few things about her mother—the caress of her hand against a cheek, the whisper of her fine gown against the floor as she walked, the faint memory of a sweet scent and a pretty smile. "But I was barely five. I have far fewer memories of her than I'd like. I imagine losing not one parent but both in your twenties must be much worse."

A muscle tightened in his jaw and he shifted in his chair. His dark gray eyes became, if possible, even darker. Gabrielle felt the shift in the air around them—the way the sun suddenly seemed cold against her shoulders, the way her stomach clenched in reaction to it. To him. But the difference today was that his ferocity was not directed at her.

"It was a difficult time," he said, his voice clipped. He frowned. "But the media frenzy which followed was far worse." His lips thinned. "Such cowardly dogs! So many veiled suspicions—so much rumor and innuendo. As if the truth were not tragic enough."

"That's terrible," Gabrielle murmured, careful to keep her voice quiet, soothing—because she had the feeling he would stop talking altogether if she interrupted him, and she was not entirely sure that if that happened he would not resume intimidating her as he had before. Why was she not more worried at the prospect? Or did she imagine that now that she knew exactly how dark and masterful he was, how he could devastate her—and how she would enjoy it—she would no longer be susceptible to him?

"In truth, there was a part of me that was relieved," he said after a moment, his gaze fixed somewhere in the distance. "I am not proud of it. My parents were focused entirely on themselves. They were not caretakers. My father was, I think, desperately in love with my mother. With her rages, her affairs, her demands. But she was never satisfied with an audience of only one."

Gabrielle had read about his vivacious, famously temperamental mother. Vittoria Garnier had been flamboyant, reckless and luminously beautiful—and, as such, irresistible to the tabloid press, who had fawned over her and skewered her in equal measure. No one ever thought about the child in these situations, did they? Not then and not now. No one ever thought to question what it might be like to see your parents' marriage ripped apart in such a public, horrible way. Your paternity questioned, your mother's lovers cataloged for all the world to see, your privacy up for grabs to the highest bidder with the basest intentions.

Gabrielle felt a deep pang of pity for the child Luc had been, growing up in the midst of such a circus.

But she did not dare to express that to him.

"You have a history with that one man?" she asked then. "The one outside the restaurant last night?"

"Silvio Domenico," Luc said, with disgust, his face turning to stone. "And before you ask, yes—he *is* the same man I was filmed punching in the face at my parents' funeral. 'Grieving Garnier Heir in Graveside Brawl' I believe the headlines screamed." His mouth twisted. "Such dignity. Such respect for the mourning process." She wasn't sure if he meant the tabloids or—worse—himself.

"What happened?" Gabrielle asked. She didn't know why he was talking to her like this, but she was fascinated by this glimpse inside of him. He was so intensely guarded, and yet he was sharing his past with her. Of his own volition.

"He is a piece of filth," Luc said, his eyes blazing. "He is not fit to be scraped from beneath a shoe!" He muttered something obscene in Italian. "But none of this can matter today. It is all in the past."

Not so much in the past, Gabrielle thought with a flash of insight, if the fact that her flight had landed him in the papers again had triggered so much rage. Was it possible that all that fury had not been directed at Gabrielle personally, but at the specter of his mother all those years before?

"I am so sorry," she said, then searched his face, wishing she had not heedlessly wandered into the minefield of his past that way. The fact that she hadn't known made no difference. "I had no idea when I ran that it would affect anyone but me."

Something passed between them, electric and intense. Gabrielle was aware of the wind chimes in the nearby trees, the faint sounds of traffic in the distance, but she was otherwise held spellbound by his commanding gray gaze, unable to look away from him.

"I accept that," he said at length, turning to reach for his phone as it rang, signaling the end of the moment.

He answered the call in French, excusing himself from the table with a quick word and moving inside.

Gabrielle watched him go. He moved with the same focused intent and leashed power that he did everything else. It was only when he disappeared from view that she realized she had not taken a full deep breath since she'd stepped out onto the deck.

She nearly laughed. It seemed her armor worked as well on Luc Garnier as on anyone else—which astonished her.

Because already you believe he is somehow superhuman, she chided herself. *He is only a man.*

But she remembered the way he'd touched her, the way she'd writhed in his arms, and she doubted it.

CHAPTER ELEVEN

GABRIELLE stood on the elegant terrace high over the city of San Francisco and watched as the last of the day sank over the horizon, the beautiful northern Californian city lighting up all around her as darkness claimed it fully. The sun took the warmth of the day with it, and Gabrielle shivered slightly as evening gathered around her. She pulled her silk wrap closer over her bare shoulders, but made no move to go inside.

She could hear Luc's voice echo from behind her, inside the library in the luxurious penthouse suite into which he had retreated to make some business calls. She was just as happy to take a few moments to herself to try to process the past few weeks. To try to breathe.

Had it been only a month? It seemed like so much longer. But it had been nearly four full weeks since Luc had appeared at Cassandra's front door in the Hollywood Hills and everything had changed. *She* felt changed. What worried her was that she couldn't decide if she had changed in the way she had feared so much—what if she'd lost her ability to discern whether or not she had lost herself? Didn't *losing herself* mean that she might not be able to tell?

Luc had arrived in such a fury, but the storm had passed during that long, exquisite first night. It was almost as if Luc had woken up the following morning a different man. He was not suddenly easygoing or relaxed, of course—he was still Luc Garnier, and Gabrielle imagined he could never be affable or pleasant as some men were—but he had changed. He had gone out of his way to be courteous—solicitous, even.

That same day he had swept Gabrielle off for an afternoon trip up the matchless California coast. He had taken her on a helicopter ride over pretty Catalina Island, then out to dinner in the charming town of Santa Barbara, with its mix of Spanish, Mediterranean and Moorish architecture that again reminded Gabrielle of her home in Miravakia. After a dinner of spicy Cajun food, a car had whisked them away, up into the foothills, to the luxurious San Ysidro Ranch, which managed somehow to be as unpretentious as it was elegant. Their exclusive and private cottage house had been a little gem, hidden away in the trees along one of the creek side paths on the ranch property.

And all the while, Luc had talked to Gabrielle as if she was a human being—his wife and not merely his newest business acquisition. Gabrielle had been in very real danger of being swept off her feet by this far more accessible version of Luc— until she'd discovered her own bags at the cottage.

"What is this?" she'd asked, momentarily confused by the sight of them. "Why are my bags here?" It would have been one thing to find a single overnight bag—but she'd seen her entire suite of travel bags lined up neatly against the wall.

"I had everything sent ahead," Luc had said, as if that should have been obvious. He'd studied her for a moment. "Will you not be more comfortable?"

"I do not need *all* my bags, surely?" Gabrielle had said, suspicion sparking in her gut—especially when he'd turned away from her and pulled out his ever-present PDA. "How long will we be away from Cassandra's house? One night? Two?"

"We are not going back," Luc had said, without glancing up from the PDA in his hand. He'd scrolled through a message, frowned, then slid the device back into his pocket. He'd strolled across the room and fixed himself a drink, all without turning to see her astonishment. Suddenly the reality of her situation—of her marriage and her husband—had come flooding back to her. How could a single afternoon have so bewitched her? How could she have forgotten for a moment?

"Of course I have to go back!" she had cried. She'd refused to let the easy charm of the ranch cottage distract her. So what if there was a soaring wood-beamed ceiling and a stone fireplace with a cracking fire within? She refused to be seduced by *furnishings*. "You had no right to just…*decide* that I wasn't returning to Cassandra's house!"

"Are you angry that I did it, or angry that I didn't ask you first?" Luc had asked mildly, settling himself on one of the bright sofas.

He had seemed as perfectly at ease surrounded by the rustic Western décor as he had in Miravakia's grand cathedral. It was as if he molded whatever room he found himself in to his own specifications, and it had seemed to Gabrielle, glaring at him from beside the grand four-poster bed that dominated the room, as if the cottage had been created with Luc Garnier in mind. It was maddening.

"I am angry that you seem to have no regard whatsoever for my feelings on this or any other issue," Gabrielle had replied. Perhaps the shockingly romantic day had lulled her into a false sense of security. It was the only thing that could explain her sudden boldness.

"We are on our honeymoon, are we not?" Luc had asked, still in that mild way. But Gabrielle had felt a frisson of alarm—or awareness—skitter down her spine. There had been steel beneath his tone.

"I…I don't know…" she had said. Honestly. She'd sucked in a breath and dared, "I've told you that I think this marriage was a mistake."

She'd expected the rage she'd seen the night before—the sardonic remarks, the intimidation, the blistering fury. But he had not done any of the things she'd expected.

"So you have," he'd said. He had been unreadable in that moment, only watching her from across the room. He'd risen to his feet, never taking his eyes from hers, and inclined his head. "The fault is mine, I think. Perhaps I need to concentrate on more exciting honeymoon activities than today's touristy adventures. Perhaps that would put you in a better frame of mind where our marriage is concerned?"

"I don't think *activities* are going to change the fact that I—" Gabrielle had begun, but her words had dried up on her tongue, because he'd pulled the tails of his shirt from his trousers with a quick jerk of his wrists. His dark brows had arched—challenging her.

"I beg your pardon?" he had said, his mild tone at odds with the sudden sexual heat that had filled the room. "You were saying?"

Then, still maintaining that disturbing, intoxicating eye contact, he'd slowly unbuttoned the shirt and shrugged out of it. She had been the one to blink, to let her gaze fall—indeed, she'd been powerless to resist.

Gabrielle had not been prepared for the sight of him in the cheery light of the cottage and the fire instead of the dark of the previous night's bedroom. His chest was all hard planes and fascinating dips, the wide expanse of his pectoral muscles narrowing to a tight abdomen and lean hips. Dark hair dusted his muscles, making him seem even more impossibly male. He was gorgeous. Beautiful. And Gabrielle had been seized with the urge to taste every bit of his golden skin that she could see.

But then he'd made everything even worse by raking his trousers off, stepping out of them stark naked.

"What are you doing?" Gabrielle had managed to whisper, while her heart had hammered at the walls of her chest and the blood had pumped so loudly in her ears she'd thought it might permanently deafen her.

He'd stood before her with arrogant nonchalance and without a shred of modesty. But then he had nothing to be modest about. Gabrielle hadn't been able to help herself—her eyes had been drawn almost against her will to that place between his legs that she had *felt* the night before—in the kind of detail that it made her feel dizzy to remember—but had previously only *seen* on sculptures in museums.

She'd gulped. If she'd been wearing pearls, she might have clutched them. His maleness had hung thick and proud before him, and as she'd looked at it, it had stirred to life. She'd felt her body respond—her breasts grow heavy, and that wet, coiling hunger roll to life in her groin, fanning out and lighting her afire. She had been fascinated. Her body had simply wanted him. Again. *Always.*

As if his male organ had read her mind it had thickened—hardening until it stood away from his flat belly.

Her eyes had flown to his, silver and amused in the firelight.

"I am going to sit in the hot tub out on the patio," Luc had said lazily. He'd reached over and picked up his drink, as urbane and sophisticated as if he had been dressed in full black tie. "Perhaps you would like to join me?"

Gabrielle had gaped at him, her breathing erratic. His naked body had been all she could think about—the sight of all that bare skin and maleness making her feel wild and mad and jittery.

"I've only been in a hot tub in the spa," she'd said. Idiotically.

"This will be different," he'd promised, amused. He'd held out his free hand, commanding and regal, making her feel distinctly overdressed by comparison. She had wavered, her body clamoring for her to throw herself at him while her mind warned her that the bags were a lesson she could not afford to ignore—so peremptory and arrogant and—

But then he'd smiled. One of his rare, heartbreaking smiles. One that flashed that fascinating dent in his lean jaw and made his eyes gleam like highly polished platinum.

"Trust me," he'd said.

And she'd found herself moving toward him without another thought…

Gabrielle shivered on the terrace in San Francisco—but not from the cold. She darted a look over her shoulder, but Luc was still indoors. She could still hear his voice—the dark, rich caress of French when he talked to his assistants, the lyrical lilt of Italian when he spoke to his right-hand man.

She would never look at a hot tub the same way again.

And that had only been the first night.

Luc had hired a sexy little convertible and they'd meandered their way along the spectacular California coast, their bags turning up in one luxurious suite after the next in places Gabrielle had only ever read about. Big Sur, the Carmel Valley, Monterey. Gabrielle had hardly known where the rugged beauty of the California coastline left off and her husband's began. He'd made love to her every night, over and over, with a ferocity that had made her toes curl and her heart sing, the nights bleeding into the days until she felt as aware of his body as she was of her own.

He was more dark magic than man, she thought, and she knew she was spellbound, enchanted. Every night, she tried to resist him. Every time he touched her she tried to hold something of herself in reserve—to keep some small part of herself safe. But now as she stood with all of San Francisco laid out before her, she was forced to wonder what that small, hidden part of her mattered when every other fiber of her being seemed to dance to his tune at his command. How could she have allowed this to happen? Unlike her father, whom she had blindly followed for years out of a sense of duty and familial obligation, and her own helpless love for him no matter how remote he seemed, she had known immediately that she should not do the same with Luc. And here she was, a scant few weeks later, turned inside out because he wished it.

The worst part was, she could summon up only the most distant kind of alarm.

Did *she* wish it? Was she pretending to want to resist him while secretly thrilling to her own surrender? Was it not surrender at all, but instead the acceptance of pure, unadulterated pleasure—something she had never permitted herself before?

Something in her suspected that it might be true—though she shoved it aside.

Someday this spell will break, she told herself now, sternly, *and then what will you have? A marriage that resembles your relationship with your father much too closely. A life completely and utterly controlled by a man you never wanted, never chose.*

But she wasn't sure she cared as much about that possibility as perhaps she should.

"Gabrielle."

Just her name on his lips and her sex melted, while the rest of her body surged to attention. *Just her name.* He was lethal. She turned to see him standing in the French doors that led out to the terrace. He was dressed all in black—trousers, and a cashmere turtleneck that made him look impossibly French even as it clung to his spectacular chest, defining his lean, tight muscles. He frowned. It no longer made her heart beat in panic—but that didn't mean she had grown immune to him. Not by a long shot.

"There is a chill in the air, and a breeze this high up," he said. "You'll catch cold."

"It's a beautiful evening," she replied, smiling. She didn't move. It was one more little rebellion, hardly noticeable at all except to that tiny part of her she hid away, tucked deep inside.

The moment seemed charged, as the city rushed into night-time below them, bridges and buildings sparkling and spreading out in all directions. Gabrielle felt an emotion she could not name roll into life inside of her and begin to grow. She didn't know if that was what made her want to weep, or if it was the odd, arrested look in his eyes—as if he was seeing her for the first time. She swallowed against it.

"You look lovely," Luc said, crossing to her. He took her hand and lifted it to his lips. Even the barest touch of his mouth against the back of her hand made her quiver. And he knew it. She could see the sure, sensual knowledge in his silvery gaze.

It is only sex, she told herself, fighting her body's instant response. *Physical chemistry. It doesn't mean anything more than that.* There was no magic, no sorcery, no spell. He was just a man, and she had never explored her passions before. It was simple, really.

She'd been telling herself some version of the same story for weeks.

She wished she believed it.

"Thank you," she said, her voice hushed. She had dressed for the evening in a simple black sheath, and had secured her hair in a low, sleek ponytail, held with a jeweled clasp at the nape of her neck.

"I apologize for abandoning you," he said, searching her face as if he could see the struggle she thought she'd hidden from view. "I'm afraid my business does not lend itself to holidays, no matter how much I might wish it to do so."

Gabrielle smiled automatically—though she knew him well enough after these intense, close weeks to suspect that it was not the business that did not lend itself to time off, it was Luc himself who refused it. But she backed away from saying such a thing—from exploring the implied intimacy that knowing anything about him suggested. She had to keep something in reserve or she would end up with nothing. Why was that so hard to remember?

"I watched the sun set over the Golden Gate Bridge," she said, smiling up at him. Light, easy. Her polite hostess mode, all surface and shine. She clung to it—determined to feel as composed as she sounded. "How could I possibly feel abandoned?"

Her eyes were dark, with no hint of green—which, Luc had come to know over the past weeks, meant she was upset. She gave no other sign. Her smile was perfect, her body at ease. Yet he could feel her distance and he hated it.

"I am glad to hear that a sunset and a foreign city are adequate replacement for me," he said dryly, watching her closely. Her lashes swept down, covering her eyes, and when she looked up again he saw humor there.

"Was that a joke?" she asked.

"I never joke," he replied in the same tone, and she laughed.

"Have you concluded your business?" she asked, angling her body away from his as he moved closer. It was subtle thing—unconscious, perhaps—but Luc noticed it. He frowned. "It must be quite late in Europe."

"I decided to let everyone sleep tonight," Luc said. "But only because I expect them to work even harder in the morning."

She crossed her arms over her torso, pulling the wrap tighter around her body. She gazed out over the city, remote and beautiful. He did not see the city arrayed at his feet—he saw only her. He wished that he could penetrate her mind, explore her secrets. He had accepted that she had this power over him—a power no other woman had ever had. He had realized that he wanted to *know* her in a way that went far beyond the carnal. He assumed it was because she was his wife; knowing that he would be with her for the rest of their lives was reason enough to have a deeper interest in her, surely? He should have expected it. And like anything else, he told himself, this urge to know her would pass in time. It had to.

"Are you a good boss?" she asked, startling him. "Do they like you?"

Luc was incredulous. "*Like* me?" he asked. He rolled his shoulders back and frowned slightly. "I've never given it a moment's thought. They obey me, or they are replaced."

"I will take that as a no, they do not." Amusement made her voice rich.

"Is that how you plan to rule your country?" he asked derisively. "As a popularity contest? I doubt you will find that the most efficient form of government."

"There is a difference between fear and respect," she replied, seeming unperturbed by his harsher tone. It occurred to him that it had been a long time since he'd managed to get under her skin with only a few words. "Surely a good ruler should strive for the latter rather than the former?"

"This is all very naïve, Gabrielle," Luc said dismissively. "Yes, it would be delightful if my employees adored me. But what should I care if they do not? As long as they work hard, perform well and remain loyal, they are rewarded. If they wish to be loved in return, perhaps they should adopt a domestic animal."

She raised her brows, looking mildly quizzical. "You do not care at all?" she asked. "You are perfectly content for them to hate you, so long as they perform their duties to your specifications? That is all you require?"

"I am their employer, Gabrielle." He did not understand why her tone set his teeth on edge, or why he felt suddenly defensive. Nor why she had developed this sudden interest in his business concerns. "Not their lover."

"I am not your lover either," she replied, a flash of anger in her voice, her eyes. "I am merely your wife. Should I hate you? Fear you? Will it matter to you as long as you are obeyed?"

He stilled. "You compare yourself to my employees?" he

asked softly, watching her face closely. "Have you taken leave of your senses?"

"I fail to see the difference in our positions," she replied coolly. Whatever anger he'd sensed in the previous moment was gone, and she was once again composed and easy. She might have been discussing the weather forecast. She even smiled at him. "It is always best to know one's place."

The words struck at him, reminding him of the way her father had said much the same thing back in Paris. As if she were an animal, or a servant. He didn't know why hearing her repeat the same sentiment bothered him when he'd agreed with it before, more or less. It was unreasonable. Irrational.

Yet he still reached over and took her shoulders in his hands, pulling her to him, closing the distance between their bodies.

She came without objection, tilting her face up toward his, though he still sensed that distance in her, no matter how close she might be physically. She was too calm, too collected. Too damned serene.

He wanted her mindless, uncontrolled, *fierce*. The way she was beneath him, astride him. On the bed, the floor— wherever they happened to find themselves. He was becoming less and less tolerant of her smooth, perfect exterior when they were in private. She used it to keep him at arm's length, he was sure of it, and it infuriated him.

"I will indulge you anything you wish," he told her, holding her still. "Including this asinine argument you seem determined to have tonight."

"Are we arguing?" she asked lightly, her eyes unreadable in the night air. "My apologies. I was merely clarifying."

"But I must tell you," he continued, as if she hadn't spoken, "I had a very different evening in mind."

"Oh?" She was so unruffled. So calm. Why did that needle him? Wasn't a woman with her poise exactly what he'd wanted? What he'd searched for with such single-minded purpose?

Luc stepped back and reached into the pocket of his trousers. He pulled out the small jeweler's box, cracked it open, and held it out before her.

"A small token," he said quietly. An uncomfortable feeling gripped him. He scowled at her, still holding out the box with the damned ring—an impulse he suddenly regretted. But he still bit out the words. "I hope you approve."

CHAPTER TWELVE

His voice had gone stiff. Formal. He even scowled down at her, as if he wanted to shout at her.

In another man Gabrielle might have called it shy—even awkward. Odd that her poking at him about *her place* had had no such effect on him—but his giving her a gift did. Or perhaps it was the gift itself.

Gabrielle swallowed carefully and looked at the ring nestled in the box, with sparkle enough to rival the hectic flash and shine of the city all around them. She dared to raise her eyes to his, and what she saw there made a fine tremor snake through her.

He did not kneel. He did not mouth pretty words. He only gazed at her. It took her breath away. Not merely the ring. But the fact that he was giving it to her like this—like some kind of backward proposal for their backward marriage.

It was perfect, somehow. And she didn't know why it should matter to her. But it did. Oh, how it mattered—how it caught at her heart and squeezed.

"The stone belonged to my mother. The original setting would not have suited you, so I had it reset." Luc took the ring from the box and then took Gabrielle's hand.

She already wore the ring he'd put there in the cathedral on their wedding day, but this felt different—deeper, more emotional. Perhaps because she knew him now—knew his scent, his touch, the timbre of his voice. Perhaps because he might be many things she was still only beginning to process, but he was no longer a stranger.

Her hand felt fragile in his much larger one—breakable.

She found she was holding her breath as he slipped the ring onto her finger. It fit perfectly, as she had known it would. She spread her fingers wide to look at the new ring—feeling far too emotional to look at him in such a fraught moment.

The stone was a large diamond, cut to dance and shimmer with any hint of light. It sat high on a simple platinum setting, and looked as if it had been specifically made to grace and flatter her hand. Gabrielle had more jewelry than she knew what to do with—she had inherited her mother's pieces, and had the entire historical collection of Miravakian Crown Jewels at her disposal—yet nothing had ever touched her so much or so deeply as this particular stone from this particular man.

He doesn't need to do this, she kept thinking, bemused. They were already married. The ring seemed so…romantic.

A concept she could not get her head around. Not as it applied to Luc Garnier, the most sensual and least romantic of men.

"It is beautiful," she murmured, staring at it, her voice hushed.

It was as if the world had hushed, too, trapping them in a bubble with only this ring and unspoken undertones that made Gabrielle's body hum with tension or emotion—she wasn't sure which.

She didn't understand the rush inside of her that threatened to sweep her away. She was afraid to look at him—afraid she might succumb to the heat that threatened to spill from behind her eyes. But she forced herself to do it anyway, and felt the force of his gray gaze burn through her, kicking up brush fires all the way to the soles of her feet and back again.

His look was fierce. Demanding. And yet she knew, with a flash of feminine intuition, that despite appearances he was at his most vulnerable. Rather than making her feel as if she had an advantage, finally, it humbled her. Made her ache.

"It suits you," he said, in the same quiet voice.

"Thank you," she whispered, unable to say anything else despite the words that crowded in her throat, nearly choking her. She reached over and laid her trembling hand on his hard cheek, her palm caressing the place where that dent appeared on the rare occasions he laughed. She was not hiding anything from him as she gazed at him—she was wide open, unde-fended. More naked than ever before.

It shook her to the core. And yet she couldn't seem to look away.

"The car is waiting," Luc murmured after a moment. He turned his mouth into her hand and his lips curled against her palm. Gabrielle blew out a soft breath. He reached up and laced his strong, clever fingers with hers and gave her a crooked, almost boyish smile that broke her heart into pieces.

He does not have to do this...

But she gave no sign of her inner turmoil. She smiled, the way she always did, and followed him out to dinner.

Luc lounged against the leather seat in the back of the car and watched Gabrielle. Covertly. She extended her hand when he checked his PDA, tilted the diamond this way and that, so it caught the passing streetlights and sent light cascading around her. He was certain she did not want him to catch her in the act, since she dropped her hand into her lap the moment he slid the PDA back into his pocket.

"There has been a change of plans," he said.

"Our dinner plans?" she asked, turning that serene coun-tenance toward him.

"No." He fought the urge to say something sarcastic, just to see if he could pry behind that mask as he had so easily in the beginning. More and more he was convinced he only saw the true Gabrielle when they were in bed. "Tonight we are going into Marin County, to a restaurant I think you will enjoy. An interesting take on classic French cuisine."

"It must be good," Gabrielle said, smiling. An expression he had not seen before—mischievous, he thought—crossed her face. "You are not just half-French, but half-Parisian, aren't you? Your palate must therefore be held to be even more discerning than a regular Frenchman's."

"Indeed," Luc said. Shadows hid her face, then bursts of light illuminated her as the car made its way through the city and toward the wild beauty of Marin County, just across the Golden Gate Bridge. "I believe I have been called particularly discerning even for a Parisian."

"I feel sorry for the chef," she said, clearly teasing him now, and Luc felt torn.

On the one hand he wanted her to continue looking at him with that bright humor in her eyes. He craved it. But on the other he was so unused to being teased that he wasn't certain what to do—how to respond in kind without becoming overbearing. And then, of course, there was the part of him that didn't mind being overbearing at all, if it would force her to open up to him and display her secrets.

He was not used to such indecisiveness.

"I had hoped to travel into the Napa Valley tomorrow," he said after a moment, casting the unusual feelings aside and concentrating on facts, as ever. "I have an interest in a vineyard there, and it is beautiful country. But I am afraid business calls me to London." He shrugged. "We will have to leave."

She was quiet for a moment. There was no sign of any frown between her brows, though for some reason Luc was certain there would have been if she'd showed her feelings more. He thought back to their wedding, and to that first night he had hunted her down in Los Angeles. Her feelings had overtaken her then, though she'd hidden them in public.

When had she started hiding them in private, too? He didn't like the sensation that she was hiding *from him*, specifically. That there were whole worlds in her, perhaps, that he had no access to at all.

He should at least know that they were there. Shouldn't he?

"I have not been to London since last spring," she said at last. He felt certain that was not at all what she wanted to say. "Do you go there often?"

"Often enough," he said.

"I ask because, as I am sure you know, I have a residence there," she said. "If you would care to stay in it, we can. I don't know what your usual arrangements are in London."

He remembered, dimly, the house in Belgravia that had been mentioned as part of her holdings in the marriage documents. He was more interested in her periodic return to this stiff, chilly formality with him—though at least she had stopped talking of returning to her friend's house in Los Angeles. Did that mean she had accepted their marriage after this last passionate month? He found he was not willing to ask—and he didn't know what to make of such uncharacteristic reticence on his part.

"That will do," he said finally, when he realized she was awaiting his response. "I don't know how long we will stay." Was he afraid of what she might answer if he did ask? He dismissed that possibility. Since when had he ever been *afraid* of an answer, no matter how tough the question?

"However long you wish," she said. She smiled again. That bright, easy, completely manufactured smile—the one she no doubt used on strangers. It was enraging. "I'll phone the housekeeper before we leave."

The civilized conversation was driving him insane. Luc wanted to reach beneath her manicured veneer and find the truth of her—force it out of her—so he could see it even when she sported all her sophistication and class like some kind of shield.

And then he thought, *why not?* Inside the car the barrier was raised, hiding them completely from their driver. The windows were tinted for privacy. *Why not, indeed?*

"Take off your panties," he ordered her, in the silken tone he knew would excite her.

She gasped. Color flooded her cheeks and her eyes widened.

"I'm sorry?" she said, her voice betraying her. It was husky as she tried—and failed—to summon up some outrage. "What did you say?"

"It is of no matter," he murmured. "I'll do it myself."

He turned to the side, maneuvering himself so that he knelt before her. He parted her long, gorgeously formed legs, taking care to run his hands along the elegant length of each, and kissing the curve of one knee.

"What…what are you doing?" she whispered, her voice ragged.

"You can leave your shoes on," he told her. He was tired of masks, of shields. He wanted the real Gabrielle. And he could think of only one way to access her—immediately. And if that also happened to go a long way toward rattling her composure—well, that was even better.

His hands streaked up her thighs and hooked around the sides of the flimsy panties she wore. He met her gaze as he drew them down her legs, then over the delicate heel of each shoe—and watched her mouth open on a breath, though no words escaped. He held her eyes with his as he drew one leg over his shoulder, tilting her back against the seat, sliding her bottom toward him, angling her hot center toward his mouth.

"Luc!" A desperate whisper. "Luc, you cannot…!"

But he did. He kissed her calf, the turn of her knee, the creamy skin of her inner thigh. And then he moved into the cradle of her thighs and kissed the hot, sweet core of her, already wet and swollen and ready for him. He felt her go rigid beneath him. Her hands burrowed into his hair, her legs clenched around his shoulders.

He licked the length of her furrow, reveling in her scent, her taste. He sought out the center of her desire and sucked it gently into his mouth, then repeated it all. Again and again. Until she writhed beneath him, sobbing out incoherent sounds that might have been his name.

She was like cream and truth, all woman, and more delectable than the finest Parisian cuisine. He heard her moans and knew she couldn't fake that. He felt her body stiffen and shake, and knew with deep satisfaction that she couldn't smooth that away, hide it behind her manners and breeding.

She came apart around him, arching up from the seat and crying out his name, and he knew it was real. He could taste it.

He sat up, gently rearranging her on the seat next to him and tucking her against his shoulder. Her ragged breathing was the only sound in the car—like music to his ears.

She was his. Entirely his. He couldn't abide the idea that she was hiding something—herself—from him. He wouldn't allow it.

He reached forward and scooped up her panties from the floor of the car as her eyes opened and she blinked. She was bright red, and her eyes were heavy-lidded with leftover passion. He did not have to ask if she was satisfied—he could still taste the rich wine of her arousal against his tongue. She shot him a nervous sort of look, then reached out to take the panties from him.

"I think not," he said. He smiled as her eyes widened. He took the panties—a scrap of peach-colored silk and lace that she looked at in some mixture of horror and desire—and tucked them away in the pocket of his trousers. "We can both spend the entire dinner picturing you naked beneath your clothes," he said softly.

Her breath left her in a rush. A quick look told Luc that she was aroused as much as she was dazed, and that she didn't quite know what to do about either.

But as long as he could read her—as long as he'd shocked her public mask from her face—he didn't care.

CHAPTER THIRTEEN

WITHIN moments of meeting Luc's business associates—brothers from whom he had been attempting to buy a very successful chain of family-friendly hotels in various European Union countries for the past eighteen months—Gabrielle had them all eating out of her hand. Luc could not decide if it was the effortless grace of her manners, the quiet elegance of her subtly sophisticated ensemble, or some special Gabrielle mixture that only she could produce. Whatever it was, she used it well. She had the men and their wives at ease and laughing throughout the long meal in one of London's finest restaurants, seemingly without exerting herself.

She caught his eye as he watched her across the table laden with fine linens and delicate china, and he had the pleasure of seeing her gaze warm, though she made no other outward expression. But he knew it was for him only, that private heat, and it filled him with a sense of triumph.

No masks, no shields. Not when she looked at him. Not anymore.

"Your wife is truly a gem among women," one of the men told Luc in a besotted aside during the cheese course. He was the oldest of the three Federer brothers, and the most powerful. There would be no deal without Franz Federer's approval—which was the only reason Luc had decided not to object to the way the man was staring at Gabrielle's figure, which she showed to advantage tonight in a sleeveless royal-blue shift. "Who would have expected the infamous Luc Garnier to take a wife, eh?"

It was clear to Luc that it was not the *fact* of the wife that stunned the man—but the *specific* wife that Luc had procured. It was equally clear that being called *the infamous Luc Garnier* was not exactly a compliment. Luc remembered Gabrielle's words about fear versus respect in his business, and wondered for the first time if she might have had a point after all. He had never cared much about the distinction. Maybe it was time he started.

"Even the mighty must fall," Luc said, with the wry shrug that seemed to be expected. He toyed with the delicate crystal stem of his wineglass.

"And lucky is the man who falls to a princess such as yours," Franz agreed, nodding. "Such graciousness! Such refinement!"

"I count myself lucky that I am old enough to appreciate both," Luc replied, ignoring the distaste that he felt.

He didn't understand it. He had wanted a wife who inspired this reaction in others—in men exactly like Franz Federer, in fact, whose well-known moral judgments about marriage applied only to others and never to himself. Luc had sought Gabrielle out for precisely this purpose. He'd found the single respectable woman alive who could inspire such raptures from usually dour businessmen. So why was he entertaining fantasies of planting his fist in the other man's face?

"Marriage is not for young men, it is true," Franz said, settling his considerable girth back in his chair. He patted his belly thoughtfully. His own wife, significantly and obviously younger than him, by at least two decades, had excused herself to powder her nose some time before.

Idly, Luc wondered if the woman was more interested in the waiter, who seemed closer to her in age and interests, than in her husband. She had been gone almost long enough to incite speculation.

"But it settles a man down. Even a man of your…ah… *stature.*"

Luc had heard this before, of course. *Stature* being code for *reputation.* The truth was, he was feared because he was utterly ruthless. He knew no other way. When he wanted something—hotels, land, existing companies that he felt he could operate better, Gabrielle—he went after it. And he always got what he went after. Sooner or later.

"My *stature* precedes me, does it?" Luc asked mildly. He chose not to be insulted—he wanted the hotels more than he wanted to teach Franz Federer some manners.

He kept his gaze on Gabrielle as she charmed the younger brothers and their overawed wives with her stories of growing up in a royal palace not fitted for young children.

"I can't bring myself to tell you about the rock crystal vase I nearly destroyed one day, while playing horses in a drawing room," she told them, shuddering theatrically. "It's far too incriminating, and a priceless piece of art was *this close* to being lost forever! I would have died from the shame of it!"

She made it sound like a madcap adventure worthy of an Enid Blyton book, when, unless he missed his guess, a childhood with King Josef must have been anything but pleasant. He felt a kind of pang, trying to imagine her as a little girl, locked away in that *palazzo* with her grim, fault-finding father. He rather thought there had been fewer incidents of *playing horses* than the anecdote suggested. But her audience ate it up—captivated, no doubt, by the fantasy of a reckless young princess *this close* to disaster. Luc found himself no less charmed.

"I don't mind telling you that there was some concern that you might not be the best fit for our family's hotels," Franz continued, forcing Luc's attention away from Gabrielle and her past. "And with that business with the tabloids recently…"

He shook his head sorrowfully, though his eyes were avid as he assessed Luc's reaction.

Luc smiled, though that deep, abiding rage he never seemed to conquer rolled over in his gut. He hated the tabloids. He hated Silvio Domenico and his slimy brethren more than he could express. He hated even more that Gabrielle had thrown them into the frenzy of a tabloid cycle—directly into Silvio's clutches.

But she had not planned it. She had simply run—afraid and unknowing. Luc believed her—and if he had paid closer attention to her emotional state at their wedding, and less to her father's assurances of her obedience, the entire affair could have been avoided. He blamed himself.

"You cannot believe what you read in those rags, of course," he said carelessly, as if it was of no matter to him. "They are writers of fiction and fantasy."

"All civilized men must be appalled at their prominence these days," Franz said, shaking his head in sympathy that Luc suspected was feigned. "The stalking and the lies. And yet everyone reads them!"

"They are a scourge," Luc agreed. He gestured toward Gabrielle. "As you can see, I have caught up to my runaway bride, against all the odds. Did I not read that she was tortured, somehow, by the experience? Ravaged in some way? I don't think she looks any the worse for her ordeal."

"Indeed she does not," Franz agreed. Perhaps too readily for Luc's comfort.

"The truth is that we honeymooned in America quite without incident." Luc sighed, sitting back in his chair and swirling the wine in his glass. "I wish I could tell you that it was scandalous, but it was not. I'm afraid my scandalous days now exist only in the imagination of the paparazzi. I cannot say that I regret it."

"I think she is a good influence on you," Franz said after

a moment—as if Luc had *asked* to be patronized by a man he could buy and sell several times over.

Luc set his teeth and forced himself not to react. Every sense told him that this infernal deal was about to be closed.

"I would like to think so," he said. He even thought it might be true—though he did not intend to share that with Federer, of all people.

"You seem more settled. It suits you," Franz said.

The gall of it! As if he and Luc were intimate in some way beyond his lust for Luc's money—and possibly Luc's wife!

"This is good for a man as he approaches his middle years." Franz smiled. "And it will be good, too, for our hotels."

"I am pleased to hear it," Luc said. He extended his hand.

When the other man took it, Luc smiled. A real smile this time.

The deal was done. And Luc had his wife to thank for it.

She met his eyes once more, that telltale color reddening her cheeks. Suddenly, Luc couldn't wait to show her exactly how grateful he was.

London was a cold, gray slap after the sun-drenched blues and greens of the California coast. Gabrielle pulled her silk scarf tighter over her hair to ward off the wetness as she rushed through the Brompton Road crowd toward the doors of Harrods, eager to get inside and out of the rain.

Once through the grand doors, Gabrielle pulled her scarf away from her face and shook it out slightly, damp all over, though she found it a bit exhilarating after all the sunshine she'd gotten over the previous weeks. She had thrown a light trenchcoat over a pale yellow Chanel suit better suited to California than England, and was convinced she'd landed in a puddle the depth of the Thames in her rush to get from the car into the famous department store. She felt the wet and the London grime all the way up the backs of her legs. She was cold and soaked. And she didn't care in the slightest, because Harrods worked its usual magic on her the moment she stepped inside.

Gabrielle shook the water from her scarf and tucked it in the pocket of her coat, then unbuttoned the trench as she walked through the grand rooms she'd seen so many times before. She knew it was touristy at best, and sentimental at worst, but she had never been able to shake her abiding love for the British institution that was Harrods. Whenever she visited London she made a point to visit the store, to wander through the gilt-edged displays and marvel at the soaring ceilings and marble floors. Every now and again, when she knew her father would not be around to judge her, she brought home one of their gourmet hampers, always wishing she could take it on the perfect picnic somewhere, but making do with her private rooms. Being in the bustling, lavish rooms at Harrods reminded her of being a young girl, dispatched to the nearby store with her governess *du jour* while her father tended to affairs of state. Her father would have his privacy while Gabrielle enjoyed herself wandering about Harrods, then followed it up with an afternoon cream tea. Few things had ever made her happier.

"If it isn't the delightful Mrs. Garnier," a sly voice drawled in Italian from behind her, causing Gabrielle to start, and drop the leather gloves she'd absently picked up.

She recognized the man immediately—it was the paparazzo who had so angered Luc in Los Angeles. Silvio. He leaned close, his beard grizzled and the smell of old cigarettes wafting up from his damp jeans and tracksuit top. Gabrielle forced herself not to recoil—anything she did would be held up to scrutiny and twisted into the most negative light possible. It was best to do very little.

"My apologies, Your Royal Highness," the man continued, his voice suggestive, his eyes hard, "if I've interrupted. You looked so sad just then. So alone."

"Not at all," Gabrielle said easily, finding her public smile harder to come by than usual. "I was daydreaming quite happily, I assure you. I used to come here quite often as a girl." She swept him with a quizzical look. "Have we met?"

"Your husband did not introduce us when we ran into each other in Los Angeles," Silvio replied, shifting his weight to move even further into Gabrielle's space, water glistening in his shaggy salt-and-pepper curls. "But I'm sure you remember the occasion—outside a restaurant, just a few days after he chased you to the States? I think maybe he had something to hide that night, yes?"

"Something to hide?" Gabrielle echoed. The man obviously loathed Luc. It was etched into every line on his weathered face. She found she felt much the same about *him*. She forced a light trill of laughter. "I think you misunderstand him. My husband is a private man and we were on our honeymoon. No need to read anything into it but that."

"Private people don't spend their honeymoons having dinner at the Ivy, Your Royal Highness, do they?" Silvio retorted, so close now that Gabrielle could see the brown and yellow nicotine stains on his teeth.

She was forced to shift back against the display table to put an appropriate distance between them, and her skin crawled when he smirked.

"Not if they want it to stay private."

"You still haven't told me your name," Gabrielle replied, buying time and scraping together every little bit of manners she'd ever been taught, determined to remain polite even when she wanted to run, screaming, into the streets of Knightsbridge to get away from the man. "I am afraid you have me at a disadvantage."

"I am Silvio Domenico," he said aggressively, and made a lazy sort of gesture with his hand, approximating a bow. He eyed her as he leaned against the display table, his cold gaze repellent. Gabrielle merely straightened her spine and waited.

"I feel sorry for you," he said after a moment.

"I can't imagine why," she said crisply. Repulsive man! "But I must excuse myself. I have a great many—"

"I don't think you'll want to run off just yet," the odious man interrupted, with a smile that chilled Gabrielle to the bone. "Not if you want your so-called private husband's life to stay that way."

"What on earth are you talking about?" Gabrielle asked, letting her impatience show.

Sensing that he might be losing his audience, Silvio shifted closer, his gaze alight with an excitement that Gabrielle instinctively knew could not bode well for her. Or for Luc.

"It turns out that Luc's last mistress wasn't as discreet as she was supposed to be," Silvio told her with evident delight. He paused deliberately. "You do know that Luc is famous for his confidentiality agreements, right? No roll in the hay with Luc Garnier unless you promise not to talk about it. That's the rule. He makes them all sign." He waited for her reaction with obvious enjoyment—he wanted to feed on it, Gabrielle could tell. He wanted her to react badly—to hurt.

So she refused to show him anything, however little she might personally like to hear about the women who'd come before her. Much less any documents Luc might have had those women sign—which she very much doubted was true. Who would dare sell Luc out to the press? She merely arched an eyebrow.

"That seems quite sensible, given the fact you and your colleagues follow him around the planet digging for every detail," she replied crisply.

"What surprises me is that there are always so many takers," Silvio said, with that nasty edge to his voice. "Don't see the attraction myself." Gabrielle stared at him. He laughed. "You, too? I thought he bought you?"

"This conversation is over," Gabrielle replied icily, turning to go, but his hand on her arm stopped her. She stared at it, then up at him in outrage. How *dared* he touch her? "Remove your hand! At once!"

"You know about La Rosalinda, of course?" Silvio continued, but he dropped his hand. His voice lowered, becoming even more intimate and disgusting. "The toast of Italy. What an uproar Luc caused when he dismissed *her*!"

Rosalinda Jaccino was an Italian film star. She was a world-renowned beauty—all flowing black tresses, mysterious eyes and sexy curves. The sight of her breasts supposedly caused riots. She also happened to be Luc's most recent ex-lover. Gabrielle had read all about her while researching Luc in the weeks before their marriage. She certainly didn't want to hear what this repulsive toad of a man so clearly wanted to tell her about the other woman. Just as she really, truly did not want to picture that bombshell with her husband.

In bed with her husband. That sinuous, famously curvy body wrapped around his—

Those are not helpful images, she told herself dryly. And if Luc had wished to marry La Rosalinda he would have done so. Instead he had looked the world over and chosen Gabrielle.

But there was no time to ruminate on her marriage—she was trapped in the leather goods section of Harrods unless she wanted to cause a scene. Which she did not. She knew, somehow, that Silvio would stop at nothing to tell her whatever it was he had clearly tracked her down to tell her. She would just as soon he did not share whatever it was with half of London.

"What is it you want?" she asked with great patience, wishing she could escape into the Egyptian Hall next door. If this awful little man tainted her Harrods experience—one of the few truly happy memories of her childhood—she didn't know how she would stand it.

"It is not what *I* want," Silvio said. "It is what I think you will want—once you know what I know about La Rosalinda and your husband."

He made the word *husband* sound like a particularly filthy curse.

"Surely you did not come to talk to me about my husband's former lovers?" Gabrielle asked, with as much dignity as she could muster. "I must confess that I am not interested in them." She shrugged. "I am sorry if that disappoints you. And, while this has been a charming interlude, I really must—"

"Don't dismiss me, Your Royal Highness." The man's voice went cold. Brutish. His eyes were flat. "I don't think you'll be quite so high and mighty if I go straight to the papers with what I have, will you?"

"What *do* you have?" Gabrielle asked, fighting to keep her voice even. A trickle of foreboding ran through her, making her skin feel itchy.

"I have a tape." He laughed, still so close that Gabrielle could smell the tobacco on his breath, along with a hefty hint of onions. "Well, not exactly a tape. More digital than that—but the end result is the same, isn't it?"

"A tape of what?" Gabrielle asked through her teeth, unable to keep the edge out of her voice. The loathsome man was obviously enjoying himself. He tucked his hands into the pockets of his jeans and grinned at her.

"Your husband," he said, relishing the moment. "And La Rosalinda." He smirked. "The lady likes to film herself when she's in bed. And let me congratulate you, Your Royal Highness—your husband certainly knows what he's doing." He let out a wolf whistle, turning the heads of nearby shoppers. "He's the star of the show, believe me. Very accomplished."

"Don't be absurd," she said coldly, dismissively. "Luc would never allow himself to be filmed at all—much less at such a time."

"Who said she asked his permission?" Silvio retorted, his smirk deepening.

Gabrielle blinked at him. She held herself very, very still. Around them shoppers bustled this way and that, and London charged about its business, as if this wasn't happening.

This couldn't be happening.

"Why are you telling me this?" she managed to ask. But what she thought was, *poor Luc—this will kill him!*

"Unless you want the surround sound movie of your brand-new husband and his ex to air on television tomorrow night—so artistic—you better watch how you talk to me," Silvio retorted in a hiss. And then he laughed.

Vile little man.

"What do you want?" Gabrielle asked, hearing the strain in her voice as she spat the words out. Her hands curled into fists so tight she felt her nails dig into her own palms.

"Meet me back here tomorrow," Silvio said, with unholy glee in his voice. "Bring yourself, and ten thousand pounds—and I'll give you the tape." He laughed. "Bring anyone else—or tell Luc—and I'll sell the tape to the highest bidder and you can watch him perform with the rest of the world. Does that sound like a deal?"

Gabrielle could only glare at him—which made him laugh all the more.

"See you tomorrow, sweetheart," he said, and walked away.

CHAPTER FOURTEEN

"You seem unusually quiet," Luc said as the dinner plates were cleared from their places, sitting back in his chair and regarding Gabrielle with that piercing gray gaze of his. She was afraid he could see too much—see *through* her—too easily.

She tried to look at him and see what someone else might, but she felt too captured by his direct gaze to manage it. He was too virile, too masculine. The coat he wore was expertly tailored to emphasize the impressive, sculpted width of his shoulders. Across the dinner table his hard mouth crooked slightly at the corner, almost affectionately—a word she would never have thought to apply to him previously. The grand dining room of the London Ritz seemed to fade, and Gabrielle wondered helplessly if it would always be this way with him—if he would always command her attention, her focus, and bleed the light and color from the rest of the world.

She had an inkling that he probably would.

"I think that I miss the sun," she said, finding it hard to manage her usual light and easy tone. "Though this room is a fair approximation of it, isn't it?" She waved her hand, taking in the glittering chandeliers and lavish furnishings, all of which gave the famous hotel restaurant a distinct golden hue even late in the evening. "It's almost like sunshine."

She knew that she should tell him. She should have told

him already. She should have called him the moment she'd left the horrible paparazzo's presence. She should have told him as they dressed for dinner—when he'd told her he preferred the slightly more risqué Balenciaga black dress to the more classic Chanel black dress and she had changed accordingly. She'd had ample opportunity to tell him during the ride from her house in Belgravia to the Ritz, when she'd asked him about his day and told him silly stories about her minor adventures. And they'd done nothing but talk throughout dinner—even touching briefly on his past with the paparazzi, giving her many an opportunity to raise the subject.

But every time she opened her mouth to tell Luc what Silvio had said—what he'd insinuated and what he'd claimed—she couldn't do it. It would hurt Luc too much. She didn't know how to tell him that his worst fear was on the brink of being realized. Wasn't this why he had chased her in such a fury to Los Angeles? He would do anything to avoid bad press—even that dinner he'd insisted upon in California, where they'd run into Silvio. And Gabrielle realized that while she was no longer afraid of her husband, she couldn't bear to hurt him—as telling him about Silvio's plans would inevitably do. He would rage and glower, and perhaps even threaten, but she knew enough now to know that it came from a place of pain. She simply couldn't stand to cause him any more pain.

The thought startled her. When had she reached that conclusion? When had she come to understand him that way?

"Sunshine in London, surrounded by rain and cold with no end in sight?" Luc said dryly, but there was a certain tenderness in the way he looked at her, and it tugged at her heart. "I suspect you are more of a romantic than you let on, Gabrielle."

"A romantic?" She smiled. "Impossible. There's not a romantic bone in my body. My father expressly forbade it."

"Shall we put it to the test?"

She didn't understand when he stood and stretched out his

hand. She blinked at him in confusion. Then comprehension dawned, and she let out a startled laugh.

"You wish to dance?" she asked. "Here?"

Elegantly dressed couples already moved on the dance floor to the sounds of the four-piece band, but Gabrielle found it impossible to imagine the two of them among the crowd. It was so…so impractical. So very unlike Luc.

"Why not?" he asked, amusement making his silver gaze gleam beneath the chandeliers.

"Perhaps it is not I who am romantic?" Gabrielle murmured, and slipped her hand into his.

The last time—the only time—she had danced with her husband had been at their wedding, and Gabrielle found that she'd blocked out much of the experience in the chaos and excitement of what had followed. She tried to remember the details as he led her out on to a different dance floor, pulling her to him expertly. She remembered that part: the feeling of being caught up against the unyielding wall of his chest—of being held so securely she'd felt trapped, overcome.

She felt neither of those things now. Her breath seemed to tangle in her throat as she tilted her head back so she could look up at him—at the harsh, forbidding face that now seemed more dear and necessary to her than the mountains she'd stared at her whole childhood.

"The last time we danced was at our wedding," she said, aware that her voice was husky.

"I remember," he said. "You may recall that I was there and, unlike some, remained there as planned."

She ignored his dig. She even smiled.

"What I recall is that you lectured me about politically expedient spouses," she replied. She let her hand slide along his arm, testing the shape of his rock-hard bicep against her palm. "I think you meant to cow me into submission."

"Behold my success," Luc replied in a low voice, almost a growl. "I cowed you into a race across the planet."

"At your next wedding," Gabrielle said, concentrating on the part of her that felt the lightness between them, the teasing, and not the part that ached for him beneath it, "you might consider talking to your bride rather than lecturing her. I only offer suggestions," she continued hurriedly, when his eyes narrowed in warning, "because I know you are a perfection-ist and wish to improve yourself in all things."

"Careful, Gabrielle," he warned, his dark eyes hard on hers.

She did not know if it was the teasing he objected to, or the idea of a second wife. He had proved remarkably and con-sistently ill-humored whenever the idea of an end to their own marriage—however fanciful—was raised. She decided to act as if it was the former.

"Come, now," she said softly, smiling. "We are none of us so grand that we cannot take a bit of gentle teasing, are we?"

"I prefer to tease in a more private place," he replied in a silky tone. "I find the results are far more edifying."

As he had no doubt intended, she could almost feel his mouth on her skin, his flesh against hers, the hot, hard length of him moving deep within her—and all while he held her so correctly, so reservedly, and executed the steps of the waltz with faultless precision. She let out a shaky laugh.

"Do not play games with me," he suggested, a smile lurking in his gaze though his mouth remained hard, "if you cannot compete."

She knew this was the way he played with her—and that she might be the only person on earth he could be said to play with. He did not know the meaning of the word *gentle*. He did not tease—he decimated. Everything about him—from the way he carried his hard warrior's body, fashioned for combat, in elegant couture, to the way he conducted his business affairs like the wars he did not fight, to this, his marriage—

was the same. He was an unstoppable force—more machine in many ways than man. He knew nothing else, no other way of behaving.

She couldn't bear to hurt him. To cause him pain by telling him what Silvio had threatened to do. She was overwhelmed by the need to shield him, protect him.

And that was when she knew. When the truth of it hit her like a speeding train to the side of the head. She felt the blood drain from her face, from her extremities, so that everything tingled and hurt while her stomach clenched and twisted. An earthquake could not have knocked her more firmly on her behind, though he continued to hold her up and move her about the room.

"What is it?" he asked, frowning down at her. "You look as if you've seen a ghost."

"No, no," she murmured, and tucked her head against his chest, because for once in her life she could not bring herself to smile. Everything seemed too sharp, too real—the world suddenly in brutal focus when she hadn't even known it was blurred. "I am perfectly well."

But that was not precisely true.

She was in love with her husband.

Recklessly, totally and heedlessly in love with him. Even thinking the word *love* made her blood pound harder in her veins and her head swim.

Of course, she thought, the truth ringing deep inside her like a bell. *Of course.*

How could she have thought it was anything else? How had she hidden the truth of it from herself for so long?

"Look at me," he commanded her.

She felt dazed, but she complied, letting that fierce gray gaze crash into her, knowing finally that what she felt was not terror, not panic, but a bone-deep exultation. It was hard and it was true and it was love—fierce and uncompromising.

She loved him.

"I am fine," she told him. Finally she smiled. "I promise."

"Do you need to sit down?" He was already moving toward their table, but she stopped him with a hand against his steely chest. She blinked to hide the sudden tears in the backs of her eyes. She was too emotional—too full with the sudden knowledge she'd been denying herself for so long. Too long.

"No," she said. "I want to dance." He looked as if he would ignore her. "Please? I am a little tired, I think. That's all."

He searched her face, and for a moment she thought he would remove them from the dance floor after all, but he relented. He pulled her close again, and frowned down at her.

"If you feel dizzy at all, tell me," he ordered her. "I am not a mind-reader, Gabrielle."

"Indeed you are not," she murmured, and he responded with something close to a snort. But he danced, sweeping her with him, gliding them both across the floor.

The band played; the chandeliers glowed.

She loved him.

Her body had known it from the first moment she'd seen him, as she walked toward him down the aisle at their wedding. It had overwhelmed her. Her blood had sung out to him, her breath had caught, and she had wanted him despite everything. Despite the fact she did not know him, despite the fact he had been so hard, so terrifying. Her body had known all along. Even while she ran, even while she hid, even while she tried to convince herself that there was something wrong with her.

She had called it weakness, worried she was going mad, tried to hold herself apart—but none of it had made any difference. He had managed to get to her, again and again, and she'd not only let him, she'd wanted him. She wanted him now.

But more than that, more than all the rest of it, she wanted to protect him.

She could not tell him about Silvio. She refused. She would

do what she must and make sure Luc never heard about the tape. She would protect him from the thing he hated most, and she knew as she looked up at him, at his strong face set in those uncompromising lines, that she would love him desperately until the end of her days. Ten thousand pounds was getting off cheaply. She would pay twice as much, and as easily, to keep him from any more pain. She would do it happily.

"And now you smile," he said. "A real one this time."

"Take me home," she told him, her smile widening. "I think I'm interested in the kind of teasing you prefer."

As soon as the bedroom door closed behind them, shutting them away in the privacy of their suite of rooms in the grand Miravakian Belgravia house, Gabrielle turned and smiled—the kind of smile that made Luc harden instantaneously while desire roared through his body.

"My turn," she said. She seemed to shimmer in the glow of the single light left burning—the small bedside lamp she used to read, which cast the rest of the room into shadow.

"By all means," Luc agreed, tugging his tie off and opening the top button of his crisp white dress shirt. In his current state he would have agreed to anything. He couldn't take his eyes off her. She was incandescent tonight—radiant.

"You are so accommodating," she said, her eyes sparkling.

"You are different tonight," he told her as she swayed toward him, her figure displayed to breathtaking advantage in the formfitting black dress she wore so well. He'd spent the whole dinner fascinated by the delicate ridge of her collarbone. He was mesmerized now by the roll of her hips, the fullness of her mouth, the heat in her eyes. He was hypnotized.

She did not speak. She only smiled that same mysterious smile as she advanced on him and then put her hands on his body, making him smile in return with deep satisfaction because she was finally touching him. He made a low noise in the back of his throat as she ran her palms over his abdomen, then up his chest, leaving trails of sensation in her wake. She helped him shrug out of his jacket, then tossed it aside.

He nearly vibrated with a mixture of awe and lust as she sucked her full bottom lip into her mouth, worrying it, while her eyes moved over him, drinking him in. He felt it like a physical caress.

"Che cosa desideri?" he asked huskily. The room felt close and tight around them. "What do you desire?"

"You," she whispered, emotion crackling in her voice, across her lovely face. "Only you."

"You have me," he replied. Succumbing to a sudden sense of urgency, he backed her toward the huge raised bed that dominated the room as she yanked his buttons free, parting his shirt to stare greedily at his exposed skin. "You need only ask."

"I am not asking," she said, tilting her head up, heat and mischief in her gaze. "Tonight I am telling you."

"Is that so?" he asked lazily, enjoying her boldness.

"You do not like being told what to do, I know." Her lashes swept down, and then she looked up at him again. She was suddenly coquettish. She was delectable. "I want you to take off my dress."

Luc smiled. "I find that perhaps I do not mind it as much as I thought," he murmured. He reached over and smoothed his hands along her curves, feeling the heat of the skin on her bare shoulders. "There are certain things you can always order me to do."

Spinning her around, he unzipped the dress and peeled it from her, slowly exposing her creamy skin to his hungry gaze. He pushed the fabric down over the swell of her breasts as they surged against a bra made of lace and imagination more than anything substantial, then further, over the flare of her hips and the triangle of scarlet and lace that covered her mound.

"Your wish is my command," he whispered, lifting up the

heavy coil of her hair and pressing his mouth to the place where her pulse throbbed against her neck. She smelled of flowers and spice and went straight to his head—with a spike of desire to his groin.

She surprised him by turning around in his arms, stretching up to press her mouth to his. She was like heat. A rich, addictive sweetness that was all her—only her—with an underlying kick he couldn't seem to get enough of. The taste of her wrenched the desire in his gut to an even higher pitch. He raked his hands through what was left of her elegant chignon and jerked her closer, flattening her against him. He felt the push of her breasts against him, the hard ridges of her nipples like twin points of delicious agony against his bare skin, and angled his mouth across hers for a deeper, better fit. He filled his hands with the sweet curves of her bottom, pulling her tight against him, her softness directly against his throbbing groin.

She felt too good. He could eat her alive. In one gulp. But she wanted her turn, and he wanted to give it to her.

She pulled away, her eyes dark in the low-lit room. Once again that smile curved her lips. It drove him crazy. He had the sensation that the worlds he'd sensed in her were there once more—just out of reach, hidden in plain view—if he could simply decode that damned smile.

He let her push him backward toward the bed, intrigued by the new determination that tilted up her chin and brought that gleam to her eyes. She kept pushing against him, and he kept letting her move him, until he sprawled back across the deep burgundy silk dupioni coverlet. He propped himself up on his elbows and watched her. If this was how she looked when he let her take charge, he resolved to allow it more often.

Very slowly, never taking her eyes from his, she reached behind her and released the catch of her bra—pulling it off with one hand and letting her breasts fall free. He did not move—he only feasted on them with his eyes. So close, and yet out of reach, the twin globes were begging for his touch—his tongue. Then she bent and slowly stripped her panties from her body, drawing his eyes along with her as she stepped out of them. One long, shapely leg, then the next.

Luc thought he might have lost the power of speech. He ached to bury himself in her. His hands twitched with the need to touch her. And she only stood there, for a moment that seemed to stretch into infinity—her eyes as unreadable as the sea they were said to resemble.

Just when his patience was about to snap she stepped toward the bed, running her hands up his legs until they met at the waistband of his trousers. Her hair trickled across his stomach—teasing him, inciting him, driving him slowly and softly out of his mind with the most intense lust he had ever experienced.

She leaned over him and set about removing his trousers with more single-mindedness than skill. She let out a soft sigh when she released his aching hardness from behind his zipper, and took it in her warm hands, testing the weight and feel of it against her palms.

Luc had to close his eyes and grit his teeth to retain control. Barely.

"Stop," he ordered her when she leaned forward, her mouth far too close to his sex.

He jackknifed up and pulled her away from danger, his heart pounding against his chest like a drum. He kicked his trousers off, wincing as he nearly unmanned himself in his haste to get rid of his socks, his underwear, without releasing his hold on her. Her hair fell around her in a tangled curtain of dark honey, her lips were swollen slightly from his kisses, and she was without question the most beautiful creature he had ever seen.

If he did not get inside her soon he might kill them both. And her mouth would not do—not tonight.

"I told you—" she began.

"I have only so much control," he gritted out, cutting her off, his own voice guttural in the quiet room. "I am only a man, Gabrielle!"

"Are you sure?" she asked, her laughter wicked. Powerful. Then her eyes darkened—a mix of passion and something else Luc could not identify. "I think you do not trust me."

She didn't give him a chance to answer. She climbed up on to the bed, straddling his thighs, bracing herself against his chest and holding herself there for a moment—poised above him, tormenting them both.

If he had meant to answer her, he forgot. He forgot everything.

"Gabrielle—" he managed to grit out, through his teeth.

And she sank down on top of him, burying his sex deep within her, making them both groan.

Luc pushed her hair back from her face and pulled her down close as her hips began to move in that delicious, mind-numbing roll that was uniquely hers. He kissed her once, twice, and then released her, watching her rear up in front of him like some kind of goddess. She rode him until they were both panting and she was moaning—rode him until she shone with the force of it—rode him with an abandon and an intensity that he had never seen before, never dreamed of before.

And then she whispered something he was too far gone in ecstasy to hear, and rode them both over the edge.

CHAPTER FIFTEEN

LUC had no intention of playing Silvio Domenico's demented games.

He'd received the paparazzo's call at half-ten that morning, told the vile dog exactly what he could do with his lies and rumors, and dismissed the matter.

Except here he was, a little more than an hour later, walking into Harrods like a puppet on a string.

He was furious with himself. He could not imagine Gabrielle doing the things Silvio claimed she was doing—the very idea was absurd. Gabrielle, who had little or no interest in the tabloids, selling compromising photos of the two of them to Silvio? It was laughable at best.

And yet he had come.

He had left a business meeting abruptly and hailed a black cab instead of his own car, all in his haste to confirm what he already knew to be a lie.

He knew Silvio. He knew how the man operated. He was outraged that the piece of filth had dared to utter his wife's name!

His wife.

She had surprised him last night. All that passion and abandon—and her boldness. He was stirred simply remembering it. There had been an intensity to their lovemaking that he hadn't understood, but he had responded to it—how could he not? She had bewitched him, clearly. There was no other explanation. He had chosen her because she conformed to a list of attributes he'd made up years before—but he had not expected this *thirst* for her. This ravenous hunger that he could not seem to satisfy.

Maybe that was why he had come? The hunger made him distinctly uncomfortable, as it did not fade or decrease. If anything, it had only gotten worse in the time he'd known her. He hardly recognized himself when he was around her. It was as if he forgot himself. He…wanted. He wanted things he found himself unwilling to name.

It would have disturbed him had he not been far too infatuated with her to care.

That infatuation was why he had come, Luc told himself. He was here to see through whatever charade Silvio intended to show him, make it clear the scum of a man was never to invoke Gabrielle's name again, and be on his way. Nothing more, nothing less.

He stopped in the designated place, lurking behind a display case like the paparazzi he abhorred. Why was he doing this? What could Silvio possibly have to show him that would make the slightest difference to him?

"I must tell you the truth about your wife, my friend," the other man had said, making Luc feel slimy by association, simply because he'd answered the unfamiliar number on his mobile phone. "Much as it pains me, you understand?" His laughter had turned into a hacking smoker's cough.

"How did you get this number?" Luc had demanded, disgusted.

"Does it matter?" Silvio had asked, with another arrogant laugh.

"I'm hanging up," Luc had snapped. "And then I'm having you arrested for harassment—"

"She's approached me with some naughty pictures of the

two of you," Silvio had interrupted smoothly, with obvious lascivious enjoyment. "A souvenir from your honeymoon, yes? How proud you must be. I am told your—ah—*assets* are extraordinary."

"You expect me to believe that my wife wants to sell you photographs?" Luc had said derisively. He had made a succinct and anatomically impossible suggestion.

"Save it for your loving wife," Silvio had taunted him, unfazed. "And why shouldn't she make a little cash like everyone else? You're lucky she came to me. Anyone else and you would have seen it on the nightly news with the rest of the world. At least I'm giving you a little advance warning!"

Luc shook his head slightly now, and knew that his initial instinct had been correct. His coming here was a mistake. He had played right into Silvio's hands. The truth was that he *knew* Gabrielle could never conceive of such a thing—and she certainly would not be in cahoots with the likes of Silvio.

It was far more likely that Silvio was taking pictures of Luc now, as he lurked at this counter, and would later run some absurd story about it in one of the tabloids, claiming that Luc was meeting a lover—or something far more salacious. Drugs. Criminals. Who knew the depths to which Silvio might sink? He was less than a pig.

Luc was disgusted with himself.

But then he saw her, and he froze.

Gabrielle strode into the hall, looked around, and then marched directly toward the far side. She was so elegant, so refined, dressed all in snowy white. She held herself like the queen she would be one day. *What was she doing here?*

But he knew. He couldn't believe it, but he knew.

Another figure detached itself from the shadows and met her. Silvio.

It took only moments. Gabrielle held out an envelope and snatched the one that Silvio offered directly from his hand.

They exchanged only a few words. Then she turned and walked away from him, exiting the store without ever looking around. She had no idea that Luc was there.

Silvio looked in Luc's direction and shrugged, his cocky grin firmly in place, but Luc barely noticed him.

Something broke loose inside him—something sharp and jagged and dangerous. It moved through him like a howl, though he did not make a sound. It was happening again. Just as it had happened when he was a boy. The frenzy of lies, speculation—the dirt that would slime him by association and follow him like a storm cloud.

And *she* was the one doing it this time. Not his parents—forever mysterious to him, forever unknowable and lost to him. Not them, but Gabrielle. The one he had chosen because she would never do this. The one he had believed would never, *ever* do this.

He should have known better than to trust her public face—the one that had tricked him into marrying her, the one that had deceived him even after he'd had to chase her across the globe, humiliated by her defection in front of all the world. She was no better than his self-centered mother—and hadn't he known that from the first? Hadn't he expected this behavior from all the women he'd dated across the years? The more beautiful they were, the more treacherous. Hadn't he known that since he was an infant?

He hadn't realized how much he'd expected—needed—her to have nothing to do with Silvio's little demonstration until he'd seen her walk in. He hadn't realized how much he'd trusted her until he'd watched her betray him.

He hadn't known how much he could feel, no matter how little he wanted to feel.

And it had never occurred to him that his heart might be involved at all until now, when it reminded him of its existence by aching like an open wound that would never heal.

* * *

The moment Gabrielle walked into their rooms and saw Luc already there she knew something was wrong. She stopped in her tracks and stared at him.

Luc sat in the sitting area near the large fireplace, his long legs stretched out in front of him and his arm thrown out along the back of the sofa that he seemed to dwarf. He wore a dark charcoal sweater that hugged the fine muscles of his torso and a pair of dark trousers that fit him exquisitely, emphasizing his strength and power. He looked gorgeous, as ever, and his position suggested relaxation and ease, but Gabrielle stiffened. She could feel the dark tension emanate from him in waves. His gaze—cold, and a dark gray too close to black—locked to hers like a slap. A shiver of anxiety slithered along her spine.

She had not seen that particular look of his in a long time. Not since the night he'd appeared at her door in California, in fact. And she did not remember him being quite so hostile even then. She was surprised to discover he could still make her gasp in reaction simply with the force of his gaze.

"Has something happened?" she asked at once. She crossed to him, sinking down into the plush armchair facing him.

Foreboding and menace seemed to fill the room, and all he did was look at her, as if he was trying to read her. His rugged face had closed down, turned back into stone and iron—and he was once again the forbidding, menacing stranger who had so overwhelmed her originally.

She realized with some amazement that she hadn't understood how much he'd changed—how open he had become, how relatively warm and approachable—until now.

"Did you have a nice day?" he asked, in that low voice with its treacherous undercurrents. She couldn't read him at all—but she could sense that she should tread carefully, even so.

"Yes, thank you," she said automatically, her ingrained politeness kicking into gear despite her confusion. "I saw some old friends for lunch. It was lovely. And you?"

How absurdly formal! Gabrielle felt ridiculous—and then his mouth pulled to the side in obvious mockery, and the feeling intensified. She felt color high on her cheeks as his gaze—insulting and cutting—swept over her, leaving marks, she was sure.

"I, too, saw an old friend of sorts," he murmured. His tone sharpened as he leaned forward, no longer pretending to be casual. His gaze slammed into her. "Tell me, Gabrielle—and please do me the favor of being honest, if you can—where are they?"

"Who?" she asked, confused and wary.

He thought she was dishonest? She felt skittish and nervous in a way she had thought never to feel around him again. It turned out that loving him did not change the way he could get under her skin. Perhaps love only explained it. It was an uncomfortable notion.

"My friends?" she continued when he did not. "They are distant cousins, actually, and we met in Chelsea—"

"Not your friends."

His voice could have cut through steel. She nearly winced, though she caught herself. She ordered herself to calm down, to keep talking.

"Why won't you tell me what's happened?" she asked. "You look… You look so—" She broke off helplessly. What could she say? *You look as hard and remote and cold as you used to be—before I knew I was in love with you, before I believed this marriage would work?* She didn't know what was going on, but she knew that this could not possibly be the right moment for that revelation.

"You should be less concerned with how I look," he bit out, his big body seeming to vibrate with all the leashed power she could sense he wanted to release, "and more concerned with what I am about to do."

Gabrielle blinked. That was obviously a threat. But why? What could he imagine she'd done? She thought of the repugnant Silvio and their exchange at Harrods—but even if Luc knew of it, why would he take his anger out on her? Surely she was an innocent party in that mess?

"I don't know what you mean," she said, folding her hands in her lap and straightening her spine as much as she could, thinking that if he would not simply tell her what was going on she would wait him out. Hadn't she already decided that was the smartest way to handle him? He would destroy her in any straightforward contest. She wasn't sure he could help himself—that was his way. Her best bet was to endure, and wait. She had every faith he would come around in time. And that she was more than capable of surviving the storm until he did.

"Do you think your manners will help you?" he asked in a near sneer, his eyes boring into her even as he held himself firmly in check. "Do you think I will be fooled?"

"Luc, please." She searched his face, but the Luc she had come to know was gone, and in his place was this creature of granite, of glaciers and stone. As much a stranger to her as he had been on their wedding day. Her heart began to beat out a jagged, panicked rhythm. *No one said it would be pleasant to wait out the storm*, she thought. "I can't defend myself if I don't know what you're talking about!"

"Where are they?" he thundered, making her jump.

"I don't know—"

"The pictures," he bit out, fury etched across his face, making him seem as deadly as the warrior she'd sometimes fancied him to be.

"Pictures?" Had he gone mad? She had not the slightest idea what he could be talking about. She blinked at him. "What pictures?"

He launched himself up and onto his feet. Gabrielle's heart leapt to her throat—but he did not reach for her. She did not know if she was glad of that or not. He paced around the room, looking like some kind of elegant wild animal, all rangy motion and lethal energy. She stood, too, thinking it best not to have him behind her or out of sight, as any animal of prey would in the presence of so unpredictable a predator.

"The camera must be automated—and portable, obviously," he said, addressing the room in general more than her, still in that low, tense voice. "You had nothing to do with our hotel arrangements, so you could only have had moments to prepare it and put it into place. But I can't find the damned thing and I can't find any pictures." He turned back to her, his gaze flicking over her contemptuously. "But you already have what you want, don't you? Your final rebellion against your father—against me—accomplished with a few clicks of a camera lens."

"Luc." She said his name softly, trying to sound reasonable. "You are not making any sense."

His head tilted to one side, an arrogant and challenging gesture, and his eyes ran hot with molten fury—and it was directed at her. Gabrielle felt her breath hitch in her chest.

"Am I not?" he asked. Too quietly. Too precisely. Biting the words off with his teeth. "Let me tell you what does not make sense to me. The money. Why would you need it? You have your own. And even if you did not—"

"Money?" Gabrielle shook her head, warding his words away from her. "You think I am motivated by *money*? Like some desperate—?"

"Even if you did not," Luc gritted out, ignoring her, "I have more than enough money to keep you in any style you wish. So it cannot be for money. What else could motivate you? Are you not famous enough? Photographed enough? Do you aspire to the ranks of those interchangeable starlets known only because they have no shame, no lower place to fall? Or is it one last rebellious act from the supposedly obedient princess? *Tell*

me!" he demanded, louder, moving closer, yet still maintaining his distance—just outside an arm's length away.

As if he was afraid to touch her, she realized in astonishment. Was he afraid that he would hurt her? Or did he want to? Or, like her, did he suspect that if they touched his anger would disappear in the heat of their need for each other?

"I have no wish to be any of those things," she said softly.

"At first I simply wanted to destroy you," he told her, in a voice that was almost affectionate—though his eyes glittered dangerously and she knew better. "To cast you out and be done with this farce. But I cannot figure it out, Gabrielle. I cannot make sense of it."

"What do you think I've done?" she asked, holding herself still, or unable to move, perhaps, while he looked at her that way. Her breath hurt her, sawing in and out of her lungs.

"I know what you've done," he said bitterly. He shook his head. "But you were a virgin—you could not have faked it. I am sure of it." He let out a hollow sort of laugh. "Why I equate virginity with honor, I do not know. At the end of the day you are still a woman, are you not? Perhaps you planned this from the start."

Gabrielle blanched at the bleakness in his voice, then shook her head. She racked her brain for any possible issue that could have upset him this much, but couldn't think of anything.

Except her meeting with Silvio.

"There *is* something I haven't told you," she said, fighting to remain calm—or at least sound calm. "But even if you know about it, I don't know why you should be so angry with me. I thought I was doing the right thing."

"Did you?" He sounded only mildly interested—halfway to being bored—but Gabrielle knew better. She knew this was Luc at his most lethal.

"Yes," she said. She felt her confusion melt away in a rush of overdue anger that punched into her gut and hummed through her—how *could* he speak to her this way? After they had come so far? Had he been pretending all this time?

"You call this the right thing?" he said, with a nasty, sardonic inflection that made her want to slap him—an urge she had never had before in her life. "You can say this to my face?"

"Of course," she said tightly, and lifted her chin.

He could go to hell—with his anger and his coldness and this insane line of questioning, as if she was a common criminal. Who did he think he was? And here she was, so in love with him—it was infuriating.

Her hands balled into fists. She raised her eyebrows in challenge. "Of course I thought so. Why else would I meet with Silvio?"

CHAPTER SIXTEEN

"So you admit it." Luc could not believe it. He could not believe she would *defend* what she had done! He felt frozen, and yet nearly liquid with fury—all at the same time. He felt as if everything shook—as if the city of London wavered beneath his feet—but nothing moved. Not even him. "You do not even try to lie to protect yourself? You announce it freely!"

Her gaze darkened, her mouth flattening into a thin line.

"I don't know what you want me to say." She crossed her arms over her chest. Hugging herself tight or fending him off? He couldn't tell. "Why engage in this exercise? Why not simply ask me about it if you already know?"

"This is how you respond?" He was so angry he felt his hands twitch and his blood pound against his temples. His suspicion that she had planned this from the beginning—first his humiliation when she disappeared, then this betrayal to the vile tabloids just as he began to trust her—crystallized in the vicinity of his chest. "This is your defense of something so low, so disgusting, that it demeans us both?"

"I thought I was helping you!" She enunciated each word, showing her temper, no longer so perfectly composed. But even that added to his fury. *Now* she showed him cracks in her well-mannered façade? Now, when it couldn't—shouldn't—matter any longer?

The emotions he'd spent his entire adult life avoiding filled him now, in a churning mess, and they were as unpleasant and unhelpful as he recalled. Anger. Hurt. What was the point of either? He tried to wrestle the emotional wave that crested inside of him into line—to tamp it back down beneath the smooth exterior he'd worked so hard to have define him—but it was too late. He had the sudden notion that he and Gabrielle were the same—with the masks they each wore, the calm surfaces with so much hidden beneath. Too much hidden.

And what does it matter now? he asked himself bitterly. She was the one he had trusted. She was the one he had married. And yet it turned out she was the same as all the others, the same as his deceitful mother—worse, because he had believed better of her. Because she had somehow convinced him that she *understood* him. What had he been thinking?

"You thought you were helping?" He had to turn away before he did something he would truly regret. Like show her these things he didn't want to feel—all of them, in all their raw and vulnerable ugliness.

No. He would not. He could not bear to be so exposed. Not now, not ever—and certainly not after she had so betrayed him. *No.*

"Yes, I thought I was helping." She blew out a ragged breath. "Why else?"

When he turned to look at her again she had pressed her fingers to the frown between her eyes. She rubbed at it, then dropped her hand to her side. She regarded him warily, her eyes too wide and too dark—as if *he* had wounded *her* somehow!

"Silvio approached me yesterday," she said quietly. "He told me your—that there was a tape."

"Stop," Luc ordered her with a slash of his hand through the air, as if to cut her words off himself. The chaotic emotions inside him intensified—burned—fought to come out. "I cannot hear any more lies!"

"Lies?" She raised her gaze to his, anger and confusion and something else mixed together in the blue-green depths.

"I don't know what I was thinking," he raged at her, his voice like a low, angry throb in the otherwise hushed room. He could feel his own vulnerability like a sharp pain, and he hated the fact that he could not control it—could not control himself. Hated more that she had brought him to this. That she had *planned* to do this to him, and now stood before him and denied it. "I have become everything I despise. That is what is most clear to me in all of this. I am no better than my father in his day, dancing to her tune—"

"I am not your mother," she interrupted him. Her voice was even, her eyes steady on his. But he ignored her.

"This—this—*infatuation* has made me a stranger to myself," he continued, as if she hadn't spoken.

He had been bewitched, enchanted—but these were simply other ways of saying he had been played for a fool. She had played him—he who had never let his guard down before. And look what happened when he did! When he made romantic gestures to a woman who had run away from him at his own wedding! Anger. Hurt. Fear that now he had let these emotions out they would rule him. That he would become a slave to them, like his parents before him.

He had the terrible notion that it was the fact that *she* had done this that hurt—not simply that it had been done. That *she*, Gabrielle, was no different from the others. He had trusted her more—he had liked her more—

"But no more," he snapped. *No more*, damn her.

She moved toward him then, her frown melting from anger to cautious concern. She reached out to touch him—but he intercepted her hand before she could make contact with his cheek and held it out between them like a weapon. Hers or his, he did not know.

"*Je sais exactement ce que vous êtes—plus jamais ne me*

tromperez-vous," he spat out. "I know what you are, Gabrielle. I won't be fooled by you again."

"Luc—"

"This is over," he threw at her.

Even to his own ears the words sounded as if they came from far off—some faraway rage, someone else's fury. Better that than the keening mess in his gut, his fury like some kind of flu, ravaging through his body. How could this be happening to him?

"This marriage should never have happened. I should have known that no one could live up to my standards. That even in Nice you were nothing more than a carefully constructed lie. Did your father plan it? Or was that you, too?"

He could feel her pulse flutter wildly in her wrist.

"What...? Nice?" she asked, reeling. "What would my father have to do with—?" She cut herself off, trying to make sense of his angry words. "You were in Nice when I was? This past spring?"

"I followed you," he told her, without a shred of apology, forcefully—wanting to rip into her with the knowledge. Anything to make her hurt as he hurt. Anything to ease the force of it inside his own body. "I wanted to make sure you had no skeletons in your closet—no secret lovers, no dirty laundry. What does it matter now? You never saw me then, and believe me, Gabrielle, you will never see me again."

He saw the color drain from her face. He wanted to soothe her pain even as he caused it. He wanted to pull her close and crush her mouth to his. He wanted her even now, and he hated them both for it.

"You cannot mean that!" she cried.

He watched her pull herself together—he wondered what it cost her.

"This is crazy—a misunderstanding—"

"I want an annulment."

The words fell between them like stones from a great height. Gabrielle flinched, her eyes wide and shocked.

"But you… We…" She couldn't seem to form sentences. She cast around for words, her mouth working, her eyes glued to his. "We cannot *annul*, surely—?"

"I have already contacted my lawyers," he told her, taking satisfaction from the way his words hit her body like blows, making her falter on her feet. Though he still held her hand in his—a pale imitation of the way their hands had once touched and would never touch again. Why did thinking that deepen his pain? Where was the indifference that should accompany his realization that she was as fake as the rest—as untrustworthy, as disappointing? "I suggest you do the same." He sneered at her—anything to create distance, to make her like the others. "I will be claiming fraud, of course."

"Luc—" She had to clear her throat, and she sounded like a stranger, hoarse and choked. "Luc, you cannot do this."

"Why can't I?" He moved close—too close, tempting himself with the wild madness of her mouth so near to his—and bared his teeth. "You abandoned me on our wedding day. You besmirched my name across the globe. You are no better than the paparazzi scum you are so friendly with. I have no doubt you planned this with them for the maximum amount of embarrassment." He remembered he was holding on to her hand and let go of it abruptly, releasing her so she stumbled backward. "You are nothing to me."

"But—but—I love you!"

She gasped even as she said it—and her hands flew up to cover her mouth, as if she could stuff the words she'd cried back inside. Her breath came in agitated pants. Her eyes were dark and glazed with emotion, but he wanted more. He wanted her to deny that she could ever have dealt with Silvio—could have sold him out. Barring that, he wanted her to hurt, to howl. He wanted to make sure she felt every bit as empty as he did.

"I beg your pardon, Gabrielle?" He snarled her name like the snap of a whip against tender flesh. "What did you just say?"

But she surprised him. She curled her hands into fists again, and then dropped them to her sides. She was still dressed in pristine, snowy white, the only color her over-bright eyes, like the sea in a storm. The cowl neck of the top she wore showcased her delicate collarbone and the elegant line of her neck. He hated that she could look so beautiful, so regal, even now.

"I said that I love you," she said, her voice thick but her head high. Her eyes glittered, but stayed steady on his. "I do."

"You *love* me?"

It was as if she'd spoken in one of the few languages he didn't know. He pronounced the word *love* as if it were some kind of disease, as if he could be infected by saying it aloud. Inside him, something broke. He felt it—felt the rising tide of an emotion like grief that accompanied it. But he could not allow what he feared would follow any acknowledgment that her words had gotten to him. *He would not.*

He cocked his head to one side and looked at her as a snake might look at a mouse. "And what reaction do you expect me to have to this convenient announcement, Gabrielle?"

"I have no expectations." He saw her throat work. "It is no more and no less than the truth."

He let out a filthy Italian curse that made the color flood her face. Then he closed the distance between them, his palms wrapping around her bare shoulders and hauling her to him, bringing her face scant inches apart from his.

Was it love or was it madness? Or was love itself madness, as he had always believed, though he had never felt as mad as he did now? Why did he yearn to touch her, again and again, stripping them both naked and sorting it out with their bodies? It was only sex, he told himself desperately. It had to be.

"You love what I can do to your body," he snapped at her. "You love the way I make you feel. That is all. That is *nothing*!"

"I can't help what you think," she whispered back, a sob in her throat. "But I do love you. Even now."

"I am touched, Gabrielle, but somehow unimpressed with such a brave declaration at such a time," he bit out, his fingers digging into her soft flesh, though she made no sound of protest. He bent her backward in some grotesque parody of a kiss—and he loathed himself because he wanted to kiss her, to lose himself in the heady insanity of her taste, her body. "You can explain to your father that you love me—and that is why you betrayed me, that is why I am throwing you back to him like something defective."

"Luc…"

Finally. Finally her tears spilled over and flowed down her cheeks. He exulted in them—and wanted to reach inside himself and physically rip out the part of him that still wanted to protect her, despite everything.

Despite what she had done to him. Despite how little she must care for him and about him if she could do it—if, as he believed more and more with each second, she had planned this from the moment her father told her she was to marry. And there was no mistaking it. He had seen her sell him out with his own eyes.

"I would never betray you! I love you!" she cried.

How could he want so urgently to believe her—even when he knew better?

"You and your love can go to hell," he told her, with cold, brutal finality. He didn't know where it came from—but the coldness was like a savior, descending upon him and muting the turbulent mess inside him. Masking it. He forced himself to let her go. He stepped away from her and told himself he didn't care when she sank to the plush carpet before him, the marks from his fingers standing out against the pale white silk of her skin.

He had to leave her before he lost himself. That much was perfectly, terrifyingly clear.

He walked out, and he forced himself not to look back.

Gabrielle did not get up from the carpet for a long time.

It seemed to take forever for her to accept that Luc had left her—left the house, left London, *left her*—and even so, she did not fully come to terms with it until a full two weeks had passed.

He did not answer his mobile, and he did not return. He'd sent staff to collect his belongings within twenty-four hours of his departure—none of whom acknowledged her beyond a stiff announcement of their purpose. But she was still holding out a kind of desperate hope—something her father crushed in one short telephone call to London.

"You might as well come home," he barked into the phone, his displeasure evident even from as far away as Miravakia. "Your antics have lost you your husband, it seems. Best ensure they do not also lose you your throne."

Gabrielle couldn't think of any reason to stay in London if Luc had already started the process of dissolving their marriage. What would be the point? She might as well be in Miravakia as anywhere else—what did any of it matter?

She did not realize that she was in some kind of shock until she found herself back in Miravakia, ensconced in her father's *palazzo* as if she had never left. She had the sense that she was suspended in some kind of bubble, underwater, far away from whatever happened around her. In the middle of the night, when she could not sleep and could only lie awake, her body in a fever and her heart pounding with the enormity of her loss, she knew that she was hiding from the pain of Luc's desertion—afraid to really let herself feel what she was not at all certain she could survive.

She might have remained there forever—hidden away, protected, distanced entirely from what she shied away from feeling—had it not been for her father.

"You have proved yourself useless and ruined your reputation, so there can be no more trading on it," King Josef said one morning at the breakfast table, when Gabrielle had been home for some weeks. If he had broken his customary silence before, Gabrielle had not noticed. "I'm afraid I don't possess the necessary imaginative prowess to make a silk purse out of this sow's ear."

She realized two things simultaneously as she stared down at her bowl of muesli, his cold, brutal words falling around her like so many blows. One, that this was not the first time her father had spoken to her like this—not by a long shot, and this was not even the worst example of his cruelty or his callous disregard for her feelings. And two, she was not required to listen to it.

A part of the hard shell she'd gathered around herself cracked wide open.

She was done with it. With him. With his casual cruelty and his offhand treatment of her. She was required to respect him as her king, and even on some level as her parent. But that did not mean she was required to suffer his behavior for one moment more.

What was the worst that could happen? The King had already married her off to a stranger. Luc had already left her. There was no *worst*.

It was as if the sun had broken from behind the clouds.

Gabrielle raised her head and fastened her gaze on her father. It was as if she'd never seen him before. He was dressed, as ever, impeccably. His light brown hair was smoothed back from his aristocratic brow, and his handsome features were set in their usual expression of stern displeasure.

She had always disappointed him. Because she was not a boy. Because she was not able to read his mind, anticipate his needs.

Because her mother had died and left her care in his hands. Because he was a man who would always be disappointed.

She remembered thinking that he was like Luc, that they were the same kind of man, and almost let out a laugh. The two men could not be more different. King Josef was petty, mean. Luc was elemental, unstoppable. King Josef dominated a room because he thought his consequence demanded it. Luc because he could not fail to do so—it was who he was, not what he did.

Most important, Luc had made her feel free. She had been more herself with him than she had ever been before. She hadn't had to be the constrained, quiet princess that King Josef demanded for Luc. Luc had liked it when she did not hide. He'd liked her wild, free—and only with Luc had she let herself be both proper in public and unrestrained in private.

Only with Luc…

"What do you have to smile about, may I ask?" King Josef asked, bristling. He put his silver fork down against his plate with a loud clunk. "When I think of the shame you have brought upon this family, this nation, I cannot imagine I will ever smile again."

"I was thinking of Luc," she said, her mind racing—the protective shell around her was broken now, and the feelings she'd been holding at bay were rushing in.

She had spent her whole life curling up into a ball, keeping her head down and staying silent, all in the desperate hope that she might please someone who could never be pleased. Why was she doing the same thing now? Why was she responding to Luc's anger as if he were her father?

"There is no point in wasting your time with Garnier," King Josef said dismissively. "He wants nothing to do with you."

"Yes, Father," Gabrielle said impatiently. Dismissively. "I was the one in the marriage. I know what he said."

A tense silence fell over the breakfast table. Gabrielle

pulled herself away from her thoughts to notice that her father was staring at her, affront etched across every feature.

"I beg your pardon?" he said icily.

Ordinarily Gabrielle would have soothed him. Apologized to him. But then ordinarily his displeasure would have made her anxious—she would have felt horrible, fallen all over herself to fix things, yearned for some sign of approval or, barring that, no outward disapproval.

Today she found she didn't much care. She had finally had enough of trying to please him—enough of falling short.

"My marriage is none of your business," she told him. Quietly. Clearly. "I'll thank you to keep your opinions to yourself."

"Who do you think you are?" he demanded, puffing out his chest in outrage.

"I am the future queen of Miravakia," Gabrielle said, the words ringing out as if they'd been waiting years for her to voice them. She pushed her chair back from the table and stood tall. "If you cannot respect the fact that I am your daughter, and a grown woman, respect that."

"How *dare* you address me in this fashion?" King Josef barked. "Is this how you behaved during your association with Garnier? Is this why he washes his hands of you?"

"I think you mean my *marriage* to Luc Garnier," Gabrielle corrected him gently, finding that after all this time she wasn't angry with her father. She was simply done with him. She looked at him and saw a very small man, crippled by his outsize sense of himself and his need to lord it over his own daughter.

"Your marriage is over," he shot back at her.

Gabrielle thought about that, carefully placing her snowy-white linen napkin next to her plate and stepping away from the table. Why was her marriage over? Because Luc said so? Well—who gave him that right? Even Luc Garnier could not so casually sunder what God had brought together. She had heard that much of her own wedding ceremony.

"Where are you going?" her father demanded as Gabrielle turned and headed for the door, a new resolve making her square her shoulders and spurring her into action.

She loved Luc. Their weeks apart had not altered that at all—if anything they had strengthened it. His horrible reaction had not lessened her feelings either, though she remained furious that he could so easily toss her aside. It was easy to see, in retrospect, that she and Luc had been played against each other by the noxious Silvio, and that Luc, predictably, had reacted with his usual high-octane fury. She was not sure she even blamed him—hadn't she known that any hint of scandal was Luc's worst nightmare? Apparently Silvio had known it, too.

But it was high time she stood up for herself. It was past time she went after what she wanted. She was not the weak, malleable creature she had been before. She had no intention of letting Luc walk away from her without a fight.

She would respond to Luc the way *he'd* responded to her when she'd run away from him.

She would hunt him down, explain to him that he had no other option, and take him to bed.

And when she thought about it in those terms she could hardly wait.

CHAPTER SEVENTEEN

ROME was hot and Luc was surly.

He skirted a group of Spanish-speaking tourists taking pictures of themselves in front of the Fontana del Nettuno at the northern end of the Piazza Navone, barely restraining himself from berating them simply for being in his way.

He was in a foul mood, and had been for weeks. He could not pretend he did not know why.

He had left Gabrielle in London, but her ghost followed him everywhere he went. First he had gone to Paris, where his business was headquartered. Work was his *raison d'être*. It had saved him when his parents died. It had defined his existence since. And yet he'd found himself unable to concentrate. He'd looked at contracts and thought of her mysterious smile, the one he had never decoded. He'd sat in meetings and imagined he was back in bed with her, wrapped up in her arms, their mouths and bodies fused together. He *felt* her—felt her hands upon his skin, felt the ways in which she had changed him—and he despaired that this was permanent, this emotional mess that he'd become.

He thought he might be going mad. Or, worse, was already mad.

He had removed himself to his home in Rome, a penthouse apartment steps from the Piazza Navona. This was where he came to recharge his batteries. Though his mother's family maintained a villa on the Appian Way that had come to him upon her death, he had always preferred the bustle and endless motion of the city center.

Except for now. Rome, haunted by the ghosts of thousands of years, all of them indistinguishable beneath the Italian sky, now seemed haunted exclusively by the one woman Luc could not seem to escape. He saw her everywhere. He heard the music of her laughter on the breeze, glimpsed her face in every crowd and around every corner, and reached for her in his sleep only to wake, alone and furious.

No woman had ever gotten under his skin in this way.

No woman had ever gotten to him at all.

"I do not know when I will return," Luc growled into his mobile now, scowling at the usual frenzied scene spread out before him across the *piazza*. So many tourists and natives in the sun, enjoying the ease and flow of Roman life. And he, meanwhile, could not escape a woman he refused to allow himself to want any longer. She hung over Rome, the city of his heart and his youth, like a smog. She invaded him, altered him, and she was not even there.

"Capisco bene," Alessandro said over the phone. Too carefully. Too calmly. "I am capable of taking care of things at the office, Luc. You must take as much time as you need."

Luc realized that his second-in-command believed him to be nursing some kind of melodramatic romantic ailment, and let out a short laugh. How could he tell Alessandro that Gabrielle had managed to prise off the lid he had clamped down on emotions he had always denied he could ever feel? There was nothing melodramatic about it—it was all too inescapably mundane. And it was killing him.

"I am not lovesick, like a child, Alessandro," he snapped.

"Of course not," the other man replied. Obviously placating him.

It was enraging—yet Luc could do nothing but end the call.

He looked up as he approached his building, his scowl sharpening as he recognized the figure lurking near the haphazardly parked cars in front. The grizzled face and matted curls could belong to only one person: Silvio Domenico.

Exactly who Luc least wanted to see—ever, and certainly not in his current mood.

"Ah, Luc!" Silvio called, his voice heavy with mockery. "Such a beautiful day, is it not? Too bad you must spend it alone!"

As he spoke he lifted his camera and fired off a series of shots. Luc did not alter his stride as he approached—just as he did not alter his expression. The other man grinned at the sight—and not nicely.

"The strong, silent type today, eh?" he jeered. "No punches? No swearing? I am disappointed."

Luc closed the distance between them. He wanted to crush Silvio. He wanted to wrap his hands around the other man's throat, tear apart his limbs and throw them into the gutter for the dogs. But he did none of those things. He stopped, instead, when he was only a few feet away, and regarded the other man for a long, cool moment.

"I have yet to see my intimate life on the evening news," he said. "You disappoint me, Silvio."

"It's only a matter of time," the other man boasted. "There is nowhere you can go that I can't follow. Nothing you do that I won't record. No matter how rich and powerful you get, you still can't control me."

Luc waited for the usual wave of fury to crash through him, but it did not come. He thought instead of Gabrielle. He thought of the fact that no pictures had appeared anywhere—there were not even any rumors that embarrassing pictures existed, as there should have been. There was no whisper of any impropriety either in his marriage or concerning his wife. It dawned on Luc—slowly and inexorably—that there never would be.

That there had never been any photographs. There had only been Silvio, playing games, and Luc's immediate assumption that Gabrielle had betrayed him. Because everyone else had. He remembered with perfect, cutting clarity the way she had looked at him on that last evening—her eyes so wide, so dark, so filled with tears.

I love you. He heard her as clearly as if she stood behind him and whispered in his ear. *I love you.*

"Cat got your tongue?" Silvio taunted him, his lips curled.

"How tedious you are," Luc replied at length, when he was certain his voice would remain even. He eyed Silvio like the cockroach he was. "What an empty life you have made for yourself. I will endeavor to travel to more interesting places to give you a change of scenery, shall I?"

Silvio shot another round of pictures, sneering.

"Garnier, abandoned by wife, succumbs to drink and drug binge," he murmured. *"Once-feared multimillionare Garnier laid low by love—licks wounds in raunchy Roman orgy."*

Luc arched an eyebrow. "I never realized until this moment how obsessed you are with me," he murmured, feeling more like himself than he had in ages. "How sad."

"You should never have hit me!" Silvio snarled, with enough rage that Luc might have thought he referred to something that had occurred in the past decade, had he not known better.

"You should never have thrust your camera into a moment of private grief," Luc returned coolly. "Much less called my mother a whore."

"They say men marry their mothers," Silvio said, flashing a smile filled with yellow teeth and malice.

Luc's first urge was to plant his fist in Silvio's face—again. But that was reflex. When he thought about it for a moment, he nearly smiled. *I am not your mother,* Gabrielle had said. And indeed she was not. He realized now that she never had been.

"Are you calling my wife a whore?" he asked softly. He found he could not even feel the rage he ought to feel—because it was so patently absurd. Of *course* Gabrielle was an innocent. Luc was the only man who had ever touched her—he had taught her how to kiss!

"The Princess? I suppose not," Silvio murmured. "But she was so distraught at the idea of a sex tape of you and La Rosalinda that she paid me ten thousand pounds to destroy it." Silvio laughed. "As if I would turn over such a thing for so little, when it could make ten times that!"

Luc looked at him for a long moment. Could he blame Silvio? Or was it his fault for jumping to the conclusion that had supported his worst fears? She had not planned to embarrass him. There was no resemblance between Gabrielle and the others. No connection between her and the toad who stood before him. None.

"This is your revenge?" he asked at last.

"I don't need revenge," Silvio scoffed. "I have ten thousand pounds. Will you hit me again?" And now Silvio taunted him. "A broken nose this time, maybe? I wonder how much I can sue you for? A man can never have enough money."

Luc let out a laugh then. "There would be no point," he replied. He stepped around the little pig of a man and moved toward the front door of his building. "It is too absurd. By all means print that. Make a fool of yourself in front of all of Europe. With my compliments."

Silvio swore at him as he walked away, but Luc did not respond. He didn't care. It was as if Silvio had finally, after all these years of hunting him, ceased to exist.

He was far more focused on the fact that he'd called Gabrielle *my wife*. With no past tense.

Gabrielle arrived in Rome awash with memories.

It seemed like another person who had run to Rome from

Miravakia in the wake of her own wedding—run from everything she knew and the man she most assuredly did not know.

How had so much changed in so little time? She was now bound and determined to fight for the man she had run from before. Her love for him seemed to burn inside her, bright and fierce and true, and it had nothing to do with how angry she was at the way he'd treated her. How had she changed so much—so much she hardly recognized herself?

Rome was the same. The boisterous, ebullient city surged around her as she rode in a taxi from the airport—unchanged and yet always changing, ancient and new, flexing its more than two thousand years of history and beauty in the Mediterranean sun. It had not taken too much work on her part to figure out where Luc had gone. He had told her himself that he preferred Rome above all other cities, though he only went there alone, and to unwind. Meaning he visited far less than he wished.

Gabrielle held tight to the fact that he was not in Paris, working—his second-in-command had told her so himself. Surely if she meant as little to Luc as he had claimed he would barely have noticed her absence? What was she to him, after all, but another in a long line of women? She could hardly expect to have dominated his world as he did hers—and his going back to work as if she had never existed would have been confirmation of that.

But the fact that he was not in France—that he did not even seem to be working—had to be a good thing, she told herself. It reminded her of something he'd told her during that lazy trip up the California coast.

They had been in Big Sur, awed by the giant trees and the craggy coastline. The Pacific Ocean had pounded against the rocks, swelling and retreating, churning up foam, far below the little cliffside path where they'd strolled.

"I will always prefer Rome to all other cities," he had said. "It is the place I am most at home."

"Why do you not go there more often?" she had asked. Hadn't he just said he spent little time there?

"My offices are in Paris," Luc had said matter-of-factly, shrugging, a faint frown between his eyes. As if he did not understand the question. As if there was nothing else that mattered but work.

Gabrielle remembered wondering why there was such a split in him—work and home forever on different sides of the divide. She had longed, then, to comfort him somehow— though she had sensed that he would not welcome it. Now she wondered why it had never occurred to her that he worked so hard, was so driven, because he knew nothing else. He did not even know he needed comfort.

She glanced down at her left hand, at the two rings that sat on her finger. The diamond he'd given her burst into flame and rainbow in the afternoon sun, reminding her of the night he'd presented it to her. He had been so stiff, so formal. So remote. Even then she had sensed his vulnerability—had known that even a man so powerful as Luc was uncertain. Was that when she had known that he must care for her, little though he might be able to show it?

Of course he could not trust her. He could not trust anyone. He had never had anyone to trust.

His parents had abandoned him—first to play their histrionic relationship games, then in dying so young. He had never allowed anyone else near. He'd had no reason not to believe it when Silvio made up lies about her—and if Gabrielle thought about what Luc had said, the references to *pictures*, she could imagine the form those lies had taken. She could not be surprised that Luc had felt so betrayed. A month or so of love could not cancel out the lifetime of distrust and suspicion that had preceded it.

It only made her more determined.

She would love him whether he wanted her to or not. She

wouldn't stop just because he struck out at her, cast her aside. She loved him enough to know that she must never give up—she must break through, somehow, to that vulnerable part of him he kept hidden away. So that they could both be free—together.

Luc stood on the terrace of his penthouse, looking out over the rooftops of Rome. He had never brought one of his women to this place—the most private of his homes—and had had no specific intention to bring Gabrielle here, either, though he had married her.

Yet he couldn't seem to stop thinking of how much she would have loved to see the sun set over the city, creeping across the domes and steeples, the light orange and gold.

I love you.

He had called her *my wife*. Not *my ex-wife*. He had demanded that his lawyers draw up the necessary papers and then avoided their calls ever since. Today he had realized what he should have known all along—she had not betrayed him. That Silvio had played him for a fool, even played him against Gabrielle, and because he was a fool he had run with it. Embraced it. Had some part of him *wanted* to believe she was capable of such treachery? Had he *wanted* her to be his mother all over again? To confirm his darkest fears?

He couldn't seem to come to terms with what all of that meant. He who was famous for his decisiveness, his boldness.

He put his glass of wine down on the table and moved to the railing, restless. He remembered when he was younger, how he had stood in this same place and plotted the many ways he planned to increase his holdings, conquer his rivals, cut low his enemies. All of which he had done—in spades.

Now all he could think of was the mesmerizing curve of her hip, the small, pleading noise she made when she was close to her climax. Her serene, elegant smoothness and the wildness contained within it.

He was infatuated. Obsessed.

Even Rome seemed empty without her.

Luc was forced to admit defeat. It was a new and oddly uncomfortable experience.

But it seemed he could not live without her.

Had he already suspected as much in London? Was that why he'd been so quick to walk out on her? Had he been running for his life—the empty, emotionless life he had crafted so carefully and that she had destroyed forever?

He walked back into the flat from the terrace, scowling as he worked to come to terms with this new information. If he could not live without her, that meant that he had to get her back. It meant that, and it also meant a great many things he was not certain he wished to look at directly.

He turned when he heard the low chime of the elevator doors, opening inside his private foyer.

"I am so sorry, Mr. Garnier," the bellboy cried out immediately. "I know you ask that we announce all visitors, but this—"

"Hello, Luc," Gabrielle said quietly as she stepped from the elevator car.

Dio, but she was beautiful. She went straight to his head, standing there so composed and pretty, in a delicate blue jacket and skirt that he longed to rip from her body right there, tumbling them both to the marble floor.

"Gabrielle." He tasted the syllables of her name. Had he conjured her up? Had wanting her made her appear, like some genie from a childhood fairy tale?

He had showered after his run-in with Silvio, scrubbing the encounter off his skin. He'd thrown a button-down shirt on over his trousers, but neglected to fasten it—an impulse he was glad of as he watched the way her eyes caressed his chest and abdomen before they returned to his.

"I believe you forgot something," she said in her calm,

soothing voice, her gaze intent on his as she stepped toward him. The elevator—dismissed with a wave of Luc's hand—closed behind her. "In your haste to get away."

He remembered his own words, delivered so differently, so angrily, a world away. He felt something like a smile curve his mouth.

"Did I?" he asked softly, drinking her in. "And what is that?"

She tossed her head back. Defiant, bold. She was different than he remembered—more vibrant, more sure. She looked him in the eye. She was not afraid.

She was glorious.

"Your wife," she said.

CHAPTER EIGHTEEN

"I LOVE you," she told him, marching across the marble foyer and stopping when she was only inches from his hard, beloved face. "Even though you broke my heart in London. I love you, and I refuse to accept that our marriage is over."

"You have grown claws, it seems," Luc murmured in that silky way of his. "I see my absence has suited you."

She couldn't read his expression. There was something new in the way he looked at her—but it was not cold, or vicious. Hope unfurled inside her chest and mingled with the determination that had already guided her here.

"It did not suit me." She found that her hands were on her hips. "You were an ass."

His lips curved. "I thought you sold Silvio photographs," Luc said. "Compromising photographs from our honeymoon, to be precise."

He spoke rather too mildly, Gabrielle thought with asperity. But then, he did not dispute the fact that he'd been an ass.

"I paid him for a tape of you and that Rosalinda—to prevent his selling it," Gabrielle shot back. She frowned as his words penetrated. "Photographs of you and *me*?"

"You sound appalled," Luc said.

"Of course I'm appalled!" Gabrielle retorted. "How could you believe such a thing? I would never sell photographs to anyone—I am the Crown Princess of Miravakia! I am not some second-rate starlet!"

"I know who you are," he said, his eyes darkening.

"Clearly not!"

He cocked his head to the side and she stared back, her hands fisted on her hips. The air around them seemed to seethe with tension. Heat. Gabrielle's eyes felt overbright, her cheeks were too warm, and she felt as if the room was spinning, whirling. All that she could see was Luc's steady, addictive gray gaze.

"I know exactly who you are," he said, his voice a low throb that seemed to echo in her chest, along her limbs, between her legs. "You haunt me."

He looked like some kind of warrior, some avenging angel, his face resolute and fierce—and the most beautiful thing that Gabrielle had ever seen.

"I know your voice because I cannot escape it," he told her in a savage tone. "I know your touch because I dream of it. I know your scent, your voice, your walk." His voice faded away into almost nothing, the faintest whisper of sound. And yet he held himself away from her.

"Had you only talked to me about his accusations—" Gabrielle began, frowning at him even as her breath came quicker, in little pants, and her attention focused on his dangerous mouth.

"I could not," Luc said fiercely. Such a proud, difficult man. His gaze turned almost defiant. "I did not know how. And it seems he knew how best to manipulate us both."

If possible, she loved him more for the admission. She could feel the change in him, though she hardly dared dream what it might mean. He stood before her like some kind of Roman god, his chiseled torso gleaming, his dark hair thick and damp, his eyes so dark, like steel, and his cruel, delicious mouth pulled to the side in a sardonic smile.

"Why are you here?" Luc asked, his voice still and quiet, with the faintest hint of mockery. As if he knew already. "Did you hunt me down?"

"I will not grant you a divorce. I will fight an annulment. I'll fight *you*," she said, tilting her chin up.

"Why?" he asked. He moved closer, his glorious chest now within reach, his mouth a bare whisper above hers, his dark eyes boring into her, seeing into her—through her.

"Because I love you," she said softly. "Why else?"

"Ah, love," he said, hardly above a whisper. "Is that what it is? How do you know?"

"You have ruined me for other men," she told him, tilting her head back, easing ever closer, not daring to touch him but almost—almost…

"Have you tested the theory?" he asked sardonically, but his eyes gleamed with amusement.

"And if I had?" she asked, teasing him. She was not sure where her sudden sense of daring came from. She only knew that she dared. She dared anything and everything if she could have him.

"Ah, Gabrielle," he muttered, his voice thickening as he thrust a strong hand into her heavy hair, anchoring her head against his hot palm and drawing her up on her toes. "You will be the death of me."

"You love me," she said simply. She knew it deep inside, as much a fact as her need to breathe, as her own love for him.

There was a breathless, electric pause. Luc stared at her. She slid her hands around his strong neck and arched into him, pressing her aching breasts against him. He groaned, deep in his throat.

"I do, damn you," he said in a low voice, his eyes nearly silver. "I do."

His mouth covered hers, and Gabrielle surrendered herself to the kick and roll, the heat and wonder. He kissed her again and again, savage and tender, as if he could never get enough. It was an apology, and it was a covenant, and she could not tell where she ended and he began.

He bent slightly and swept her into his arms, never lifting his mouth from hers. Gabrielle had the faintest hectic impression of an elegantly appointed drawing room before he deposited her on the Oriental rug in front of a fireplace and followed her down—and then his hard chest crushed into her with delicious pressure.

Gabrielle groaned—and forgot about the room. She didn't care where they were. She cared only that she was touching him—finally. His hands stroked her, moving to her hips and hiking up her skirt so she could wrap her legs around his waist.

She struggled with the zip of his trousers and he cursed slightly. He shifted and released himself with two quick jerks. She had only a dizzy moment to look at his manhood, jutting proudly before him, and then he was thrusting into her, deep and hard and wild, and she thought no more.

She came almost instantly, shuddering around him. Luc felt the dark sorcery of her taste, her touch, overwhelm him, and he followed, shouting out her name.

But it was not magic, he knew, as he slowly came back to himself. It was love.

No wonder he had cast it aside and run from it—just as she had done in the beginning. No wonder he had so quickly grasped any excuse to leave her.

"What I know of love is twisted," he told her when her eyes fluttered open. He traced patterns along the sweat-slick skin of her thigh, still wrapped around him. "Sick."

"Then it is not love," she whispered, her sea-colored eyes calm as she regarded him.

"I do not believe in it," he said. He kissed her brow, the tip of her nose, her cheek. "I don't know how to believe in it."

"It's not in your head, but in your heart." She placed one

of her slender hands on his chest. He felt his heart kick beneath her touch. "I spent my whole life loving someone who cannot love me in return," she said. "I think love is feeling free. Not hidden away, not afraid. But finally whole—together."

She was wondrous. She was his wife. He felt a deep, primal surge of possession and emotion and knew she was right. He loved her.

Beyond rationale and reason, he was madly in love with her. Crazy with it. And the most insane part was that he no longer cared that he had lost his objectivity.

"I love you," he said fiercely, testing it out, even as he hardened once more within her. He scowled at her. "And I do not think it will ever change. I do not think you will escape it."

"Good," she whispered, and began to move her hips against him.

It would always be this way, Gabrielle thought some time later. She was wrapped in his long shirt and in his arms, enjoying the glittering Rome night from his balcony. She leaned back into his embrace, smiling.

There would be no ordinary Thursdays in their marriage, there would be only Luc. He would not be easy, and perhaps she would not be either. But they would have this passion—this wild, sweet fire that burned them both into ash—again and again. She wanted him still—again. Always.

"I will get back what you paid that little toad," Luc promised her suddenly. She could feel his voice rumble in his chest and through her. "He will not profit from my wife for a tape that does not exist. To the tune of ten thousand pounds, no less!"

"I don't care about it," Gabrielle murmured, tilting her head back to nestle against him. "I never even looked at it."

"I care." His voice was implacable. "It is the principle. He will no doubt turn it into another series of stories, but that is of no matter to me. Let him. But he *will* pay you back the money he extorted, this I promise you."

Gabrielle smiled. If he no longer cared about the tabloids, then things really had changed. What had started as a vain hope mixed with a deep resolve, and had bloomed during their impassioned lovemaking, now burst into light inside her.

They would make it. It would be all right. This was as it should be—finally.

"If you wish it," she said.

"How can you love such a man as me?" he asked her, his tone deceptively light. When she turned to face him, his eyes were hard on hers. "One who abuses you so terribly, chases you and then abandons you, believes the worst of you, accuses you of every sin imaginable?"

Gabrielle reached over and laid her hand against his cheek, making both of them take a quick, startled breath in response to the electric heat that arced between them, as if they had not made love three times already. She traced the shape of his lean jaw, then curled her fingers around his neck.

She would love this man forever.

"Well, Luc," she said, and smiled, letting him see all the light and hope and love she carried inside her. "See that it does not happen again."

He muttered a soft curse, or perhaps it was her name, and crushed his mouth to hers.

And Gabrielle knew beyond a shadow of a doubt that they had both found their way home.

At last.

* * * * *

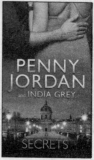
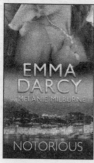
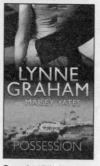

The World of Mills & Boon®

There's a Mills & Boon® series that's perfect for you. We publish ten series and with new titles every month, you never have to wait long for your favourite to come along.

Blaze® — Scorching hot, sexy reads

By Request — Relive the romance with the best of the best

Cherish™ — Romance to melt the heart every time

Desire™ — Passionate and dramatic love stories

Visit us Online

Browse our books before you buy online at
www.millsandboon.co.uk

M&B/WORLD